Italian and Italian American Studies
Stanislao G. Pugliese
Hofstra University
Series Editor

This publishing initiative seeks to bring the latest scholarship in Italian and Italian American history, literature, cinema, and cultural studies to a large audience of specialists, general readers, and students. I&IAS will feature works on modern Italy (Renaissance to the present) and Italian American culture and society by established scholars as well as new voices in the academy. This endeavor will help to shape the evolving fields of Italian and Italian American Studies by re-emphasizing the connection between the two. The following editorial board consists of esteemed senior scholars who act as advisors to the series editor.

New Reflections on Primo Levi

New Reflections on Primo Levi

Before and After Auschwitz

Edited by Risa Sodi and Millicent Marcus

palgrave
macmillan

First published in 2011 by PALGRAVE MACMILLAN® in the United States—a division of St. Martin's Press LLC, 175 Fifth Avenue, New York, NY 10010.

Where this book is distributed in the UK, Europe, and the rest of the world, this is by Palgrave Macmillan, a division of Macmillan Publishers Limited, registered in England, company number 785998, of Houndmills, Basingstoke, Hampshire RG21 6XS.

Palgrave Macmillan is the global academic imprint of the above companies and has companies and representatives throughout the world.

Palgrave® and Macmillan® are registered trademarks in the United States, the United Kingdom, Europe and other countries.

ISBN: 978-0-230-10385-6

New reflections on Primo Levi : before and after Auschwitz / edited by Risa Sodi and Millicent Marcus.
    p. cm.— (Italian and Italian American studies)
    Includes index.
    ISBN 978-0-230-10385-6
    1. Levi, Primo—Criticism and interpretation. I. Sodi, Risa B., 1957–
II. Marcus, Millicent Joy. III. Title. IV. Series.

PQ4872.E8Z767 2011
853'.914—dc22   2010049477

A catalogue record of the book is available from the British Library.

Design by Scribe Inc.

First edition: July 2011

10 9 8 7 6 5 4 3 2 1

Printed in the United States of America.

To my father, Simon Bernstein

—Risa Sodi

To the memory of my mother, Marion Marcus

—Millicent Marcus

Contents

Introduction

Millicent Marcus and Risa Sodi
Yale University

Today, at a time when Primo Levi's works inspire a voluminous stream of scholarly studies and academic conferences in all the world's major languages, and when his influence can be found in such disparate places as pop music and literature, Indian dance, contemporary film and theater, the fine arts, and more, it is astonishing to think that just two decades ago, Levi's name was virtually unknown outside of a small group of scholars and enthusiasts. During our years in graduate school (the early 1970s for one of us, the late 1980s and early 1990s for the other), Levi's texts were considered outside the canon, the work of a nonprofessional, and unlikely to achieve permanence. One of us remembers, in particular, having her 1986 application for research funds for a study of Levi rejected by a major Italian American organization because Jewish issues were judged to be marginal, and by a major Jewish American organization because Italy was judged to be marginal. Indeed, the first English-language monograph on Levi was only published in 1990 (by one of the editors of this volume).

Of course, Levi's absence from booksellers' shelves and the curricula of Italian programs in the United States and Britain in those years reflected a cultural reticence emanating from Italy itself. Both the Italian literary establishment and the surrounding national culture were unable to accommodate the searing documents issuing from the hand of this Holocaust survivor. Natalia Ginzburg's rejection for Einaudi of *Survival in Auschwitz* (*Se questo è un uomo*) was symptomatic of the threat that Levi's writings posed on two related fronts: that of literary propriety, and that of acceptable historiography. Ginzburg's judgment that the time was not ripe, in 1946, for publication of a survivor memoir was not totally unfounded but is nonetheless astounding for its timidity and lack of perspicacity. Einaudi and Ginzburg represented the Establishment; Levi—though Turinese, like them—was an outsider.

For an institutionalized literature tightly bound to concerns of genre, aesthetics, and ideological correctness, Levi's Holocaust texts were unassimilable. They contravened identifiable generic categories, exhibited no *bellettrismo*, and failed to register an activist response to injustice. By defying classification and refusing to adhere to the norms of stylistic and ideological acceptability, his work could not be contained within the traditional confines of "the literary." Levi's segregation from the literary establishment during his lifetime was corrected belatedly, only after his having won acclaim from a general readership in Italy and abroad.

Much is already known about Levi's background as a literary upstart, how even while writing his masterworks he toiled for many years in the backwaters of industrial chemistry: first, in a nickel mine, then in a jerry-rigged bedroom laboratory (replete with demijohns of hydrochloric acid and beakers full of stannous chloride), and eventually at the SIVA varnish factory. We also know that he set out to study physics at the university, landing in the chemistry department due to a fluke of (Fascist-era) timing. In *The Search for Roots*, Levi included an excerpt from his college chemistry text among the volumes that "accompan[ied him] throughout the years."[1] And yet, less is known, or remarked on, about the passion for Dante that had him winning informal recitation contests while still in high school, or his knowledge of the Italian Romantics, or his reading of classical and biblical literature. When asked to assemble his "personal anthology," Levi chose 30 texts, more than half of which would fit into any contemporary course on world literature. Thus, into his sixties, we find Levi pursuing two contemporaneous and parallel lines of endeavor: his public work in science and his after-hours work crafting literature. Is it any wonder, for example, that he found a kindred spirit in Mario Rigoni Stern? They had in common religious roots, ties to ancient Italian minorities, wartime experiences, a love of the mountains, and one other crucial factor: their nearly *a priori* exclusion from the Italian literary establishment and the label that they carried with them for years as authors of one-shot successes—*The Sergeant in the Snow* for Rigoni Stern (1953) and *Survival in Auschwitz* for Levi (1947 and 1958).

The Italian Shoah: A Submerged History

Of course, the unease with which the literary establishment greeted *Survival in Auschwitz* and Levi's subsequent Holocaust texts reflected a far deeper problem: Italy's resistance to telling the Holocaust story at all—or rather, its reluctance to confront what filmmaker Ettore Scola called "a passage little frequented, and hardly edifying of our History."² It should come as no surprise that Italian reticence about its part in the Shoah flows from a deep and complex set of motivations. In the politically polarized atmosphere of the First Republic, both the Right and the Left had strong reasons for repressing the Holocaust past. We need not belabor the Right's desire to distance itself from the historical inheritance of Fascism—in this case, the Racial Laws, which foreshadowed and facilitated the Final Solution on Italian soil. What does need explanation is the unwillingness to revisit the Shoah on the part of the Italian Left, whose impulse to critique Fascist injustice was in this case overridden by the desire to protect a certain World War II historiography. Indeed, the Left came to archive the Italian Holocaust mostly under the rubric of World War II literature about the anti-Fascist struggle—not as a testimony of the Jewish tragedy. In fact, the numbers of memoirs penned by partisans and soldiers vastly outweighed (and outsold) the exiguous number of such memoirs (less than a handful) by Italian Jewish survivors. The reasons are not surprising, given the numbers of ex-partisans and soldiers—in the tens of thousands—versus the mere eight hundred Jewish ex-deportees. The Left, indeed, actively promoted the founding of the National Association of Italian Partisans (ANPI, or Associazione nazionale partigiani d'Italia) in 1944 (while the war was still raging in the north), whereas its counterpart, the National Association of Ex-Deportees (ANED, or Associazione nationale ex-deportati) struggled for recognition by the Left, even after its founding two decades later, in 1968.

These occurrences are symptomatic of the official approach to the Holocaust commonly held by the communist and non-communist Left in Italy. Indeed, the Italian Holocaust could hardly be reconciled with the threat posed by this tragic episode to the Resistance "master narrative" on which a progressive Italian postwar class based its claims for moral authority and political clout. Both Left and Right, then, were invested in protecting a stereotype that was profoundly undermined by the Italian Holocaust story. We are referring to the myth of *italiani brava gente* (the "good Italian people," or, as a film title has it, "Italians Are Nice People").³ This persistent fallback—evident in estimable scholarly work and rampant in the popular press—portrays the populace as either victims of Fascism or warriors for the Partisan cause, thus purifying the ideal of *italianità* from the taint of passive acquiescence to dictatorship, and from active complicity with the war-mongering and genocidal policies of their ally to the North.

This convenient myth is akin to the "convenient truths" posited by Levi in "The Grey Zone" chapter of *The Drowned and the Saved*. Italy, which had been racked by civil war on one front and world war on another, and was plummeted into exhausting reconstruction at war's end, nonetheless was spared most of the turmoil and wrenching national self-evaluation experienced elsewhere in Europe during the various war crimes trials. Italy, in fact, never put its leaders or their lackeys on trial; it never called to account those who had ordered and carried out the Italian Holocaust. Unlike the Nuremberg trials in Germany or the French trials of 1947, 1984, 1994, and 1997, Italy shunned a postwar reckoning with its citizens' role in executing the Final Solution.[4] National reconstruction went beyond literal bricks and mortar to encompass the reconstruction of a national identity—blindered and recalcitrant in part, one might say—that obfuscated the role of ordinary citizens and Fascist adherents during the Shoah. For every tome and conference today that seeks to portray Italy as a nation of Palatuccis and Perlascas, there are equally numerous voices of historians and others who, while acknowledging the extraordinary efforts of those two famous men, and other men and women less celebrated than they, also point to irrefutable statistics showing Fascist officials zealous in rounding up Italian Jews, and ordinary citizens unscrupulous in selling out their Jewish neighbors for paltry sums of money or a chance to occupy their apartments.[5]

Levi himself benefited from one of the true *bravi italiani* in the form of Lorenzo Perone, the uneducated day laborer who appears as one of the unforgettable dramatis personae in *Survival in Auschwitz* and the namesake character of the short story, "Lorenzo's Return." In numerous interviews over the years, Levi credited Lorenzo with saving his life in Auschwitz through daily food drop-offs, made at considerable risk and sacrifice to himself. Levi learned after the war that many others also benefited from Lorenzo's largesse, for which he in turn refused recognition or compensation. Today, Lorenzo, along with 483 other Italians, is numbered among "the righteous among the nations," the designation given by the Jerusalem-based "Holocaust Martyrs' and Heroes' Remembrance Authority," Yad Vashem, to non-Jewish rescuers of Jews.[6] Levi's remarks about Lorenzo in *Survival in Auschwitz* are featured prominently on the Yad Vashem "Righteous Among the Nations" home page: "I believe that it was really due to Lorenzo that I am alive today; and not so much for his material aid, as for his having constantly reminded me by his presence . . . that there still existed a just world outside our own, something and someone still pure and whole . . . for which it was worth surviving."[7]

Toward a New Historiography

We hope that this volume will add to the chorus of voices that seek to reconfigure perceptions of the Shoah in Italy according to rigorous scholarship in the fields of history, psychology, literature, political philosophy, and others, and counter—or even put to rest—longstanding, unhelpful, factional, and antiquated notions of *italiani brava gente*. Indeed, with the end of the Italian First Republic and the resulting process of political reconfiguration, the World War II historiographies that served the old political orders have given way to alternative readings of that traumatic past. With respect to the Shoah, the floodgates opened with an outpouring of books, films, conferences, memorializations, and official commemorations that, since the 1990s, shows no sign of abating as of this writing.

At the same time as late twentieth-century political currents were shifting, social strains in the form of surging immigration induced many in Italy to ponder the role of "the other" within the framework of the national self-image. Large numbers of East European arrivals, freed by the fall of the Iron Curtain, joined African and Asian immigrants, rattling the nearly monolithic—that is, Roman Catholic and white—Italian majority culture. It was at the confluence of the waves of immigration from the East and South and the fall of the First Republic that Italy began to look more closely at its oldest minority, the Italian Jews. Just as scholarly work on Levi was scant before the 1990s, so publications about Italian Jewry remained a niche industry through the 1980s, confined largely to Italian Jewish publishers and Italian Jewish markets. The unexpected groundswell of attention that marked the years of increased immigration coincided with a marked uptick in scholarly and popular works of Italian Jewish interest. In particular, Holocaust literature—both survivor narratives (Pekelis, Pappalettera, Zargani, Sonnino, Padoan, and others) and Holocaust-related fiction by non-Jewish authors (Loy, Pederiali, Maurensig, De Luca, Maraini, and others)—were published, and republished (in this last regard, one thinks of the republication, 40 years after the fact, of the survivor memoirs by Liana Millu and Giuliana Tedeschi).

Levi both participated in this surge (by penning forewords and introductions) and benefited from it (through increased attention to a newly perceived *corpus* of Italian Holocaust literature). It added heft and depth to his profile and galvanized the scholarly world, engendering comparatist, cross-national, and cross-disciplinary work with Levi's *oeuvre* at its core. With the anticipated milestone publication of Levi's collected works in English (joining not one, but two, anthologies of his collected works in Italian), it seemed fitting and timely to bring together top scholars from three continents writing in English on Levi. Thus, the following volume grows out of a 2008 Yale University international conference, "Primo Levi in the Present Tense: New Reflections on His Life and Work Before and After Auschwitz," and features scholars hailing from Italy, the United Kingdom, Australia, and various parts of the United States.

New Reflections: Chapter by Chapter

Stanislao Pugliese opens this volume by considering Levi's politics and involvement in two anti-Fascist movements, Justice and Liberty (*Giustizia e libertà*) and the Action Party (*Partito d'Azione*). His study, "Primo Levi's Politics: *Giustizia e Libertà*, the *Partito d'Azione* and 'Jewish' Anti-Fascism," leads in two directions: an excursus through the sociopolitical milieu that produced such Jewish anti-Fascists as Nello and Carlo Rosselli, Carlo Levi, and Primo Levi; and a teleological inquiry into the essentially antihumanistic nature of Fascism, its descent into genocide and Holocaust, and what Pugliese suggests was a "second fall of man." These two lines of inquiry, which also take in Heidegger, Todorov, Wiesel, and Eco, ultimately lead to challenging reflections on the resurgence of Fascistic discourse in contemporary Italian politics and on why Levi's political thinking does not occupy a bigger place in contemporary criticism.

Nancy Harrowitz appeals to Italian Jewish historian Arnaldo Momigliano's concept of "parallel nationalization" in order to explore Primo Levi's pre-deportation Jewish identity. In Momigliano's view, Jewish identity ceased to exist, supplanted by a new *italianità*, subsequent to mid-nineteenth-century Jewish emancipation from the ghettos and inclusion in the post-unification state. By looking at both Momigliano's theoretical construct and the self-fashioning of his own Jewish identity, she casts light on disconcerting, or at least curious, statements by Levi—for example, his assertion in *The Periodic Table* that "it had not meant much to me that I was a Jew: [. . .] I had always considered my origins as an almost insignificant but odd fact, a small cheerful anomaly, like having a crooked nose or freckles." Harrowitz takes Levi's statement as her starting point, interrogating it in the light of positions advanced by Momigliano and others, such as Gramsci and Lombroso, to dissect the notion of an "Italy without anti-semitism" (Gramsci), or the erasure of Jews to effect an erasure of bigotry (Lombroso). Her essay, "The Itinerary of an Identity: Primo Levi's 'Parallel Nationalization,'" provocatively scrutinizes this best known of Italian Jewish authors and his efforts to circumscribe—or circumvent—the problematics of Jewish identity.

"Primo Levi and Holocaust Memory in Italy, 1958–1963" is an inquiry, by Robert Gordon, into a crucial quinquennium for "memory culture" in Italy. While Levi might appear to have been quiescent during this five-year period marking the interval between Einaudi's reprinting of *Survival in Auschwitz* (1958) and the publication of *The Reawakening* (1963), Gordon argues that two parallel step changes were instead underway. The first, proper to Levi, culminated in his unexpected reemergence in 1963 as the Campiello Prize winner; and the second, extended to Italian postwar culture in general, concluded with a dramatically expanded public interest in and awareness of Italian Holocaust issues. Gordon illustrates the elements that informed this period of historical ferment with a wide-ranging exploration of four broad categories of collective memory: (1) nonfiction works in Italian (by De Felice, Caleffi, Piazza, Debenedetti, Bruck, and others) and Italian translations of seminal foreign works (by Antelme, Frank, Shirer, Poliakov, among others); (2) fiction, film, and literature in Italian and in Italian translation (by Bassani, Ginzburg, Schwartz-Bart, Pontecorvo, De Sica, and others); (3) events permeated by public memory, such as the Eichmann trial or the fifteenth anniversary celebration of liberation; (4) and events directly related to Jewish memory, such as the founding of the Center for Contemporary Jewish Documentation (1955) or several historiographic series appearing in Jewish journals. Gordon concludes with tantalizing speculations on the post-1963 public fall-off of attention—both to Levi and to Italian Holocaust "memory culture."

Trauma theory, as proposed by Freud, informs Jonathan Druker's study, "Trauma and Latency in Primo Levi's *The Reawakening*." Levi's second memoir, Druker posits, not only follows Freud's three stages of trauma but is itself a literary representation of the second stage of latency (defined as "an interval of forgetfulness between the primary exposure and the appearance of pathological symptoms") bracketed by stages one (the initial shock) and three (the onset of recurring traumatic memories). Druker further suggests that Soviet Russia functions in the work as a geographical, chronological, and cultural site of latency with crucial implications for addressing the Holocaust as a problem born of (Eastern? Western?) European history and culture. Parallels thus emerge between and within the liminal spaces of Holocaust geography, and between and within the survivor and the survivor-as-narrating-persona. Distinguishing itself from previous interpretations of *The Reawakening* that focused on Levi's picaresque journey and its colorful cast of characters, Druker's analyses of the book and the two films it spawned is an invitation to take Levi studies in a new direction.

Translation of various and unexpected sorts is the thread running through Lina Insana's essay, "The Witness's Tape Recorder and the Violence of Mediation." She argues that Primo Levi's translation acts, as well as the act of being translated, reveal unique tensions in his works and his "subject position," and that these tensions in turn offer a unique perspective on his writings, his *weltanschaung*, and his thought. Taking a close look at the 1980 essay, "Translating and Being Translated," where, for Levi, the first term evokes an "arduous task" and the second, physical violence, Insana argues that Levi was fully aware of the different levels of mediation at work in his Holocaust prose and other writings. By discussing and analyzing the roles played by such seemingly disparate elements as the tape recorder (literal and metaphoric), Levi's German translator, his letter of presentation of *The Search for Roots*, and the fictional "Torec" virtual reality machine, Insana investigates the gap between Levi's theories of translation and the duty he felt owed him by readers of his work. How was Levi to control a vulnerable, open text (his testimony), and how are his readers to address the "profound violence" of reading?

In "The Strange Case of the *Muselmänner* in Auschwitz," Joseph Farrell confronts one of the most stubborn "cruxes" of Holocaust scholarship. After surveying the mysteries surrounding the origin and meaning of the term, Farrell approaches the central paradox of Levi's approach to those individuals who seem to have surrendered their humanity before the onslaughts of the Nazi concentrationary regime. Farrell traces Levi's evolving relationship to the "drowned" in his Auschwitz taxonomy, using the perspective of Giorgio Agamben, first as a resource and then as a foil, before proposing his own reflections on Levi's *Muselmänner*. While Agamben's recourse to the Western Humanist tradition provides a powerful context for judging the enormity of the Nazis' crime against the dignity of humankind, this position leads the philosopher to a state of incomprehension with respect to Levi's own contemptuous and dismissive representation of Null Achtzehn and his doomed *Muselmänner* comrades. While sharing Agamben's bewilderment, Farrell insists on probing ever deeper into the motives behind Levi's wholesale repudiation of the "drowned" and his concomitant sympathies for the "saved," no matter how ambiguous their means of arriving at that state. In the end, Farrell achieves a nuanced understanding of Levi's position vis-à-vis the *Muselmänner*, once the radical change in attitude, signaled by the elevation of this group to the status of "genuine witnesses" in the pages of *The Drowned and the Saved*, is taken into account.

Among the most significant developments in recent Levi scholarship has been its increasingly expansive reach—its extension beyond the limits of his Holocaust writings to embrace the entirety of Levi's literary corpus. That this "accidental author" came by his vocation as a result of atrocious historical circumstance is well known but it does not diminish the critical interest and value of those writings that owe no direct debt to Levi's Auschwitz ordeal. Far from depriviledging the testimonial writing, the increasing scholarly attention to Levi's "minor works" serves to flesh out our understanding of the overall literary agenda within which *Survival in Auschwitz*, *The Reawakening*, and *The Drowned and the Saved* took shape. One study to offer such a holistic view of Levi's trajectory is Marina Beer's "Primo Levi and Italo Calvino: Two Parallel Lives." What emerges from this comparison is a series of symmetries: both writers published their first works in 1947, inspired by their experiences during World War II; both achieved the status of *maître à penser* through prolific journalistic activities; both delighted in the genre of the short story; and both became the Italian writers with the widest readership abroad. Equally striking are the intersections: Calvino's editorial work as Levi's "first reader" and his promotional work to shape Levi's public image as an author. As Beer demonstrates, the influences between them were "reciprocal and bi-directional," especially given Calvino's and Levi's shared predilection for the fantastic and the cross-fertilization of their many stories written in that mode. But most of all, it was the commonality of their outsiders' position with respect to the contemporary Italian literary scene that bound them, thanks to their unfashionable insistence on merging "two cultures" by bringing technological inquiry and scientific curiosity to bear on the workings of the literary imagination. But Beer's attentiveness to the parallelisms of these two literary lives does not blind her to their radical points of departure. For the purposes of this volume, one of the most striking patterns to emerge is Calvino's avoidance of the Jewish themes that are present instead in Levi's work, in keeping with the general Leftist impulse to subordinate the Italian Holocaust narrative to that of the anti-Fascist struggle.

The impulse in recent Levi studies to go beyond his Holocaust writings and entertain a more holistic approach to his literary corpus finds a pointed example in Elizabeth Scheiber's "*L'immagine di lui che ho conservato*: Communication and Memory in *Lilìt e altri racconti* (*Moments of Reprieve*)." The publishing history of *Lilìt* reveals, in microcosm, the tension between an exclusive focus on Levi's Holocaust writings and a more integrated approach to his literary production as a whole. As Scheiber explains, the original Italian collection mixes Auschwitz tales with others that are unrelated to the Holocaust experience, whereas the American edition limits itself to stories issuing from the Lager. Scheiber examines the consequences of this editorial decision and draws two lessons of interest for Levi criticism. She begins by questioning the appropriateness of the subtitle to the US edition—*A Memoir of Auschwitz*—which associates these writings with the genre of autobiography, or more generally, chronicle. Instead, she argues that these tales defy definition as memoir for the very reasons that prompted Levi to exclude them from *Survival at Auschwitz*, that is, they were "nonessential" to the testimonial project of that early work. According to Scheiber, what unifies the Auschwitz-related tales in *Lilìt* is a focus on writing as an overarching theme—the foregrounding of problems in communication, intertextual links, testimonial impulses, and injunctions to potential readerships—and she suggests that the non-Holocaust related stories (the *altri racconti*) share this metatextual focus. Consequently, the US edition does a disservice to the vital coherence of Levi's anthology by severing the Lager stories from the "other tales," thereby downplaying their collective exploration of the impulse to generate narratives and the responsibilities incumbent upon receiving them.

Though Levi was known to compare *Survival in Auschwitz* to a "weekly industrial report," Lawrence L. Langer sees this disclaimer of literary merit as far more than a mere example of the "modesty topos." In deemphasizing the aesthetic aspects of his Holocaust memoir, Levi was seeking to avoid charges of invention and exaggeration that would undermine the credibility of his account. In his essay "The Survivor as Author: Primo Levi's Literary Vision of Auschwitz," Langer invokes his own studies of oral survivor testimonies to prove that Levi's narrative, by contrast, abounds in literary devices—from the structuring motif of the epic journey to the specific and climactic borrowings from Dante. Langer argues that literariness is used both to enhance the power of the testimony and to "disable" its own aestheticizing influence. His essay seeks to interrogate Levi's double objective by devoting considerable attention to "The Canto of Ulysses" (chapter 11 of *Survival in Auschwitz*). According to Langer, any consolation in that chapter that may derive from the recourse to so venerable a literary heritage (Dante and even Homer) is undone by the episodes of disgrace and physical privation that immediately precede and follow it. Even more damning (in the literal sense) is the vast disparity between the Hell of Dante's devising, where, according to a divinely ordained and humanly intelligible system of justice, punishment is an organic expression of the corresponding sin, and the Nazi "inferno," where suffering is universal, undeserved, and meted out according to the most arbitrary and incoherent governing principles. In a stunning interpretive move, Langer suggests that "The Canto of Ulysses" functions as a "dramatic enactment of its author's deepest fear in writing about Auschwitz"—that Levi may also be charged with the sin of abusing his rhetorical powers and using a literary practice that casts doubt on the truth claims of his testimony.

Among the first to understand and promote Levi's achievement outside Italy was Nicholas Patruno, whose essay "How It All Started: A Personal Reflection" offers an account of one scholar's pioneering forays into this field of studies. Woven into Patruno's memoir is a small treasure trove of archival findings—insights gleaned from documents consulted at the Einaudi archives and from conversations with Levi's friends and colleagues in Turin. What emerges is a series of glimpses into Levi's relationship to his literary career: his involvement in editorial decision making, his monitoring of translations, his preoccupation with reviews, and even his alertness to financial matters. Of great interest are his negotiations over the titling of translated works and his exchanges with Calvino over the placement of "Argon" within the text of *The Periodic Table*. But Patruno pointedly concludes by noting that engagement with Levi studies goes beyond the confines of scholarly research to enter the classroom where, over the course of many years, he sought to reach new generations of students with the literary power and moral urgency of Primo Levi's lesson.

Mirna Cicioni takes up Levi's invitation to look at *If Not Now, When?* through the lens of the American Western and, with careful attention to detail and analytical rigor, traces the ethos and structures of the two. Bringing to bear a set of critical tools seldom trained on Levi's works, Cicioni pulls together the works of Slotkin and Tompkins, and Spinazzola and Della Colletta, to state her case that *If Not Now, When?* is not only a take on the Western from a modern, Italian/Eastern European, Jewish, partisan perspective, but also an "anti-historical novel" (*romanzo antistorico*) that calls into question the possibility of absolute historical knowledge itself. As the title of her essay—"Levi's Western: 'Professional Plot' and History in *If Not Now, When?*"—indicates, Cicioni takes Will Wright's idea of the "professional plot" Western, formulated in his seminal *Six Guns and Society*, and applies it to films such as *The Wild Bunch, The Magnificent Seven*, and *The Professionals*, in preparation for her analysis of common "professional plot" elements, themes, and characters in *If Not Now, When?* By focusing on this seldom explored work of Levi's, Cicioni not only adds to our understanding of Levi's *oeuvre* but also elucidates his novel in a dynamic new way.

One of Levi's obsessive concerns was the inevitable failure of human language to meet the challenge of Holocaust representation. In the absence of a "new harsh language" (Levi's term), his writings had to maintain an ongoing mindfulness of the chasm between the vocabulary of free men and their referents in the world *al di qua del filo spinato* (on this side of the barbed wire). That mindfulness, as Ellen Nerenberg points out in her essay, "Mind the Gap: Performance and Semiosis in Primo Levi," led the writer to seek the tightest possible control over the signifying process of his Holocaust texts. The "gap" of Nerenberg's title—the distance separating signifier and signified—grows ever larger in the case of performance, where Levi's prose language of Holocaust witness is adapted to the conditions of spectacle—be it in the form of theater, cinema, or radio broadcasts. Herein lies one of the major paradoxes of Levi's testimonial mission. While on the one hand, performance forces Levi to yield absolute control over his signifiers, on the other hand, it dramatically increases the size of the public that can be reached by the testimony. Furthermore, thanks to the collective conditions of the audience's experience, performance helps to demonstrate the profoundly political potential of Levi's work. In her survey of the performances of Levi's work during his lifetime, Nerenberg charts the writer's "changing relationship to the linguistic signification of the Holocaust over time." Beginning with analyses of the "hidden theater" within testimonial writings such as *Survival in Auschwitz* and *Moments of Reprieve,* Nerenberg then considers the theatrical and radio adaptations of Levi's first memoir. Drawing from her research in the Einaudi and RAI archives, Nerenberg offers accounts of several radio broadcasts in which the literal process of giving voice serves to interpret and complement Levi's writings in surprising and powerful ways.

In Conclusion

Given Primo Levi's pioneering struggle to break through his culture's Holocaust silence, and given the brilliance of his literary production, it should come as no surprise that the recent swell of Italian Holocaust revisitations would revolve around his central achievement. Significantly, the scholarly focus on Levi's survivor testimony has spilled over into his non-Holocaust writings and, from there, to his century and his intellectual milieu. The essays collected in this volume explore much of his major and many of his minor writings, the genre shifts of his works, his ties to major writers of his time, and the political, psychological, and historical contexts of his literary production.

Levi wrote in his Preface to *The Search for Roots,* "Only the dead can no longer change and no longer put out other roots, and for this reason only the dead are entitled to criticism."[8] His seeming authorization of critical studies like the one at hand is gratifying; but the notion that the dead can no longer generate new cultural roots strikes us as singularly inappropriate to Levi's case. Given that the public and scholarly perception of Levi, and the interest in him and his works, has flourished since his untimely death in 1987, we propose that—as he put it—"new shoots have broken through" and that the recent critical studies by the scholars presented here are deeply rooted in the ideas that Levi allowed to germinate over a lifetime of literary production.[9]

Notes

1. Primo Levi, *The Search for Roots* (Lanham, MD: Ivan R. Dee, 2003), 5.
2. "[U]n brano poco frequentato e poco edificante, della nostra Storia." From Ettore Scola's preface to the screenplay *Concorrenza sleale* (Turin: Lindau, 2001), 5.
3. Though commonly known as *Attack and Retreat,* Giuseppe De Santis's 1965 film, *Italiani brava gente,* was retitled "Italians Are Nice People" by *New York Times* film critic Bosley Crowther in his February 4, 1966

review for that newspaper. http://movies.nytimes.com/movie/review?res
=9E01E1DC1338E637A25757C0A9649C946791D6CF.

4. In 1987, Klaus Barbie was convicted of crimes against humanity. "In 1994,
Paul Touvier, who was responsible for the massacre of seven Jews in Lyon during World War II, was tried and condemned to life in prison. A third trial, in
1997, focused on Maurice Papon, a senior official responsible for Jewish affairs
in Bordeaux. Papon's trial was different from the other two because they were
killers, whereas Papon was a bureaucrat who signed the death warrants for
1,560 French Jews, including 223 children. Papon was found guilty for crimes
against humanity and was sentenced to ten years in jail. The trial served as a
pretext for reexamining France's role in the Holocaust. Debate arose about
the Vichy regime's involvement in rounding up, deporting, and murdering
French Jews." See http://www.jewishvirtuallibrary.org/jsource/vjw/France
.html#Holocaust.

5. Giovanni Palatucci and Giorgio Perlasca were Fascists who went to extraordinary (and, in the case of Palatucci, fatal) lengths to protect Jews from deportation. Their heroic endeavors became the stuff of two films, *Senza confini* by
Fabrizio Costa (2001) and *Perlasca: Un eroe italiano* by Alberto Negrin (2002),
as well as studies including Marco Coslovich's *Giovanni Palatucci: Una giusta
memoria* (Atripalda: Mephite, 2008) and Enrico Deaglio's *La banalità del bene*
(Milan: Feltrinelli, 1991), translated as *The Banality of Goodness: The Story of
Giorgio Perlasca* (Notre Dame, IN: Notre Dame University Press, 1998).

6. See http://www1.yadvashem.org/yv/en/righteous/statistics.asp#detailed. Italy, Germany, and Slovakia register roughly the same number of Righteous Among
the Nations: 484, 463, and 498, respectively. The largest number, 6195, comes
from Poland; the smallest—1—from Chile, Georgia, Japan, Luxembourg,
Montenegro, Portugal, Turkey, and Vietnam.

7. See http://www1.yadvashem.org/yv/en/righteous/about.asp.

8. Levi, *The Search for Roots*, 8.

9. Ibid., 8.

Part I

Politics, Nationalism, and Collective Memory

Primo Levi's Politics

Giustizia e Libertà, the Partito d'Azione and "Jewish" Anti-Fascism

Stanislao Pugliese

More than twenty years ago, the Italian chemist, writer, and Holocaust survivor Primo Levi fell to his death from the stairwell of his apartment building in Turin. Within hours, a debate exploded as to whether his death was an accident or a suicide and, if the latter, how this might force us to reinterpret his legacy as a writer and "survivor." Elie Wiesel, Cynthia Ozick, Philip Roth, Diego Gambetta, and Susan Sontag, among many others, weighed in with thoughtful and sometimes provocative commentaries, but the debate over his death has sometimes overshadowed the larger significance of his place as a thinker "after Auschwitz."

"It is barbaric," thundered Theodor Adorno, "to write poetry after Auschwitz."[1] Adorno's dictum has perhaps been misunderstood. He was not arguing for a taboo to be placed on any representation of the Holocaust, but that the Shoah represented a break in the ontological status of *Homo sapiens* that resulted in the impossibility of a traditional aesthetic. "After Auschwitz," Adorno argued, "events make a mockery of the construction of immanence as endowed with a meaning radiated by an affirmatively posited transcendence."[2] Levi himself hints at this in commenting on the "simple and incomprehensible" stories the inmates tell each other in the evenings: "Are they not themselves stories of a new Bible?"[3]

We are forced, after the Fall of contemporary humanity, into an impossible double bind: the necessity of recording, reflecting upon, and representing an event for which we do not have the proper conceptual or linguistic tools. "Then for the first time," realized Levi, "we became aware that our language lacks words to express this offense, the demolition of a man."[4] While recognizing our linguistic and hence conceptual poverty, Levi might have argued instead that, after Auschwitz, there could be no poetry (nor art) that was not—in some sense—about Auschwitz.

His own response can be found not only in his memoir of the concentrationary universe, *Survival in Auschwitz*, but in his subsequent *The Reawakening*, as well as his poems, essays, and science fiction. For if science had been corrupted—first by social Darwinism, racism, imperialism, then harnessed to the cause of genocide by National Socialism—and if humanism seemed to be an inadequate bulwark against moral and political bankruptcy, Levi still insisted that science and humanism were our only hope against a recurrence of madness.[5] But this hope rested on a new variant of humanism, no longer naïve, tinged with tragedy and wary of the future. Perhaps thinking of his situation in Turin in the early days of Fascism and war—similar in some ways to that described by Giorgio Bassani in his novel *The Garden of the Finzi-Continis*—Levi admonished us: "After Auschwitz," he wrote, "it is no longer permissible to be unarmed."[6]

Closely related to Levi's intellectual, philosophical, and cultural position was a political stance of consistent, fervent, and ongoing anti-Fascism and left-wing politics. He often spoke and wrote for anti-Fascist partisan organizations in Italy, such as the National Association of Ex-Political Deportees (ANED, or Associazione nazionale ex deportati politici; later "in Nazi Camps"—nei campi nazisti—would be added to the association's title) and the National Association of Partisans of Italy (ANPI, or Associazione nazionale partigiani d'Italia). On other occasions, I have remarked on this political legacy of Levi's; here, I would simply ask the question: why has his political thinking been all but erased from the critical commentary in the United States?[7]

This erasure reveals the flaws of a certain cultural critique. It was only thirteen years after the end of World War II that Levi already discerned a disturbing reality: the naïve illusion that fascism was dead. Instead, he sensed that it was "very far from being dead; it was only hidden, encysted. It was keeping quiet, to reappear later under a new guise, a little less recognizable, a bit more respectable, better adapted to the new world that had issued from the catastrophe of World War II which fascism itself had provoked."[8]

Levi's analysis of the Holocaust did not stem from a counter-Enlightenment critique but from a deeply felt humanism. Auschwitz was the logical culmination of fascism, "its most monstrous manifestation," but one could also have fascism without the camps.[9] Fascism begins by denying the fundamental freedom and equality of human beings, proceeds to burning books, and, as foreseen by Heinrich Heine, ends by burning people. (Although many know Heine's famous 1821 aphorism, few might know that he was referring to the burning of the Koran by the Spanish Inquisition.) Lest we pride ourselves on having escaped this malediction, Levi has some sobering words. "Every age has its own fascism," he darkly warned in a 1974 essay,

> and we see the warning signs wherever the concentration of power denies citizens the possibility and the means of expressing and acting on their own free will. There are many ways of reaching this point, and not just through the terror of police intimidation, but by denying and distorting information, by undermining systems of justice, by paralyzing the education system, and by spreading in a myriad subtle ways nostalgia for a world where order reigned, and where the security of the privileged few depends on the forced labor and the forced silence of the many.[10]

I would argue that Levi recognized the Holocaust as "a second fall of man," in that we could never again conceive of human beings in the same way as before. "Consider that this has been," he writes in the poem "Shemà," on January 10, 1946. This event has erupted into history; we have witnessed what men can do to other men; if it has happened, it can happen again, and we can never return to an imagined state of innocence, no matter how fervently desired. On a more personal note, Levi recalled the days in the transit camp at Fossoli as "a condemnation, a fall, a reliving of the biblical stories of exile and migration. However, it was a tragic fall in which despair was tempered with the surprise and pride of a rediscovered identity."[11]

The conceit of the Holocaust as a second fall has now become so accepted that we might easily fail to grasp its significance. "At Auschwitz, not only man died," laments Elie Wiesel, "but the idea of man."[12] The title of Eva Hoffman's meditation on the post-Holocaust world, *After Such Knowledge*, explicitly argues for our changed moral status.[13] Emil Fackenheim predicted that "all authentic future philosophers and Christians would be sick with permanent fear."[14] The critic George Steiner equates the Holocaust with an act of suicide—as Dustin Kidd parses, one that is "inspired by hatred of the condemning best that is in man. The Holocaust signifies a second Fall of Man, one that is chosen in full awareness of the consequences; and we have burned the garden behind us."[15] Curiously, the greatest philosopher of the twentieth century, Martin Heidegger, speaks of "a second fall of man," but for the German thinker, perhaps haunted by his own tainted relationship with National Socialism—which he never condemned, even after the Second World War—this was a fall into banality, not brutality. The only similarity with other post-Holocaust thinkers is that for them and for Heidegger, this was a fall from which no redemption was possible.

This rendering of the Holocaust as a "second fall of man" has not gone unchallenged. Harold Kaplan critiques the literature of the Holocaust that "has been dominated by demands for meaning as if the world faces an eternal day of judgment focusing on a new more drastic version of 'original sin,' a second fall of man."[16] Yet I imagine Levi, the secular Jew, would have agreed that humankind's ontological status has been irrevocably altered.

When Primo Levi was born (July 31, 1919), the Jews of Italy had already assimilated into Italian social, cultural, and political life. As has often been pointed out, two non-practicing Italian Jews, Sidney Sonnino and Luigi Luzzati, each became prime minister, and the most highly decorated officer in World War I was Emmanuele Pugliese. Although there was antisemitism, often cultivated by the Catholic Church, Zionism found only a small foothold in Italy. Typical was the historian Nello Rosselli, younger brother of the more charismatic Carlo.[17] A member of the Young Italian Jewish Federation (Federazione Giovanile Ebraica Italiana), Nello spoke at a Zionist conference in Livorno in November 1924 and eloquently explained his ties to Judaism. Confessing that he did not attend synagogue on the sabbath, that he was ignorant of Hebrew, that he did not support the Zionist cause, and that he did not observe any of the religious practices demanded by his religion, Nello asked, "How then can I call myself a Jew?"

> I call myself a Jew . . . because . . . the monotheistic conscience is indestructible in me . . . because every form of idolatry repels me . . . because I regard with Jewish severity the duties of our lives on earth, and with Jewish serenity the mystery of life beyond the tomb . . . because I love all men as in Israel it was commanded . . . and I have therefore that social conception which seems to me descends from our best traditions.[18]

When Fascism came to power in 1922, it carried with it no innate antisemitism. But an alliance with Nazi Germany laid the foundation for tragedy. Levi, like most Italians—Jew and Christian alike—was shocked when the Fascist regime published a "Manifesto of the Racial Scientists" in the summer of 1938. The following autumn, the regime promulgated a series of antisemitic laws patterned on the Nuremberg Laws in Nazi Germany. In the chaos of the Second World War, Levi joined the militant underground Resistance but was captured in December 1943. In February 1944, he was sent to Auschwitz; he managed to survive through a fortuitous combination of his extensive knowledge of chemistry, the humanity of a precious few other prisoners, and simple luck. His memoir of life in the extermination camp, *Survival in Auschwitz*, has claimed its rightful place among the masterpieces of Holocaust literature. When the camp was liberated by the Red Army in January 1945, Levi began a picaresque odyssey, as recounted in *The Reawakening*. His last work, *The Drowned and the Saved*, is arguably the most profound meditation on the Shoah.

Although best known for these works on the concentrationary universe, Levi did not want to be known as a "Holocaust writer"; he aspired to the simple title of "writer," without any adjective ("Holocaust," "Italian," or "Jewish"). In addition to his Holocaust masterpieces, Levi also wrote poetry, essays, science fiction, and a novel concerning Jewish partisans in World War II. His testimony was not only, as he stated, "to bear witness" but also to search for an ethical line of conduct and moral reasoning based on classical humanism yet cognizant of humanity's changed moral status after Auschwitz.[19]

In their search for a common definition of fascism, historians and political philosophers from Benedetto Croce to John Rawls have sometimes adopted the metaphor of disease. Fascism, they write, was a virus, a virulent malady, a political affliction, a moral disorder, an ethical sickness. It attacked all that was healthy in European civilization (the Enlightenment tradition, rationality, humanitarianism, and all the freedoms associated with classical liberalism) and ended with the deaths of tens of millions of innocents and the rotting corpses of Benito Mussolini and Adolf Hitler.[20]

As with other forms of totalitarianism, Italian Fascism sought to strip away the private sphere from the individual and turn it over to the state. On another front, it inflated language to its own ends so that rabid nationalism and distorted history became the common tongue of empire. For many, the antidote to the bombastic, inflated rhetoric of Fascism was the seemingly plain and simple language of American literature; it was no coincidence that the anti-fascist writer Cesare Pavese and others spent the 1930s translating Whitman, Melville, Thoreau, Anderson, and other great American writers of the nineteenth and early twentieth centuries.

In the face of the grandiose (and often ridiculous) claims of Fascist rhetoric, writers and others took refuge in the simple pleasures of the quotidian. To combat the attempt of the Fascist state to seize control of the family through social legislation (preventing abortions, outlawing contraception, taxing bachelors, granting stipends to large families), some writers, such as Natalia Ginzburg, whose husband, Leone, was killed by the Gestapo in Rome, fell back to the familial and domestic scenes of the hearth. Primo Levi instead turned to science.

"Every age has its own fascism," Levi warned, and it would be facile to imagine that our age is immune from such temptations. As Isaiah Berlin perceptively noted:

> Few things have done more harm than the belief on the part of individuals or groups that he or she or they are in sole possession of the truth: especially

about how to live, what to be and do and that those who differ from them are not merely mistaken, but wicked or mad, and need restraining or suppressing. It is a terrible and dangerous arrogance to believe that you alone are right; have a magical eye which sees the truth, and that others cannot be right if they disagree.[21]

Another extraordinary Levi from Turin—Carlo—had written of the perennial danger of our "fear of freedom" in a powerful and provocative 1939 essay, as World War II was beginning.[22] Moreover, it was in his anthropological masterpiece of empathy and understanding, *Christ Stopped at Eboli*, that he warned of an eternal attraction to Fascism:

> We cannot foresee the political forms of the future, but in a middle-class country like Italy, where middle-class ideology has infected the masses of workers in the city, it is probable, alas, that the new institutions arising after Fascism, through either gradual evolution or violence, no matter how extreme and revolutionary they may be in appearance, will maintain the same ideology under different forms and create a new State equally far removed from real life, equally idolatrous and abstract, a perpetuation under new slogans and new flags of the worst features of the eternal tendency toward Fascism.[23]

In a speech delivered at the Casa Italiana at Columbia University (today the Italian Academy for Advanced Studies) on April 25, 1995, to commemorate the fiftieth anniversary of the liberation of Italy, Umberto Eco traced a typology of what he called "Ur-Fascism."[24] Here, I would like to place Eco's Ur-Fascist (quotes in italics) into dialogue with Levi, using the latter's essays from *The Periodic Table*.

As Eco points out, the Ur-Fascist insists on a cult of tradition while, in "Uranium," Levi praises "the boundless freedom of invention of one who has broken through the barrier and is now free to build himself the past that suits him best" (199). The Ur-Fascist stands for the rejection of modernism, whereas Levi, in "Potassium," suggests that "the truth, the reality, the intimate essence of things and man exist elsewhere, hidden behind a veil" (56). Fascism embraces irrationalism, whereas Levi, in "Iron," was filled with "disgust at all the dogmas, all the unproved affirmations," and felt a "dignity" in chemistry and physics as "the antidote to fascism" (42). The Ur-Fascist insists on action for action's sake; Levi recounts his decision to join the Resistance in "Gold": "Extremely insecure about our means, our hearts filled with much more desperation than hope, and against a backdrop of a defeated, divided country, we went into battle to test our strength" (130). For the Ur-Fascist, disagreement is treason; and Levi confessed in "Gold" that, while they proclaimed themselves anti-fascists, "Fascism had its effects on us, as on almost all Italians, alienating us and making us superficial, passive, and cynical" (128). Fascism has an innate fear of difference; Levi instead sings the praises of difference in "Zinc": "In order for the wheel to turn, for life to be lived, impurities are needed, and the impurities of impurities in the soil, too, as is known, if it is to be fertile. Dissension, diversity, the grain of salt and mustard are needed: Fascism does not want them, forbids them, and that's why you are not a Fascist; it wants everyone to be the same, and you are not" (34). Fascism makes an appeal to a frustrated middle class; Levi noted with the astuteness of a sociologist in "Nickel," the "ironic gaiety of a whole generation of Italians, intelligent and honest enough to reject Fascism, too sceptical to oppose it actively, too young to passively accept the tragedy that was taking shape and to despair of the future" (63).

The Fascists live in fear of being humiliated by the ostentatious wealth and force of their enemies; in "Nickel," Levi takes up Cesare Pavese's dictum to embrace "the two experiences of adult life": success and failure. "We are here for this: to make mistakes and to correct ourselves, to stand the blows and hand them out" (75). The Fascist rants that pacifism is trafficking with the enemy because life is permanent warfare; Levi, in "Vanadium," argues that "the enemy who remains an enemy, who perseveres in his desire to inflict suffering . . . one must not forgive him: one can try to salvage him, one can (one must!) discuss with him, but it is our duty to judge him, not to forgive him" (222–23). Whereas the Fascist has nothing but contempt for the weak, Levi, in discussing the village simpleton in "Argon," writes in biblical fashion that "the simple are the children of God and no one should call them fools" (7). Under Fascism, everyone is educated to become a hero in the cult of death; Levi defuses this decadent cult in "Gold," writing of his own seemingly impending death: "I harbored a piercing desire for everything, for all imaginable human experiences, and I cursed my previous life, which it seemed to me I had profited from little or badly, and I felt time running through my fingers, escaping from my body minute by minute, like a hemorrhage that can no longer be stanched" (137). For Eco, the Ur-Fascist transfers his will to power to sexual matters; Levi is frank and remorseless in recounting his failures with women. Besides the memorable, "feminizing" image of his pistol—an object notorious for its phallic connotations ("it was tiny, all inlaid with mother of pearl, the kind used in movies by ladies desperately intent on committing suicide" [131])—he laments in "Phosphorus" that his "inability to approach a woman was a condemnation without appeal which would accompany me to my death, confining me to a life poisoned by envy and by abstract, sterile, and aimless desires" (125). Fascism must be against "rotten" parliamentary governments; but the antifascists, emerging "out of the shadows"—men "whom Fascism had not crushed"—spoke of others, of Antonio Gramsci, Gaetano Salvemini, Piero Gobetti, Carlo and Nello Rosselli, and told Levi and his companions that "our mocking, ironic intolerance" of the old order "was not enough" (129–30). Finally, according to Eco, Ur-Fascism speaks Newspeak; but Levi saw through the veil of sanctity with which the regime wrapped itself: "Fascism was not only a clownish and improvident misrule but the negator of justice; it had not only dragged Italy into an unjust and ill-omened war, but it had arisen and consolidated itself as the custodian of a detestable legality and order, based on the coercion of those who work, on the unchecked profits of those who exploit the labor of others, on the silence imposed on those who think and do not want to be slaves, and on systematic and calculated lies" (129–30).

An example of Levi's willingness to problematize the categories of traditional humanism is his concept of the "grey zone," contained in the second chapter of his last work, *The Drowned and the Saved*. Since much has been written on this, I would here like to approach the idea through a tenuously related work, Tim Blake Nelson's 2001 film, "The Grey Zone."

Just as Levi refused to embrace an easy Manichean division of the concentrationary universe into evil Nazis and innocent victims, Nelson rejects sanctifying the victims. Levi was one of the first to point out the moral contagion that infected the inmates, and focused on the extreme situation of the *Sonderkommando* at Auschwitz. Both the Italian writer and the American filmmaker were struck by the moral choices made by Miklós Nyiszli, a Hungarian doctor who "volunteered" for the *Sonderkommando* in exchange for the safety of his wife and daughter (both of whom survived the camps). On clearing out a contingent of Jews from one of the gas chambers, the *Sonderkommando* discovers a young girl who has miraculously survived the Zyklon B. The discovery of the girl changes the moral calculations of the *Sonderkommando*.

Although not depicted in the film, an episode recounted by Nyiszli and mentioned by Levi also deserves mention here because it accurately reflects the sense of moral corruption institutionalized in the camps, even away from the gas chambers or crematoria. One evening, a soccer match is organized between the SS and the *Sonderkommando*. "The teams lined up on the field," recalled Nyiszli. "They put the ball into play. Sonorous laughter filled the courtyard."[25] Levi not only paints a grim portrait of the same event, but points out its larger moral significance, hearing in this episode only satanic laughter, for the Nazis have won the game before it is even played: "It is consummated, we have succeeded, you no longer are the other race, the anti-race, the prime enemy of the millennial Reich . . . we have embraced you, corrupted you, dragged you down to the bottom with us . . .

dirtied with your own blood . . . you too, like us and Cain, have killed the brother. Come, we can play together."[26]

Yet even in this modern *Inferno*, there are the lessons of humanism. One is taught to Levi by the Austrian veteran of the Great War, Steinlauf, who convinces Levi that:

> precisely because the Lager was a great machine to reduce us to beasts, we must not become beasts; that even in this place one can survive, and therefore one must want to survive, to tell the story, to bear witness; and that to survive we must force ourselves to save at least the skeleton, the scaffolding, the form of civilization. We are slaves, deprived of every right, exposed to every insult, condemned to certain death, but we still possess one power, and we must defend it with all our strength for it is the last—the power to refuse our consent.[27]

Compare Levi's passage with that of the Catholic noblewoman Pelagia Lewinska, also a prisoner at Auschwitz:

> At the outset the living places, the ditches, the mud, the piles of excrement behind the blocks, had appalled me with their horrible filth . . . And then I saw the light! I saw that it was not a question of disorder or lack of organization but that, on the contrary, a very thoroughly conscious idea was in the back of the camp's existence. They had condemned us to die in our own filth, to drown in mud, in our own excrement. They wished to debase us, to destroy our human dignity, to efface every vestige of humanity, to return us to the state of wild animals, to fill us with contempt toward ourselves and others. But from the instant I grasped the motivating principle . . . it was if I had awakened from a dream. I felt under orders to live . . . And if I died at Auschwitz it would be as a human being. I was not going to become the contemptible, disgusting brute my enemy wished me to be.[28]

One of the most commented upon passages of Levi's work is the chapter "The Drowned and the Saved" in his first book. Yet the ringing manifesto in defense of humanism on its first page is sometimes overlooked:

> We are in fact convinced that no human experience is without meaning or unworthy of analysis, and that the fundamental values, even if they are not positive, can be deduced from this particular world which we are describing . . . We do not believe in the most obvious and facile deduction: that man is fundamentally brutal, egotistical and stupid in his conduct once every civilized institution is taken away, and that the Häftling is consequently nothing but a man without inhibitions. We believe, rather, that the only conclusion to be drawn is that in the face of driving necessity and physical disabilities many social habits and instincts are reduced to silence.[29]

Whereas the other inmates have scratched their numbers onto the bottom of their tin soup bowls, and Clausner has written "Ne pas chercher à comprendre," Levi and Alberto have insisted on carving their own names.

Tzvetan Todorov has perceptively called our post-Holocaust humanism "an imperfect garden."[30] Indeed, while science and humanism may permit a precarious return to the garden, it is a garden that we must share with the serpent. But there are other beasts in the garden that are not as pernicious: the centaur, for example. As both a chemist and a writer, Levi felt the divorce of science from humanism to be the tragic flaw of the twentieth century. He reveled in his stance straddling two worlds. "I am a centaur," he once wrote enigmatically, as all men and women are centaurs: "a tangle of flesh and mind, divine inspiration and dust."[31] He insisted that his role as a scientist, chemist, and technician were complementary and not contradictory to his status as a writer and humanist. As he remarked in an interview with American writer Philip Roth, "In my own way I have remained an impurity, an anomaly, but now for reasons other than before: not especially as a Jew but as an Auschwitz survivor and an outsider-writer, coming not from the literary or university establishment but from the industrial world."[32]

Primo Levi was an essayist and a prolific writer for various Italian newspapers; we today might recognize him as a "public intellectual." It was in his "other" work, such as *The Monkey's Wrench* and *The Periodic Table*, which Levi did not perceive as divorced from his Auschwitz experience, that he offered a possibility of living in a post-Holocaust world. Here, Levi redeemed the idea of work for us, transforming it from a curse to a blessing. He would reverse the perverse irony of *Arbeit Macht Frei* and insist that, indeed, work *could* make one free. Work well done; work as the expression of *techné*, of craft, of the intellect. The Italian bricklayer Lorenzo Perone, finding himself in the camp as a slave laborer and befriending Levi, refuses to build shoddy walls. Not only does he slip Levi and Alberto extra rations of bread and soup for six months but, by his example of "work well done," teaches Levi an important lesson: "Lorenzo was a man; his humanity was pure and uncontaminated, he was outside this world of negation. Thanks to Lorenzo, I managed not to forget that I myself was a man."[33] These were paeans to the dignity of work, "especially," Levi insisted, "the work of the craftsman as modern analogue of the search for adventure and creativity . . . a theme valid for all times, all places and all social structures."[34]

Yet, Levi suffered from depression most of his life and this could not all be blamed on Auschwitz. Sometimes, he could find respite in writing, but the completion of a work or a specific task, such as the translation of Kafka's *The Trial*, could thrust him into the darkest despair. Toward the end of his life, with the appearance of Holocaust deniers and historical "revisionists," he was again haunted by the shadow of Auschwitz. Often compared to Elie Wiesel, there is one major difference: Wiesel had the gift of faith, however tormented by the reality of the Shoah. Wiesel has spent the last sixty years in a continuous dialogue and debate with his God; Levi, the atheist, had the benefit of no such interlocutor. Instead, he had only the foundation of classic humanism: "I was helped by the determination, which I stubbornly preserved, to recognize always, even in the darkest days, in my companions and myself, men, not things, and thus to avoid that total humiliation and demoralization which led so many to spiritual shipwreck."[35]

"I became a Jew in Auschwitz," he once wrote, comparing the concentration camp to a "university" of life.[36] Yet he could also paradoxically admit in an interview late in life, "There is Auschwitz, and so there cannot be God."[37] Rather than seek to untangle these contradictions, Levi embraced them. It was perhaps his last lesson to us.

Notes

1. From his 1949 essay "Cultural Criticism and Society," reprinted in *Prisms*, trans. Samuel and Shierry Weber (Cambridge, MA: MIT Press, 1967/1981), 17–34.

2. Theodor Adorno, *Negative Dialectics*, trans. E. B. Ashton (New York: Seabury Press, 1973), 361.

3. Primo Levi, *Survival in Auschwitz*, trans. Stuart Woolf (New York: Collier, 1961), 59.

4. Ibid., 22.

5. Here, the reader should know that an essay in the book *Primo Levi and the Fate of Humanism after Auschwitz* (New York: Palgrave, 2009), by one of this volume's contributors, Jonathan Druker, offers a radically different interpretation than the one presented here.

6. From "Vanadium," in *The Periodic Table*, 223.

7. "Trauma/Transgression/Testimony," in *The Legacy of Primo Levi*, ed. Stanislao G. Pugliese (New York: Palgrave, 2005), 3–15, and in a paper, "Primo Levi's Politics," at the conference "Primo Levi in the Present Tense: New Reflections on His Life and Work Before and After Auschwitz," organized by Millicent Marcus and Risa Sodi at Yale University, April 2008.

8. Afterword, "Why Auschwitz?" in *Shema: Collected Poems of Primo Levi*, trans. Ruth Feldman and Brain Swann (London: Menard Press, 1976), 45–46.

9. Ibid., 51.

10. Primo Levi in *Il Corriere della Sera*, May 8, 1974; reprinted in *L'assimetria e la vita*, ed. Marco Belpoliti (Turin: Einaudi, 2002); translated as "The Past We Thought Would Never Return," in *The Black Hole of Auschwitz*, trans. Sharon Wood (New York: Polity Press, 2005), 34.

11. "Itinerary of a Jewish Writer," in *The Black Hole of Auschwitz*, 164.

12. Elie Wiesel, *Legends of Our Time*, trans. Stephen Donadio (New York: Avon, 1970), 230.
13. Eva Hoffman, *After Such Knowledge: Memory, History, and the Legacy of the Holocaust* (New York: Public Affairs, 2004).
14. Emil L. Fackenheim, *To Mend the World: Foundations of Post-Holocaust Jewish Thought* (Bloomington: Indiana University Press, 1994), 303.
15. Dustin Kidd, "The Aesthetics of Truth, The Athletics of Time: George Steiner and the Retreat from the Word," December 7, 1998. http://xroads.virginia.edu/~ma99/kidd/resume/steiner.html.
16. Harold Kaplan, *Conscience & Memory: Meditation in a Museum of the Holocaust* (Chicago, IL: University of Chicago Press, 1994), 150.
17. For the only biography in English, see Stanislao G. Pugliese, *Carlo Rosselli: Socialist Heretic and Antifascist Exile* (Cambridge, MA: Harvard University Press, 1999).
18. The best study of Nello Rosselli's religious beliefs is Bruno Di Porto's essay "Il problema ebraico in Nello Rosselli," in *Giustizia e Libertà nella lotta antifascista*, ed. Carlo Francovich (Florence: La Nuova Italia, 1978), 491–99. Rosselli's speech is quoted in Renzo De Felice, *Storia degli ebrei italiani sotto il fascismo*, 89–90; English translation in Susan Zuccotti, *The Italians and the Holocaust* (New York: Basic Books, 1987), 246.
19. See especially Robert S. C. Gordon, *Primo Levi's Ordinary Virtues: From Testimony to Ethics* (Oxford: Oxford University Press, 2001).
20. See Stanislao G. Pugliese, "The Antidote to Fascism," in Carla Pekelis, *My Version of the Facts* (Evanston, IL: Marlboro Press/Northwestern, 2004), vii.
21. Isaiah Berlin, "Notes on Prejudice," in *New York Review of Books*, October 18, 2001, 12.
22. Carlo Levi, *Paura della libertà* (Turin: Einaudi, 1946); reprinted in *Scritti politici*, edited by David Bidussa (Turin: Einaudi, 2001), 132–204; for a recent English translation, see *Fear of Freedom*, trans. Adophe Gourevitch, ed. Stanislao G. Pugliese (New York: Columbia University Press, 2008).
23. Carlo Levi, *Christ Stopped at Eboli*, trans. Frances Frenaye, with a new introduction by Mark Rotella (New York: Fararr, Straus, & Giroux, 2006), 252.
24. Umberto Eco, "Ur-Fascism," *New York Review of Books*, June 22, 1995, 12–15.
25. Miklos Nyiszli, *Auschwitz: A Doctor's Eyewitness Account* (New York: Arcade, 1993), 57–58.
26. Primo Levi, *The Drowned and the Saved*, trans. Raymond Rosenthal (New York: Summit, 1988), 55.
27. Levi, *Survival in Auschwitz*, 36.
28. Pelagia Lewinska, *Twenty Months at Auschwitz* (New York: Lyle Stuart, 1989), 141, 150; quoted in Rubenstein, *After Auschwitz*, 186–87.
29. Levi, *Survival in Auschwitz*, 79.
30. Tzvetan Todorov, *Imperfect Garden: The Legacy of Humanism* (Princeton, NJ: Princeton University Press, 2002).
31. "Argon," in Levi, *The Periodic Table*, 9.

32. "A Conversation with Philip Roth," in Levi, *Survival in Auschwitz* (New York: Touchstone, 1996), 185.

33. Ibid., 94, 111.

34. "Itinerary of a Jewish Writer," in Levi, *The Black Hole of Auschwitz*, 164.

35. "Afterword," trans. Ruth Feldman, in Levi, *The Reawakening*, trans. Stuart Woolf (New York: Collier, 1986), 217.

36. Ferdinando Camon, *Conversations with Primo Levi*, trans. John Shepley (Marlboro, VT: Marlboro Press, 1989), 68.

37. Ibid.

2

The Itinerary of an Identity

Primo Levi's "Parallel Nationalization"

Nancy Harrowitz
Boston University

In 1975, Primo Levi published a troubling description about what his Jewish identity meant to him in the year 1941. This passage appears in *The Periodic Table*, the story of his life as a chemist: "In truth, until precisely those months it had not meant much to me that I was a Jew: to myself, and in contacts with my Christian friends, I had always considered my origins as an almost insignificant but odd fact, a small cheerful anomaly, like having a crooked nose or freckles; a Jew is somebody who at Christmas does not decorate a tree, who should not eat salami but eats it anyway, who has learned a bit of Hebrew at thirteen and then has forgotten it."[1] The political scene at the time was rapidly shifting. The Fascist racialist doctrine of the purported impurity of Jews had become diffuse. Levi was learning what exclusion meant for Jews, as it became difficult for him to remain at the university because of the antisemitic Racial Laws of 1938–1939. Despite the claims he makes to the contrary, the fact of being Jewish was already much more significant than the "small cheerful anomaly" he notes, as not only Levi but also the entire Jewish community of Turin was then suffering under laws eliminating Italian Jews' civil rights.

Yet Levi's representation of his Jewish identity has a rather sweet nostalgic tone, evoking, for example, his bar mitzvah at age 13—which itself is a complicated symbol of an often rapid learning of the tradition and, for many Jews, the equally quick forgetting of the same. His description, however, while appearing on the surface to be innocuous, has another side to it. One of the similes that Levi employs to represent the "cheerful anomaly" of Jewishness—namely, a "crooked nose"—tells a different story. The figure of the purportedly "Jewish" nose had already been used in antisemitic discourse for many decades in Europe to great harm to the image of Jews, and now was being used widely in Fascist anti-Jewish propaganda.[2] How could Levi then describe a persecuted Jewish identity in Fascist Italy as "cheerful," as random and potentially "cute" as the revealing nose that was often used as a goad to hatred and derision?

The exploration of what Jewish identity meant to Levi during Fascism raises important questions: what did it mean to be a Jew in Fascist Italy, or more to the point in Levi's case, what did it mean to be an Italian Jew who did not seem to acknowledge the antisemitism surrounding him, despite overwhelming evidence to the contrary? Anti-Jewish campaigns began in the early 1930s with radio broadcasts, newspaper articles, the expulsion of foreign Jews, antisemitic children's novels, and finally the Racial Laws. As part of what one can call his rhetoric of denial, Levi gave a lecture to the Jewish community in 1938 that had as its topic the astounding thesis that antisemitism was at an all-time historical low. How could Levi still make this claim in 1938?

Born in 1919, the year Mussolini's party was formed, Levi was educated within the strictures of Fascism. As the years of Fascism wore on, more and more attempts were made to achieve national homogeneity. Theories purporting common racial origins of all Christian Italians were propagated beginning in the early 1930s. These claims excluded from *italianità* a generation of patriotic Italian Jews, many of whom had fought in World War I or swore a strong allegiance to the monarchy, often naming their sons and daughters after the king and queen. The Racial Laws of 1938–1939 were the culmination of this exclusion, resulting in many hardships for Italian Jews. After the Racial Laws, after their painful expulsion from a new, Fascist-defined Italian national identity, where could the civic identity of Italian Jews reside? How did they negotiate within themselves this painful change in their civic status?

Primo Levi's transformation of life-altering antisemitism into a benign image of a cheerful crooked nose is, as I will demonstrate, representative of a set of strategies that he adopted to contain or transform a prejudice that ultimately challenged his Italian identity, which he held near and dear. However, before we further explore Levi's understanding of his Jewishness and what it meant in the Italian context, the notion of Italian Jewish identity itself must be contextualized historically in order to understand what tensions were at play for him.

A clear relation exists between Levi's approach to his identity in *The Periodic Table* and the development of Jewish identity before and during Fascism.[3] I would argue that Levi's strategies of Jewish self-representation are the direct result of a genealogy of denial regarding antisemitism in Italy that began decades before and strongly influenced Levi's generation. Levi's unwillingness to acknowledge the life-altering prejudices surrounding him in Fascist Italy is not only a strategy to contain and, therefore, minimize the bigotry, but it is also a marker of a denial whose historical roots lie in myths regarding Jewish emancipation during and after the 1860–1861 unification of Italy.

An examination of some crucial moments in the development of a post-ghetto, post-unification Jewish identity in Italy will shed some significant light on Levi's representation of his own Jewishness and help understand the apparent contradictions found in his representation.

Conditions for Jews in Italy by the late eighteenth century, after almost three hundred years of ghetto life, were among the worst in Europe. In 1796, Napoleon exerted his influence, at the beginning of what was known as the Jacobin triennium, in Italy. Announcing the immediate emancipation of the ghettos, proclamations went into effect in northern cities and towns declaring that the gates of the ghettos should immediately come down and that Jews thereafter were to be granted full civil rights. This dramatic change in the status of northern Italian Jews had differing effects: in some towns, the gates were indeed pulled down; in others, Jews were afraid of the reaction of their Gentile neighbors and so wanted the gates to remain intact as protection. After the departure of the French troops, there were attacks on Jews all over Italy, as they were seen to be supporters of the French who had brought them freedom. A Catholic group from Modena that called itself *Viva Maria* marched into the small towns of Siena and Senigallia and began murderous pogroms during which at least 26 Jews were killed and hundreds wounded.[4] Later, Jews quickly became part of the initiative to bring unification to the country, and often fought in the battles from 1848 to 1861.

The construction of a new Jewish identity in Italy after the unification was both an exciting and a terrifying proposition. On the one hand, integration was not difficult in some respects, because the Italian Jews already belonged linguistically to the area in which they resided and they enjoyed a much higher rate of literacy than non-Jewish Italians did. After the final emancipation from the ghettos and then unification in 1860–1861, Jews integrated into all levels of Italian society, even, within the span of one or two generations, attaining high posts within the government. Yet, on the other hand, antisemitic campaigns and discussions regarding the visibility of Jewish religious and cultural practice and how those differences could be suppressed—the so-called Jewish question—were ongoing. Many members of the clergy, arguing against any acceptance of Jews unless they fully assimilated and converted, maintained antisemitic movements throughout the end of the century.[5]

After unification, Italy, too, was not immune to the debate in the rest of Europe regarding the cultural and religious visibility of Jews. In the 1890s, prominent Italian criminologists and anthropologists, such as Cesare Lombroso, Paolo Mantegazza, and Enrico Ferri—both Jewish and non-Jewish—discussed the ability and necessity of the Jews to assimilate fully. It was generally held, as the historian Mario Toscano puts it, that the prevailing culture "stigmatized Jews and Judaism as holdovers of an archaic identity rendered obsolete by the progress of reason and science."[6]

The degree to which this pressure was felt can be measured by the writings of the criminologist Lombroso on the Jewish situation. Lombroso, himself a Jew, wrote a 1894 book titled *L'antisemitismo e le science moderne* (Anti-Semitism and Modern Science), in which he refutes pseudoscientific claims based on purported physical evidence that the Jews were an inferior and dangerous "race." He alleges, however, that Jews brought antisemitism upon themselves through the visibility of their "atavistic" religious practices. Lombroso cites as particularly harmful the wearing of skullcaps and prayer shawls, circumcision, and even the use of Passover matzos.

As a solution to antisemitism, Lombroso proposed that the total assimilation of Jews would ensure the removal of any perceptible difference. The last chapter of his book recommends a happy merger between Jews and Christians that would result in all Jews becoming Christian—in other words, the complete erasure of Judaism, resulting, thereby, in a complete erasure of bigotry.

There are, however, two aspects of Lombroso's speculation about, and investment in, Jewish identity that are quite revealing of the tensions at play in the creation of a postunification Jewish identity. The first is his choice to write about antisemitism in what was essentially a protective response due to increased pogroms in Eastern Europe in the 1890s. Even though he was clearly unsympathetic to Orthodox Jewish practice, he did believe that Jews could get out of harm's way by eliminating their visible differences. Second, Lombroso evidently continued to ponder the issue of Jewish identity and Zionism well after his book on antisemitism appeared.

In 1897 and 1898, only three years after the publication of *Anti-Semitism and Modern Science*, Lombroso traveled to Russia, where he met with young Zionists. He subsequently wrote articles for the Austrian press in support of Zionism (this, after attacking Zionism a few years previously), and thus appeared fully to embrace a Jewish identity (and a Zionist identity, as well), rather than ducking his Judaism under the guise of a mediating scientific gaze. Ultimately, he gave an interview in Amsterdam, published in 1901 by a Jewish newspaper in Italy, in which he baldly stated that he was a Zionist because he was a Jew, and as a Jew he did not know if it were possible not to be a Zionist.[7] He had evidently developed a much broader notion of what

Jewishness could be and was now proposing that an openly Jewish and Zionist identity was acceptable. No longer was he content with the erasure of Judaism that he had proposed only a few years before.[8]

In his subject position as a scientist during the development of extremely pejorative biologically based theories regarding Jews, Lombroso was working within an antagonistic environment. Lombroso's earlier writings can be interpreted as a reaction to such hostility, as he was a Jewish scientist writing against Jewish difference due to the pressure to conform exercised by his scientific discipline. The sentiment about Jewish assimilation voiced in *Anti-Semitism and Modern Science* reflects Lombroso's own desire to be able to assimilate fully into his profession. As Alexander Stille asserts, "the nature of the Jewish community was determined by the political needs of the larger society," and so Lombroso, at least for a while, became the scientifically "neutral" Jew who projected society's desire that the "Jewish question" be solved by assimilation.[9] Even this stance, however, did not protect him from vicious antisemitic attacks from colleagues who had worked closely with him for years, one of whom stated that Lombroso's "thought" was not Italian.[10] And yet, despite these tensions, he ultimately reclaimed a secular Jewish identity for himself, thus demonstrating a resiliency about this very identity.

From the middle to the end of the twentieth century, the Jewish community was torn between a desire to become as fully integrated as possible into Italian society and a desire to maintain its Jewish identity despite this acculturation. Lombroso's situation exemplifies these tensions and demonstrates, as well, that an uncomplicated integration into either a scientific society or a secular one without resistance was not possible for Italian Jews during this period. It should be remembered that Lombroso was a highly influential figure not only during his time but also for generations afterward. Primo Levi's father, for example, was a great admirer of Lombroso, and his books were a constant presence in Levi's childhood home.

The next important moment in the history of postunification Jewish identity in Italy comes in the writings of the distinguished Italian Jewish historian, Arnaldo Momigliano. Also from Piedmont, Momigliano was known for his research on many topics—classical studies as well as modern. He took a vivid interest in the history of Italian Jews, and wrote many essays on the subject over a span of 50 years, collected in a book titled *Essays on Ancient and Modern Judaism* (*Pagine ebraiche*, or "Jewish Pages," in the original) and published in Italian in 1987. Momigliano left Italy after the war, and lived abroad for most of his remaining career. After the betrayal of Italian Jews by the Fascists, Momigliano preferred the condition of an expatriate.

In 1933, Momigliano published a review essay of a book by Cecil Roth on the history of the Jews of Venice, in which he codified beliefs regarding Jewish identity in Italy. Momigliano's influence is crucial in order to understand the representation of the civic status of Italian Jews and the genealogy of denial that influenced Levi.

Momigliano writes that the unification of Italy in 1860–1861 resulted, for Jews coming out of the recently opened ghettos, in a process that came to be called "parallel nationalization." He begins by taking Roth to task for a lack of historical perspective: "Finally, a detail among details, an episode among episodes, we read of the passion and commitment with which the Jews of Venice cooperated in the defense of the Republic in 1848. But this cannot be viewed as a simple episode, one among many in the history of the Jews of Venice; indeed, it is the very conclusion of the entire history of the Jews of Venice."[11]

Arguing that, for the Jews of Venice, unification posed the end to their history, Momigliano raises an intriguing question about the nature of their identity in relation to their history and their patriotism. Taken literally, his assertion could mean that Venetian Jews were either no longer Jewish or no longer Venetian, because a new civic identity had superseded both. Yet clearly, it is their Jewish identity that dissolved under the equalizing pressure of the new *italianità*. It would be unimaginable to suggest the complete disappearance of any regional identity in Italy. It would appear in contrast, however, that it was instead quite acceptable to propose the dissolution of a marginalized and marginalizing identity, such as Jewishness.

Momigliano continues with his thesis regarding the development of national identity and the ways in which that development affected different groups in Italy:

> The history of the Jews of Venice, like the history of the Jews of any other Italian city, is essentially the history of the development of their Italian national consciousness. This development (and we should bear this in mind) does not ensue from a *pre-existing* Italian national consciousness so that Jews had to become part of an already formed Italian national consciousness. The development of an Italian national consciousness for Jews is parallel to the formation of a national consciousness by the Piedmontese, the Neapolitans, or the Sicilians; it is part of the same process and characterizes the process itself. Just as from the beginning of the seventeenth century to the nineteenth century, regardless of previous events, the Piedmontese and the Neapolitans have become Italian, Jews living in Italy have at the same time become Italian. Obviously, this has not prevented Jews from retaining, to a greater or lesser extent, Jewish peculiarities, just as the fact of becoming Italian has not stopped the Piedmontese or the Neapolitans from

retaining regional characteristics. When the gates of the ghettos were opened, this process was, generally speaking, already accomplished.[12]

Momigliano's argument is based on the fact that Italy is a country whose history before unification was characterized by foreign invasion, strong regional identities, and the diffuse use of dialects rather than a standard language outside of literary practice. Jews in Italy were closely tied linguistically to the communities in which they lived because they spoke the local dialects and were usually identified from the outside as members of that region.

Since all of Italy required Italianization in order to create a new national identity, Momigliano reminds us that, before unification, there were no "Italians."[13] As the new, nationalized society learned to identify and construct itself, so were the Jews part of this process. But at a certain point, Momigliano's analysis becomes an unparallel comparison: he tells us that, after the establishment of a national consciousness, Jewish "peculiarities," as opposed to regional "characteristics," remained. We can imagine what those regional characteristics might be—food, accent, dialects—but what were Jewish peculiarities?

The term "peculiarities" that Momigliano uses takes us back to the so-called Jewish question of the nineteenth century. It resonates with the anthropologists' debates that regarded purportedly strange Jewish customs as standing in the way of emancipation: Jews could not become full citizens of any state unless they abandoned their customs, which were inextricably linked to their religious practice. Those "peculiarities"—in other words, "differences"—stand at the heart of cultural and religious identity. Momigliano is simultaneously accepting—perhaps reluctantly—the Jewish difference that remained after unification and marking it through the uneven choice of language he adopts to describe it.

Momigliano's theories about Italian Jewish identity might have gone relatively unnoticed had it not been for the reaction of Antonio Gramsci, whose statements regarding a lack of antisemitism in Italy became widely disseminated: "There is no anti-Semitism in Italy for the very reasons Momigliano mentions—that a national consciousness developed and established itself after having overcome two cultural forms [. . .] it goes without saying that the overcoming of Catholic cosmopolitanism and the ensuing formation of a lay spirit, not only independent but at odds with Catholicism, caused Jews to develop a national consciousness and to abandon Judaism."[14]

In this passage, Gramsci takes two big leaps: first, stating that there is no antisemitism in Italy, and then claiming that Jews abandoned Judaism precisely because they had adopted a national identity. Has Gramsci merely clarified Momigliano's syllogism, or has he rather created a false syllogism out of Momigliano's terms? The theme of "Judaism without Jews" was an integral part of discussions and debates regarding Jewish emancipation all over Europe. Gramsci, however, went much further than Momigliano. For Gramsci, parallel nationalization signifies one identity ceding entirely to the next—in other words, total assimilation without any leftover "peculiarities." Lombroso's earlier desire for an assimilation that would end antisemitism is reflected in Gramsci's claim regarding the abandonment of Judaism.

By the early twentieth century, beliefs regarding an ease of integration and lack of antisemitism had solidified into the twinned concepts of Momigliano's "parallel nationalization" and Gramsci's "Italy without antisemitism." Past pressures regarding assimilation were seemingly forgotten as an emerging Jewish identity became fused and infused with patriotic ideals, a process that had begun with Jews fighting for unification. Despite Gramsci's apparent hyperbole, his analysis ultimately became the dominant myth regarding the emancipation, citizenship, and integration history of Jews in Italy. Looking at the actual history of emancipation, however, it becomes clear that these analyses are based more on illusory ideas than on the realities of the situation. The path to emancipation was not the uncomplicated one that Momigliano suggests, and both Momigliano and Gramsci's analyses are simplistic and misleading.

In Momigliano's case, the experience of the Holocaust changed his views dramatically. Momigliano wrote another essay in 1984, titled "The Jews of Italy," in which he speaks of ghetto life and linguistic variables, and of how different life was for Jews depending entirely on the region in which they lived.[15] He writes of wondering, when traveling through Italian towns, if Jews had been expelled, if they had been excluded from public life, and how and if the Jews who had lived there survived. The essay has a poignant and regretful, commemorative tone, even before the reader arrives at the moment when Momigliano speaks of having lost 11 family members, including his parents, to the Holocaust. In another essay, titled "Storie e memorie ebraiche del nostro tempo" (Jewish History and Memory in Our Time) and written at about the same time, Momigliano discusses Mussolini's failed relationships with Italian Jewish intellectuals—several of whom ended up leading the resistance movement—and with Italian Jewish women such as Margherita Sarfatti. He suggests that the Racial Laws "were an attempt to liquidate his own past."[16] History had made clear to Momigliano the fallacies of the notion of "parallel nationalization."[17]

Momigliano's case brings up important questions regarding the relationship of Jews to national identity. What can the term expatriate mean to Jewish citizens whose civic status is removed by their country? What could the term "patriate" have meant to a people whose identity was legally removed through the Racial Laws? What could their connection have been to an Italy that had rejected them as citizens? Momigliano's expatriate status is an example of precisely what his generation of Italian Jews lost during Fascism—namely, a concept of an Italy where they belonged, an Italy that was still their homeland. Momigliano understood this and preferred to stay away physically, rejecting an Italy that had rejected him, by refusing to come back after the war.

Levi represents the history of the Jews in Italy as a series of vignettes emphasizing the idiosyncratic and the colorful. In *The Periodic Table*, he celebrates the Jewish difference of his ancestors while simultaneously erasing or circumscribing the antisemitism, both in the distant past and in his own youth, which would later challenge his civic identity as a "legitimate Italian." Jewish difference is containable by limiting it to a "small amusing anomaly." His logic resembles Gramsci's and Lombroso's in that the existence of prejudice is dependent on the presence of Jewish difference. If his own and that of his "ancestors" can be relegated to a small amusing anomaly, then this must mean that the antisemitism surrounding him may be insignificant as well.[18] To a certain degree, Lombroso's trajectory of the denial, then acceptance, of his Jewish identity mirrors Levi's. Toward the end of his life, Levi gave a talk titled "L'itinerario di uno scrittore ebreo" (The Itinerary of a Jewish Writer), in which he seems fully to accept a designation that he had previously resisted, that of "Jewish writer," given to him by the outside world.[19]

Does Levi's circumscription of the problematics of Jewish identity dovetail with other mythologizing discourses about Fascism? In postwar Italy, a new version of myths regarding the nature of antisemitism within Italy emerged. For many years after the war, murderous measures taken against Jews in Italy by the Fascists were blamed on pressure from Hitler, as if no indigenous form of antisemitism or persecution was possible. These myths are finally being put to rest, although not without resistance. Historians such as Giorgio Fabre and Mario Toscano have found ample documentation that Mussolini had conducted campaigns to suppress Jews before Hitler came to power, and that the deportation of Jews after the German invasion of 1943 was not carried out by Nazis acting alone but more often by the Fascist militia.[20] Despite much evidence to the contrary, myths still prevail in Italy about Fascism, and there is a need for ongoing scholarship.[21]

What were the stakes for Levi in the version of Jewish life he gives in his works and in the highly creative story of his family's integration that he presents in *The Periodic Table*? Furthermore, we could also ask what the stakes were for Momigliano in 1933 in his theory of parallel nationalization.

We can speculate that the *italianità* of a civic Jewish identity, fed by Jews fighting for unification and at a new high after the intense patriotism of World War I, was deeply unsettled by rising antisemitism under Fascism and by the Fascist political regime, whose first aim was to bolster national identity—a concept indeed dear to the hearts of Italian Jews because of their past nationalism. It was an extremely difficult moment for a people whose identity for almost one hundred years had been invested in the new Italian nation and who now faced a new antisemitism presented as part of a nationalism that could—and in fact, did—unseat their civic identity.

One could say that the warnings were all there for Levi and Momigliano's generation; the question of whether or not Jews should be treated as full citizens had been in play since emancipation. But in most cases, the battle was won—or so Italian Jews thought. The issue, however, came around again, this time with Mussolini, who in the early 1930s began to paint Italian Jews as Zionists whose purportedly divided loyalties had to be questioned. The process of questioning Italian Jews' identity as not truly Italian—a process that eventually led to the removal of civic status through the Racial Laws—had in fact begun much earlier.

Levi's relationship to Italy and to his Jewishness was very different: he lacked the critical distance that Momigliano took, even though we can see that in the 1930s, with his parallel nationalization argument, Momigliano had initially fallen into the trap of the blind civic investment of Levi's generation. Levi differs from Momigliano in the following not insignificant respect: after the war, Levi is unable to look at Fascist Italy with Momigliano's same critical eye. Momigliano clearly understands the relationship between Nazi persecution and Fascist collaboration, as he tells us that Holocaust deportations were carried out by Nazis and Fascists in alliance, even before other historians were in agreement on this very important point. Momigliano's nostalgia was reserved for a lost past that preceded the loss of civil rights in Fascist Italy, and he did not romanticize a problematic history. Levi, on the other hand, represents his own past in Fascist Italy primarily through a sentimental perspective that undermines the strength of the prejudice that he and other Italian Jews suffered during the time.

Levi says in an oft-cited interview that the Holocaust gave him a Jewish identity—that it sewed a yellow star onto his heart.[22] But, unlike Momigliano, what it did not seem to do was to allow him a critical distance from a sort of nostalgia for his childhood and adolescence in Fascist Italy. Feeling himself to be foremost an Italian, Primo Levi seemingly could not reconcile his self-image with the realities of exclusion and betrayal that was Italy for Italian Jews after the mid-1930s. A late nineteenth-century antisemitic attack carried out against Levi's own family can be seen as a sign of what was to come two generations later.[23] Rather than the "lowest ebb" of antisemitism, as Levi asserts in his talk of 1938, he finds himself willingly blind in the middle of intense antisemitism that was not by any means a historical anomaly ascribable to Hitler's influence on Mussolini.[24]

Levi's understanding of Italian Jewish identity raises questions about the consequences of acculturation and integration, cultural accommodation, and the relationship between national identity and Jewish identity for Italian Jews. Through an analysis of the broader context in which Levi developed as a writer, we may better understand his dilemma, caught between devotion to Italy and persecution by the Nazi and Fascist regimes.

Notes

1. "Per vero, fino appunto a quei mesi non mi era importato molto di essere ebreo: dentro di me, e nei contatti con i miei amici cristiani, avevo sempre considerato la mia origine come un fatto pressoché trascurabile ma curioso, una piccola anomalia allegra, come chi abbia il naso storto o le lentiggini; un ebreo è uno che a Natale non fa l'albero, che non dovrebbe mangiare il salame ma lo mangia lo stesso, che ha imparato un po' di ebraico a tredici anni e poi lo ha dimenticato" (*Opere*, 1997, 1:770). Levi, *The Periodic Table*, trans. Raymond Rosenthal (New York: Schocken Books, 1984), 35–36.
2. See Sander Gilman, *The Jew's Body* (New York: Routledge, 1991).
3. The historian Renzo De Felice is another figure of Levi's generation who tended to exculpate Fascism and the role played by Fascist antisemitism in the Holocaust. One may speculate that his reasons were similar to Levi's and to the young Arnaldo Momigliano's.
4. *Storia d'Italia*, ed. *Corrado Viventi*, vol. 11, *Gli ebrei in Italia* (Milan: Einaudi, 1996), 1136–37.
5. Despite evidence to the contrary, the historian Mary Gibson argues that there was no "Jewish question" in Italy for the following reason: "Race was most often linked to the 'Southern Question' [. . .] the belief that two different races inhabited the North and the South provided a barrier to the government's ambition to homogenize the peninsula and make new 'Italians' [. . .] this focused attention on southerners, rather than two other groups more familiar to European racial theorists, the Jews and black Africans." Gibson, *Born to Crime: Cesare Lombroso and the Origins of Biological Criminality* (Westport, CT: Praeger, 2002), 101.
6. Mario Toscano, "Italian Jewish Identity," in *Jews in Italy under Fascist and Nazi Rule: 1922–1945*, ed. Joshua Zimmerman (Cambridge: Cambridge University Press, 2005), 43.
7. Cesare Lombroso, *L'antisemitismo e le scienze moderne* (Torino: Roux, 1894). See Delia Frigessi, *Cesare Lombroso* (Milano: Einaudi, 2003), 320–23, for a discussion of Lombroso's Zionism. For more discussion of Lombroso's Jewish identity, see David Forgacs, "Building the Body of a Nation: Lombroso's *L'anti-Semitismo* and Fin-de-Siècle Italy," *Jewish Culture and History* 6 (2003):

96–110, and Nancy Harrowitz, *Anti-Semitism, Misogyny, and the Logic of Cultural Difference: Cesare Lombroso and Matilde Serao* (Lincoln: University of Nebraska Press, 1994).

8. The question remains whether Lombroso would have accepted what he had called atavistic Orthodox religious practice at this time, or whether his new-found tolerance was only for a politicized secular Judaism.

9. Alexander Stille, "The Double Bind of Italian Jews: Acceptance and Assimilation," in *Jews in Italy under Fascist and Nazi Rule: 1922–1945*, ed. Joshua Zimmerman (Cambridge: Cambridge University Press, 2005), 43. Stille's term "double bind," for Italian Jews caught between a desire for acceptance and the demanded price of assimilation, is very useful for understanding the situation of Levi and many others in his generation.

10. For an extended analysis, see Mario Toscano, *Ebraismo e antisemitismo in Italia: Dal 1848 alla guerra dei sei giorni* (Milano: FrancoAngelo, 2003).

11. Arnaldo Momigliano, *Essays on Ancient and Modern Judaism*, ed. Silvia Berti, trans. Maura Masella-Gayley (Chicago, IL: University of Chicago Press, 1994), 225.

12. *Ibid.*

13. For more contextualization of Momigliano and the atmosphere surrounding the questions of identity after emancipation, see Paolo Bernadini, "The Jews in Nineteenth-Century Italy: Towards a Reappraisal," *Journal of Modern Italian Studies* 1, no. 2 (1996): 292–310.

14. Antonio Gramsci, *Further Selections from the Prison Notebooks*, ed. and trans. Derek Boothman (Minneapolis: University of Minnesota Press, 1995), 104.

15. Arnaldo Momigliano, "The Jews of Italy," in *Essays on Ancient and Modern Judaism*, ed. Silvia Berti, trans. Maura Masella-Gayley (Chicago, IL: University of Chicago Press, 1994).

16. Arnaldo Momigliano, *Pagine ebraiche*, edited by Silvia Berti (Turin: Einaudi, 1987), 145. Translation mine.

17. Momigliano had a difficult time under Fascism: he was given a chair in Roman history at the extraordinarily young age of 28 only to lose it two years later because of the Racial Laws, which expelled Jewish professors and students from the universities. He then went to England as an expatriate where he survived the war by teaching history. He was offered a chair in Turin after the war but refused to come back to Italy, preferring to stay in his new homeland, but always describing himself as a Piedmontese.

18. For a discussion of *The Periodic Table* with regard to Levi's representation of his ancestors, see Alberto Cavaglion, *Notizie su Argon: Gli antenati di Primo Levi da Francesco Petrarca a Cesare Lombroso* (Turin: Instar Libri, 2006), in which Levi states that the characters in the "Argon" chapter of *The Periodic Table* were not Levi's direct ancestors at all but rather fictionalized composite sketches of elders of the community.

19. Primo Levi, "Itinerary of a Jewish Writer," in *The Black Hole of Auschwitz* (Malden, MA: Polity Press, 2006), 128–29.

20. Giorgio Fabre, *Mussolini razzista. Dal socialismo al fascismo: La formazione di un antisemita*. (Milan: Garzanti Libri, 2005), and Liliana Picciotto Fargion, *Il libro della memoria. Gli ebrei deportati dall'Italia (1943–1945)*, 2nd ed. (Milan: Mursia, 1992).

21. See, for example, Millicent Marcus, *Italian Film in the Shadow of Auschwitz* (Toronto: University of Toronto Press, 2007).

22. Ferdinando Camon, *Conversazione con Primo Levi* (Milano: Garzanti, 1991).

23. In the 1880s, Levi's grandfather had a bank in the small town of Bene Vagienna that was driven out of business, and the family driven out of town, by an anti-semitic Dominican friar. It is not clear exactly what Levi knew or did not know about the particulars of this episode; it appears that older family members did not discuss it willingly. See Ian Thomson, *Primo Levi* (London: Random House, 2002) for more details.

24. See Giorgio Fabre, *Mussolini razzista: Dal socialismo al fascismo: la formazione di un antisemita* (Milan: Garzanti, 2005), *Il contratto: Mussolini editore di Hitler* (Bari: Dedalo, 2004), and Susan Zuccotti, *The Italians and the Holocaust* (New York: Basic Books, 1987) for discussions of Mussolini's anti-Semitic policies.

3

Primo Levi and Holocaust Memory in Italy, 1958–1963

Robert S. C. Gordon

University of Cambridge

A certain standard account of Primo Levi's early career as a writer goes as follows: *Survival in Auschwitz* appears in 1947 with the small Turinese publisher De Silva, having been rejected by Einaudi, on the advice of Natalia Ginzburg and probably also Cesare Pavese. It is produced in a small print run, has a few positive reviews, but is then largely forgotten outside local circles. When Einaudi picks up and republishes the work, with minor modifications, in 1958, it is a significant success. Levi is persuaded, a short time thereafter, by friends such as the anti-Fascist jurist and historian Alessandro Galante Garrone, among others, to write further on his wartime experiences. The result is the publication of his narrative of return, *The Reawakening*, in 1963, an "Odyssey" to complement the "Iliad" of *Survival in Auschwitz*. If anything, *The Reawakening* is even more of a success, winning the first Campiello Prize, selling in large numbers, and swiftly being adopted as a book in schools.

In the period from 1958 to 1963, then, Levi passed from relative obscurity to having a public profile and a public voice for the first time, as both a witness and a writer. This step change, however, is not only (indeed, perhaps not primarily) to be explained by the sheer power and inherent quality of his work. The period of Levi's emergence coincided to a striking degree with a similar step change within what we might call the wider "memory culture" of the Holocaust in Italy (and not only Italy). Roughly outlined, the path followed by that memory culture since the war had gone from an early period (mid-1940s) of personal, often locally published and locally read, firsthand accounts of the concentration camps, on to a marked phase of retrenchment and silence from the late 1940s until the mid-1950s, and on, finally, to a period of dramatic growth of interest in and awareness of what we now call the Holocaust or the Shoah in the late 1950s and early 1960s. Even from this rough sketch, it is clear how Levi's path, from the first to the second edition of *Survival in Auschwitz* and on to *The Reawakening*, runs in closely parallel directions, suggesting that his profile over the period between 1958 and 1963 (and indeed throughout his career) needs to be understood in close relation to—as both symptom of and causal factor in—contemporary, wider changes in the public field of representation and knowledge of the Holocaust.

This chapter aims to survey that field and, by doing so, to raise a series of issues relating to how collective memory and knowledge of the past itself has its own periodization, and how there are different layers of causation and agency in the building of that history of memory; how factors national and international, individual and collective, participant and general, commercial and intellectual, all intervene to shape networks of representation and to settle the conventions at work within the field. As Samuel Moyn has argued in his study of a specific moment of Holocaust controversy in France, "dominant memory paradigms" can be seen to shift at particular moments, evinced in both quantitative and qualitative change.[1] What follows is an attempt to trace such a paradigm shift in Holocaust memory in Italy, centered on the years between 1958 and 1963. It surveys different bodies of Holocaust-related cultural material and data from those years, sampling from four overlapping areas of output: nonfiction book publishing; fiction in books and films (and other forms of literature); mediatized events and other forms of public memory; and the specific sphere of Jewish memory.

Nonfiction

The period of the late 1950s and early 1960s saw the publication of a varied range of important testimonial and historiographical material on deportation and the concentration camps. In the area of testimonial writing about concentration camps by both Jewish and former anti-Fascist political deportees,[2] there had already been significant publications since 1954, such as the highly successful *Si fa presto a dire fame* (It's Easy to Say Hunger) by the socialist ex-partisan Piero Caleffi, or the memoir of a Triestine Jewish victim who died shortly after returning home in 1945, Bruno Piazza's *Perché gli altri dimenticano* (Because the Others Forget).[3] Further new firsthand accounts were published during 1959 and 1960: for example, Mario Bonfantini's *Un salto nel buio* (A Leap in the Dark) told of the writer's escape from a deportation train from Fossoli; and Emilio Jani's *Mi ha salvato la voce* (*My Voice Saved Me: Auschwitz 180046*), of the author's singing as part of his life in Auschwitz.[4] Perhaps the most significant debut work of testimony in this period, however, was Edith Bruck's *Chi ti ama così* (*Who Loves You Like This*), a strikingly intense memoir of Bruck's experience of deportation as a young girl from Hungary to Auschwitz, survival, emigration to Israel, and subsequent "escape" from an oppressive new homeland to a life in Italy.[5]

Two other kinds of book were produced through publishing operations, symptomatic of a growing interest in Holocaust-related material: republications of earlier Italian works of testimony from the mid-1940s, and translations of significant foreign works (often also originally published in the immediate postwar years). Republication is, of course, best illustrated by the case of *Survival in Auschwitz*, but two other important works of the mid-1940s, one regarding Jewish deportation, the other partisan capture, confirm the trend. The former is Giacomo Debenedetti's *16 ottobre 1943* (*October 16, 1943*), his chronicle of the round-up of Rome's Jews first published in book form in 1944 and reissued by Il Saggiatore in 1959.[6] The latter is the account by Piero Chiodi of his time as a partisan and camp prisoner: *Banditi* (Bandits), first published in 1946 and reissued in 1961.[7] Translations, as with Caleffi and others noted above, were already appearing to some resonance a few years before, in the mid-1950s. Anne Frank's diary, published in Dutch in 1947, was already well on its way to becoming a global phenomenon in 1954, when Einaudi produced the first Italian edition.[8] In the same year, Einaudi also published Robert Antelme's memory-cum-analysis, *La specie umana* (*The Human Race*).[9] The trend continued into the 1960s with translations of two key "pre-testimonial" texts, the diaries of David Rubinowicz and Emmanuel Ringleblum, accounts of the Warsaw ghetto written and recovered from the rubble of genocide.[10] Also in the category of translated firsthand accounts, although from the opposite perspective and written in retrospect, was the autobiography and apologia by the founding commandant of Auschwitz, Rudolf Höss, written from his prison cell before his execution in 1947 and translated, again by Einaudi, in 1962.[11]

Höss's autobiography was introduced by a translation of the preface to the English edition by the British military jurist and official at Nuremberg, Edward, Lord Russell of Liverpool.[12] Russell had also been the author of the most widely read summary account of Nazi crimes, *The Scourge of the Swastika*. This work, and that of several other important foreign historians, was also translated in and around the late 1950s and early 1960s, appearing alongside the beginnings of a corpus of historiography in Italian. Russell's work was published as *Il flagello della svastica* in 1955 by Feltrinelli, the Marxist-oriented publishing house that had only begun operating in 1954 and went on to publish Piazza and Bonfantini, as we saw above.[13] In the same year, Léon Poliakov's first discrete, documented history of the genocide, *Harvest of Hate: The Nazi Program for the Destruction of Jews in Europe*, was translated also, as *Il nazismo e lo sterminio degli ebrei*.[14] 1962 saw two further highly significant translated contributions: Gerald Reitlinger's *Final Solution* (*La soluzione finale*), specifically focused on the Final Solution and following on from Poliakov, and American journalist and historian W. L. Shirer's general history of Nazism, *Rise and Fall of the Third Reich* (*Storia del Terzo Reich*).[15]

Finally, Italian historians also began contributing serious work to this nascent field of Holocaust historiography. A rich example, with autobiographical underpinnings, came from a writer of Polish origin, Alberto Nirenstajn, who had moved to Palestine from Poland in 1936, joined the Allied Jewish Brigade and fought in Italy before settling in Florence. Drawing on his own background and knowledge, he collated a powerful history of the Warsaw ghetto, published in 1958 as *Ricorda che ti ha fatto Amalek* (Remember What Amalek Did to You).[16] Piero Caleffi, now a Socialist Senator, followed up *Si fa presto a dire fame* in 1960 with *Pensaci uomo!* (Think about It!), a collaborative work of popular history put together with graphic designer and former Communist Resistance fighter Albe Steiner, combining a short historical introduction on the history of Nazism and the Final Solution with fully 120 pages of photographs of the camps and their victims.[17] By far the most significant work of original research, however, was Renzo De Felice's *Storia degli ebrei italiani sotto il fascismo* (History of the Italian Jews under Fascism), important not only because it marked De Felice's first foray into a field he would come to dominate in subsequent decades, nor only because it marked a sea change in attention paid to the specifically Italian history of Fascist antisemitism and its relations to Nazi antisemitism and genocide. The book also created a political storm in its own right, causing Radical Party politician Leopoldo Piccardi to lose his post, having been tainted with antisemitism by De Felice's research, and leading to a split in the party. This is a first, dramatic indication of the role at the heart of civic and political culture and at the heart of the problematic Fascist legacy that antisemitism and the Holocaust would come to take up at the end of the twentieth century.[18]

Fiction, Film, Literature

In conventional descriptions of Levi's *The Reawakening*, a feature commonly used to distinguish it from its predecessor is its markedly more writerly, narratively inventive—in short, "fictional"—quality. Once again, this story of a development in Levi's personal literary style runs parallel to and is infused by a larger trend, a flow of new autobiographical, semifictional and purely fictional literature on the Holocaust appearing in Italy in these same years. As with work in testimony and history, the flow included works by Italians, works translated, and works centered both on Italy and on the wider European genocide.

The Reawakening appeared from Einaudi in 1963, as did Natalia Ginzburg's family memoir Lessico famigliare (Family Sayings), which while by no means a work of Holocaust literature, nevertheless gave a striking cultural profile to the very particular world of the Jewish, anti-Fascist intelligentsia of Turin.[19] In the muted but powerful figure of her husband, Leone Ginzburg, tortured and murdered by the Nazis in Rome, or in her feckless but principled brothers, Ginzburg built Jewish figures of iconic victimhood and heroism—figures of a sort of displaced Holocaust—for Italian anti-Fascism. A few months earlier, in 1962, a third major text had paved the way for both Levi and Ginzburg, marking an extraordinary moment for Italian Jewish narratives of antisemitism shadowed by the Shoah: this was Giorgio Bassani's Il giardino dei Finzi-Contini (The Garden of the Finzi-Continis), which had itself been preceded by two other volumes of memories of Jewish Ferrara under Fascism: Cinque storie ferraresi (Five Stories of Ferrara) and Gli occhiali d'oro (The Gold-Rimmed Spectacles).[20]

The trio of Bassani, Levi, and Ginzburg offer powerful evidence for a general opening toward mainstream literary representation of the Holocaust, although all of them approach that topic from an oblique or even implicit angle, telling local stories, following premonitory moments or aftereffects, or exploiting the looming shadow of the genocide in readers' minds. An interesting partial exception to this rule is Edith Bruck, who followed Levi's path in producing a second, more fictionalized Holocaust text after her Chi ti ama così (Who Loves You Like This): Andremo in città (We Will Go to the City), which includes a story of a child's-eye fantasy of salvation.[21]

If we turn to the field of translated fiction, we find two examples of powerful and widely successful novels, both international casi letterari and translated into Italian in 1959–1960, which did nothing to shirk the head-on representation of the concentration camps and of the genocide. First, the Israeli survivor-writer known as Ka-Tzetnik 135633 (the pseudonym was his concentration camp—Kozentrationslager, or KZ—number) wrote the international bestseller La casa delle bambole (House of Dolls; 1953): republished by Mondadori in 1959, it was into its seventh edition within nine months.[22] Set in a camp brothel, La casa delle bambole was one of the first "controversial" Holocaust fictions, one of the first major works to establish a trend more commonly associated with the 1970s, the "sexualization" of the Holocaust. The second work was André Schwarz-Bart's

1959 Prix Goncourt-winning novel *Le dernier des justes* (*The Last of the Just*), a grand meditation on and intense depiction of the camps—ending in the gas chambers—recast into narrative through Jewish history and the Talmudic legend of the Thirty-Six Just Men (once again, a representational operation not without its risks and controversy). It was published in Italy by Feltrinelli in 1960 and was into its tenth edition by 1963.[23]

In the ambit of fictional narrative or semifictional narrativization of the Holocaust, it makes sense to consider film narratives also. As Millicent Marcus has penetratingly shown, this same period saw the first major, if somewhat disconnected, instances of Holocaust filmmaking in Italy.[24] As with written narratives, they show evidence of attention both to the Holocaust as an international phenomenon and to specific local, Italian aspects of this history, as well as its oblique relations with other major national narratives, such as the Resistance. Three films from 1959 to 1961 are worth mentioning. 1959 saw the release of Gillo Pontecorvo's second full-length fiction film, *Kapò*, a film that has nothing direct to say about Italy whatsoever (it begins in France before moving to a *Lager* setting), but which was nevertheless deeply influenced by the conflation of Pontecorvo's Resistance experience, his Jewish origin and the persecution suffered by his family, and his reading of Primo Levi.[25] Also in 1959, Roberto Rossellini's film *Generale Della Rovere* told an affecting and emblematic tale of a con man (played by Vittorio de Sica), taken into prison and used as an informer by the Nazis who encourage him to pose as the eponymous general of the title, and who comes to embody and believe the role he is playing.[26] At the very end of the film, the partisan prisoners that the 'general' now refuses to betray are set alongside a group of Jewish prisoners destined for deportation and death, conflating, as the moral and historical climax to the film, resistance and genocide. And in 1961, Carlo Lizzani released *L'oro di Roma* (*The Gold of Rome*), a dramatic—at times melodramatic, at others, ethnographic—reconstruction of the persecution of Rome's Jewish community by the Nazis and their Fascist collaborators in 1943.[27] The handsome young hero of the film (played by Gérard Blin) ends the film by choosing to assert himself as both Jew and Italian, going on the run to join the Resistance. Both Lizzani and Rossellini (and indeed, De Sica) draw a very direct line of connection in film history to the legacy of neorealism, suggesting that aspects of the Holocaust were now posing key ethical and aesthetic questions having to do with what stories a "civic" or committed or "national-popular" filmmaker should be telling. At the same time, it is striking to note the faint praise and relative neglect of all these three films in general histories of Italian film, as if the story of the Holocaust struggled to establish itself as a core film-historical imperative.

One final, quite distinct "literary" dimension to the emergence of the Holocaust as part of the broad cultural landscape from the late 1950s is worth noting—that is, the ways in which a vocabulary of the Holocaust began to spread as a shared shorthand, a normalized idiom, in fields well beyond the strictly testimonial, through the dissemination and metaphorization of words such as Auschwitz, *Lager*, and *genocidio*. This hugely important and still largely unexplored process was underway, for example, in Salvatore Quasimodo's 1956 collection, *Il falso e vero verde* (The Green True and False), which includes his poem "Auschwitz," or in several works by Pier Paolo Pasolini, from his 1962 poem "Monologo sugli Ebrei" (Monologue about the Jews), to the "Israel" section of his poetry collection, *Poesia in forma di rosa* (Poetry in the Form of a Rose; 1964), where Pasolini stages a sustained and highly strained identification between several of his roles as outsider, persecutee, self-denying bourgeois, intellectual (and so on) and the emblematic figure of the Jew. Over the following decade, Pasolini would famously go on to develop his critique of consumerism and the anthropological changes it had wrought on Italy as a new "genocide."[28]

Events and Public Memory

High-end book publishing of testimony, history, or fiction, and a growing use of a vocabulary of the Holocaust among literary intellectuals, tell us relatively little about wide-scale cultural changes, although they may well be both symptom and cause of this. Several of the books noted earlier, however, had a popularizing or educational form or agenda (for example, Caleffi's *Think About It!*) and cinema—even high-end, committed cinema—stretches to include a far wider audience than the printed book. And there is further evidence of a mass or collective dissemination of Holocaust awareness in the period in the form of mediatized events and public forums devoted to the topic.

One epoch-making media event of the early 1960s dominates all accounts of the growth in global awareness of the Holocaust: Eichmann's capture and his trial and execution in Jerusalem, between 1960 and 1962. Italy was no exception here. Though only one Italian witness (Hulda Cassuto) spoke at the trial and one session was devoted to Italy (on May 11, 1961), Italian newspapers such as *Corriere della sera* and *La stampa* ran daily dispatches from the court.[29] As many as eight "instant" books, as we might now call them, were published on Eichmann in Italian between 1961 and 1963, several going into multiple editions; and that excludes the first Italian edition, in 1964, of the most famous document to emerge from the trial, Hannah Arendt's hugely controversial *Eichmann in Jerusalem*. The chief prosecutor, Gideon Hausner, published his opening address in several languages (prefaced in Italy by Levi's friend Galante Garrone), and in a moment of high courtroom drama, reflected in media coverage, the survivor-writer we have already encountered, Ka-Tzetnik 135633, stood as one of the many survivor-witnesses.[30]

As part of the media event surrounding Eichmann, several popular magazines ran features on the trial or other aspects of the Holocaust. The popular history magazine *Storia illustrata (Illustrated History)* was one of these: Primo Levi's first published interview came in a round table on the Eichmann trial for *Storia illustrata,* in 1961.[31] Among other features on the Holocaust, the same issue ran an article by Gerald Reitlinger, indicating that his book, *The Final Solution,* was being prepared for Italian publication (1962) in the wake of the Eichmann trial. *L'espresso* also ran more than one feature on Eichmann, including an account by one of the court correspondents and author of one of the instant books, Sergio Minerbi, and a tie-in to the upcoming release of Lizzani's *The Gold of Rome.*[32]

Although this concerted interest was a relatively new phenomenon, there had been coverage of a more sporadic and sensationalist kind in magazines in preceding years. The focus of interest in these earlier pieces was typically the grotesque criminals and monsters of the Nazi era and the war, and much less the victims and the human suffering inflicted. Thus, *Storia illustrata,* which only began publishing in 1957, had already run several articles on individual Fascists and Nazis, military aspects of the war, Nuremberg, and Hitler (including a July 1959 piece on why he hated the Jews), and, among these, a single article, in March of 1960, on the genocide. In April 1960, *L'espresso* had run a sensationalist inquiry into the so-called *Pantera nera* (Black Panther), an infamous Roman Jewish woman who had informed on her neighbors to the Nazis.[33]

Media-driven events and coverage comingled with another strand of public event of a more local and traditionally collective kind: commemorations, public discourses, exhibitions, conferences, and the like. There was an intense program of such initiatives touching on Italy's sense of its own past as a result of a dual anniversary around 1960 and 1961: the fifteenth anniversary of the Liberation, in 1960, and the centenary of the unification of Italy, in 1961.[34] Cycles of public lectures were held in major cities, including in Turin, Milan, Rome, and Bologna, drawing large, cross-generational crowds. On occasion, but not always, specific space was allotted to the history of antisemitism and genocide: Caleffi spoke on the topic in the Milan cycle in 1961; Norberto Bobbio gave a public lecture at the Turin synagogue in January 1960; and, as has only recently been uncovered, Primo Levi and Giorgio Bassani shared a platform for perhaps the only time during the Bologna lectures.[35]

Exhibitions also began to proliferate. A key example, which has recently been researched with great acuity by Marzia Luppi and Elisabetta Ruffini, was the travelling exhibition, partly sponsored by ANED, called the "National Exhibit of Nazi Lagers," which opened in Carpi in 1955 and worked its way around the country, finishing in Turin 1959. At the Turin showing, Primo Levi undertook his first serious public speaking engagement.[36] In Rome, also in 1959, the National Gallery of Modern Art hosted a less known, but equally resonant exhibition—"International Monument at Auschwitz (Italian Committee)"—to mark the international architectural competition to design a monument for the main concentration camp site at Auschwitz. The level of Italian involvement in the international competition was strikingly high. The Italian committee (a subcommittee of the International Auschwitz Committee) included Carlo Levi, Alberto Moravia, Ignazio Silone, and Piero Caleffi. The competition's first-round winners included three Italian architectural studios (out of seven chosen winners) and, in the second round, two out of three groups (all three were then asked to collaborate on the final project design).[37] The point here is not how many Italians won how many prizes, but rather, the evidence the competition and the exhibition offer of the newly heightened profile of the Holocaust in Italian public culture, and of the desire to present oneself as involved in such events and initiatives.

Jewish Memory

Although our principal focus has been on the increasing spread of awareness, representation, and general talk of the Holocaust beyond circles of individual victims and their communities and out into the wider culture, it is important, finally, to note also evidence from within those communities of this same shift. This means, in particular, registering responses from the Jewish community. Generalizing, we can say that there is evidence of both a reactive and, at times, anxious response to—and also a proactive influencing of—the leap in Holocaust awareness we have seen.

The proactive mode is perhaps clearest if we return to the field of historiography. From within the Jewish community, the early 1960s saw a concentrated effort at launching a formal historiography of the specifically Italian and Fascist phenomenon of antisemitism as part and parcel of a serious historiography of the Nazism, Fascism, the war, and the genocide. The key case is one already mentioned above, De Felice's *History of the Italian Jews under Fascism*, a work that, quite apart from launching De Felice's career as a historian of Fascism, was significant for having been commissioned and funded in collaboration with Einaudi by the official board of the Union of Italian Jewish Communities (*Unione delle comunità israel-itiche italiane*). At least two other important historical works addressing the same field of Fascist antisemitism appeared in the same period from within the ambit of key Jewish institutions: first, the recently formed Center for Contemporary Jewish Documentation (*Centro di documentazione ebraica contemporanea*, or CDEC, founded 1955) published a series of essays in three volumes between 1961 and 1963, edited by Guido Valabrega and col-lectively entitled *Gli ebrei in Italia durante il fascismo* (Jews in Italy under Fascism),[38] and secondly, the influential Zionist journal, *Rassegna Mensile di Israel* (*Monthly Jewish Review*), published a series of densely researched articles by the Israeli historian Meir Michaelis between 1961 and 1963.[39]

This opening out toward, and sponsoring of, concerted historical work on the part of groups within Italian Jewry was, however, not without its anxieties, evident in the way that some corners of the community reacted to the proliferation of Holocaust material we have been tracing. This is evident, for example, in the mixed responses in the pages of *Rassegna Mensile di Israel,* whose dual focus on Italy and Israel at times sat uneasily with either a secularizing or a Holocaust-centered vision of Jewish iden-tity. While there is a striking growth in reviews and articles on the Holo-caust, not infrequently worries are expressed about either the attitudes on display or the possible excesses of interest in such matters. Thus, to give three instances by three leading contributors to *Rassegna Mensile di Israel,* Giorgio Romano criticized Giacomo Debenedetti for his depiction of the victims of persecution as "lay" or lapsed Jews; Dante Lattes carried on an intense polemic with Salvatore Quasimodo over some antisemitic com-ments by the latter; and G. L. Luzzatto reviewed Bassani's *Garden of the Finzi-Continis* with some hostility for its risky mix of reality and fiction.[40]

A final review from *Rassegna Mensile di Israel* serves also to recall a wider socioreligious context to this anxiety: in 1962, a group of South American Jesuits writing collectively under the pseudonym Maurice Pinay published a fierce antisemitic tract entitled *Complotto contro la chiesa* (*Plot Against the Church*), describing a vast Jewish conspiracy to destroy the Church and discerning perversely even a Jewish hand behind the Holocaust (as a tactic for establishing a state of Israel). The book was written specifi-cally in an attempt to halt the liberalization of Church attitudes to the Jews under John XXIII (whose papacy coincided with the period from 1958 to 1963) and the Second Vatican Council. The book was reviewed with rigor-ous hostility by Renzo De Felice in *Rassegna Mensile di Israel,* but its pres-ence and profile point to a delicate moment in the history of the Church's role in public life and Jewish identity in Italy in relation to that—one that was about to explode into international controversy in 1963 with the first staging of Rolf Hochhuth's play *Der Stellvertreter* (*The Deputy*), with its accusations of the church's passive complicity in the Holocaust.[41]

Conclusion

As we have seen, an eclectic mass of output and activity relating to the Holocaust emerged in Italy around the years between 1958 and 1963, just as Primo Levi began his public role as Holocaust survivor and writer. In many ways, the raw quantitative aspect of what has been described above contains the principal argument of this chapter: that Levi's trajectory coincided with, contributed to, but was also necessarily shaped in turn by this wider acceleration of interest in the Holocaust and by the beginnings of a cultural field of Holocaust talk in Italy. Some further, tentative analytical conclusions, and some patterns to be discerned within and around that eclectic output, are also possible.

First, we can surmise that around 1960, with the war now 15 years past, the time was ripe for a general, detached reassessment of aspects of its history, including the genocide, and we can see this temporal shift coinciding with a moment of diversification in the publishing and media industries so that scholarly, educational, and broadly popular (high-, middle- and low-brow) material all find space for covering this new angle on the recent past. Distance also means that a "memory" culture, *strictu senso*, emerges strongly for the first time at this moment (both Bassani and Ginzburg write memory-framed narratives), alongside documented historiography. This dual development complements a tendency to shift away from interest in the evils of Nazi leaders to the experience of victims. Such changes in media and in attitude also reflect the wider changes most commonly associated with the years from 1958 to 1963 in Italy, that is, the changes of a sociocultural and economic nature that make up the so-called boom or economic miracle and that contributed to a loosening of cultural values boundaries (as was the case with John XXIII and Vatican II), to the diversification mentioned above, and to the start of a generational shift (for example, the CDEC was set up by the youth organization of the Jewish community).

Another form of the crossing of boundaries is evident in the crucial role played by translation, indicating the transnational nature of the Holocaust and its discourses and representations. There was an intense commerce across borders in Holocaust material, with local operators (publishers, but also translators, authors of prefaces, among others) inflecting and appropriating foreign material as their own. In the latter respect, the very prominent role played by the Turinese publisher Einaudi is particularly worthy of note.[42] Finally, the material gathered here does not so much make up the first phase in which the Holocaust had been addressed in Italy—private and smaller-scale works, often by survivors and their associated networks such as ANED, had been produced ever since the war—but rather the first time the Holocaust entered the general public sphere and public discourse, the first time the media saw it as a discrete event capable of attracting readers, and the first time writers used the vocabulary of genocide as a malleable element of shared cultural and public knowledge. Primo Levi, in his move from testimony to a form of testimonial-narrative literature, and in his first steps into the public arena of interviews and lectures, was prominent in this shift and indeed would soon emerge as the single most influential individual voice responsible for shaping the vision of the Holocaust in Italy.[43]

It would be tempting to imagine a smooth and linear progress from this moment toward the peak of hyper attention to the Holocaust reached in Italy (and elsewhere) in the late twentieth century. But this would be a misconception. After this flurry in the early 1960s, as indeed before, lines of continuity were uneven and shifting. The Church issue noted above would quickly become a focus of immense new controversy following Hochhuth; the Auschwitz trial in Frankfurt, starting in 1963, would replicate some of the mediatized buzz of the Eichmann trial; and the student movements of the late 1960s and the generational battles over the legacies of Nazism and Fascism would revive and sustain the issue of the Holocaust in new ways. And yet, there is also a sense in which the years after 1963 mark a falling off, a moment of exhaustion after the first truly wide-scale wave of interest in Holocaust, after all the attention paid to Eichmann and the rest; or perhaps a first moment of registering the risks that an excess of (superficial) attention might amount to another form of silence: certainly many reviews in *Rassegna Mensile di Israel* begin at this point with rather weary comments on the mountain of material now appearing. Odd as this may seem, we have some evidence for it from Primo Levi himself, in a (to our ears) extraordinary statement from an interview in 1963, following the publication and success of *The Reawakening*.[44] Asked whether or not he had more to write on the Holocaust, Levi is blunt and unambiguous (and tellingly wrong) in his reply:

[interviewer:] "So you're all done with the experience of the camps?"
[Levi:] "Absolutely, not another word. Nothing. I've said everything I had to say. It's all over."[45]

Notes

1. Samuel Moyn, *A Holocaust Controversy. The Treblinka Affair in Postwar France* (Waltham, MA: Brandeis University Press, 2005).

2. It is a marker of what is still an early moment in the history of Holocaust awareness that these two categories continue to overlap and merge here.

3. Piero Caleffi, *Si fa presto a dire fame* (Milan: Edizioni Avanti!, 1954; 6th ed. 1958); Bruno Piazza *Perché gli altri dimenticano* (Milan: Feltrinelli, 1956).

4. Mario Bonfantini, *Un salto nel buio* (Milan: Feltrinelli, 1959); Emilio Jani, *Mi ha salvato la voce* (Milan: Ceschina, 1960). For this and all contemporary testimonies, see the bibliographical material in Anna Bravo and Daniele Jalla, eds, *Una misura onesta* (Milan: Franco Angeli, 1993).

5. Edith Bruck, *Chi ti ama così* (Milan: Lerici, 1959).

6. Giacomo Debenedetti, *16 ottobre 43* (Milan: Il Saggiatore, 1959; 1st ed. 1944).

7. Piero Chiodi, *Banditi* (Turin: Einaudi, 1961; 1st ed. 1946).

8. Anne Frank, *Diario* (Turin: Einaudi, 1954; 1st ed., *Het Achterhuis*, 1947).

9. Robert Antelme, *La specie umana* (Turin: Einaudi, 1954; 1st ed., *L'Espèce humaine*, 1947).

10. David Rubinowicz, *Il diario* (Turin: Einaudi, 1960); Emmanuel Ringelblum, *Sepolti a Varsavia* (Milan: Mondadori, 1962).

11. Rudolf Höss, *Comandante ad Auschwitz* (Turin: Einaudi, 1960; 1st German ed. 1958).

12. From 1985, Einaudi published it with a new preface by Primo Levi, now in *Opere*, ed. Marco Belpoliti (Turin: Einaudi, 1997), 2:1276–83.

13. Edward Russell of Liverpool, *Il flagello della svastica* (Milan: Feltrinelli, 1955; 1st ed., *The Scourge of the Swastika*, 1954).

14. Léon Poliakov, *Il nazismo e lo sterminio degli ebrei* (Turin: Einaudi, 1955; 1st ed., *La Bréviaire de la haine*, 1951).

15. Gerald Reitlinger, *La soluzione finale* (Milan: Il Saggiatore, 1962; 1st ed., *The Final Solution*, 1953); W. L. Shirer, *Storia del Terzo Reich* (Turin: Einaudi, 1962; 1st ed., *The Rise and Fall of the Third Reich*, 1960). Reitlinger's work had already been extensively summarized in 1953–54 by Luigi Meneghello (under the pseudonym Ugo Varnai), in the Olivetti journal *Comunità* n.s. 22, no. 4 (December 1953–April 1954), 16–23, perhaps the earliest signal of a turning point toward serious work on the Holocaust in Italy.

16. Alberto Nirenstajn, *Ricorda che ti ha fatto Amalek* (Turin: Einaudi, 1958).

17. Piero Caleffi and Albe Steiner, *Pensaci, uomo!* (Turin: Einaudi, 1960). A similar combination of text and photographs also characterized Domenico Tarzizzo, ed., *Ideologia della morte: Storia e documenti dei campi di sterminio* (Milan: Il Saggiatore, 1962).

18. Renzo De Felice, *Storia degli ebrei italiani sotto il fascismo* (Turin: Einaudi, 1961). On the Piccardi affair, see De Felice's comments in Renzo De Felice, *Rosso e Nero* (Milan: Baldini e Castoldi, 1995), 150.

19. Natalia Ginzburg, *Lessico famigliare* (Turin: Einaudi, 1963).

20. Giorgio Bassani, *Cinque storie ferraresi* (Turin: Einaudi, 1956); *Gli occhiali d'oro* (Turin: Einaudi, 1958); *Il giardino dei Finzi-Contini* (Turin: Einaudi, 1962).

21. Edith Bruck, *Andremo in città* (Milan: Lerici, 1962).

22. Ka-Tzetnik 135633, *La casa delle bambole* (Milan: Mondadori, 1959; 1st ed. 1953).

23. André Schwarz-Bart, *L'ultimo dei giusti* (Milan: Feltrinelli, 1960; 1st ed. 1959).

24. Millicent Marcus, *Italian Film in the Shadow of Auschwitz* (Toronto: Toronto University Press, 2007).

25. Gillo Pontecorvo, *Kapò* (Italy: Cineriz, 1961). See Carlo Celli, *Gillo Pontecorvo* (Lanham, MD: Scarecrow, 2005), 15.

26. Roberto Rossellini, *Generale della Rovere* (Italy: Zebra Film, 1959).

27. Carlo Lizzani, *L'oro di Roma* (Italy: Ager Cinematografica, 1961).

28. See Salvatore Quasimodo, *Tutte le poesie* (Milan: Mondadori, 1984), 203–4; Pier Paolo Pasolini, *Opere*, vols. 1–10, ed. Walter Siti (Milan: Mondadori, 1998–2003), 5:511–17 ("Il genocidio"); 9:1211–27, 1338–46 (poetry).

29. See Manuela Consonni, "The Impact of the 'Eichmann Event' in Italy, 1961." *Journal of Israeli History* 23, no. 1 (2004): 91–99.

30. Gideon Hausner, *Sei milioni di accusatori* (Turin: Einaudi, 1961).

31. Now in "Primo Levi," in *Voice of Memory: Interviews 1961–87*, ed. Marco Belpoliti and Robert S. C. Gordon (New York: New Press, 2000), 179–83.

32. *L'espresso*, April 30, 1961, 7. Regular trial reports for *L'espresso* were filed by Manlio Cancogni. Minerbi's book was called *La belva in gabbia: Eichmann* (Milan: Longanesi, 1962).

33. "Pantera nera," *L'espresso*, April 16, 1960, 21–23.

34. These dates also coincided with a period of dramatic institutional crisis in government and public order triggered by the so-called Tambroni affair, when neo-Fascists entered the government coalition.

35. See Levi, "'Deportazione e sterminio di ebrei' di Primo Levi, con una nota di Alberto Cavaglion," *Lo straniero* 11, no. 85 (July, 2007): 5–12. The Milan, Rome, and Turin lectures were published, respectively, as *1945–1975: Fascismo, antifascismo, Resistenza, rinnovamento*, ed. Marco Fini (Milan: Feltrinelli, 1962); *Lezioni sull'antifascismo*, ed. Piergiovanni Permoli (Rome: Laterza, 1960); *Trent'anni di storia italiana: 1915–1945: Dall'antifascismo alla Resistenza*, ed. Franco Antonicelli (Turin: Einaudi, 1961).

36. See Marzia Luppi and Elisabetta Ruffini, eds., *Immagini dal silenzio: La prima mostra nazionale dei Lager nazisti attraverso l'Italia 1955–1960* (Modena: Nuovagrafica, 2005).

37. The Italian architects and artists involved were Andrea Cascella, Pietro Cascella, Pericle Fazzini, Giorgio Simoncini, Tommaso Valle, and Maurizio Vitale.

38. Guido Valabrega, ed., *Gli ebrei in italia durante il fascismo*, vols. 1–3 (Milan: CDEC, 1961–63).

39. This work would feed into the major study, Meir Michaelis, *Mussolini and the Jews: German-Italian Relations and the Jewish Question in Italy, 1922–1945* (Oxford: Oxford University Press, 1978).

40. Giorgio Romano, "Rassegna delle riviste," *Rassegna Mensile di Israel* 5 (1960), 228 (on Debendetti); Dante Lattes, "Tu quoque Quasimodo?" *Rassegna Mensile di Israel* 1 (1961), 3–5; G. L. Luzzatto, "Il giardino dei Finzi-Contini," *Rassegna Mensile di Israel* 5 (1962), 239–40.

41. Maurice Pinay, *Complotto contro la chiesa* (Rome, 1962), and Renzo De Felice, "L'ultima maschera," *Rassegna Mensile di Israel* 1 (1963), 63–68. Hochhuth's play was first staged in Berlin in 1963 and then in London and New York in 1964. It was published in Italian in 1964 (*Il Vicario*, Milan: Feltrinelli, 1964), and an attempt was made to stage it in Rome in 1965, with Gian Maria Volonté in the lead role, but it was blocked by a police raid on a legal technicality.

42. In the notes to this chapter alone, there are references to 16 books on the Holocaust published by Einaudi in the period 1958–1963.

43. See Robert S. C. Gordon, "Which Holocaust? Primo Levi and the Field of Holocaust Memory in Post-war Italy," *Italian Studies* 61, no. 1 (2006): 85–113.

44. Alberto Cavaglion makes this contrary argument in his preface to *Immagini dal silenzio*, 12.

45. Belpoliti and Gordon, eds., *The Voice of Memory*, 82.

Part II

Unbearable Witness

4

Trauma and Latency in Primo Levi's *The Reawakening*

Jonathan Druker
Illinois State University

Primo Levi's second book, *The Reawakening*, describes his liberation from Auschwitz and his nine months as a "displaced person" as he waits and wanders through Eastern Europe and the Soviet Union, finally returning home to Italy in October 1945. This memoir usually has been read as a spirited odyssey, or as a lively, picaresque account that affirms the value of community, or as the story of Levi's metaphorical "rebirth" after the Holocaust.[1] Gian-Paolo Biasin brings nuance to the conversation in saying that the book describes a journey "haunted by the memories of the horrors past . . . which project their long shadow over the whole narration."[2] I would go even further: the historical trauma of Auschwitz does not merely color Levi's second memoir but dictates its form and, therefore, its meaning. That is to say, the structure of *The Reawakening* closely follows the three stages of trauma posited by Sigmund Freud, which I summarize here.[3] First, there is the initial shock, which is so extreme and unexpected that the subject cannot immediately absorb its impact; then, there is the latency period, an interval of forgetfulness between the primary exposure and the appearance of pathological symptoms; and finally, there is the onset of recurring traumatic memories that may last a lifetime.

This chapter offers a close reading of *The Reawakening* as a literary representation of latency bracketed in its initial and closing pages by elements of the first and third stages of Freudian trauma—specifically, by the last days in Auschwitz and the first days at home. Trauma theory has not been used previously to analyze the structure and content of this book even though its original title, *La tregua* (The Truce), clearly suggests a hiatus or a dormant period after one battle and before the next. An interpretive strategy alert to the symptoms of trauma not only sheds light on what Levi's book says, but also on how it works in psychological and historical terms. This critical approach enables us to see that, in the memoir, Soviet Russia functions as a geographical, chronological, and cultural site of latency, as the place of forgetfulness and evasion. My claim is that *The Reawakening* effectively positions the Holocaust as a problem born of European history and culture that cannot be addressed either intellectually or psychologically in Russia, a land "on the margins of civilization" (192).[4] With its postwar chaos, featureless landscape, and unintelligible language, Russia signifies here the antithesis of the Enlightenment and all that is European, including, I will argue, the Germans' rational and efficient approach to genocide.[5] Levi was captured by the Italian Fascists and, as a Jew, handed over to the Germans who deported him to Auschwitz. Both physically and culturally, Europe is the site of trauma in his texts. As recounted on the last page of *The Reawakening*, the latency ends and the trauma reveals itself only when, by reaching his own corner of Europe in Turin, he becomes a survivor in the fullest sense. This circumstance might lead us to surmise that, before reaching home, survivors of trauma inhabit a liminal space that prevents them from recalling their worst memories.

A qualification is in order: in this highly mediated literary text, the opposite of a raw diary, Levi the survivor is a narrating persona that cannot simply be equated with the chemist, writer, and Holocaust survivor named Primo Levi. Therefore, this artful form of autobiography offers no easy path to Levi's unconscious, nor is it useful to read the book as one long suicide note, as some have suggested.[6] However, the text itself can be interpreted by means of Freudian concepts. The psychoanalytic reading of *The Reawakening* I propose here differs greatly from most other readings of the text, which concentrate on Levi's remarkable portraits of the individuals encountered during his long odyssey—Russians, Poles, Italians, Germans, and more—and on the friendships Levi develops with unforgettable characters like "the Greek" and Leonardo. These readings are valid, and the idea of friendship—Robert Gordon has called it one of Levi's "ordinary virtues"—is a central concern in virtually all of the author's books.[7] However, in trying to understand *The Reawakening* as a Holocaust text, I find that its structure is even more important than its content. If the book represents latent trauma, then the engaging characters and their amusing adventures are diversions from the traumatic legacy of Auschwitz, which only reveals itself in the final pages. As such, the picaresque episodes featuring the good-natured rogue Cesare are deployed as much for evasion as for pleasure. Instead of dwelling on characters and details of the plot, my reading is attentive at the macro level, that is, to the three stages of trauma that structure the work, and also at the micro level, which includes the many metaphors secreted in the text that manifest trauma by indirection.

Irving Howe's brief comment on *The Reawakening* is perceptive and lends support to my approach. While not referring to trauma specifically, he noted the opposition between the plot and the affective core of the book. "Outwardly, along the skin of the narrative, *The Reawakening* appears to follow the traditional pattern of picaresque . . . But in basic spirit the book is anti-picaresque. Between the external form of the narrative and its inner vibrations of memory there is a strong nervous tension."[8] Explaining the origin and significance of this tension is the purpose of this reading.

Several general points may be made at the outset. First, a traumatic experience is not easily mastered, not easily sequestered in the past, and not easily narrated. It is not just that trauma confounds representation, whether in testimony or other forms of discourse. It is also the unrepresentable or untranslatable qualities of terrible experiences that contribute to traumatization.[9] Second, Levi's testimony helps us to see that the traumatized individual, beset by disturbing memories, never really returns from the site of trauma and never brings his troubled history to a close. Rather, as Freud remarks, "he is obliged to *repeat* the repressed material as a contemporary experience, instead of . . . *remembering* it as something belonging to the past."[10] Third, reflecting on unmastered memory in *The Drowned and the Saved*, Levi notes that a historical trauma perpetually links the perpetrator to the victim. "The memory of a trauma suffered or inflicted is itself traumatic because recalling it is painful or at least disturbing. A person who has been wounded tends to block out the memory so as not to renew the pain; the person who has inflicted the wound pushes the memory down, to be rid of it, to alleviate the feeling of guilt . . . [Both] victim and oppressor . . . are in the same trap."[11] This victim-perpetrator dynamic—each requires the other—enables us to see that the narrator's trauma is not his alone since the Holocaust impinges on the historical consciousness of Germany, Italy, and all of Europe. Unable to put the past behind him, the Holocaust survivor embodies the guilty history of the entire continent. Indeed, his ongoing trauma is symptomatic of Europe's own nightmare: the repressed fear that its civilization produces as much darkness as light, as much violence and destruction as creation.

The Reawakening opens with a two-stanza epigraphic poem whose rather obscure meaning is made clearer on the final page of the book, in which Levi describes the pleasures of his homecoming and "the liberating joy of recounting [his] story."[12] However, the reader also learns that bearing witness does not free Levi the survivor from his traumatic memories: there is no "talking cure." In these concluding paragraphs, written in late 1962, 17 years after his return, he states that he is still plagued by a recurring "dream full of horror," "a dream within a dream," or rather a peaceful dream about normal life among family and friends that is shattered by an anguished nightmare. "I am alone in the center of a grey and turbid nothing," Levi narrates, "and, I *know* what this thing means . . . I am in the Lager once more and nothing is true outside the Lager. All the rest was a brief pause, a deception of the senses, a dream" (emphasis in original). The former inmate's irrational fear, which periodically escapes from his unconscious, is that his waking life is a dream while his nightmare—that he was never liberated from the camp—is reality. This recurring incubus always ends, as does the book we have been reading, with "a single word, not imperious, but brief and subdued. It is the dawn command of Auschwitz, a foreign word, feared and expected: get up, "*Wstawać*" (194). The word is Polish, the second most important administrative language in Auschwitz after German.

This persistent nightmare that comes unbidden, unfolding "each time in a different way" (193), shows that the survivor has not mastered his terrible experience. Instead, the concluding passage of the book reveals that a deep psychic wound remains open after all these years. The behaviors described here are recognizable symptoms of what we now call posttraumatic stress disorder, a condition commonly known as shell shock when Freud wrote the following about traumatized World War I combatants: "Dreams occurring in traumatic neuroses have the characteristic of repeatedly bringing the patient back into the situation of his accident, a situation from which he wakes up in another fright."[13] Levi the survivor, who awakes once again in fear even though he is safe at home, clearly presents the symptoms of trauma. He is haunted by an experience that he can neither forget nor assimilate. The story does not end in liberation because the return from Auschwitz is never fully incorporated into the psyche. Having read the last page of *The Reawakening*, it is not difficult to interpret the book's epigraphic poem, untitled here but in Levi's collected poems titled "Alzarsi" (perhaps best translated in this case with the imperative, "Get up!," and "Reveille" in Feldman and Swann's translation in *Collected Poems*, which I adopt here). The first stanza is set in Auschwitz, and the second stanza is set at home after his liberation. The poem was written in early 1946, less than three months after he returned from his long ordeal:

Dreams used to come in the brutal nights,
Dreams crowding and violent
Dreamt with body and soul,
Of going home, of eating, of telling our story.
Until, quickly and quietly, came
The dawn reveille:
      Wstawać
And the heart cracked in the breast.

Now we have found our homes again,
Our hunger is quenched,
All the stories have been told.
It is time. Soon we shall hear again
The alien command:
   Wstawać.

11 January 1946[14]

The first stanza articulates concisely in verse ideas expressed in more detail in the "Our Nights" chapter of *Survival in Auschwitz*.[15] Since the poem and Levi's first book were written contemporaneously, the consistency in language and thought is not surprising. The memoir describes how the prisoners are transported beyond the barbed wire by incessant and urgent dreams of food, of home, and of telling their terrible Holocaust tales. However, the overwhelming presence of Auschwitz impinges on the illusory escape promised by sleep. The inmates' dreams are always interrupted by the soft but peremptory wake-up call that returns them to the brutal reality of the camp, which, as the poem says, leaves "the heart cracked in the breast." In both the poem and Levi's first book, the reveille provokes quiet dread. "For the whole duration of the night, cutting across the alternating sleep, waking and nightmares, the expectancy and terror of the moment of the reveille keeps watch. [. . .] Very few sleep on till the *Wstawać*: it is a moment of too acute pain for even the deepest sleep not to dissolve as it approaches. The night guard knows it, and for this reason does not utter it in a tone of command, but with [a] quiet and subdued voice [. . .]."[16] The brief respite from the daily suffering that sleep affords makes the return to consciousness all the more agonizing.

It is evident that the second stanza of the poem is a concise formulation of the last two paragraphs of *The Reawakening*. The notable consistency here between the verses written just weeks after his homecoming and the prose penned many years later suggests that Levi's trauma had not diminished much over time. Initially, the dreams of the first stanza seemed to have been realized: he is home and fed and has told his incredible tale, but this deception ends with the forceful three-word sentence, "it is time"— time once again for the command that compels obedience, for the reveille that signals the onset of a trauma that resists narrative closure.

Why does Levi choose "Reveille" written so many years earlier, as the epigraph for *The Reawakening* when the book deals only briefly with Auschwitz in the beginning and spends only four pages at the end describing his return to Italy? It can be argued that these bookends, Auschwitz and Turin, are essential to understanding the significance of his nine-month parenthesis. In a sense, the story unfolds in the gap between the two stanzas, that is, in the period between his stay in the camp and his homecoming. The gap on the page is thus equivalent to the latency represented by Russia in the book itself. Put another way, the poem can be read as a miniature account of the three stages of trauma, from the initial experience, to a period of forgetfulness (expressed by the blank space between the two stanzas), to the onset of the recurring nightmare. If the prominently placed poem announces the trauma of Auschwitz as the book's main theme, then, at same time, this epigraph suggests that most of what the book narrates—the months in Russia—is digressive. The gap in the poem indicates a necessary blankness—itself an apt metaphor for the unconscious—between two distinct struggles: the event from which the trauma originates and the aftereffects.

It would be difficult to exaggerate the importance of the word *Wstawać* in Levi's literary representations of Holocaust trauma. "The foreign command," issued in a language at once familiar and unfamiliar, is positioned emphatically as the last word of both the poem and *The Reawakening*, and is mentioned numerous times in *Survival in Auschwitz*. While Levi makes the literal meaning clear—get up!—it is evident that aspects of the word remain beyond the ken of ordinary experience. The trauma that *Wstawać* represents cannot be named by an Italian word because its sound—more than its definition—is what summons Levi the survivor to Auschwitz again. That is to say, *Wstawać* represents trauma by means of its untranslatability. In this, Levi has found an effective literary strategy for overcoming the difficulty of rendering trauma into language. Furthermore, we are reminded by the word *Wstawać* not to lose sight of the fact that the scars left by Auschwitz are specific and have lasting consequences, not only for the victims, but also for the perpetrators and, to a lesser degree, for all of the citizens of Europe who still live on that tainted ground and with that tainted history.

The beginning of *The Reawakening* follows directly from the end of *Survival in Auschwitz*, with the liberation of the concentration camp by the Red Army on January 27, 1945. At the arrival of four Russian soldiers on horseback, the survivors feel a mixture of joy and shame (2). They have been dehumanized and have suffered unimaginable indignities that will isolate them for all time from ordinary people as represented here by the soldiers, who, Levi asserts, as witnesses, undoubtedly feel some measure of shame that such a crime against humanity occurred, "that it should have been irrevocably introduced into the world." Here, Levi's use of words like "irrevocable" and of metaphors of staining and scarring can be read as representations of trauma. "We [survivors] should have liked to wash our consciences and our memories clean from the foulness that lay upon them," Levi writes, "[but] we felt that this should never happen, that now nothing could ever happen good and pure enough to rub out our past, and that the scars of that outrage would remain within us forever, and in the memories of those who saw it, and in the places where it occurred and in the stories we should tell of it" (2). The Holocaust not only wounds the participants, but also the land and even the language that must be called upon to describe the events.

The traumatized state of the victims, and of the perpetrators and bystanders, too, is further revealed by means of metaphors of infection that suggest an incubation period between exposure to the disease and a clear manifestation of its symptoms. "This is the awful privilege of our genera-tion," Levi writes, "no one better than us has ever been able to grasp the incurable nature of the offence that spreads like a contagion. It is foolish to think that human justice can eradicate it. [. . .] It returns as ignominy upon the oppressors, it perpetuates itself as hatred among the survivors, and swarms around in a thousand ways, against the very will of all, as a thirst for revenge, as a moral capitulation, as denial, as weariness, as renuncia-tion. These things, at that time blurred, and felt by most as no more than an unexpected attack of mortal fatigue, accompanied the joy of liberation for us" (2–3). At the end of this passage, Levi suggests that his full understand-ing and articulation of the traumatic legacy of Auschwitz is possible only after a period of reflection, but not at the liberation, not when his views were still "blurred." The inability to process a shocking experience in its immediate aftermath is consistent with the first stage of trauma. As Cathy Caruth puts it, "the [traumatic] event is not assimilated or experienced fully at the time, but only belatedly, in its repeated *possession* of the one who experiences it."[17] Only after reaching the third stage of trauma, having passed through the latency period of this contagion, can Levi represent the first stage; only in retrospect can he describe in its inchoate form the disturbing event that will later possess him.

It is ironic that after descriptions of the permanent stains left by Ausch-witz, the Russians subject Levi to the second of three baths that marked important transitions in his unwilled journey. The Nazis provided the first one, a "bath of humiliation" that welcomed Levi to the concentrationary universe; the last one—"functional, antiseptic, highly automatized [*sic*]"— was provided months later by the Americans. Consistent with his other descriptions of the benign and primitive Russians, Levi describes his sec-ond bath, at hand of two robust Soviet nurses, as "extemporaneous and crude" but also humane. In all three baths, Levi remarked, "it was easy to perceive behind the concrete and literal aspect a great symbolic shadow, the unconscious desire of the new authorities, who absorbed us within their own sphere, to strip us of the vestiges of our former life, to make us new men, consistent with their own models" (8). This second bath marks

Levi's transition from a concentration camp inmate—categorized by the Germans as a subhuman slated for extermination—to a displaced Italian under Russian control. In the following pages, Levi will mention several times that the Russians had no interest in making fine distinctions among the various sorts of Italians under their care. Their treatment was the same whether they were faced with ex-soldiers, ex-forced laborers, ex-inmates of Auschwitz, Communists, Monarchists, Fascists, or Jews (126). The Russians make Levi a "new man," however superficially, whose previous life and sufferings are supposed to be washed away by the cleansing waters of the bath, enabling a forgetful state in which the trauma of Auschwitz recedes temporarily into his unconscious as he makes his way to eastward.

The Reawakening is structurally and thematically continuous with Survival in Auschwitz because his nine-month odyssey was decisively framed by Auschwitz, first as a real place and then as a nightmare. This framing alters the significance of the long middle section set in Russia and Russian-occupied Poland. What might have been a narrative of rebirth becomes instead one of latent trauma marked by forgetfulness and evasion. As Levi tells it, time seems to stand still in the vast Russian landscape so unlike home. "In no . . . part of Europe, I think, can you walk for ten hours, and always remain in the same place, as if in a nightmare: always with the same straight road in front of you, stretching to the horizon, always the same steppe and forests on both sides, and behind your back yet more road stretching to the other horizon, like a ship's wake" (115). Space is a common analogy for memory; the empty horizons of Russia represent a featureless amnesia. For the displaced Italians, Russia is the blank space of waiting, a place outside of history, neither here nor there, a "regime in limbo," a "land of dreams" and of "the sleep of reason" (142; 91; 159).

Drawing on a long, unscientific tradition, Levi represents Russia as Europe's other and opposite. Europe is the land of the Enlightenment; Russia is unenlightened and even primitive.[18] The most extreme version of this idea was put forward by the Nazis, who saw the Slavs, among other peoples, including the Jews, as Untermenschen. In The Reawakening, and in other books of his, too, Levi describes the Russians with affection, as if they are erratic but loveable children. However, their supposed lack of orderliness and rationality, so unlike the Germans, leaves more space for humane acts. The Russian bureaucracy that governs the displaced Italians is not ill-intentioned, just stupid and negligent. "The Russians, in contrast to the Germans, possess little talent for fine distinctions and classifications" (103). Later, Levi adds, "we had already noticed that the Western religion (German in particular) of differential prohibitions has no deep roots in Russia" (108). And again: "The Germans, in analogous circumstances, would have covered the walls with bilingual placards, beautifully printed . . . and threatening the death penalty. The Russians, in contrast, allowed the ordinance to spread by itself, and the march to the other camp to organize itself" (114). In all of these comparisons, the Russian mind differs from the rational Western one, which Levi associates with the Nazis but also, implicitly, with the Italians and himself. At one point, the displaced Italians write and perform an allegorical play, "The Shipwreck of the Spiritless," in which the Russians are figured as primitive cannibals intent on devouring the marooned Italians who only want to go home. However, the implied violence of this unsophisticated barbarism is surely benign when compared to the methodical, civilized violence unleashed by the Nazi obsession with "differential prohibitions."

The need for Russia to function as the geographical, chronological, and cultural site of latency, and not as a site of trauma, may explain Levi's silence on two points. First, although he did not personally observe traces of this violence, he also does not mention, even in passing, that much of the Holocaust took place in the lands far to the east of Auschwitz through which he traveled on his long journey home.[19] Second, he suppresses or forgets the staggering war crimes of Stalin and the Soviet Army that would certainly have been known to him by time he completed the book.[20] In conversation with Philip Roth, Levi indicates that his presentation of the Soviet Union (i.e., as benign and backward) is "objective." He adds that a thaw in the Cold War allowed him, in 1961, to broach the topic "without being called a philo-Communist by the right wing and a disruptive reactionary by the powerful Italian Communist Party."[21]

Davide Ferrario and Marco Belpoliti's 2006 film, *La strada di Levi* (*Primo Levi's Journey*), adapts *The Reawakening* in a far more successful way than Francesco Rosi did in 1997.[22] I will not offer an analysis of the film here but only wish to point out that Ferrario and Belpoliti are faithful to Levi's experience of the East, even though the film is set in the post-Soviet world of 2005 instead of the Soviet one of 1945. Neither in Levi's book nor in Ferrario and Belpoliti's film is the East a site of Holocaust trauma. In both works, the East is Europe's other: a place of neglect rather than action, an exotic land where, even now, horses are still an important means of transport. By 2005, global capitalism had made superficial incursions—evidenced by T-shirt logos and the like—but it is only when the film crew reaches Budapest, bright with neon, that the Western viewer experiences a familiar setting.

Levi has a similar sensation in 1945. After days of uncomfortable train travel, he arrives in Romania, where the familiar Latinate names are "a delicate philological pleasure," and finally, in Hungary, where, he remarks without irony (although it would certainly be appropriate in the case of the Holocaust victims), "we now felt ourselves in Europe, protected by a civilization which was ours" (183). At first, this sense of feeling at home as Europeans is conveyed simply when, for example, Levi notes, "the suburbs of Vienna were ugly and casual like those we knew at Milan and Turin" (186). But the homeward journey darkens at the sight of "Vienna undone and the Germans broken," producing in Levi and his companions "[an] anguish, which was mixed up with [their] misery, with the heavy, threatening sensation of an irreparable and definitive evil which was present everywhere, nestling like gangrene in the guts of Europe and the world, the seed of future harm" (187–88). This is a strong image of the infection that quietly lurks, of the latent traumatic memories of the War and certainly of the Nazi genocide that will return to poison Europe. The traces of the Holocaust, which are found throughout the continent and in the survivors themselves, are inescapable reminders of this toxic history.

The final chapter of the book, "The Awakening," takes place in Italy and, first, in Germany, a nation in close geographical proximity to Levi's home and not so very foreign to a Northern Italian. Now in Munich, on German soil, the question of what the Holocaust will mean to the present, since it is now of the past, is very much on Levi's mind:

> Did [the Germans] know about Auschwitz, about the silent daily massacre, a step away from their doors? . . . If they did not, they ought, as a sacred duty, to listen, to learn everything, immediately, from us, from me; I felt the tattooed number on my arm burning like a wound. [. . .] I felt that everyone should interrogate us, read in our faces who we were, and listen to our tale in humility. But no one looked us in the eyes, no one accepted the challenge; they were deaf, dumb, and blind . . . still prisoners of their old tangle of pride and guilt. (190–91)[23]

The metaphorical burning on Levi's tattooed arm is an apt representation of his psychological trauma that, the reader is made to feel, would have been relieved if these anonymous Germans had listened and apologized; instead, it is exacerbated and turned inward when no acknowledgment is made. The force of this renunciation, of this unwillingness to own a traumatic history, is subverted in Rosi's adaptation of The Reawakening. At just this moment in the narrative, in Munich, Rosi introduces a scene of atonement in which a German prisoner of war, on seeing Levi's striped jacket and yellow star, drops to his knees and places his hand on his heart.[24] This stiff and preachy film is successful in some respects, but it fails in this instance to convey faithfully the survivor's decades-long isolation resulting from the belated and partial acknowledgment among Germans that the Holocaust was a great crime committed on their behalf. Rosi's gesture is anachronistic but not altogether mistaken if he means to describe our present moment. Now, 70 years after the events, the memory of the Holocaust seems permanently woven into Germany's national narrative. Even if the perpetrators and enablers of this traumatic violence never passed completely out of the latent period, their children and grandchildren are beginning to recover the suppressed memories.

Crossing the Brenner Pass into Italy in October 1945, Levi notes that his "less tired companions celebrated"—he means the forced laborers and ex-soldiers who had not passed through the extermination camps—while he and fellow Holocaust survivor, Leonardo, "remained lost in a silence crowded by memories." Reckoning the past and calculating their losses was impossible to do in Russia, so far from home, but this is no longer the case.

> Of 650, our number when we had left [as deportees to Auschwitz], three of us were returning. And how much had we lost, in those twenty months? What should we find at home? How much of ourselves had been eroded, extinguished? Were we returning richer or poorer, stronger or emptier? We did not know; but we knew that on the thresholds of our homes, for good or ill, a trial awaited us, and we anticipated it with fear. We felt in our veins the poison of Auschwitz . . . Soon, tomorrow, we should have to give battle, against enemies still unknown, outside ourselves and inside. (192)

These few words are a highly effective statement of what the Holocaust bequeaths to each survivor: a catalogue of loved ones lost; a diminished sense of self and dignity; but also the unending challenge, the "trial" of living with trauma, of struggling with the poison inside that will not be purged.

It is not surprising that the challenges of the homecoming make Levi regret the end of his purposeless roaming in the East. "The months just past, although hard, of wandering on the margins of civilization now seemed to us like a truce, a parenthesis of unlimited availability, a providential but unrepeatable gift of fate" (192).[25] It is significant that he views his experience of the colorful characters and their picaresque adventures as "a truce" or "a parenthesis," as a kind of latent period that has now finished. The larger story, whose impact cannot have been felt until this moment of homecoming, is his condition as a traumatized survivor. It has already been posited that the opening chapter of *The Reawakening*, describing Levi's "blurred" perception of the legacy of Auschwitz, represents the first stage of the posttraumatic stress disorder, in which the traumatic event is not yet assimilated, and that the nightmare that closes the book represents the third and final stage, in which the trauma is truly experienced for the first time. It is unusual in a memoir that its final page should bring the entire story into focus and determine its meaning, but this is the case for

The Reawakening. The obscure crisis presented in the epigraphic poem has arrived and is now unambiguous. "For those who undergo trauma, it is not only the moment of the event, but of the passing out of it that is traumatic," says Caruth, adding, "*survival itself*, in other words, *can be a crisis*."[26] The structure of trauma is such that only *after* surviving a life-threatening experience, and only *after* forgetting it, does the memory return with its full psychic force. In this sense, Levi's homecoming is not only a return but also a departure toward a new, difficult life conditioned by his own near-death experience and the deaths of hundreds of his fellow deportees.

The Reawakening recounts a tale of erring and forgetfulness that resembles the generalized repression of Holocaust memory in Europe from the end of World War II until, roughly, the Eichmann trial in the early 1960s. In Western Europe (e.g., in Italy and France), postwar governments memorialized their resistance movements rather than recalling the extent to which their nations had collaborated with the Nazis. In Germany, the suffering of the non-Jewish population dominated public discourse. This studied avoidance of Europe's traumatic history relating to the Nazi genocide, this evident period of latency, might account for the delayed recognition in Italy of Levi's first book, *Survival in Auschwitz*. The belated completion and publication of *The Reawakening*, which first appeared in print in 1963—even though Levi began to write some of its pages as early as 1946—coincided with a new and not wholly untroubled fascination with the Holocaust, decades after it occurred.

Of course, remembering the Holocaust survivor has always been problematic. She or he is a threat to society's integrity, to its self-perception and its cognitive framework. "The survivor . . . is a disturber of the peace," wrote Terrence Des Pres.[27] This is true, in part, because the survivor is a subject of trauma who remembers obsessively the otherwise forgotten violence on which cultures are founded and through which national histories lurch forward. This is why the memory of the Holocaust cannot be wholly suppressed or contained: the repressed does indeed return. *The Reawakening* shows that Levi's personal history is tightly connected to awful events that traumatized victims of the Holocaust but, also, to varying degrees, perpetrators, bystanders, and ultimately, entire nations. His memoir of return illustrates Caruth's claim that history and trauma are inexorably linked. "History, like trauma, is never simply one's own," she writes, "history is precisely the way we are implicated in each other's traumas."[28]

Notes

1. *The Reawakening*, trans. Stuart Woolf, with afterword, "The Author's Answers to His Readers' Questions," trans. by Ruth Feldman (New York: Macmillan, 1987). See, for example, Isabella Bertoletti, "Primo Levi's Odyssey: The Drowned and the Saved," *The Legacy of Primo Levi*, ed. Stanislao Pugliese (New York: Palgrave Macmillan, 2005), 105–18. Bertoletti states that "the infernal sorrows of the Lager are replaced in *La tregua* by a mood of exuberance" (112). On the picaresque aspects of the memoir, see JoAnn Cannon, "Storytelling and the Picaresque in Levi's *La tregua*," *Modern Language Studies*, 31, no. 2 (2001): 1–10. Henceforth, all references to this edition will be included in parenthesis in the text.

2. Gian-Paolo Biasin, "The Haunted Journey of Primo Levi," in *Memory and Mastery: Primo Levi as Writer and Witness*, ed. Roberta S. Kremer (Albany: State University of New York Press, 2001), 10.

3. Sigmund Freud, *Moses and Monotheism*, trans. Katherine Jones (New York: Vintage Books, 1967), 84.

4. In *The Reawakening*, Levi very often uses the term "Russia" and "Russian" when, for greater historical accuracy, he might have written "Soviet Union" and "Soviet." The first three paragraphs of the book are typical. In his description of the arrival of the Red Army at Auschwitz, Levi employs the word "Russian" four times while the word "Soviet" does not appear (1). Levi's usage speaks to the commonly held notion in Western Europe that the Soviet Union was just the latest iteration of the Russian Empire and that Russia dominated the other Soviet republics both politically and culturally. Levi describes Germany's conqueror as "Victorious Russia" (107); he and the other prisoners contend with "the Russian Command" (114); and he describes "Russian trains," not Soviet ones (67). It is noteworthy that Levi never actually touched Russian soil during his many months in the Soviet Union. After passing through Poland and before reaching Western Europe, he traveled through Ukraine, Belarus (Levi often calls it "White Russia"), Romania, and Hungary. Nevertheless, Levi and the other Italians speak of being detained in Russia (146); of confronting "the immense, heroic space of Russia" and "the Russian summer" (113); of struggling with the Russian language (120). Another commonly held notion shaping Levi's account is that eastern Russia was not wholly "European" despite the strict cartographic definition. According to Neumann, many Western intellectuals of the 1950s considered Russia more Asian than European, and thought that Russia, nomadic and barbarian, was the antithesis of sedentary, civilized Europe. Iver B. Neumann, "Russia as Europe's Other," *Journal of Contemporary European Studies* 6, no. 12 (1998): 26–73.

5. On the idea that the Holocaust was enabled by the Enlightenment, see, for example, Max Horkheimer and Theodor W. Adorno, *Dialectic of Enlightenment: Philosophical Fragments*, ed. Gunzelin Schmid Noerr, trans. Edmund Jephcott (Stanford, CA: Stanford University Press, 2002).

6. See Alexander Stille, "The Biographical Fallacy," *The Legacy of Primo Levi*, 209–20. In support of the idea that Auschwitz killed Levi 40 years after the liberation, "even Levi's son, Renzo, was quoted as saying: 'Read the conclusion of *The Truce* and you will understand'" (209).

7. See Robert S. C. Gordon, *Primo Levi's Ordinary Virtues: From Testimony to Ethics* (Oxford: Oxford University Press, 2001), particularly the chapter on friendship, 219–36.

8. Irving Howe, "Introduction," Primo Levi, *If Not Now, When?*, trans. William Weaver (New York: Summit Books, 1985), 12.

9. "The difficulty many (but not all) survivors of the Holocaust have in expressing their experiences can be explained by the fact that the nature of the events that happened to them is in no way covered by the terms, positions, and frames of reference that the symbolic order offers to them. In short, the problem which causes trauma is not the nature of the event by itself or any intrinsic limitation of representation per se, but the split between the *living* of an event and the availability of forms of representation through which the event can be *experienced*." Ernst van Alphen, "Second-Generation Testimony, Transmission of Trauma, and Postmemory," *Poetics Today* 27, no. 2 (2006): 482; emphasis in original.

10. Sigmund Freud, *Beyond the Pleasure Principle (excerpt)*, in *The Freud Reader*, ed. Peter Gay (New York: W. W. Norton, 1989), 602; emphasis in original.

11. Primo Levi, *The Drowned and the Saved*, trans. Raymond Rosenthal (New York: Random House, 1989), 24.

12. This, and the quotations that follow, until otherwise noted, come from Levi, *Survival in Auschwitz: The Nazi Assault on Humanity*, trans. Stuart Woolf (New York: Collier Books, 1993), 93.

13. Freud, *Beyond the Pleasure Principle*, 598.

14. Primo Levi, *Collected Poems*, trans. Ruth Feldman and Brian Swann (London: Faber and Faber, 1988), 10.

15. Levi, *Survival in Auschwitz*, 59–64.

16. Ibid., 63.

17. Cathy Caruth, "Trauma and Experience: Introduction," in *Trauma: Explorations in Memory*, ed. Cathy Caruth (Baltimore, MD: Johns Hopkins University Press, 1995), 4–5; emphasis in original.

18. Iver B. Neumann, *Russia and the Idea of Europe: A Study in Identity and International Relations* (London: Routledge, 1996).

19. Lucy S. Dawidowicz reports that, in 1941–1942, the *Einsatzgruppen* were active in places that Levi passed through on his journey home, including eastern Poland, Ukraine, and Belarus, all of which were parts of the Soviet Union at the time. The *Einsatzgruppen* and other police units killed around two million victims. See *The War against the Jews, 1933–1945* (New York: Bantam Books, 1976), 171.

20. Krushchev's 1956 speech, in which he denounced Stalin's purges and war crimes, was much discussed that summer in the Italian press. See Elena Dundovich, "Khrushchev: Contemporary Perspectives in the Western Press," in

Wilfried Loth, ed., *Europe, Cold War, and Coexistence, 1953–1965* (New York: Frank Cass Publishers, 2004), 190–200.

21. "A Conversation with Primo Levi," in *Survival in Auschwitz: The Nazi Assault on Humanity*, 183.

22. *La strada di Levi* [Primo Levi's Journey], directed and adapted by Davide Ferrario, screenplay by Marco Belpoliti, Primo Levi, and Davide Ferrario (San Lorenzo in Campo: Rossofuoco Productions, 2006), film; *La tregua* [The Reawakening], directed by Francesco Rosi, adapted from Primo Levi (New York and Santa Monica: Miramax Films, 1997), film.

23. A case can made for using the word "wound" rather than "sore," as Stuart Woolf does, to translate the Italian, *piaga* (Primo Levi, *Opere 1*, 1997, 392).

24. "Rosi added several scenes that betray the mood of the book. Most disturbing is the addition of an atonement scene . . . Rosi appropriated this act of atonement from German chancellor Willy Brandt's kneeling before the Warsaw ghetto monument in 1970." Marla Stone, "Primo Levi, Roberto Benigni, and the Politics of Holocaust Representation," in *The Legacy of Primo Levi*, ed. Stanislao Pugliese (New York: Palgrave Macmillan, 2005), 141.

25. Later, Levi qualified that statement as follows: "In its historical reality, my Russian 'truce' turned to a 'gift' only many years later, when I purified it by rethinking it and by writing about it." "A Conversation with Primo Levi," in *Survival in Auschwitz: The Nazi Assault on Humanity*, 183.

26. Cathy Caruth, "Trauma and Experience: Introduction," *Trauma: Explorations in Memory*, 9; emphasis in original.

27. Terence Des Pres, *The Survivor: An Anatomy of Life in the Death Camps* (New York: Oxford University Press, 1976), 210.

28. Cathy Caruth, *Unclaimed Experience: Trauma, Narrative, and History* (Baltimore, MD: Johns Hopkins University Press, 1996), 24.

5

The Witness's Tape Recorder and the Violence of Mediation

Lina Insana

University of Pittsburgh

Introduction

The analysis of Primo Levi's sizeable testimonial, literary, and essayistic production has tended, over the years, to be subject to what I'll call a centripetal approach that seeks to draw together its threads, themes, and images. One of the gestures I'd like to make in the present chapter is to suggest that from within Levi's *oeuvre* emerges an opposing, centrifugal force.[1] This is a force governed in part by a logic of the reactive and productive capacities of difference—the "mustard seed" as Levi writes in *The Periodic Table*—and driven by Levi's many contradictions, both in his evolution over time and the tensions engendered by his multiple and overlapping subject positions: assimilated Jew, survivor, chemist, public intellectual, cultural icon, and so on.[2] To this end, my comments in the present chapter will show that translation—the totality of the ways in which Levi translated and wished to be translated—is emblematic of this fact and offers a study in how we might better use Levi's tensions to explore his writings, his worldview, and his thought.

I have, in other forums, focused extensively on the way in which translation functions as a metaphor for the challenges and mechanisms of Holocaust testimony in Levi's *oeuvre*. In this context, I have argued that Levi's translation practices are consistently interventionist and activist, and that they tend more often than not to undermine or even reverse their source text.[3] This results in a foregrounding, variously, of the witness's reacquisition of agency through the translation process, of the very real challenges of transmission, and of translation's unique ability to figure the witness's mediating role in the transmission of Holocaust testimony, as well as the anxieties that emerge from that role. These anxieties manifest themselves textually in sites of translation such as Levi's mediations of Dante and Kafka, but also paratextually in Levi's commentaries on translation and other kinds of mediation. Interestingly these latter texts suggest two specific—and very different—tropes of translation that are helpful in understanding Levi's bifurcated notion of translation, a notion that, as it turns out, depends entirely on where Levi sees himself in the chain of translational acts.

Translating and Being Translated

Primo Levi's essay "Tradurre ed essere tradotti" (Translating and Being Translated), first published in 1980 as "Lasciapassare per Babele" (Pass to Babel), plots out the difficulties of both terms in the essay's later—and better-known—title. The first term, the act of translating, is variously described as a thankless job (a counterintuitive fact, Levi says; the reversal of Babel *should* draw the gratitude of all human kind); a trap-laden terrain where false cognates, idioms, and culturally specific signifiers lie waiting in ambush ("agguato") for the unsuspecting but well-meaning translator; the domain of a poorly remunerated figure within both intellectual and commercial economies; and a process requiring the kind of art not taught or teachable in schools. In short, translating is "a more *arduous* task" (emphasis mine) than can be remedied by the mere awareness of such snares as false friends, because of the "superhuman" difficulty of transmitting the "expressive force" of a text from one language to another.[4]

Belying the ostensibly equal valence given to both terms in the essay's title is the scant, one-paragraph conclusion in which Levi comments on the diametrically opposed role of "being translated." Here, the position of being the author translated by someone else is described primarily in terms of imposed, unwanted passivity and imprisonment: "a kind of work that belongs neither to the work week nor to the weekend; as a matter of fact, it's not work at all, it's a semi-passivity," similar to that of being operated on or psychoanalyzed.[5] The staccato list of feelings that assail the poor passive translated author frames the discourse in even more striking terms: he feels, by turns, or all at once, "flattered, betrayed, ennobled, x-rayed, castrated, leveled, raped, adorned, killed" by the translator of his or her work.[6] This rhetoric of brutal physical violence (highly sexualized, we should say) whose agent "has poked his nose and fingers into [the author's] entrails" is in tension with Levi's description just a few pages earlier of a translator (much like himself) who must "lower himself into the personality of the author" to detect the many dangers presented by the text.[7] In the process of translating, it is the translator who must risk his well-being for the greater linguistic good, but from the perspective of the translate*d*, the stakes are even higher: invasive prodding, mutilation, and even death. Risky business in either case, but it is clear that translating for Levi is decidedly *not* the same as being translated, and indeed the two terms end up being the bearers of very different codes of interpretation and conduct, translatorly and otherwise.

On the other hand, the two processes as described by Levi do share at least one fundamental characteristic: a respect for the unity between place and language, between experience and its linguistic expression. A consideration of this commonality helps us to understand better what, exactly, is at stake in Levi's seemingly divergent theories and practices of translation. Namely, it suggests that, on either side of the equation, to express the Holocaust in a code different from the locus of its linguistic and cultural logic is arduous, to say the least, and that Levi is aware of the various levels of mediation that bring his language, and the testimony it carries, farther and farther away from its source text. Moreover, it suggests that Levi's interpretive gestures are part of a lifelong struggle to gain power over the signification of the Holocaust, to articulate from the position of the survivor despite *and* against the commanding logic of the event, its own unique mode of articulation, its own grammar, its own language.

Levi's comments on the active term in "Translating and Being Translated" represent a kind of translator's *apologia*, a defense against potential criticisms of inaccuracy or excessive license, and ultimately a plea for the translator as being "the only one who truly reads a text, reads it profoundly, in every crease, weighing and valuing every word and every image, or perhaps discovering its gaps and missteps."[8] This passage constructs the translator as a privileged figure whose intimate knowledge of the text puts him in a position to assess even its shortcomings. What it does not make explicit is the extent to which Levi as a translator in fact felt compelled to correct those gaps and missteps in the service of goals that reached beyond the source text and into his own aesthetic, moral, and ethical world view—in sum, to enact the same intrusive violence on the source text that he describes from the position of the translatee. The difference, in the end, is one between the holistic investment suggested by the notion of "lowering oneself into" the source text's author and the more violent and even deadly paradigms of interaction imagined by Levi's anxieties of passivity in the signification of the Holocaust—specifically *his* Holocaust. I propose to place both of these modes of translation in open dialogue with Levi's discussion—in the "Lettere di tedeschi" (Letters from Germans) section of *The Drowned and the Saved*[9]—of having *Survival in Auschwitz* translated into German, and with his private reflection on the process of constructing his "antologia personale" (personal anthology), *The Search for Roots*.

The Witness's Tape Recorder

After a career of troubling the text to accommodate the reader (as Friedrich Schleiermacher[10] would say), of recontexting and subverting the Ancient Mariner and Dante's poet *and* pilgrim, of reshaping and "correcting" writers like Presser and Kafka, Levi in the 1985 essay "Letters from Germans" (the last proper chapter of *The Drowned and the Saved*) selects the curious image of the tape recorder to articulate what he hoped Heinz Reidt's German translation of *Survival in Auschwitz*[11] would be. In that essay, Levi develops an antidote to the kind of potentially annihilating and castrating violence that for him characterized "being translated": "In a certain sense, it was not so much a matter of translation as of a restoration: it was, or I wanted it to be, a *restitutio in pristinum*, a retranslation into the language in which the events had happened and to which they owed themselves. It should have been, more than a book, a recording tape."[12] The idea that the translation from Italian into German should represent a restoration of the source text of Auschwitz compels us, first, to see the Holocaust as a source text that demands translation. By this theory, Levi's text is ostensibly diminished by its attempts to reproduce the *Lager* "original," since it expresses itself in a language not inherent to the events and their logic. It also suggests that Levi's claim for the desirability of this kind of reverse signification process represents, in effect, an attempt to test the truth value of the Italian translation that lies between the German source text of Auschwitz and the German translator's attempt to recapture it. This circular or "back" translation is a common process in legal and technical translation fields, a check to ensure that the first translation was "faithful" enough to be rendered unproblematically back into its "original" state.

Despite its currency in technical translation practice, however, this prospect is quite a different one in the literary and testimonial spheres, where the possibility of a quality-control check on Levi's and Reidt's "reproductions" of the Holocaust is illusory, at best. At worst, it seeks to occult the layers and levels of difference that lie, on one hand, between the *Lager* and Levi's rendering of it, and on the other, between *Se questo è un uomo* and *Ist das ein Mensch*. These layers and levels include temporal differences; a double spatial dislocation; the rerouting of the system of signification out of the German cultural space via Levi and his Turinese, integrated Enlightenment subject position; the host of linguistic differences at play between the *Lager*'s corrupt German, its use within Levi's elegant Italian narrative, and its recontextualized appearance in postwar German prose. But most importantly, Levi's comments suggest that he conceives of the various seasons in the life of his testimony in fundamentally different ways, and thus as subject to essentially different theories and ethics of translation. Levi's description of his goals for the German translation, in this same part of *The Drowned and the Saved*, suggests the slippery nature of his notions of originality and reproduction. "At the time, I was spurred on by a scrupulous sense of *superrealism*; I wanted for nothing to be lost in that book, and especially in its *German garment*, of that bitterness, of that violence done against language, that I had tried so hard to *reproduce* in the Italian *original*" (emphasis mine).[13]

"That I tried so hard to *reproduce* in the Italian *original*": Levi's *Survival in Auschwitz* is thus constructed as a site of oscillation between imperfect reproduction and originality, between the "superrealist" mimesis of a source or object and the sacred utterance—harking back to romantic notions of translation's evocation of divine creation—of the "original" testimonial word. Levi's paradoxical terminology in fact walks a line between translating—in his own earnest effort to reproduce the German source text of the *Lager*—and being translated, between control and its relinquishment.

If the first stage of the testimony's life—Levi's translation from the German of the Third Reich to his measured, rational Italian—is couched in terms of derivation, interpretation, analysis, even lack or inadequacy, the second phase, the *restitutio in pristinum* into German, is described in terms of the stability of a source text that can be recaptured and reinstalled as the primary bearer of truth and meaning. Moreover, for Levi, the process of returning to that fixity entails none of the violence and change (adornment, castration, rape, murder) described in the last paragraph of "Translating and Being Translated." Rather, it amounts to a corrective restoration of the most organic and peaceful kind, neither adding nor subtracting from the source text to be transmitted, and eliminating any and all anxieties that Levi might feel about the violence wrought by normal translation. In the return to his original's "original," Levi would have us believe, the violence is neutralized, the process externalized from the bodies of translator and translatee alike—and the various source texts in question remain intact.

The Violence of Mediation

As an emblem for the ways in which translation can come to stand for the whole of an albeit tension-filled Levian testimonial value system, Levi's comments tell us this: that each of these phases or translation *acts* is linked to an essentially different translatorly "*task*," or duty, and that translating is not necessarily the same as being translated, in either practical or ethical terms.[14] Specifically, I would suggest that Levi, in this particular instance, deploys these delicately balanced tropes of translation as strategies of containment for the German language, and that Levi's desire to return his story to its originary linguistic state ultimately emerges from the need to allow the German language only the space it needs to perform for the reader the historical violence of the camps and the violence done to the German language *by the camps*. Levi is not willing, however, to inflict new violence—the inevitable violence of translation—on his testimonial text. If German, the language of the offence (and the violence) is acceptable within the safe confines of Levi's appropriation of it, then the German language and culture must not be set free to do new translatorly violence, to enact new offenses on Levi's now-sacred testimonial text: in other words, to "x-ray" it, "rape" it, or ultimately "kill" it.

We have noted, however, that Levi's anxieties about the danger associated with close reading and mediation are not limited to translations from and into the German language. Striking evidence of this comes in the form of Levi's letter to Einaudi editor Giulio Bollati on the occasion of his submission of the *Search for Roots* manuscript in September 1980 (written, remarkably, less than two months before "Translating and Being Translated"): "I have felt more laid bare in making this choice than in writing books. I have never undergone psychoanalytic treatment or surgery; this work has seemed to me equivalent to those. It has felt like having my stomach opened, or rather, like being in the act of opening it myself, like Mohammed in the ninth Bolgia and in Doré's illustration."[15]

Doré's illustrations of Dante's *Inferno* recur frequently as signposts of anxiety in Levi's essays, most notably in his piece on "Fear of Spiders" ("Paura dei ragni") in *Other People's Trades*. In language uncannily similar to that used to explore the "essere tradotti" term in Levi's "Translating and Being Translated" essay, Mohammed's splayed torso is proposed as a figure for the violence of reading and textual examination, the body of the man as it stands for the "laid bare" text, or *corpus*, of the writer. Here, the violence is of the writer's own doing as he examines—and then opens for the examination of others—his textual genealogy. Levi's idea of *corpus* is thus expanded to embrace not only his own textual production but also the body of texts that have helped to form him, to compose his own textual body. As Belpoliti writes of the *Search for Roots* preface, this is the closest that Levi comes to an explicitly Freudian self-reading: "The roots of the title are thus the parts of himself—of the writer—that plunge into the subterranean, earthy part [of himself], and therefore the most complex and disquieting."[16] If specific texts are threatening for linguistic, cultural, or historical reasons, Levi's more general comments regarding his work in *The Search for Roots* suggest an awareness of the difficulty of his own potential mediation by his readers, and a reluctance to have undue violence done to any of his figured bodies: textual, evidentiary, and testimonial alike.

What are the implications of Levi's double standard for broader testimonial issues within Levi's *oeuvre*—one translation theory applied to his own testimonial task and quite another applied to the duty owed to him by potential translators or interpreters of his work? What are, for Levi, the ethical differences between translating and being translated? Moreover, can we discern, in the space between these two processes, a space, or gap, that illuminates Levi's work in a more global way? If translating and being translated come to mean essentially different things for Levi, what does this say about his role as interpreter of the Holocaust? What is the relationship, in the end, between theoretical notions of translating and being translated, and the practical dynamics of testimony?

Ultimately, Levi's various uses and abuses of translation constituted textual sites of exploration in which the mechanics, challenges, and ethics of testimony came under his sophisticated gaze. Through this process, his activist translations came to symbolize and authorize new agencies, a subjecthood reclaimed after its brutal destruction in the *Lager*. Levi's theorizations of these processes, though, tend to underscore the danger inherent in such close readings as translation demands; unraveling Babel, as we well know from *Survival in Auschwitz*, is no easy task. But being translated—both in theory and in practice—was a far more threatening prospect for Levi. He was notoriously controlling of his foreign-language translators, meticulously checking their work while it was still in progress, and even stopping publication of the first French translation of *Survival in Auschwitz*. Its potential for "flattery" and "ornamentation" aside, being translated ultimately represented for Levi an offense against his testimonial agency and a threat to the integrity of his testimonial signs. Even when the threat is figured as a more textually corporeal one (as the body of his textual influences *cum* textual self) and even when it is Levi himself doing the violent prodding, an open text is always a vulnerable one.

Levi's two views of translation are radically different. One recognizes only the violence imposed on a text when it is mediated and on a translator when he or she mediates it. The other amounts to an idealized testimonial fantasy of pristine source texts and an externalized, neutralized model of return and restitution, healing and reversal of the failures (such as Levi's Italian rendering of the corrupt sign systems of the *Lager*) of mediation. Taken together, they indicate a whole constellation of testimonial anxieties on Levi's part, not only in the early stages of his production, when ineffability, transgression, and traumatic reoccurrence are of principal concern, but in its later stages, as well, when the danger of textual mediation comes into collision with its absolute necessity.

Is there a lesson to be learned from this gap between translating and being translated? Should mediators of the Holocaust source text do as Levi says—or as Levi *does*? Should we, lured by the appeal of documentary transparency, seek an untroubled return to the pristine "origin" of the event? And if so, do we risk coming to the same sad end as Levi's Mr. Simpson, whose Torec machine offers externalized and simulacral "tape recordings" of realities with which to engage too easily, too temporarily, too weakly?[17] Perhaps, instead, we must come to terms with the violence of "profound" reading that Levi saw so clearly, and with the fact that any attempt to represent the Holocaust is necessarily inscribed with our role as mediators, interpreters—to wit, translators of the event.

Notes

1. As Robert S. C. Gordon writes in the introduction to the *Cambridge Companion to Primo Levi*, "The different foci and scales of Levi's concerns and the racking movements between them, both centripetal and centrifugal, are crucial to understanding the energy behind his work" (xviii).
2. "Perché la ruota giri, perché la vita viva, ci vogliono le impurezze, e le impurezze delle impurezze: anche nel terreno, come è noto, se ha da essere fertile. Ci vuole il dissenso, il diverso, il grano di sale e di senape" (Primo Levi, *Il sistema periodico*, in *Opere*, ed. Marco Belpoliti (Torino: Einaudi, 1997), 1:768. ["So that the wheel may turn, so that life may live, impurities are necessary, as are impurities of impurities: even in the earth, as we know, if it is to be fertile. Dissent, difference, the grain of salt and the mustard seed—they are all necessary"]. This and all citations have been taken from the two-volume 1997 edition of Levi's *Opere*, edited by Marco Belpoliti. All translations from the Italian are mine.
3. Lina N. Insana, *Arduous Tasks: Primo Levi, Translation, and the Transmission of Holocaust Testimony* (Toronto: University of Toronto Press, 2009); Lina N. Insana, "In Levi's Wake: Adaptation, Simulacrum, Postmemory." *Italica* 86, no. 2 (2009): 212–38.
4. Primo Levi, "Tradurre ed essere tradotti," in *L'altrui mestiere*, in *Opere*, 2:733.
5. "Tradurre," 2:734.
6. Ibid.
7. "Tradurre," 2:733, 734.
8. Ibid., 734.
9. Primo Levi, *The Drowned and the Saved*, trans. Raymond Rosenthal (New York: Summit Books, 1988).

10. Friedrich Schleiermacher, "On the different methods of translating," in *Western Translation Theory from Herodotus to Nietzsche*, ed. and trans. Douglas Robinson ([0]Manchester: St. Jerome, 2002), 233.

11. Primo Levi, *Survival in Auschwitz*, trans. Stuart Woolf (New York: Collier, 1961).

12. Levi, *I sommerse e i salvati*, in *Opere*, 2:1128.

13. Ibid.

14. On translation as task and duty, see the canonical essay by Walter Benjamin, "The Task of the Translator," in *Illuminations: Essays and Reflections*, ed. Hannah Arendt; trans. by Harry Zohn (New York: Schocken, 1969), as well as the rich response tradition that has emerged in its wake; Derrida's "Des tours de Babel," in *Difference in Translation*, ed. and trans. Joseph Graham (Ithaca, NY: Cornell University Press, 1985) is particularly illuminating for its focus on the afterlife, or the *sur-vie*, that translation issues.

15. "Note ai testi" (Notes on the Texts), in *Opere*, 2:1576–77.

16. Ibid., 1578.

17. Of the fifteen stories contained in Levi's first published collection of short stories, *Storie naturali* (*Natural Stories*, 1966), six revolve around the relationship between the narrator and a certain Mr. Simpson, the sales representative for an office machines company, NACTA, that builds photocopiers and devices for other kinds of more or less fantastic reproduction. In the story that brings an end to both the "Mr. Simpson" series and the entire collection, "Trattamento di quiescenza," reproduction is carried to its simulacral extreme. When NATCA develops a virtual reality machine, the "Torec" or "Total Recorder," Mr. Simpson finally succumbs to the lure of machine-aided ease, surrendering his very experience of reality. Significantly, his demise is signaled by a conclusion in which Mr. Simpson ends his days alone, reading only *Ecclesiastes* and serially "experiencing" the death of others through the Torec, to which he is now hopelessly addicted.

6

The Strange Case of the
Muselmänner in Auschwitz

Joseph Farrell

University of Strathclyde

Fateless, the semi-autobiographical novel written by Imre Kertész, the Hungarian Jewish writer who was awarded the 2002 Nobel Prize for Literature, draws on the author's experiences in Auschwitz and in other concentration and labor camps.[1] Gyuri Koves, the novel's 16-year-old protagonist—the age of Kertész himself at his arrest—is initiated into the ways of the camp by Bandi Citrom, a fellow Hungarian inmate who is only slightly older but who has longer experience of life in the Lager. Inside the camp, they see a crowd of people with the letter L for Latvian inscribed in the center of the yellow star they are obliged to wear, and in the midst of the throng, Gyuri detects a separate grouping of "peculiar beings who at first were a little disconcerting." Kertész describes this latter group in greater detail:

> Viewed from a certain distance, they are senilely doddering old codgers, and with their heads retracted into their necks, their noses sticking out from their faces, their filthy prison duds that they wear hanging loosely from their shoulders, even on the hottest summer's day they put one in mind of winter crows with a perpetual chill. As if with each and every stiff, halting step they take one were to ask: is such an effort really worth the trouble? These mobile question marks, for I could characterize not only their outward appearance but perhaps even their very exiguousness in no other way, are known in the concentration camps as *Musulmänner* or Muslims, I was told. Bandi Citrom promptly warned me away from them: "You lose any will to live just by looking at them," he reckoned, and there was some truth in that, although as time passed, I also came to realize that it takes more than just that. (38)

The passage from Kertész is the verbal equivalent of a savage caricature by George Grosz, with the *Muselmänner* depicted as having their heads drawn down into their shoulders, their noses protruding, and they themselves compared to crows in winter.[2] The zoological imagery is forceful, and by being equated with animals, the *Muselmänner* are *ipso facto* reduced to a state of dubious humanity or at least distanced from the rest of their kind. It is a harsh, unforgiving portrait, and indeed, there is nothing more striking in this and in comparable descriptions than the sheer pitilessness of the representation. "No one felt compassion for the Muslim, and no one felt sympathy for him either. The other inmates, who continually feared for their lives, did not even judge him worthy of being looked at," write Ryn and Klodzinski, in the first study of the subject of the *Muselmann*.[3] Even the term "pitilessness" is inadequate, since the feeling aroused by the *Muselmänner* is frequently more akin to fear and loathing. On a later occasion, Bandi Citrom presents them as representing not only a reprehensible level of personal degeneration but also a danger against which Gyuri must guard. In an echo of Primo Levi's encounter with Steinlauf in *Survival in Auschwitz*, the mentor reproaches his young charge for neglecting personal hygiene, thereby letting himself fall to the level of the *Muselmänner*, and insists on scrubbing his body vigorously. The episode causes Gyuri involuntarily to call to mind the earlier dismissal by Bandi Citrom of the "Muslims" as "carriers of pestilence" (173).

In its refusal of compassion or fellow feeling, as in virtually every other particular, Kertész's account conforms to the characterization of that category of inmates identified by the strange term *Muselmann*. The terminology seems to have been in use in several of the Lagers, and even where nomenclature differed, inmates everywhere recognized the distinctiveness of the grouping, none more so than Primo Levi. Perhaps no aspect of camp life has drawn so much comment or has been the object of such sustained attempt to incorporate the notion into some coherent narrative. The *Muselmänner* have troubled translators and puzzled commentators, biographers, and historians, as well as those analysts and philosophers, such as Bruno Bettelheim and Giorgio Agamben, who have set themselves the task of dissecting the experience of the Lager for what it reveals not only of life at the extreme at a specific point in history but for what it says about the very nature of the human being, and of the point of contact and contrast between the human and nonhuman.[4] Interpretations of the ethical or existential meaning of the experience of the *Muselmänner* have, in other words, been central to various disputes about life in the Lager.

In times like ours, concerned with linguistic proprieties, there is a certain embarrassment over the very term "Muslim," viewed as indelicate, improper, perhaps even provocative in view of the supposed modern "clash of civilizations." In many ways this unease, although secondary, is akin to distaste over the use by writers like Mark Twain of racial language, like the word "nigger," once acceptable but now considered offensive and derogatory. This uncertainty, which is both linguistic and ethical, has created dilemmas for translators. In *Survival in Auschwitz*, Primo Levi himself used the standard Italian word, *musulmano*, and only in a footnote when introducing his discussion of the category does he employ the German term *Muselmann*.[5] However, even although Levi had opted for the familiar Italian term, Stuart Woolf, in the first English translation of *Se questo è un uomo* (published in the United Kingdom under the title *If This is a Man* and later in the United States as *Survival in Auschwitz*[6]) preferred the pseudo-German form *musselman* (with a double *s* and a single *n*) throughout. Strangely, on the page where he first uses the term, he also reproduces Levi's original footnote with Levi's spelling, *Muselmann* (94). In *The Drowned and the Saved*, Levi employs both the German and the Italian.[7] Bettelheim, writing in 1961, chooses the English *Moslem* or even the now unfamiliar term *Mohammedan*, but Agamben, like his English translator, prefers the German.

The retention of the German in an English translation of the various works under discussion is comprehensible, since the use of a foreign term is a distancing device that diminishes the prospect of offense, and it will be convenient here to follow this practice, which locates the word in the realm of specialist, technical usages. The origin of the use of the term has been disputed, and if there is no agreement or clarity here, it cannot be said *tout court* that it has nothing to do with Islam as a religion, although it could certainly be said that any connection is based on a mistaken assessment of Muslim belief. In the *Drowned and the Saved*, Levi offers, cursorily, two possible etymologies, although he agrees that neither is "very convincing." These are "fatalism, and the bandaging around the head which might be taken to resemble a turban" (77). Bettelheim too accepts the notion of Islamic fatalism as a possible explanation of the currency of the term, even if he criticizes the too ready acceptance of this interpretation of Islam that lay behind it. As he writes, "In the camps, they were called Moslems (*Musulmänner*) because of what was erroneously viewed as a fatalistic surrender to the environment, as Mohammedans are supposed to blandly accept their fate."[8]

Agamben debated various etymologies of the term, but he too concluded that the most plausible was an association with a deeply rooted western prejudice that saw Muslim belief and practice as imbued with a sense of fatalism. It is worth noting that Agamben distinguishes here between "Muslim" and "*Muselmann*," confining the latter to the special sense given it inside the camps:

The most likely explanation of the term can be found in the literal meaning of the Arabic word Muslim: the one who submits unconditionally to the will of God. It is this meaning that lies at the origin of the legends concerning Islam's supposed fatalism, legends which are found in European culture starting from the Middle Ages (this deprecatory sense of the term is present in European languages, particularly in Italian). But while the Muslim's resignation consists in the conviction that the will of Allah is at work every moment and in even in the smallest of events, the *Muselmann* of Auschwitz is instead defined by a loss of will and consciousness. (45)

In her biography of Levi, Myriam Anissimov offers another explanation: "The adoption of the term '*Muselmann*' or '*Muselmänner*' to denote prisoners in the last stages of exhaustion has been attributed to a Polish doctor, Fejkiel, who apparently compared a group of prisoners to a group of praying Arabs."[9]

It is clear that the most frequently repeated interpretation draws on the concept of "fatalism," meaning that the *Muselmann* is defined by the idea of resignation or surrender to destiny, to power, to fear, to helplessness, to the inexorable process of the demolition of the human. The *Muselmann* thus presented is a creature drained of all power of resistance, therefore bereft of will, determination, pluck, and guile, so in essence a man passively resigned to fate or to outcomes decided outside himself. Resignation involves the impossibility of resistance and the reconciliation to a life of despair, and renders hope itself redundant. The *Muselmann* is the creature who can be regarded as having bowed to fate, an idea that came to torment Imre Kertész. Perhaps as a result of his youthful experiences with Nazi brutality, Kertész in his fiction became more obsessed than any other modern writer with notions of an implacable, ineluctable destiny or fate, so a recurring situation in his work concerns characters who fall victim to arbitrary savagery, perhaps in a totalitarian system. Several of his novels focus on the plight of the individual caught up purely at random, not as the consequence of any decision or fault, in the power machinery of the police state, any police state, of any ideology. His idea of destiny has much in common with that in Greek tragedy, and the title of his first book, *Fateless* (or *Fatelessness*), indicates a state of mental confusion that leads the protagonist, Gyuri, to come to believe that he had, incomprehensibly, lived out someone else's fate. Kertész's later novel, *Detective Story* (1977), is set in an unnamed Latin American country and features a torturer who had been reading the history of Auschwitz and who calls all opponents of the régime, whatever their beliefs, "Jews." Fate represents unreason, both cosmic and individual, and is thus the antithesis of hope. It is not overstating the case to say that Kertész sees powerless humans everywhere in the same light that *Muselmänner* were viewed in the Lager, but he extends to his fictional creations a measure of pity he denies the original *Muselmänner*.

The *Muselmänner* as presented in witness writings challenges the idea of humanity, as well as of sovereignty and justice, that Giorgio Agamben wishes to espouse. In spite of a philosophical vision deeply rooted in classical thought, Agamben saw Auschwitz as representing a point of historical rupture, rather as Adorno did, although in a different intellectual framework. His three works, *Homo Sacer, Remnants of Auschwitz*, and *State of Exception* can be viewed as a kind of trilogy.[10] His is a philosophical panorama sufficiently wide to incorporate Aristotle as well as Walter Benjamin, and it has even been said that the parameters of Agamben's vision are Aristotle and Auschwitz. He undertakes an ethico-political examination of the relations between justice, power, violence, and law that allows him to define the sovereignty of nations in terms of the lives of the citizens, which in Nazism is resolved in the *Blut und Boden* (blood and soil). Increasingly, Agamben was drawn to the uncomfortable notion that the core of sovereignty lay in the power to take life and, more controversially, his thought focused on the Lager, which he seems to have viewed as an almost inevitable consequence, not of historical antisemitism, but of western views of sovereignty, founded as he believed them to have been on Greek political philosophy. The *Muselmann* tormented him, not particularly on a humanitarian level, but because the *Muselmann*, viewed as the "dead man walking," incarnated the dilemma of the human-nonhuman, thereby putting into sharp relief Agamben's theories of sovereignty, even more than of Humanism. Implicitly, although Agamben does not highlight this aspect, the *Muselmann* challenges the traditional Humanist notion of humankind. Agamben used several of the Holocaust witness-writers for his analysis and discussion, but relied particularly on Primo Levi, and subsequent discussion of this aspect of Levi's testimony has to take into account Agamben's work.

However, it seems to me that there are significant changes in Primo Levi's view of the *Muselmänner* between the books *Survival in Auschwitz* and *The Drowned and the Saved*, and that Agamben failed to give due weight to these developments. Levi can be as harsh as Kertész in his depiction of the *Muselmänner*. As is known, in addition to providing the title of his long reflective work, the Drowned and Saved are also fundamental categories in Levi's vision, and the *Muselmann* is *par excellence* the drowned or drowning man. His fate does not arouse any compassion in Levi: "With the mussulmans, the men in decay, it is not even worth speaking [...] even less worthwhile making friends with them, because they have no distinguished acquaintances in camp, they do not gain any extra rations." Most devastatingly and witheringly of all, he comments on their inevitable fate: "And in any case, one knows that they are only here on a visit, that in a few weeks nothing will remain of them but a handful of ashes in some near-by field and a crossed-out number on a register. Although swept along without rest by the innumerable crowd of those similar to them, they suffer and drag themselves along in an opaque intimate solitude, and in solitude they die or disappear, without leaving a trace in anyone's memory" (95).

There is no mistaking the echoes of Dante's *Inferno* in the reference to the anonymous crowds of souls swept along in a climactic turbulence, incapable of exercising personal control, resigned to the surrender of all individuality. In the *Limbo* circle of *Inferno*, there are groups of souls whose plight draws only haughty contempt from Dante and Virgil as they observe their punishment, and that kind of disdain seems to be the mark of Levi as he describes a group with whom he feels, at least in *Survival in Auschwitz*, no kinship. The question of just punishment has no relevance for the accounts of the *Muselmann* or any other inmate in Auschwitz, but the issue of the lack of kinship, the breaking of bonds of common humanity, is intriguing, even shocking. The language of the almost nonchalant, *poco-curante* dismissal of their final fate as "a handful of ashes in some near-by field and a crossed-out number on a register" clashes with the compassion-ate and enraged descriptions that Levi gives elsewhere of the Nazi project of the "demolition of man."

What is most surprising in this presentation is that it pays no heed to the offense done to the *Muselmann*. Plainly, the obligation Levi felt as a "witness" was precisely a sense of duty to chronicle the offense to humanity that was the Holocaust, to ensure that the memory of it did not fade, and his fear, which took shape in a recurring dream, was that on his return he would not be believed. To a modern reader, the *Muselmann* must appear as the supreme victim of that offense, but the colors employed in describing him do not convey that sense of victimhood. The *Muselmann* is a figure of reproach, an inadequate, pathetic figure who has failed. The underlying philosophy of Auschwitz is uncompromisingly Hobbesian, as Levi himself says, and the *Muselmann* is a fugitive who flees the "war of all against all," and who thereby puts himself outside the realm of the "human." To some extent, this was the consequence of the experience of Auschwitz, and Levi is clear and precise about the return to the "human" by the inmates. In *Survival in Auschwitz*, he situates the return at the point when, while await-ing the Russians, one of the band of survivors proposes that Levi and those who had gone searching for food and firewood should be given an extra portion of bread (160). In *The Drowned and the Saved*, too, he placed that reclamation of the "human" at liberation, when inmates felt themselves "becoming once again men, that is responsible" (53), implying that the acceptance of responsibility is the prime element of the definition of the human. The *Muselmann* had failed to accept that element of responsibility, and—crucially—there is no suggestion that the Nazi atrocities lay behind that failure. The *Muselmänner* themselves bear the guilt for acquiescing in a condition of subhumanity.

No critic living in warmth at home, as Levi puts it in the introductory verses to *Survival in Auschwitz*, has a right to criticize, but he has a duty to understand. At one level, it appears clear what the *Muselmann* represents: the fundamental element in his characterization relates to the abandonment of hope, of struggle, and therefore of responsibility. The *Muselmann* has given up on inner resistance and hope, but this is another of the paradoxes in Levi's presentation, for elsewhere he writes eloquently about the futility of hope for all *Häftlinge*. In his account of the haunting, empty days at the end of the war, after the German guards had fled, leaving in Auschwitz only the sick and the weakened, Levi wrote how he and the survivors struggled to adopt a vision that was incompatible with the mindset they had acquired over the preceding months. The Soviet army was known to be in the vicinity, but although their arrival was imminent, none of the Auschwitz inmates was quite convinced of it: "Because one loses the habit of hoping in the Lager and even trust in one's own reason. In the Lager, it is useless to think, because events happen for the most part in an unforeseeable manner: and it is harmful because it keeps alive a sensitivity which is a source of pain, and which some providential natural law dulls when suffering passes a certain limit" (171).

The loss of hope was not, then, a characteristic of the *Muselmänner* alone, but it is they who express this absence of hope in the most extreme way. There is, equally, no doubting Levi's preference for the Saved, for those who resist, in whatever manner. It is worth examining the brief pen portraits that Levi sketches in *Survival in Auschwitz* of fellow inmates, but it is impossible not to note there is only one of the Drowned *Muselmänner*, as against four of the plucky Saved. Null Achtzehn is the sole *Muselmann* recorded in anything resembling individual traits, but every word, every stroke of the pen, conveys a sense of the poverty and near worthlessness of his being. Not even his name is given, since Null Achtzehn means Zero Eighteen, the final three figures of the number engraved on his arm. Levi speculates, "It is as if everyone was aware that only a man was worthy of a name, and that Null Achtzehn is no longer a man" (42). This last notion—that Null Achtzehn is no longer a man—is central to Levi's depiction of the *Muselmann*, but it is equally central to his dissection of the dehumanizing aims of Auschwitz.

The objective of the Nazis is not only the destruction of a race, but also the demolition of the human by the elimination of all the innate qualities, the dignity and craving for respect and self-respect that make up the self-image of humankind. Perhaps it is not accurate to talk of "innate" qualities, since these attributes are those conferred on humanity in the western humanist tradition, to which Levi adhered. In Auschwitz, the Nazis sought to destroy men and demolish Man, and with the *Muselmänner* in general, and with Null Achtzehn specifically, they had succeeded. Null Achtzehn gives every appearance of being "empty inside," and indeed of being "nothing more than an involucre, like the slough of certain insects which one finds on the banks of swamps, held by a thread to stones and shaken by the wind" (42). He is the man everyone wishes to avoid being paired with on work projects, since he lacks not only physical strength but also all astuteness, all energy, all ability to reduce unnecessary effort. It is he who causes Levi to injure himself, requiring him to be confined for a dangerous period in the hospital block. The final words on Null Achtzehn are acid: "He carries out all the orders he is given, and it is foreseeable that when they send him to his death, he will go with the same total indifference" (43).

The tone, attitude, approach in the pen portraits of those who by virtue of inner qualities, which Levi describes objectively without expressing judgment, will belong to the Saved is strikingly different. There is a hierarchy in Levi's assessment and a hierarchy among the inmates, but his reactions and feelings toward the various categories are complex and subtle, not amenable to facile analysis. The first distinction, which might correspond to the division between the Cartesian and Hobbesian spheres of life, is the moral separation between what is permissible and acceptable inside the camps and what would be tolerated outside. Levi's euphemism, which recurs in all his works, for life inside Auschwitz is the simple Italian term *laggiù*, that is, "down there." In the chapter titled "The Drowned and the Saved" in *Survival in Auschwitz*, he talks about a "pitiless process of natural selection" that occurs "down there" and indicates that there is a "third way" in well-regulated, civil society but which "does not exist in the concentration camps" (89–90). Inside the camp, it is plain that his sympathies are with the guile, the strength of character, the sheer moral and physical force of the Saved, although it must be added that his thumbnail sketches are deeply ambiguous. He mentions and commends various individuals—Chaim for his belief, Robert for his wisdom, Baruch for his courage, and recounts in greater detail and with greater reserve the stories of Schepschel, Alfred L., Elias, and Henri. Schepschel drew admiration because he had successfully indulged in petty theft to guarantee survival, but he was prepared to hand over an accomplice to be flogged since he had believed that such an action would assist his own condition. Alfred L. kept himself well-turned-out, brought attention to himself by his adherence to regulations, so making himself eligible for special consideration. Elias prospered because, although he would have been shunned as mad or criminal outside, in Auschwitz his qualities were those needed to attain status. Henri cultivated those who held power, perhaps even by granting sexual favors, thereby making him central to a power network likely to assist him to survive. Levi's respect for the latter is limited, since he concludes that, at the time of writing and in liberty, he has no wish "to see him again" (100).

Whatever the *Muselmann* in Auschwitz finally represents, the most disconcerting element—for the contemporary reader—in many records is a distancing that borders on, and frequently becomes synonymous with, contempt. In her interview with Franz Stangl, commandant of Treblinka, Gitta Sereny found that people like him had entertained the same feelings. "They were so weak; they let themselves do anything. They were people with whom there was no common ground, no possibility of communication— this is where the contempt came from."[11]

In the taxonomy of camp life, they were the ostracized rejects, a subspecies that represented a danger to their fellows. Perhaps here, too, it is necessary to have recourse to the opposition between the Cartesian and the Hobbesian. In the opening paragraph of the first chapter of *Survival in Auschwitz*, Levi describes how he had, until his arrest, inhabited a world of "civilized Cartesian phantoms" (13); inside Auschwitz, as he repeats on several occasions, he found a Hobbesian universe, marked, in the words of *The Drowned and the Saved*, by the "continual war of all against all" (108). Human beings were reduced to the state of nature, where primal instincts ruled, where the social contract was ignored, where culture was a trivial irrelevance. The *Muselmänner* were the most obvious casualties, but a Hobbesian hierarchy of values had no room for compassion.

By the time of writing *The Drowned and the Saved*, Levi had another dilemma over the *Muselmänner*, concerning who had the right or the duty to speak for them. It has been believed from Herodotus onward that history is written by the victors, and truth is, in the graphic phrase used by Simone Weil, "the fugitive from the victor's camp." In retrospect, reconsidering the Hobbesian war that was Auschwitz, Levi came to different conclusions. Hobbesian Truth, or testimony, was of necessity written by the survivors, the Saved, but the survivors were haunted by a sense of guilt. Levi, who had a deep sense of his obligations as a witness-survivor, was aware of the paradox, developed by Agamben, that the real witness was the *Muselmann*, who by definition could not deliver testimony. "We survivors are an anomalous as well as tiny minority: we are those who through prevarication, ability or luck did not touch the bottom. Those who did, those who saw the Gorgon, did not return to give their accounts, or returned dumb, but it was they, the *Muselmänner*, the drowned who were the genuine witnesses, they whose deposition would have had a general significance. They are the rule, we the exception" (64). Levi agrees, in *The Drowned and the Saved*, that he had come to this conclusion after deep thought and reading the testimony of others, but this is a profound change of heart, for he had not worried unduly over the memory of the *Muselmänner* in the earlier *Survival in Auschwitz*.

And yet, for Auschwitz, the point of arrival, the very measure of success, is the *Muselmann*. For Auschwitz, the Saved are failures. It is in this sense, it seems to me, that Levi came to see them, the supposedly subhuman relicts who dragged out their existence without hope, without resistance, as the only genuine witnesses. It is the *Muselmänner* who express, and who force the reader of witness or historical accounts to confront the sheer awfulness of the Nazi project. It is they who have intrigued subsequent commentators or philosophers, such as Bettelheim or Agamben, who are driven not to make sense of Auschwitz but to incorporate it into some system of life and death. These were the creatures who were stripped of all humanity and of those characteristics that western Humanism regarded as intrinsic to the human being and that render them deserving of respect—reason, dignity, freedom of will and of judgment. All this has been wrenched from the *Muselmänner*, with the devastating consequence that they were not deemed worthy of the normal human response to suffering humanity—compassion. It is in this context that Primo Levi uses, with regard to them, the most terrible words that he uses with regard to any human being: that "their death was not really death." These words launch Agamben into a metaphysical turbulence that seems to me wholly inappropriate. Physical death and the pain and humiliation that precede it are not, in any literal sense, subject to ontological flexibility.

Agamben displays an irritating refusal to distinguish between the aesthetic and ethical realms. He writes, "The Muselmann as Levi describes him, is the site of an experiment in which morality and humanity are called into question" (63). The *Muselmann*, he adds, exists in a sphere in which "not only categories such as dignity and respect but even the very idea of an ethical limit lose their meaning" (63). Ethics concerns acts, not being; humanity, not Humanism; and the need to observe ethical standards concerns the witnesses and philosophers as well. Primo Levi, implicitly but forcefully, revised in *The Drowned and the Saved* the more forthright views he had accepted in *Survival in Auschwitz*. That is the real measure of ethical judgment.

Notes

1. Imre Kertész, *Fateless,* trans. Tim Wilkinson (London: Vintage Books, 2006). References are to this edition and are given in the text.

2. There is, strangely, no agreement among authors on the correct spelling of the term. The contemporary German word is *Muslim*, while *Muselmann* is a recognized form that is no longer in current use, except in the specialized sense given to it in Auschwitz. The form *Musulmann* is not German but has been employed by some writers. I have decided to follow the usage employed by the original writers in quotations, but will myself use the form *Muselmann*.

3. Quoted by Giorgio Agamben, *Remnants of Auschwitz, trans. Daniel Heller-Roazen* (New York: Zone Books, 2002), 43. In further references to this study, page numbers will be included in the body of my text.

4. Bruno Bettelheim, *The Informed Heart*, 2nd ed. (London: Paladin, 1970).

5. Primo Levi, *Se Questo è un uomo*, now in *Opere*, vol. 1, ed. Marco Belpoliti (Turin: Einaudi, 2000), 84. All references to Levi in Italian are to this edition and are given in the text by volume and page number.

6. Primo Levi, *If This is a Man* and *The Truce*, trans. Stuart Woolf (London: Penguin, 1979); *Survival in Auschwitz*, trans. Stuart Woolf (New York: Touchstone, 1996). References to the English translation will be to this later version and page numbers will be included in the body of the text.

7. Primo Levi, *The Drowned and the Saved*, trans. Raymond Rosenthal (London: Abacus, 1988). In further references to this work, page numbers will be included in the body of the text.

8. Bettelheim, *The Informed Heart*, 141.

9. Myriam Anissimov, *Primo Levi: The Tragedy of an Optimist*, trans. Steve Cox (London: Aurum Press, 1996), 423.

10. Giorgio Agamben, *Homo Sacer: Sovereign Power and Bare Life* (Stanford, CA: Meridian: Crossing Aesthetics, 1998); *State of Exception* (Chicago, IL: University of Chicago Press, 2005).

11. Gitta Sereny, *Into that Darkness: An Examination of Conscience* (New York: Random House, 1983), 313.

Part III

Strategies of Communication and Representation

7

Primo Levi and Italo Calvino

Two Parallel Literary Lives

Marina Beer

University of Rome "La Sapienza"

Contemporary Italian scholarship has matched up Italo Calvino with a number of Italian writers of his time: Cesare Pavese, Elio Vittorini, Franco Fortini, Leonardo Sciascia, Carlo Emilio Gadda, Pier Paolo Pasolini, and even Benedetto Croce, to name just a few. The same cannot be said of Primo Levi: both during his lifetime and after his death Levi cut a solitary figure in the current critical and scholarly discourse—let alone in the eye of the common reader—standing out as unique and extraordinary within the Italian literary scene. An anomalous author who is considered an "outsider to literature," Levi is unique because of his overtly claimed "hybrid" and amphibious nature: witness to the Holocaust, but also professional writer of fiction; writer and poet, but also chemist and scientist; Jew, but also Italian—and one might go on with a fairly lengthy list of *oxymora* very familiar to every scholar of Levi. His *appartatezza* in the literary establishment during his lifetime had as a consequence his belated and posthumous acclamation as a full-fledged writer by most Italian literary critics. His "uniqueness" among the established classics of the Italian literary canon is still reflected by his uncertain position as outsider in current textbooks and general Italian reference works on the Italian Novecento.

Furthermore, Levi is rarely compared to his contemporaries. He does not seem to belong to any literary current; his theoretical problems seem to stem only from his experience of the Lager (which is greatly but not solely at the root of his literary vocation and practice) and not from his keen consciousness of the contemporary world and of contemporary literature. In a recent book on Italo Calvino, Mario Barenghi notes the symmetry in popularity between the two contemporary Italian authors most representative abroad, Italo Calvino and Primo Levi: "Calvino dies suddenly in the mid-Eighties, on the eve of the diffusion of the new technologies. [. . .] He becomes a great contemporary classic worldwide and he is recognized as such precisely in this cultural and historical context; together with Primo Levi, he becomes the twentieth-century Italian writer most popular and most studied abroad."[1] But as we shall see, there are also well-grounded biographical and literary motives for pairing Primo Levi with Italo Calvino, motives that cut deeply into the historical and imaginative world of the two writers.

Among Levi's friends and correspondents, the literary insiders were actually very few. His only steady relationships with "professional" writers have been with two outsiders like himself: Mario Rigoni Stern and Nuto Revelli.[2] Apparently, most of Levi's literary correspondents belonged to the milieu of his publisher Einaudi[3]—although much is still to be learned about the actual network of his literary friends. In fact, his most important and life-long literary correspondent and acquaintance was, by far, Italo Calvino himself: since 1961, but quite certainly even earlier, Calvino (then a literary editor at Einaudi) actually became Primo Levi's first reader, with all the consequences for Levi's writing entailed in this crucial role. As Giulio Einaudi recalls, even before Calvino wrote the cover jacket of *La tregua* (*The Reawakening*) in 1963, Levi would bring all his typescripts to Calvino and would allegedly accept (with few exceptions) the suggestions of his mentor. Furthermore, Calvino was not simply the first reader of Levi's work; he also became the same critic who imparted the "instructions for use" to the general common reader, the author of the "paratexts" (book covers, jacket flaps, *fascette*, editorial notes) that conveyed to Levi's readers the interpretive clues to his books and helped them construe their image of Levi as an author. Calvino's paratexts also influenced professional criticism and reviews. Thus, Calvino (himself a great artist in crafting his own image as an author) was also partly responsible for the public image of Levi as a writer and an opinion maker—and one wonders to what extent that portrait also mirrored some features of Calvino himself.

From the very start of their literary careers, Calvino and Levi were coupled. They both published their first work in 1947 (Calvino, *Il sentiero dei nidi di ragno* [*The Path to the Spiders' Nests*], Einaudi, 1947; Levi, *Se questo è un uomo* [*Survival in Auschwitz*], Da Silva, 1947). One might wonder how much of that similarity was rooted in the historical conditions that determined their literary vocation (World War II, for both) and how much of it was actually in them from the very start, so that it could be perceived as a distinct affinity in quality and intensity by onlookers, such as their first reviewer, Arrigo Cajumi. However, in considering the parallel sequence of their books (see *Appendix*), the question of reciprocal influence may also arise. We may well ask how much their peculiar two-way readership might have developed into a mutual "mirror making," a *spemet*, as in Levi's tale "The Mirror Maker."[4] This paper will try to suggest an answer.

I will begin by listing some parallel facts. The first review of Calvino's *The Path to the Spiders' Nests* and of Levi's *Survival in Auschwitz* was written by Arrigo Cajumi and printed in Turin's *La Stampa*, November 26, 1947, under the caption "Immagini indimenticabili" (Unforgettable Images). Cajumi identified antithesis as the interpretive key to what he considers to be the "most significant books on World War II": Levi is "self-restrained and stern," Calvino is "bawdy, inventive and youthful," and if "the pale light of dawn" shows at the end of Calvino's book, Levi's work ends up "black and dismal."[5] (One must not forget that *Survival in Auschwitz* in the De Silva 1947 edition lacked the last, cathartic chapter, added in the Einaudi 1958 edition). Thus, *allegro* Calvino and *pensieroso* Levi start off together on their journey through Italian literature.

The follow-up to this first critical response was a review of *Survival in Auschwitz* published by Calvino himself in the daily newspaper of the Italian Communist Party, *L'Unità*, on May 6, 1948, in which Levi's book is said to contain "pages among the most beautiful in World War II literature."[6] Calvino's review stressed the outstanding value of Levi's book among the many memoirs from the camps that circulated in postwar Italy,[7] but his second move was to consider it mostly as a part of World War II literature about the anti-Fascist struggle and not as a testimony to the Jewish tragedy in it. In fact, this was the official approach to the Shoah (a denomination not yet in use at the time), held in common by the Communist and non-Communist Left in Italy. Calvino, as we shall see, tended to stick to this approach until the end, and constantly underestimated the surfacing of Jewishness and of Jewish themes in Levi's writings.

After Levi's enrollment as an Einaudi author in 1955,[8] the proper acquaintance of Calvino and Levi began. (Calvino had been working for Einaudi since 1947 and became editor at Einaudi in the 1950s). In 1961, Levi sends the typescripts of some "fantastic" stories to Calvino: probably "L'amico dell'uomo" (Man's Friend), "I mnemagoghi" (The Mnemogogue), "Quaestio de centauris," "Un discepolo" (A Disciple), "La carne dell'orso" (Bear Meat), and then later "Ferro" (Iron) in *Il sistema periodico* (*The Periodic Table*), and "Capaneo" ("Rappoport's Testament").[9] Some of them had already been published between May 1960 and August 1961 in the weekly, *Il mondo*.[10] Calvino answers on November 22, 1961:

> *Dear Levi,*
> *I finally read your short stories. The science-fiction ones (one should better say the biological-fictional ones) keep attracting me. The device*

of your imagination, triggered by scientific-genetic evidence as a start-ing point, has a great power of intellectual and poetical suggestion, the same [power of] suggestion as [that produced] by Jean Rostand's genetic and morphological variations. With your humanism and your finesse, you avoid the traps so easy to fall into when trying to stage intel-lectual experiments in literary molds of this kind.[11]

Calvino seems to be far less benevolent about "realistic" stories like "Capa-neo": "as a matter of fact those are fragments of *Survival in Auschwitz*, and if taken apart from the body of that narrative they aren't but sketches" ("sono frammenti di *Se questo è un uomo* che, staccati da una narrazione più ampia, hanno i limiti del bozzetto"). He ends up acknowledging his deep-rooted likeness to Levi: they both partake in "a common civilization," and they both share a culture that stands out as "different" against the backdrop of current Italian literature ("Forse i tuoi racconti mi piacciono soprattutto perché presuppongono una civiltà comune che è sensibilmente diversa da quella presupposta da tanta letteratura italiana").

In 1963, Italo Calvino wrote the text on the book cover for *La tregua* (*The Reawakening*)[12] and he also published a short novel, *La giornata di uno scrutatore* (The Watcher),[13] recounting the long day of Amerigo, a Communist poll-watcher on duty at the polls in "Cottolengo," a two-hundred-year-old institution for the handicapped and the mentally ill in Turin, a "city within the city." The dream-like description of the nightmar-ish universe of the "city Cottolengo" and the quest for "what is humane" in a "subhuman world" echo the two Auschwitz books by Levi, but especially the second one, as noted by Pier Vincenzo Mengaldo.[14]

In approximately the same years, Italo Calvino was working on *Cos-micomics*, first published in periodicals in 1964—a book defined on the book jacket by the author in the 1965 edition as "a sort of *Natural History* written by a bragging Pliny, or else a grotesque counterpoint to the poem by Lucretius."[15] The writing of *Cosmicomics* overlaps approximately with the publication of short stories in periodicals by Levi, and his first projects for a collection of modern tales in the early 1960s, projects submitted to Calvino as a reader for Einaudi. Finally, in 1966, the first collection of short stories by Primo Levi, *Storie naturali* (*Natural Histories*), was published with a jacket blurb by Calvino.[16] The book is signed with the pen name of "Damiano Malabaila" and the stories are introduced in an editorial note by Calvino that defines them as "divertissements." Levi himself adopts almost the same concepts in his presentation of his stories as "jokes, moral mouse-traps."[17] In an interview held in 1968, Primo Levi told his Croatian transla-tor Mladen Machiedo that Calvino owed the first idea for *Cosmicomics* to one of Levi's stories, "Il sesto giorno" (The Sixth Day), sketched as early as

1946–1947[18] (a manuscript version of this story dated December 22, 1957 is housed in the Einaudi Archives), and that Calvino had acknowledged his debt in the dedication he wrote on the first leaf of Levi's copy of the 1965 edition.[19] With a circular move, Levi dedicates his story "Il fabbro di se stesso"[20] to Italo Calvino: "Since Italo Calvino has taken the cue for his *Cosmicomiche* (Cosmicomics) from my "Sixth Day," I ask his forbearance to borrow his QfWfq for a story I have in mind now."[21] The story was ultimately published in *Vizio di forma* (The Sixth Day and Other Stories) and dedicated "A Italo Calvino," and retells an abridged version of the history of the universe as told in *Cosmicomics* and *t zero* (*T con zero*, 1967). The narrator's voice echoes QfWfq in summarizing the evolution of animal life on earth, and the story is both fantastic and scientifically correct in its details. It can be read as an answer to some of Calvino's metaphysical variations on scientific issues, a sort of reassessment and correction of the Calvinian narrative of the adventure of matter, something like a vindication.

Certainly, Levi considered Calvino to be a master in the art of the short story. An homage to Calvino's craft as a storyteller is found in "Breve sogno" (Brief Dream, in *Lilít*): "Riccardo did not entirely dislike the new situation. It reminded him immediately of grotesque or erotic tales staged in a train by Tolstoj or Maupassant, or of a beautiful *novella* of the same 'railway genre' by Italo Calvino."[22] Implicit influences from Calvino are easily discovered in the description of the earth seen from the moon in "Visto da lontano" (in *Vizio di forma*); in the moral fable "Una stella tranquilla" (A Tranquil Star)[23] in *Lilít e altri racconti*, about the death of a *nova*; in the Resistenza story "Ospiti" (Guests, in *Lilít*); and in the metaliterary tale "La ragazza del libro" (Girl in the Book); but also in the disquieting "Ammutinamento" in *Vizio di forma* (Mutiny, in *The Sixth Day and Other Stories*), a tale of fictional botanics very close to Calvino's botanical sensibility and imagination.[24] The influence seems thus to have been to some extent reciprocal and bidirectional. Calvino is a model for Levi, but also Levi for Calvino, if we think back to Calvino's 1961 letter, quoted previously. Calvino underlines his particular liking for "Quaestio de centauris," a story he will deal with again some years later (in 1984) in his review of an anthology of Italian fantasy short stories, *Notturno italiano*.[25]. Levi's skill in retelling the myth is highly praised as a typical feature of Italian literature, a familiar theme in these later years, from *Perché leggere i classici* (Why Read the Classics?) to *Lezioni americane* (Six Memos for the Next Millennium),[26] and Levi is made equal to a mythological storyteller as removed from him as the surrealist artist and writer Alberto Savinio. Like Savinio, Levi is classified among the literary offspring of Ovid's *Metamorphoses* and placed in the same category as Calvino himself, who chose Ovid and Lucretius as the guiding spirits of literature in the journey to the new millennium.

Calvino as editor tried to have a significant role in the final shaping of the sequence of *Il sistema periodico* (*The Periodic Table*, 1974). In a letter dated October 12, 1974, he mantains that "Argon," the narrative dedicated to Piedmontese Jewry, should be moved to the central section of the book and criticizes its position as the opening chapter, arguing that the story itself is "weak." "It should probably stick out less if moved to the middle of the book (for example: homecoming from deportation; finding the surviving relatives; reflection on family continuity in the past)."[27] The final argument is interestingly extra-rhetorical in an "oulipien" sense:[28] "If the sequence of chapters is arranged according to the atomic weight of the elements [. . .] I have no objections."[29] Significantly, Calvino suggested that Levi tone down the "free" Jewish theme by making it merge into the narrative of Jewish persecution and appear as a fragmentary family chronicle. Levi did not accept Calvino's advice and "Argon" remained the opening chapter of the book.

It should be noted that Calvino remained consistent throughout in his modest appreciation of Jewish topics in Levi's writing. In his review of *La ricerca delle radici* (*Search for Roots*, 1981),[30] there is no explicit reference to Levi's choice of the *Book of Job* as having to do with Jewishness, and the text by Isaac Babel's "L'ebreo a cavallo" (The Jew on Horseback) receives almost no notice at all as being Jewish, nor does the choice of Scholem Aleichem's *Tewje the Milkman* or Paul Celan's "Todesfuge" (Death Fugue).[31]

From *Marcovaldo* (1963) onward, Calvino's role was also relevant to the intense Italian debate on literature, industry, and the representation of workers from which Levi's *La chiave a stella* (*The Monkey's Wrench*) originated as a late and controversial offspring in 1978. Primo Levi's subsequent activity as authoritative reviewer and creative opinionist in the daily press (*Il Giorno, La Stampa*) owes much to Calvino's model of cultural journalism—a genre that for Calvino, as well, verged on the fictional and creative (*Palomar [Mr. Palomar], Sotto il sole giaguaro [Under the Jaguar Sun]*).

In 1978, Calvino began collaborating with the translator and literary critic Sergio Solmi on the Italian version of Raymond Queneau's *Petite cosmogonie portative* (*Small Portable Cosmogony,* 1950), a poem of "Lucretian" inspiration in six cantos. The natural history of matter is the topic of this encyclopedic dissertation in Alexandrine verses, written in a dense baroque language full of neologisms and puns. Calvino wrote the commentary, very much an encyclopedic work by itself. He had met Queneau and the French group of *oulipien* writers in the 1960s.[32] When *Piccola cosmogonia portatile* was finally published in 1983, Primo Levi wrote a passionate and sensitive review of the book.[33] Queneau's poetry opens up a new path of reflection for the chemist-writer. It reinforces his idea of literature as an encyclopedia of modern science and a bridge between the "two cultures," and brings him closer to the aesthetic problem of *scrivere oscuro* (obscure writing), a style of writing that Levi rejected in principle as morally unfair, although he came to terms with it in his later years.[34] In fact, Levi had been called upon by Calvino and Solmi to help unravel the chemical allusions in Queneau's poem. The "Queneau connection" between Calvino and Levi continued until the death of the former. In the last days of his life, in August 1985, Calvino was engaged in the translation of the final part of Queneau's *Petite cosmogonie portative* "Le Chant du Styrène" (The Song of the Styrene), which had not been included in the 1983 Einaudi edition. He called once more upon Levi to help him, and the chemist-writer worked out some solutions over the phone. When Calvino died suddenly, Primo Levi accepted this last bit of versified chemistry as a legacy.[35]

The familiarity with Queneau's style since the early 1980s exposed Primo Levi to the complexities of a properly literary style so different from his own in connection with one of his main subject matters, chemistry, and the representation of matter in literature. Thus, he deepened his insights on the issue, which he found so problematic, of *scrivere oscuro*. Levi would treasure this experience in his translation of Kafka's *The Trial* (*Il processo di Franz Kafka*, Einaudi: Turin 1983), since the Czech writer was, for him, one of the masters of *scrivere oscuro*. In fact, scientifically minded Levi considered clarity and exactitude to be the main qualities in literary writing in general and in his own writing in particular.

In his lengthy review of *Altrui mestiere* (*Other People's Trades*) in 1985,[36] Calvino insists on the Levian motive of "penetrare la materia" a true "lezione" in ethics and aesthetics for both the profession of the chemist and that of the writer: Levi "enumera lezioni valide per entrambe" (enumerates valid lessons for both [professions]). Calvino quotes some Levian reflections on exactitude, anticipating his "*lezione americana*" (American Lesson) on "Exactitude": "The habit of penetrating matter, of coming to terms with its composition and structure, of predicting its properties and behavior, leads to an 'insight' [*in English in the text*], to a mental attitude of concreteness and brevity, to the constant struggle to go beyond the surface of things. Chemistry is the craft of sifting, of weighing and defining: three exercises most useful also to those engaged in describing facts or in giving body to their fantasies."[37] Nevertheless, in drawing his literary map of the new millennium for the Norton Lectures, Italo Calvino did not include Primo Levi among his companions on this utopian path, not even in a footnote.

One may wonder why Levi was not mentioned. It is difficult to speculate why. However, some clues may be found in the answers that both Calvino and Levi gave to the "*Pourquoi écrivez-vous?*" (Why Do You Write?)

questionnaire that was circulated among writers by the French newspaper *Libération* in 1985.[38] Levi gave nine answers:

1. Because one feels the impulse or the need for it
2. To amuse someone or to amuse oneself
3. To teach somebody something
4. To make the world better
5. To circulate your ideas
6. To fight off anxiety
7. To be famous
8. To be rich
9. Out of habit.[39]

Calvino's answers seem to contradict Levi's responses, one by one. Unlike Levi, Calvino does not, in fact, write out of "impulse": "I always write with effort, with a violence upon myself"; if Levi wants to teach something, Calvino admits to "not having any pedagogical vocation"; and if Levi thinks he is trying to make the world better, Calvino writes that he mistrusts "those who pretend to make the world better"; where Levi admits that he writes "to circulate his ideas," Calvino discloses his mistrust for his own ideas, "too often proven to be wrong." Calvino ends up with only three answers, three messages from within the prison-house of literature, from the Count of Monte Cristo's cell:

1. Because I am dissatisfied with what I wrote and I wish to correct it in some way.
2. Because reading X, I happen to think "How much I would like to write like X!"
3. To learn something I don't know.[40]

On the verge of the new millennium, it would be difficult to imagine two self-portraits as inversely symmetrical as these two. In the background of Levi's "ethical" writing, we see the finite "unwritten world" he strove to survive, to live in, to know, and to describe, whereas Calvino, who really looks like Levi's *Doppelgänger*, stands up alone to face the infinite, fickle, and endlessly changeable universe of self-generating written signs, a forerunner of a cybernetic future.

Appendix: Parallel Abridged Chronology of Levi's and Calvino's Works by Date of Publication (1947–85)

Calvino	Levi
1947	**1947**
Il sentiero dei nidi di ragno	*Se questo è un uomo* (De Silva)
1949	
Ultimo viene il corvo	
1952	
Il visconte dimezzato	
1956	
Fiabe italiane	
1957	
Il barone rampante	
1958	**1958**
Racconti	*Se questo è un uomo* (Einaudi)
1959	
Il cavaliere inesistente	
1960	
I nostri antenati	
1963	**1963**
Marcovaldo	*La tregua*
La giornata di uno scrutatore	
La speculazione edilizia	
1964	**1964–1967**
Le cosmicomiche (first published in the weekly "Il caffè" and in the daily newspaper" Il giorno")	publishes some of his stories in the daily newspaper "Il giorno"
1965	
Le cosmicomiche (Einaudi)	
1967	**1966**
Ti con zero	*Storie naturali*
1969	
Il castello dei destini incrociati	
La lettura (antologia scholastic anthology)	
Osservare e descrivere	
1970	
Gli anni difficili	
1971	**1971**
Dall'opaco	*Vizio di forma*
1972	
Le città invisibili	
	1975
	Il sistema periodico

Appendix: Parallel Abridged Chronology of Levi's and Calvino's Works by Date of Publication (1947–85) *(continued)*

Calvino	Levi
1978 Begins the translation of *Petite cosmogonie portative*, by Queneau	**1978** *La chiave a stella*
1979 *Se una notte d'inverno un viaggiatore*	
	1981 *Lilít* (1975–1981) *La ricerca delle radici* (1976–1981)
1982 Prefazione to the *Storia naturale* of Plinio *Piccola guida alla cosmogonia portatile*	**1982** *Se non ora, quando*
1983 *Palomar*	
1985 "La canzone del polistirene" (translation of "Le chant du styrene," by Queneau)	**1985** *L'altrui mestiere*

Notes

1. "Calvino scompare d'improvviso, a metà degli anni Ottanta, nel pieno della sua attività, alla vigilia della diffusione delle nuove tecnologie [...] E' in questo contesto storico-culturale [...] che assurge al rango di grande classico contemporaneo: sul piano internazionale, accanto a Primo Levi, il più noto e studiato fra gli scrittori italiani del Novecento." Mario Barenghi, *Italo Calvino: Le linee e i margini* (Bologna: Il Mulino, 2007), 25.

2. Mario Rigoni Stern (1921–2008), a well-known World War II writer, soldier on the Russian front, and author of a classic, *Il sergente nella neve* (1953). His other works include *Il bosco degli Urogalli* (1962) and *Storia di Tönle* (1978); Nuto Revelli (1919–2004), officer on the Russian front, member of the Resistance and writer: *Mai tardi: Diario di un alpino in Russia* (1946); *La guerra dei poveri* (1962); and *L'anello forte: La donna—Storie di vita contadina* (1985), a book of oral history.

3. See Carole Angier, *The Double Bond: Primo Levi—A Biography* (New York: Farrar, Straus, & Giroux, 2002). The Italian translation is *Il doppio legame: Vita di Primo Levi* (Milan: Mondadori, 2004).

4. "Il fabbricante di specchi," in *Racconti e saggi*, in Primo Levi, *Opere III* (Turin: Einaudi, 1990), 871–74; see, in English, *The Mirror Maker: Stories and Essays* by Primo Levi, trans. Raymond Rosenthal (New York: Schocken Books, 1989). A "spemet" is "uno *specchio* metafisico ... che riproduce la tua immagine quale essa viene vista da chi ti sta di fronte."

5. A. Cajumi, "Immagini indimenticabili," now in *Primo Levi: Un'antologia della critica*, ed. Ernesto Ferrero (Turin: Einaudi, 1997), 303–5.

6. Italo Calvino, "Un libro sui campi della morte. *Se questo è un uomo*" in *L'Unità*, 6 maggio 1948; now in *Primo Levi*, ed. Ferrero, 306–7 (my translation). See also Italo Calvino, "La letteratura italiana sulla Resistenza," in *Saggi*, ed. Mario Barenghi (Milan: Mondadori, 1995), 1499.

7. Such as Liliana Millu, *Il fumo di Birkenau* (Florence: Giuntina, 1947), and Bruno Piazza, *Perché gli altri dimenticano* (Milan: Feltrinelli, 1956). On these memoirs and on Italian Holocaust literature, see Marina Beer, "Memoria, cronaca e storia: Forme della memoria e della testimonianza," in *Storia della Letteratura italiana*, vol. XI of *Il Novecento: Le forme del realismo*, ed. Nino Borsellino and Walter Pedullà (Milan: Federico Motta Editore, 2001), 595–621.

8. Levi was enrolled in 1952 as translator and editor, but the Einaudi edition of *Se questo è un uomo* was printed as late as 1958. See Marco Belpoliti, Cronologia, in Primo Levi, *Opere*, 1:85–86.

9. Belpoliti, "Note ai Testi," in Primo Levi, *Opere*, 2:1428–40.

10. They were eventually to be collected in *Storie naturali* and in *Vizio di forma*. Their English translations can be found in *Moments of Reprieve*, *The Sixth Day and Other Stories*, and *A Tranquil Star*.

11. "Caro Levi, ho letto finalmente i tuoi racconti. Quelli fantascientifici, o meglio fantabiologici mi attirano sempre. Il tuo meccanismo fantastico, che scatta da un dato di partenza scientifico-genetico ha un potere di suggestione intellettuale e anche poetica, come lo hanno per me le divagazioni genetiche e morfologiche di Jean Rostand. Il tuo umanismo e il tuo garbo ti salvano bene dal pericolo in cui incorre di solito chi si serve di stampi letterari per esperimenti intellettuali di questo tipo" (my translation), in Italo Calvino, *Lettere* (Milan: Mondadori, 2000), 1:695–96. Jean Rostand (1894–1977) was a well-known biologist and highbrow writer of popular biology. Passages from one of his books were also selected by Levi in his anthology *La ricerca delle radici* (*Search for Roots*).

12. Primo Levi, *La tregua* (Turin: Einaudi, 1963). See Belpoliti, *Note ai Testi*, in Primo Levi, *Opere*, 2:1423–24.

13. Primo Levi, *La giornata di uno scrutatore* (Turin: Einaudi, 1963).

14. Pier Vincenzo Mengaldo, "Lingua e scrittura," in Levi, *Opere*, 2:vii–viii. Mengaldo refers to chapter 5 of *La giornata*: "Era tutto il mondo di fuori a diventare parvenza, nebbia, mentre questo, di mondo, questo del 'Cottolengo,' ora riempiva talmente la sua esperienza che pareva il solo vero"; and see Levi, *La tregua*, 422–23.

15. My translation. In Italo Calvino, *Le cosmicomiche* (Turin: Einaudi, 1965), book jacket: "la sequenza delle storie compone le avventure di Qfwfq in una sorta di 'Storia naturale' d'un Plinio fanfarone o di controcanto grottesco al poema di Lucrezio."

16. Belpoliti, "Note ai Testi," in Levi, *Opere*, 2:1433–34.

17. In Levi, *Opere*, 1:1431.

18. Now in *Storie naturali*, and in Primo Levi, *The Sixth Day and Other Tales*, trans. Raymond Rosenthal (New York: Summit Books, 1990). See Belpoliti, *Note al testo*, in Levi, *Opere*, 1:1438. For the original text, see Mladen Machiedo, "Riječ će preživjeti: Razgovors Primom Levijem," in *Republika* 1 (1969). Stories from *Le cosmicomiche* had been first published in *Il Caffè* in 1964, but there is no evidence of publication of "The Sixth Day" in a periodical. Calvino might have read it in manuscript. See the letter by Calvino to Primo Levi, November 22, 1961 in Calvino, *Lettere*, 1:695–96.

19. In considering Calvino's non-realistic writings, one should not forget the vigorous Italian tradition of chivalric poems and fairy tales that Calvino was also exploring, in the same years, with his collection of fairy tales, *Fiabe italiane* (*Italian Folktales*, 1956), and with the novels of the chivalric trilogy *Our Ancestors* (1957–1959)—*I nostri antenati: Il barone rampante, Il cavaliere inesistente, Il Visconte dimezzato* (*Baron in the Trees, Nonexistent Knight, The Cloven Viscount*)—up to *Castello dei destini incrociati* (*Castle of Crossed Destinies*, 1969) and *Orlando furioso raccontato da Italo Calvino* (Orlando Furioso Told by Italo Calvino, 1970).

20. In Primo Levi, *Vizio di forma*. See *I racconti: Storie naturali, Vizio di forma, Lilít* (Turin: Einaudi, 1996).

21. My translation. "Calvino ha preso spunto per scrivere *Le Cosmicomiche* da un mio racconto, *Il sesto giorno*, pubblicato in una rivista prima che nelle *Storie naturali*, perciò mi ha regalato il suo libro con una dedica molto cordiale. Adesso, invece, vorrei chiedere io il permesso a lui di prestarmi il suo QfWfq su cui ho già un racconto in mente." Quoted by Belpoliti, in Levi, *Opere*, 1:1444.

22. "A Riccardo la nuova situazione non spiacque. Gli accese immediatamente il ricordo di episodi ferroviari nei racconti di Tolstoj e di Maupassant, di almeno venti storielle ferroviarie grottesche o galanti, di una bella novella, essa pure ferroviaria, di Italo Calvino"; Levi, *Opere*, 3:576. The "novella" (in the sense of Boccaccio) he is referring to is "L'avventura di un viaggiatore" in *Gli amori difficili* (*Difficult Loves*).

23. Primo Levi, *A Tranquil Star: Unpublished Stories*, trans. Ann Goldstein and Alessandra Bastagli (New York: W. W. Norton, 2007).

24. It should not be forgotten that both of Calvino's parents were distinguished professional botanists, his mother being the first woman botanist to hold an academic position in an Italian university.

25. "Un'antologia di racconti 'neri,'" review of *Notturno italiano*, ed. Enrico Ghidetti e Leonardo Lattarulo (Rome: Editori Riuniti, 1984), in Calvino, *Saggi*, 2:1694–95.

26. "L'evocazione moderna dei miti classici, tra ironica e affascinata [. . .] è affrontata dagli scrittori italiani con la familiarità e l'agio di chi si trova a casa sua. Penso soprattutto a Savinio, la cui estrema confidenza con la mitologia non è mai irriverenza parodistica ma identificazione con le sue perpetue trasformazioni polimorfiche. E penso anche che su questa linea si trova perfettamente il bellissimo racconto sui centauri che chiude *Notturno italiano*, di Primo Levi, scrittore di formazione quanto mai diversa da Savinio. *Le*

Metamorfosi insomma continuano la loro vita metamorfica nella letteratura d'oggi." Italo Calvino, *Saggi*, 2:1695.

27. ". . . darebbe meno nell'occhio se il capitolo lo spostassi a metà del libro. (Per esempio: ritorno dalla deportazione; ritrovare i famigliari scampati; riflessione su che cosa è stata questa continuità famigliare)." Italo Calvino to Primo Levi, October 12, 1974, in Calvino, *Lettere*, 1:1203. (my translation).

28. For Calvino's involvement with *Oulipo*'s poetological theories, see note 32.

29. Ibid.: "Ma se i capitoli seguono un ordinamento per peso atomico, non parlo più."

30. Primo Levi, *The Search for Roots: A Personal Anthology*, trans. Peter Forbes (London: Allen Lane, 2001).

31. See Calvino, *Saggi*, 2:1133–37.

32. *Oulipo*, that is *Ouvrage de Littérature Potentielle*, was a poetological movement initiated by the French poet and writer Raymond Queneau (1903–1976) in 1960 and joined by scientists, poets, writers, and artists, and is still active today. "Poetic" discourse could be generated by a set of combinatory rules (linguistic, rhetorical, and narratological) that deconstructed literature in a structuralist sense. Among its members were the artist Marcel Duchamp, the novelist Georges Perec, and Italo Calvino, who was very much influenced by this idea of literature. Calvino had already translated Queneau's *Les fleurs bleus* (*I fiori blu*, Turin: Einaudi, 1967), which turned out to be a tour de force in the baroque style, which was very unusual for him.

33. "La *Cosmogonia* di Queneau," in Levi, *Opere*, 3:732–36.

34. See, in the same collection of articles, "Dello scrivere oscuro"; Levi, *Opere*, 3:633–39.

35. "Il canto del polistirene," translated by Italo Calvino, was printed by Scheiwiller in 1985. On this, see Maria Sebregondi, "Triangolazioni," in *Riga* 13 (1997): 500–503 (the issue is dedicated to *Primo Levi*, and edited by Marco Belpoliti). From Primo Levi's work on "Canzone del Polistirene" originated, in part, the project of the book that Levi never completed, *Doppio legame* (Double Bond), the letters of a chemist to a lady, a modern version of an eighteenth-century epistolary didactic genre (see Angier, *The Double Bond*, 657).

36. "*L'altrui mestiere* di Primo Levi," *La Repubblica*, March 6, 1985, in Calvino, *Saggi*, 2:1133–41.

37. My translation: "L'abitudine a penetrare la materia, a volerne sapere la composizione e la struttura, a prevederne le proprietà e il comportamento, conduce a un *insight*, ad un abito mentale di concretezza e di concisione, al desiderio costante di non fermarsi alla superficie delle cose. La chimica è l'arte di separare, pesare e distinguere; sono tre esercizi utili anche a chi si accinge a descrivere fatti o a dare corpo alla propria fantasia," quoted in Calvino, *Saggi*, 2:1141.

38. See "Perché scrivete? Io ho detto che," *La Repubblica*, March 31–April 1, 1985. This is a re-elaboration of the answers to the questionnaire of "Libération," *Pourquoi écrivez-vous? 400 écrivains répondent*, numéro hors série [22], March 1985, p. 83, which can be found in Calvino, *Saggi*, 2:1861–64. For Levi's answers, see "Perché si scrive?" in *Opere*, 3:615–18.

39. "1) Perché se ne sente l'impulso o il bisogno; 2) Per divertire o divertirsi; 3) Per insegnare qualcosa a qualcuno; 4) Per migliorare il mondo; 5) Per far conoscere le proprie idee; 6) Per liberarsi dall'angoscia; 7) Per diventare famosi; 8) Per diventare ricchi; 9) Per abitudine." In Levi, *Opere*, 3:615–18 (my translation).

40. "1. Perché sono insoddisfatto di quello che ho scritto e vorrei in qualche modo correggerlo. 2. Perché leggendo X mi viene da pensare "Ah, come mi piacerebbe scrivere come X! 3. Per imparare qualcosa che non so." In Calvino, *Saggi*, 2:1864 (my translation).

8

"L'immagine di lui che ho conservato"

Communication and Memory in
Lilít e altri racconti (Moments of Reprieve)

Elizabeth Scheiber

Rider University

When Primo Levi's collection of short stories, *Lilít*, appeared in English as *Moments of Reprieve*, it was a truncated volume, containing only one section of the original. It also bore the subtitle *A Memoir of Auschwitz*, an allusion to the content, since the text deals primarily with Levi's experiences in the concentration camp and exclusively with Holocaust topics. While the slim volume of *Moments of Reprieve* benefits from a sharper focus on Holocaust writing, its removal from a broader context of tales of disaster and crisis means that readers are deprived of the rich intratextual references among the stories. In particular, writing emerges in *Lilít* as an overarching theme that unifies the volume, and the comments on writing about the Holocaust take their place among thoughts on writing in general. The first part of this chapter will examine Levi's introduction to the English language collection and show how his stated goals undermine the subtitle of the volume. In the second section, I will examine some of the themes of writing present in the Holocaust stories. In the final section, I will study stories from the Italian volume in which echoes from the Auschwitz material can be found, looking in particular at sections where Levi appears to answer an earlier query.

Moments of Reprieve opens with a preface, missing from the original collection of *Lilít e altri racconti*, in which Levi appears to defend his authorship of the stories that follow. He compares the impetus of this collection to that of his first published books. Despite some differences in

Levi's explanation of what led him to write, he makes it clear that he felt *impelled* to write, and as such, *Se questo è un uomo* (*Survival in Auschwitz*) and *La tregua* (*The Truce*) emerged from a sense of duty to events. Having witnessed the Holocaust, he felt obligated to talk about what he had seen there: "I had the feeling I had performed a task . . . I had seen and experienced things that appeared important not only for me, things that imperiously demanded to be told. And I had told them, I had testified."[1] The preface shows, too, that Levi did not intend simply to tell his story. His work as witness to the Holocaust included the selection and elimination of events as he traced the "fundamental features" of his experiences (vii). In other words, Levi did the work of any writer, including what he considered essential and omitting what he considered superfluous. In interviews, it becomes clear that Levi was concerned with the impact his writing would have, and his writing aimed to create an emotional response within his readers. With Anna Bravo and Federico Cereja, Levi explained that he omitted the events narrated in "Cerium" in *The Periodic Table* from *Survival in Auschwitz* because he "felt that the note of indignation should prevail." He considered his first work to be a "testimony . . . an act of witnessing."[2]

The stories in *Moments of Reprieve* owe their inception to a different impetus, although there is still an element of obligation implied in Levi's description. Where the emphasis was on the essential in his first works, in these short stories Levi pauses to reflect on the "inconsequential." In his preface, Levi claims that "a host of details [from the Lager] continued to surface in my memory and the idea of letting them fade away distressed me. A great number of human figures especially stood out against that tragic background" (vii–viii). Here, Levi no longer talks about things or events, but about "details" and "human figures." These "human figures" that stand out in Levi's memory ask him to "help them survive and enjoy the ambiguous perennial existence of literary characters" (vii). The word ambiguous is usually taken to mean something that has many meanings or interpretations, that presents something puzzling to the reader or listener, but the etymology describes a situation of exile. The word comes from the Latin *ambigere*, to "wander." Characters are, in a sense, wanderers in the author's imagination and, as literary characters, they are now ciphers or symbols or allegorical figures to be interpreted by readers.

Levi also informs the reader why these tales were left out of *Survival in Auschwitz*, that is, why these tales were considered nonessential. The people and settings of the tales are unusual against the background of the concentration camps. Although the tales were written at different times, they are unified by a central, dominant character: "Each of them [the tales] is centered on one character only, who is never the persecuted, predestined victim, the prostrate man" (viii). Herein lies the crux of his creative inspiration: these characters stand out from the mass of concentration camp victims. Somehow they were not altered by the concentrationary universe: "The protagonists of these stories are all 'men' beyond all doubt, even if the virtue that allows them to survive and makes them unique is not always one approved of by common morality" (viii). These stories are about singular men who stand out. They are the opposite of the *Muselmänner* and they are also not to be confused with ethical men, that is, the people whose actions reflect what is right to do with regard to others. Although Levi doesn't say it here, it is clear enough from what he does say in this preface, as well as in the stories themselves, that Levi perceives these men as having qualities different from his own. They are opposites of him as well. For Levi, these stories owe their interest as stories to the fact that these particular characters existed in the concentration camp, that something about their inner character made them unique in that universe, that they remained "men" despite the horror they encountered. It is the mystery of this situation that Levi wants to show his readers. Because the stories are focalized through Levi, who generally appears as a neutral observer with little personality of his own, the mystery stays intact. The characters remain opaque. We, the readers, do not know what motivates them or how it is possible that they do not succumb to the situation.

In addition to focusing on unusual individuals, the setting of these tales is equally atypical for Auschwitz since it is rarely tragic. The encounters occur in a moment of calm, the "moment of reprieve" as reflected in the English title. Levi describes the settings as "bizarre, marginal moments of reprieve, in which the compressed identity can reacquire for a moment its lineaments" (vii). Two stories in particular illustrate this moment of calm in a dramatic way: "Rappoport's Testament" ("Capaneo" in the original), which takes place in an air raid shelter as bombs rain down, and "Lilith," where the narrator and his interlocutor Tischler meet in a large drain pipe to escape a rain storm. In other stories, the moment of reprieve is less spectacular—pauses in work that the narrator uses to write or barter goods.

The focus on unusual personalities encountered in the Lager and on atypical scenery problematizes the subtitle of the English edition: *A Memoir of Auschwitz*. Certainly, the generally understood meaning of *memoir* as a form of autobiography is not quite exact. Even if the term is broadened to mean an account or chronicle, the term is imprecise. To start, of the fifteen stories of the volume, only eight deal with Levi's direct experience. "The Cantor and the Barracks Chief" takes place in the camp, but it is a story of the camp recounted to Levi rather than having been directly witnessed. "The Quiet City" relates the malaise of an Aryan German at the camp whom Levi heard of through shared acquaintances but never encountered. It is also one of the stories not included in the original Italian work. "Cesare's Last Adventure" and "Lorenzo's Return" concern friends from the camp but deal with a return from the camps, the former in a light-hearted register, the latter in a dark, pessimistic vein. "The Story of Avrom," "Tired of Imposture," and "Story of a Coin" are encounters through literature. Levi reinterprets the characters with his own meditations on ethical behavior. While they take place during the Second World War, they do not deal with experiences in the Lager. The choice of subjects aside, it is difficult to conceive of these stories as a "memoir of Auschwitz" since they depict unique individuals and not the general conditions of the camp. Even though Levi has included stories on various personalities from the camp (Poles, Hungarians, Roma-Sinti, common criminals, and the like), it is odd to conceive that a "memoir" of Auschwitz would focus so sharply on the marginal cases. Using a metaphor borrowed from photography, the stories in *Moments of Reprieve* only depict the situation of Auschwitz through its negative. Undoubtedly, in using the subtitle, the publishers wanted to convey to the reading public the fact that the volume contained tales of the Holocaust, but it is misleading.

More than stories that inform us about the Holocaust, the tales of *Moments of Reprieve* speak of the difficulty of understanding the motivations of others, especially when that understanding must cross cultural and linguistic boundaries. These are tales about the mystery of the other, who, because of a cultural difference or an unusual character trait, defies comprehension. In addition, the tales speak of the difficulty of communicating our own understanding to others through the depiction of various forms of communication. The problematic of conveying meaning infects the narrative. The narrator foregrounds the narrative process (both oral and written). In fact, it is not an exaggeration to say that all of the tales of *Lilít e altri racconti* (not merely the Holocaust tales present in the English *Moments of Reprieve*) manifest a hypertextuality. They feature storytellers, writers, poets, scribes, and others in the act of narrating, transcribing, reading, and remembering literature. The narrator as participant in the tale, listening to the internal narrator communicate a story, or as "eavesdropper," listening in on his characters' exchanges, reflects on the nature of communication and poses questions about the possibility of reaching understanding.

The opening story, "Rappoport's Testament" ("Capaneo"), inaugurates the themes of writing by creating a sense of duty to the title character and launching the narrator on his task of writing. Both English and Italian titles reference the act of writing, albeit in markedly different ways. The English title refers to a segment of the text in which Rappoport, who declares that he intends to write a book containing his philosophy after the war, asks Levi and the other character in the story, Valerio, to write his tale down in the event that Rappoport does not survive the war. For Andrea Rondini, Rappoport "bequeaths to the narrator the task of writing and recounting."[3] In effect, in a sort of *envoi*, Levi ends "Rappoport's Testament" by claiming, "So I considered it my duty to perform as best I could the task with which I was entrusted" (8).[4] Writing becomes his inheritance and duty. Imbued with a sense of responsibility, Levi becomes the writer who tells other people's stories for them because they cannot. At the same time, the stories allow Levi to substitute his own ethical philosophy for Rappoport's hedonistic views. The Italian title, on the other hand, creates an intertext through a reference to a character in Dante's *Commedia* and Greek mythology. Just as Rappoport suddenly calls Capaneus to Levi's mind, so we, the readers, compare and contrast Rappoport to the character in the *Inferno*. In studying the intertext, we can extract Levi's "lesson" about the Holocaust: that survival in Auschwitz was primarily due to luck.

The character of Rappoport takes shape in a brief encounter when Levi and another Italian, the overweight, pitiful Valerio (Rappoport's foil), take refuge during an air raid, and the experience of bombs dropping nearby punctuates the story. The two Italians are soon joined by the vibrant, arrogant, title character, whom Levi describes as a sort of Lager swashbuckler: "shrewd, violent and happy [. . .] He lived in the Camp like a tiger in the jungle, striking down and practicing extortion on the weak, and avoiding those who were stronger; ready to corrupt, steal, fight, pull in his belt, lie, or play up to you, depending on the circumstances" (3–4).[5] In the course of the encounter, Rappoport chastises Valerio and Levi for their lack of vitality and their fear of the bombs dropping close by. Rappoport's sangfroid, even disdain, at the bombs is what evokes Capaneus in Levi's mind.

After Levi rebukes Rappoport, the latter quickly responds that it is not a question of nerve but of philosophy, which he imparts to the Italians. As a preamble, his arrogance is apparent: "If you can use it, fine. If not, and you get out of here alive and I don't, which would be rather strange, you can spread it about and maybe it will be of use to somebody. Who knows? Not that it matters much to me, though. I don't have the makings of a philanthropist" (7).[6] Moving on to his philosophy, he describes an egocentric epicureanism: "Well, here it is. While I could I drank, I ate, I made love, I left flat gray Poland for that Italy of yours; I studied, learned, traveled and looked at things. I kept my eyes wide open; I didn't waste a crumb. I've been diligent; I don't think I could have done more or better. Things went well for me; I accumulated a large quantity of good things, and all this good has not disappeared. It's inside me, safe and sound. I don't let it fade; I've held on to it. Nobody can take it from me" (7).[7] Despite his current status, Rappoport feels that it would require more than he has suffered to take away the precious good he has acquired: "To tip the balance, it would take many more months of camp, or many days of torture" (7).[8] As he winds up his speech, the reader perceives the full force of his arrogance and vitality as Rappoport defies Hitler: "So in the sad event that one of you should survive me, you will be able to say that Leon Rappoport got what was due him, left behind neither debits nor credits and did not weep or ask for pity. If I meet Hitler in the other world, I'll spit in his face and I'll have every right to [. . .] because he didn't get the better of me" (8).[9] Rappoport is forced to yell the last five words when a bomb strikes close by.

It is hard to know how much of the real Rappoport we see in this encounter and how much is filtered through Levi's imagination of Capaneus. What we can see is that this Holocaust incarnation of the mythical figure has undergone a transformation. In the Greek tragedy, Capaneus exhibits *hamartia*, a tragic flaw or missing the mark. His arrogance incenses Zeus who seeks retribution by striking him down. In Aeschylus' play *Seven against Thebes*, Capaneus is a warrior who stands on the wall of Thebes and declares that not even Zeus could stop him from entering the city. As proof of the contrary, Zeus strikes him down on the wall with a thunderbolt. Dante Christianizes Capaneus and places him in hell, where he must pay for his sin of arrogance by receiving a rain of flames for eternity. In the *Inferno*, therefore, divine justice is served. Even though Capaneus insulted a deity that is not the Christian God, he receives punishment: Capaneus is doomed to spend eternity lying on the ground under the rain of fire in the Seventh Circle of Hell with the blasphemers and people who are violent against God. Dante notices him in particular because he does not seem to care about the rain of fire. Capaneus overhears Dante's question to Virgil and answers for himself: "Qual fui vivo, tal son morto" (As I lived, so I died; *Inferno* 14.51). During his response to Dante, he curses Jove so that God should not have "vendetta allegra" (glad vengeance; *Inferno* 14.60). Virgil chastises him by reminding him that he is being punished for his "superbia" (arrogance; *Inferno* 14.64). Virgil then turns to Dante and quickly informs him of Capaneus's identity and, most importantly, that he held God in disdain. Rappoport, as a modern incarnation of Capaneus, shows the same spirit of defiance. He does not appear shaken during the air raid and declares he would spit in Hitler's face if he saw him after death. Having studied medicine, he is not a soldier, but Levi's description creates the image of a concentration camp warrior looking for ways to survive amid torture, illness, and famine. Also in Levi's story, Rappoport's arrogance is not a fatal flaw; instead, it preserves him from sinking into despair amid the horror.

In part, the tale of Rappoport underscores the inability of stories from the past to capture what Levi experienced in Auschwitz. The old myths have ruptured, and we are left with an expectation about life that can never be fulfilled. As often happens in the writings of the Holocaust, authors show the inability of traditional story lines to capture life history. Alvin Rosenfeld has written, "[Holocaust] literature has not occasioned any new kinds of writing, but it has greatly complicated all the literary forms it has occupied and seems to be in the process of breaking them down in an effort to find some new, more adequate measure of chronicling a radical evil and the range of human responses to it."[10]

As the story comes to an end, Levi catches a glimpse of Rappoport evacuating the camp in what we now call the Death March. Although he does not know for sure, Levi speculates that Rappoport did not survive. But, his arrogance is not the cause of his downfall. No deity intervened to cause his death. His fate is the luck of the draw, some random event beyond his control. In Auschwitz, what was once *hamartia* elevates a person above the crowd to what Levi described in the preface as a "uomo" (man).

Since Rappoport presumably died in the camp's evacuation, we can never know what he may or may not have thought of Levi's portrait. Our image of him is filtered through Levi. In effect, this is also the case with the other real people whom Levi transformed into characters. However, there are passages where the author appears to call for a response from the subjects of his portraits. As he begins the final chapter of "Il giocoliere" (The Juggler), he wishes that someone from the category of the common criminals would write his memoir of the Lager: "I often asked myself what kind of humanity was massed behind their symbol, and I have regretted that none of their ambiguous brigade has, so far as I know, told his story" (15).[11] In another tale, "Il discepolo" (A Disciple), Levi hopes that someone with whom he connected in the camp would read the tale and recognize himself. The tale depicts a new arrival at the camp, Bandi, a sincere, hardworking Hungarian with a gift for happiness. Levi tries to teach him to escape work and to "organize" food, but Bandi seems horrified at these lessons. Eventually though, the Hungarian witnesses the reception of a letter from Levi's family, an event that represents a glimmer of hope that there is something for him beyond Auschwitz. Levi has the impression that Bandi understands the import of the letter and shares with joy what the letter symbolizes. As Levi introduces the reader to Bandi, he expresses his hope that his fellow inmate will read this text one day: "I only wish that, by some not-impossible miracle, the page might reach him in the corner of the world where he still lives, perhaps, that he might read it and recognize himself in it" (28–29).[12] The wish recalls the poetic gesture of *envoi*, in which a writer would close a poem by wishing the poem to hurry to the beloved and be pleasing to her.

A partial response to Levi's wish can be found within the pages of the Holocaust material in "Il ritorno di Lorenzo" (Lorenzo's Return). As he opens the story, Levi admits that he had not written more about Lorenzo before because his friend was still alive. Writing about a living person "ties" the author's hands because such a task "verges on the violation of privacy and is never painless for the subject" (107).[13] The start of the tale reflects Pirandellian thought as Levi continues his reflection on literary portraits: "Each of us, knowingly or not, creates an image of himself, but inevitably it is different from that, or, rather, from those (which again are different from one another) that are created by whoever comes into contact with us. Finding oneself portrayed in a book with features that are not those we attribute to ourselves is traumatic, as if the mirror of a sudden returned to us the image of somebody else" (107).[14]

As Levi closes the introduction to Lorenzo's story with the philosophy of literary portraits, he maintains the Pirandellian tone by refusing to choose whose version of a person is more accurate: "What the 'true' image of each of us may be in the end is a meaningless question" (108).[15] The beginning of "Lorenzo's Return" occasions a pause in our reflection on literary portraits and encounters. As an answer to his *envoi* to Bandi, it would appear that the Hungarian would not recognize himself in the pages of Levi's work if he were to read them. The Pirandellian tones are also bound up in the problematic communication depicted in the pages of these tales. As Levi attempts to capture these encounters in a written form, he is aware that his perceptions are filtered through his language and culture.

Clearly, the stories contained in *Moments of Reprieve* are less about the conditions in Auschwitz than about Levi's encounters with people different from himself. Many tales, like "Lorenzo's Return" and "The Juggler," foreground the insolvable situation of the author who simultaneously experiences the desire to describe a unique individual and the inability to do so. Another such tale is "Lo zingaro" (The Gypsy). When the Germans offer the inmates the opportunity to write to their families, Grigo, a newly arrived inmate who is illiterate, asks Levi to write his letter for him. Levi assumes that Grigo is like other newly arrived inmates, ignorant of the laws of the Lager, but he agrees to help for a ration of bread. As they begin the process of dictating, Levi realizes how different the two men are. He calls the love letter "complicated" and admits he does not understand the meaning of the questions Grigo asks his fiancée (43). Grigo talks about making a doll for his fiancée, a doll that could possibly pull him out of Auschwitz, and it is clear to Levi that he comes from a different place (44–45). During the course of their encounter, Levi realizes that Grigo is more resourceful than other new arrivals. As the Roma-Sinti prisoner produces both a photo of a young girl and a knife that he has sneaked into the camp, Levi feels his admiration grow (44). However, the final stroke is when the letter is completed, and Grigo hands Levi a knife and his bread so that Levi may cut the portions: "I was surprised that Grigo already knew the rule, but then I thought that perhaps it applied also outside the Camp, in the to me unknown world from which Grigo came" (45).[16]

In part, in telling these stories, it seems that Levi wanted readers not only to comprehend others better but also to develop a deeper understanding of themselves. "Il re dei Giudei" (Story of a Coin), in which Levi reinterprets the life of Chaim Rumkowski, makes an appeal to readers to learn a lesson from this story. As Levi describes Rumkowski's action, he also judges the man, stating that he believes that Rumkowski saw himself as a messiah and wanted the good of his people (123). At the same time, Levi sees the man as being intoxicated by his own power (126). Surprisingly, Levi uses this very unusual man to create an image of the Everyman: "We are all mirrored in Rumkowski, his ambiguity is ours" (128).[17] Like Rumkowski, who hoped to prolong his life by cooperating with the Germans, and thereby send others to their death, we lose sight of our own mortality: "Like Rumkowski, we too are so dazzled by power and money as to forget our essential fragility, forget that all of us are in the ghetto, that the ghetto is fenced in, that beyond the fence stand the lords of death, and not far away the train is waiting" (128).[18]

The story that closes *Moments of Reprieve* also closes the first section of the Italian collection *Lilít*. By connecting the unusual case of Rumkowski to humanity in general, Levi creates a transition from the concentration camp to the everyday world. While *Moments of Reprieve* works well as a stand-alone volume, however, the addition of the other stories in *Lilít* creates a richer arena for the themes of writing, communication, and portraits. There is not space to examine all the echoes of these themes throughout the volume, so this chapter will examine a small number.[19] "Cara mamma" (Dear Mom) contains a relationship between one who dictates a letter and a scribe, as in "The Gypsy." In this story, a scribe transcribes a letter from a Roman soldier stationed in Britannia to his mother. The Roman begins by saying that the former scribe had died and that this made letter writing more difficult because the Roman had used the former scribe's services enough that he did not have to explain who he was and where he came from, and "everything one needs to know so that a letter speaks like a messenger would."[20] Reminders of Levi's experience with Grigo emerge. While the Roman's voice is the primary voice we hear throughout the story, it is clear that the current scribe does not always agree with it. When the Roman insults the sport of log throwing, the scribe inserts his own voice: "I, scribe, write here but I protest. Log throwing is an ancient and noble art that the uninitiated cannot understand."[21]

As if in answer to Levi's *envoi* in "A Disciple" and his introduction to "Lorenzo's Return," Levi depicts a situation in which a person encounters herself in a book. In "La ragazza del libro" (The Girl in the Book), Umberto, who discovers he is vacationing in the town where the subject of an interesting book lives, confronts the woman in question. In the book, the woman is described in idealized terms as "tireless and indestructible, a good shot when necessary, extraordinarily vital: a Diana-Minerva grafted onto the opulent body . . . of a Juno."[22] When the woman reads the book, she claims not to recognize herself in that person, saying "I would like to be the girl in the book: I would be happy also just to have been her, but I never was."[23] The woman's words echo Levi's words when he said it was impossible to decide whose image is the "true" one. As she turns the topic to what she presumes interests Umberto, her love affairs, she declares, "Well, they are fine where they are: in my memory, faded, withered, with a trace of perfume, like a collection of dried flowers. In yours they have become shiny and bright like plastic toys. I don't know which are more beautiful. You choose."[24]

While many of the characters in Levi's stories negotiate culture and language in their attempt to communicate, Levi shows that communication is not easy within one's own language.[25] "Decodificazione" (Decoding) places together two men from the same town who know each other. The story opens as a sort of mystery in which Fascist symbols are discovered painted on various signs. The narrator finally tracks down the culprit, but the solution does not resolve the mystery. Instead, it asks a bigger question about why a nice boy from a decent family would act in such a way. As the author confronts Piero, the young man responsible for these graffiti, he learns that the teenager is fed up with life. His course is already decided: he will become a judge, he says, "to bring justice. So that people pay; so that everyone pays his debts."[26] As the two talk, the boy drops a series of objects into the creek below them. While the narrator realizes that the boy has prepared this scene, he does not comprehend the significance of the ritual. His incomprehension leads him to meditate on the messages people leave for others:

> I thought too about the basic ambiguity of the messages that each of us leave behind from birth to death, and about our profound inability to reconstruct a person through these, the man who lives beginning from the man who writes: those who write, even only on walls, write in a code that is uniquely their own, and that others do not know; even those who speak. Only a few can transmit clearly, express, express themselves and make themselves clear: Some could but don't want to; others would like to and don't know how, most neither want to nor know how.[27]

The narrator's words seem to express a worry on the part of Levi. While he wants the reader to be able to identify with his characters and ask themselves ethical questions, he seems to worry that he is speaking in his own code, dropping mysterious objects into the stream for others to decode, and being misunderstood.

The final tale of the Italian collection problematizes the preceding content. "Breve Sogno" (Short Dream) shows the power of literature to ignite our imaginations about ordinary events as it shatters the very expectations that literature has created. In this tale, the main character, Riccardo, encounters a young woman on a train, and he immediately begins to anticipate a romantic adventure. Focalized entirely through Riccardo, the narration depicts his agitation as he struggles to find words to communicate with the young woman, even to ask her to visit Naples with him. The narrator creates rich intertexts by alluding to writers such as Tolstoy, Maupassant, and Calvino, who had written stories or scenes about chance encounters on trains, but the main intertext refers to Petrarch. Not only is the title of the short story taken from one of Petrarch's most famous poems, the young woman also is carrying an old copy of *Il canzoniere*, which she reads briefly before falling asleep and letting the book drop. Riccardo, who aspires to literary fame, has a fitful sleep in which he dreams he is a poet laureate, Petrarch himself perhaps, and that his traveling companion is Laura. He briefly poses the ethical dilemma of creating his own image of a woman with the purpose of loving that image and thereby becoming famous while at the same time being with a flesh-and-blood woman (580).

Though he may dream of becoming a poet, Riccardo appears to lack words. The story is told through thoughts and images. Riccardo says very little and is not even able to tell a version of his story to the woman. Even a topic she initiated (an allusion to Dante's *Inferno* and Pisa) appears to hold no interest for her when he begins to elaborate on the view of the islands from Pisa. She yawns and stretches out to go back to sleep. In part, it may be that the young woman intimidates Riccardo. She is described not in idealized terms but rather realistically: robust and pudgy (578) as well as having robust and pudgy hands (577). Riccardo muses over an interesting vestimentary detail: that the girl's pants have leather patches on the inside of her thighs. About these, Riccardo muses about the possibility of her riding a broom as he simultaneously rejects her being a witch (578). However, given their location, these patches on her thighs indicate some kind of sexual protection and a boundary to a romantic adventure. A bigger impediment still to his speaking is the young woman's speech. She is English and has learned Italian primarily from fourteenth-century literature, notably that of Dante and Petrarch. Her unusual turns of phrase cause Riccardo to pause and wonder about language. As she asks, "Might we stretch out our limbs (membra)?"[28] Riccardo remembers a verse by Petrarch in which the word "membra" appears and muses, "No Italian would ever say 'membra.'

It is one of those words that can be written but not uttered, because of one of our mysterious national taboos."[29] Riccardo continues to reflect on other structures that Italians do not use. His thoughts depict a malaise with respect to a supposed native tongue, in which he as a Piedmontese would rather be "skinned alive" than use the remote past. But more than that, the written language proves richer than the spoken because of its surplus of words: "Of five words that the dictionary relates, one at least is ineffable (or unspeakable), like curse words."[30] The young woman, as a foreigner, does not have the stigma of these words that Riccardo the native does, so her speech is richer than his, even if her pronunciation has a strong English accent (580).

However, her richness of language does not dissuade Riccardo. It only intimidates and silences him. Finally, though, as the train arrives in Naples, his stop, he collects his thoughts and finds the courage to ask her to join him on a visit to the city. At this point, he feels that he himself has become an object, but not the kind of object that she had been under his gaze. He could only take in the surface of her body without reading into her. His initial examination, inspired by a Sherlock Holmes story, had not revealed much to him (577). Even a closer inspection while she was asleep revealed little: "A sleeping face, or anyway a face that does not talk, does not express much: it can be either rough or delicate, intelligent or stupid; you can only distinguish it when it becomes animated with words"[31] He needed her to tell her own story, for her appearance was a cipher. As the train arrives in Naples, her gaze strikes him as penetrating him and reading him like a book: "He turned around and encountered the gaze of the girl. It was a steady and kind gaze, but with an undertone of expectation: it seemed that she could read clearly into him, as in a book."[32] He asks her to join him, get off the train, and enter the real world, but she shakes her head no. She then quotes Petrarch, mispronouncing the word for dream "*sogno*" as "sogh-no." As Riccardo corrects her, whatever spell the woman had on him seems broken and he is able to get off the train.

Just as the first story appears to launch the collection by bequeathing to the narrator the duty of writing his philosophy, the last story appears to invite the reader to leave the fantasy world of literature for the real world. Through the use of intertext, the train in "Breve sogno" is not simply the place of the literary encounter. It is also the symbol for adventure and the unexpected as well as the vehicle for two strangers to come together and find some kind of understanding. But like Piero and the narrator from "Decoding," they do not appear to connect. The young woman seems to read Riccardo, but does she really understand who he is?

This study has examined certain elements in Levi's *Lilít*, showing some of the problems with cutting the first section from the rest of the collection, and ways in which the stories collected in *Moments of Reprieve* can really stand on their own. There is still much to be studied in these works. The compact stories convey a great deal in a short space, and scant attention has been paid to them beyond the autobiographical references. What Levi said of Rumkowski's stories could apply to any of them: "A story like this goes beyond itself: it is pregnant, asks more questions than it answers, and leaves us in suspense; it cries out and demands to be interpreted because in it we discern a symbol, as in dreams and signs from heaven, but it is not easy to interpret" (126).[33]

Notes

1. Primo Levi, *Moments of Reprieve: A Memoir of Auschwitz*, trans. Ruth Feldman (New York: Penguin: 1986), vii. Unless otherwise noted, all translations of *Lilít* will reference this edition and page numbers will be included in the body of the text.
2. Marco Belpoliti and Robert Gordon, eds., *The Voice of Memory: Primo Levi, Interviews 1961–1987* (New York: New Press, 2001), 223.
3. My translation of "lascia in eredità al narratore il compito di scrivere e raccontare," in Andrea Rondini, "La scrittura e la sfida: Una lettura di '*Lilít*' di Primo Levi," *Studi novecenteschi* 59 (2002): 239. Unless otherwise noted, all translations from the Italian are mine. I will include the original Italian passages in these notes.
4. "stimo doveroso eseguire del mio meglio l'incarico che mi è stato affidato." See Primo Levi, *I racconti: Storie naturali, Vizio di forma, Lilít* (Turin: Einaudi, 1996), 378. All references to the original Italian text of the stories in *Lilít* will be to this edition.
5. "astuto violento e allegro [. . .] Viveva in Lager come una tigre nella giungla: abbattendo e taglieggiando i piú deboli ed evitando i piú forti, pronto a corrompere, a rubare, a fare a pugni, a tirar cinghia, a mentire o blandire, a seconda delle circostanze" (375).
6. "Se vi serve, tanto meglio; se no, e se voi ve la cavate e io no, che sarebbe poi strano, potrete ripeterla in giro, e verrà magari a taglio a qualcuno. Non che me ne importi molto però: non ho la stoffa del benefattore" (377).
7. "Ecco: finché ho potuto, io ho bevuto, ho mangiato, ho fatto l'amore, ho lasciato la Polonia piatta e grigia per quella vostra Italia; ho studiato, ho imparato, viaggiato e visto. Ho tenuto gli occhi bene aperti, non ho sprecato una briciola; sono stato diligente, non credo si potesse fare di piú né meglio. Mi è andata molto bene, ho accumulato una grande quantità di bene, e tutto questo bene non è sparito, ma è in me, al sicuro: non lo lascio impallidire. L'ho conservato. Nessuno me lo può togliere" (377).
8. "Per guastare il mio bilancio, ci vorrebbero molti mesi ancora di Lager, o molti giorni di tortura" (378).

9. "Perciò, nel caso deprecabile che uno di voi mi sopravviva, potrete raccontare che Leon Rappoport ha avuto quanto gli spettava, non ha lasciato debiti né crediti, non ha pianto e non ha chiesto pietà. Se all'altro mondo incontrerò Hitler, gli sputerò in faccia con pieno diritto [. . .] perché non mi ha avuto" (378).

10. Alvin Rosenfeld, *A Double Dying: Reflections on Holocaust Literature* (Bloomington: Indiana University Press, 1988), 6.

11. "mi è capitato più volte di domandarmi quale sostanza umana si assiepasse dietro al loro simbolo, e di rimpiangere che nessuno della loro ambigua brigata abbia (che io sappia) raccontato la sua storia" (383).

12. "vorrei che, per qualche miracolo non impossibile, questa pagina lo raggiungesse nell'angolo del mondo dove forse ancora vive, e lui la leggesse, e ci si ritrovasse" (392).

13. "sfiora la violenza privata, e non è mai indolore per che ne è l'oggetto" (428).

14. "Ciascuno di noi si costruisce, consapevolmente o no, un'immagine di se stesso, ma essa è fatalmente diversa da quella, o meglio da quelle, a loro volta fra loro diverse, che vengono costruite da chi ci avvicina, e trovarsi ritratti in un libro con lineamenti che non sono quelli che ci attribuiamo è traumatico, come se lo specchio, ad un tratto, ci restituisse l'immagine di un altro" (428).

15. "Quale poi sia l'immagine 'vera' di ognuno di noi, è una domanda senza senso" (428).

16. "Mi stupii che Grigo conoscesse la regola, ma poi pensai che essa era forse in vigore anche fuori del Lager, nel mondo a me sconosciuto da cui Grigo proveniva" (404).

17. "in Rumkowski ci rispecchiamo tutti, la sua ambiguità è la nostra" (444).

18. "Come Rumkowski, anche noi siamo così abbagliati dal potere e dal denaro da dimenticare la nostra fragilità essenziale: da dimenticare che nel ghetto siamo tutti, che il ghetto è cintato, che fuori del recinto stanno i signori della morte, e che poco lontano aspetta il treno" (444).

19. Andrea Rondini has examined many connections among these stories. His own study, which does not separate the Holocaust material from the rest, shows how the tales intertwine to make a cohesive collection.

20. "tutto quello che occorre sapere affinché una lettera parli come parlerebbe un messaggero" (501).

21. "Io scrivano qui scrivo ma protesto. Il lancio del tronco è un'arte antica e nobile, che un profano non può capire" (502).

22. This translation is from *A Tranquil Star*, trans. Ann Goldstein and Alessandra Bastagli (NewYork: W. W. Norton, 2007), 132. The original reads: "instancabile e indistruttibile, brava a sparare quando occorreva, portentosamente vitale: una Diana-Minerva innestata sul corpo opulento . . . di una Giunone" (553).

23. Ibid., 135. The original reads, "Mi piacerebbe essere la ragazza del libro: mi accontenterei anche solo di esserlo stata, ma non lo sono mai stata" (555).

24. Ibid. The original reads, "Ecco stanno bene dove sono: nella mia memoria, scoloriti e secchi, con un'ombra di profumo, come fiori in un erbario. Nella

sua sono diventati lucidi e chiassosi come giocattoli di plastica. Non so quali siano più belli. Scelga lei" (555).

25. In the Holocaust stories, most characters use German as a *lingua franca* even though it is usually not their native tongue. Many of the stories of the second section of *Lilít* also depict cross-cultural communication, such as "I costruttori di ponti" (The Bridge Builders) and "Cara mamma" (Dear Mom). The third section, also, opens with "Gli stregoni" (The Witch Doctors), about ethnographers attempting to capture the language of a "primitive" people.

26. "per fare giustizia. Perché la gente paghi; ognuno paghi i suoi conti" (566).

27. "Pensavo anche alla essenziale ambiguità dei messaggi che ognuno di noi si lascia dietro, dalla nascita alla morte, ed alla nostra incapacità profonda di ricostruire una persona attraverso di essi, l'uomo che vive a partire dall'uomo che scrive: chiunque scriva, anche se solo sui muri, scrive in un codice che è solo suo, e che gli altri non conoscono; anche chi parla. Trasmettere in chiaro, esprimere, esprimersi e rendersi espliciti, è di pochi: alcuni potrebbero e non vogliono; altri vorrebbero e non sanno, la maggior parte né vogliono né sanno" (567).

28. "Si può distendere le membra?" (581).

29. "nessun italiano dirà mai 'membra,' è una di quelle parole che si possono scrivere ma non pronunciare, per via di un nostro misterioso tabù nazionale" (581).

30. "Su cinque parole che il lessico riporta, una almeno è ineffabile, come le brutte parole" (581).

31. "Un viso dormiente, o comunque un viso che non parla, non esprime molto: può essere indifferentemente rozzo o delicato, intelligente o sciocco; lo puoi distinguere solo quando si anima nella parola" (579).

32. "si voltò, e si trovò davanti lo sguardo della ragazza. Era uno sguardo fermo e gentile, ma con una connotazione d'attesa: sembrava che lei gli leggesse dentro in chiaro, come in un libro" (582).

33. "Una storia come questa non è chiusa in sé. è pregna, pone piú domande di quante ne soddisfaccia, e lascia sospesi grida e chiama per essere interpretata perché vi si intravvede un simbolo, come nei sogni e nei segni del cielo, ma interpretarla non è facile" (442).

9

The Survivor as Author

Primo Levi's Literary Vision of Auschwitz

Lawrence Langer
Simmons College

In the Preface to his *Genealogy of Morals*, Friedrich Nietzsche resolved "to traverse with quite novel questions, and as though with new eyes, the enormous, distant, and so well hidden land of morality—of morality that has actually existed, actually been lived; and does this not mean," he asked, "virtually to discover this land for the first time?" Some such limited project must have been in the back of Primo Levi's mind as he began to set down his account of the fate of morality in a place called Auschwitz. As we know, so alien and disturbing was its terrain that editors failed to discern the value of his account, and when it did appear under the imprint of a small publishing house only two years after the war, most general readers proved no more enthusiastic. Why? Alluding to his friend the philosopher and psychologist Paul Rée, Nietzsche announced his desire "to point out to so sharp and disinterested an eye as his a better direction in which to look, in the direction of an actual *history of morality*, and to warn him in time against gazing haphazardly in the blue after the English fashion. For it must be obvious which color is a hundred times more vital for a genealogist of morals than blue," Nietzsche continued, "namely *gray*, that is, what is documented, what can be confirmed and has actually existed."[1] Although, unlike Nietzsche, Levi had no grandiose plan to investigate the whole moral past of humankind, the two shared an interest in a pragmatic inquiry into the nature and value of morality in their time, though Levi's focus was as narrow as Nietzsche's was broad. Neither was interested in gazing into the blue for an answer, and readers who *were* must have been puzzled and perhaps even frightened by works like *Survival in Auschwitz* that arrived shrouded in clouds of gray.

Indeed, *Survival in Auschwitz* is Primo Levi's search for a genealogy of morals in a culture of destruction that Nietzsche could never have imagined. Although the chapter called "The Gray Zone" only appears in Levi's last published work, his first may be read as a prologue to his mature effort to decipher the new moral shading that the concentration and death camp experience had added to the spectrum of human behavior. The difficulty of the task was compounded by the motto of the camp that Levi discovered soon after his arrival: not the cynical *Arbeit Macht Frei*, but its more truthful and often paralyzing companion, *"Hier ist kein warum"*—"There is no 'why' here." When he began to speak of and then to write down the details of his ordeal, he was faced with the challenge of recording a reality so unfamiliar to his audiences that it resisted both the asking and the answering of simple questions. How, for example, should one respond to the following query, which turns up in the opening pages of *Survival in Auschwitz*: "If you and your child were going to be killed tomorrow, would you not give him to eat today?"[2] Levi's narratives of Auschwitz could not be pursued in a conventional interrogative voice, analyzing motives for conduct—whether by the abusers or the abused—in a logical discourse that would lead naturally to transparency and illumination, and perhaps eventually to comprehension. Indeed, I suspect that from the outset he was more concerned with prodding his readers to reflect on what happened than to hope to understand it. With an obvious glance at Nietzsche, he called one of his chapters "This Side of Good and Evil," and he ended it with an invitation to his readers "to contemplate the possible meaning in the Lager of the words 'good' and "evil,' 'just' and 'unjust'; let everybody judge . . . how much of our ordinary moral world could survive on this side of the barbed wire" (86).

Several portraits of Primo Levi have emerged over the years, some of which he has contributed to, and a principal one is the view that the episodes of *Survival in Auschwitz* are merely transcriptions of the stories he had been telling about his camp experience to whomever would listen, including strangers on trains, from the moment he returned to Turin. This has led to an underestimation of the literary quality of Levi's first work, since he insisted through most of his life that its episodes were merely written versions of the oral testimonies that had preceded them. But anyone familiar with a substantial number of the videotaped survivor accounts now available to researchers will quickly perceive that his oft-repeated view represents a naïve hope rather than an established fact. One has only to compare a transcribed testimony with Levi's memoir to see that he has written a work of literature in spite of his professed intentions to the contrary. Toward the end of his life, in a late interview, he was still asserting in regard to *Survival in Auschwitz*, "I had one precise idea in mind, and it was certainly not to write a work of literature. It was rather to bear witness, and a witness is all the more credible the less he exaggerates . . . I was afraid that the events related might be taken as inventions."³ But there are visible loopholes in his argument, among them the premise that oral testimonies do not contain exaggerations, or that listeners do not regard some of the most extreme oral accounts of atrocities as partial inventions. Levi was hesitant to acknowledge that when the Holocaust is the subject, charges of exaggeration and invention are unavoidable because the content seems so foreign to those who did not share in the experience.

In addition to his fear that literary ambitions might mar the accuracy of his narrative, Levi shared with Adorno the concern that the writer's devotion to the beauty of language and form might somehow convert for the better the irreducible ugliness and brutality of the Holocaust ordeal, an apprehension that led to Adorno's notorious conclusion, later modified, that writing poetry after Auschwitz was barbaric.⁴ In another interview, in response to a question involving the memoirist's tendency to create "literary" characters, Levi responded: "As far as I remember, I tried not to do this in *Survival in Auschwitz*, but I gave in to the temptation quite frequently in *Lilít* [1981, translated in a truncated version as *Moments of Reprieve*, 1986]. By then I'd become a writer. The man who wrote *Survival in Auschwitz* wasn't a writer in the normal sense of the word, he wasn't looking for literary success, and he had no illusions, no ambitions to create a beautiful end product."⁵

Although like Adorno, Levi felt a legitimate anxiety about the danger of aestheticizing the horror of Auschwitz, anyone familiar with the harrowing accounts of that camp in the stories of Tadeusz Borowski (written even *earlier* than Levi's *Survival in Auschwitz*) will realize how possible it is to disable the beauty implicit in creative endeavor and, through an unsentimental style and ironic tone, to make form a servant to rather than a ruler of the formless. This is exactly what Levi does in *Survival in Auschwitz*. There is a frame surrounding the narrative that could only be a result of literary vision. It begins with a transition from the order of normal life to the disorder of Auschwitz, and ends with a slow and painful climb back from the isolation of physical and moral chaos in the camp, against which there is no permanent or effective defense, toward a restoration of the communal support, both physical and moral, that is the hallmark of civilized behavior. The shift is from powerlessly watching people die to effectively helping people live. That shift betrays a momentum in the narrative that is characteristic of what we call literature; it is not to be found in oral testimony. Although Levi denies that he was a writer at the outset of his career, he is the one who decided what to include and what to omit, and especially the arrangement of episodes, which, as we shall see, has a marked effect on our response to the text. In addition, as we are eased into the random existence of Auschwitz, time loses its meaning, future and past dissolve, and the present moment, the present morning and evening of each day, looms as the prevailing index of chronology. Regular temporal sequence returns only after the Germans have evacuated the camp, when Levi begins to date the entries, and "the last ten days" cease to be random but a race against time to preserve the lives of those handfuls of companions dying in his barrack.

And there are further examples of balance in the narrative that we do not find in oral testimonies. Very early in the text, Levi tells us that of the 45 people in his boxcar only four saw their homes again (17–18), a survival rate of less than 10 percent. He then expands the numbers to inform us that about 80 percent of the men and women in his convoy were sent to the gas chambers upon arrival, and that only 96 men and 29 women entered one of the Auschwitz camps. To the nonwriter Levi, this may have seemed like an objective statistic, the kind of numerical analysis that could have turned up in an industrial report, but to the reader of literature it is a carefully planted detail, reinforced by the information that two months later, only 40 were still alive (49). It prods consciousness into a shock of recognition— that we are about to enter a domain where life and death are no longer the opposite poles of a chronological journey beginning with birth and ending with physical demise, but have been mingled into a new inseparable twinship that I have called "deathlife" to designate the experience of dying *while* one is living, of being dead and alive at the same time, a paradox that the nonwriter Levi might have resisted but that infiltrated his tale in spite of himself. Indeed, Levi admitted to one of his biographers that after the nightmare intensity of the camp, "I had the sensation that I was living . . . but without being alive."[6] The narrative rhythm of this theme reaches fruition during the last ten days, when in spite of the common effort of Levi and the two "healthy" Frenchmen in his barracks to restore the normal chronology of living and dying to their ill companions, half of them fail to survive despite the arrival of the Russians in Auschwitz. When Philip Roth described the closing episode of *Survival in Auschwitz* as "Robinson Crusoe in hell,"[7] he unwittingly contradicted Levi's repeated assertion that all he wanted to do was to "bear witness" in his memoir. Many survivors in their oral testimony ask a version of the question "How shall I make you understand what Auschwitz really was?" Primo Levi circumvents that question by patiently—one is reluctant to add "unwittingly" here—organizing a literary structure to do just that.

Roth's allusion to Robinson Crusoe raises reverberations of literary association that may not have been evident to the reader and perhaps not even intended by Levi, but the connection nonetheless demands response and provokes interpretations. One cannot imagine searching for literary precedents to "mere" oral testimony. Challenged by the instinct to stay alive in an environment that provides no external support, Crusoe draws on a resourcefulness that enables him to achieve his desire. Roth's reaction to Levi's need to find life support "from the chaotic residue of a ruthlessly evil island" elicits both agreement and correction from Levi. "What struck me there, as throughout the book," Roth comments, "was the extent to which thinking contributed to your survival, the thinking of a practical, humane, scientific mind."[8] Using Robinson Crusoe as a model—and Levi freely admits "I truly did feel like Robinson Crusoe"—one can easily figure out the tactics required to enhance if not ensure the possibility of survival.[9] But Levi turns the conversation from similarity to contrast, stubbornly reserving his right (as he so often does) to disagree with his interviewer, insisting that after the requirements of entering the camp in good health and knowing German, luck rather than resourcefulness was the dominant factor in one's survival. Moreover, in defining Auschwitz as a place that is both "monstrous" and "new," he confirms his determination to make Survival in Auschwitz a departure from, rather than an extension of, traditional memoirs, whether fiction or nonfiction. In other words, he had an authorial strategy in mind, and although he repeats to Roth what he has said so often before, that he had "no literary intentions" when writing the book, that his model was "the 'weekly report' so often used in factories," the reader has a right to be baffled by this assertion, since the "matter of Auschwitz" bears no similarity whatsoever to the contents of an industrial weekly report.[10] Levi may unconsciously address the problem when he petitions Roth, "Please grant me the right to inconsistency: in the camp our state of mind was unstable, it oscillated from hour to hour between hope and despair. The coherence I think one notes in my books is an artifact, a rationalization, a posteriori."[11]

The response of readers and critics to the most celebrated (and the most literary) chapter in Survival in Auschwitz, "The Canto of Ulysses," pays little heed to this remark. These few pages, which ought not to be separated from the surrounding text, have become the equivalent of the Warsaw Ghetto Uprising in Primo Levi's Auschwitz narrative, a beacon of hope that seems to dim the moral despair prevalent in most of its other episodes. One of Levi's biographers has unleashed an astonishing, not to say breathtaking, tribute to this brief segment: "If one day," says Carole Angier, "there is a new Holocaust, and we can save only one chapter of one book from the twentieth century, it should be this one: Chapter 11 of If This Is a Man [Survival in Auschwitz], "The Canto of Ulysses," in which a 24-year-old Italian tries to remember, recite and explain Canto 26 of Dante's Inferno to a 22-year-old Frenchman in Auschwitz."[12] Given the literary achievement of a full century and the numberless outstanding candidates for rescue, why such extraordinary praise for this particular fragment? It appears to allow the reader to salvage from the detritus of Auschwitz some vestige of the cultural memory of the prisoners that the Germans were determined to destroy, and of the human dignity associated with it. It momentarily shifts our attention from Levi's lamentable state to the courage and prowess of the mythological Ulysses, whose voyage, in both purpose and end is quite contrary to Primo Levi's from Italy to Auschwitz.

Victor Brombert responds to the pages with equal enthusiasm: "The spanning of Greek and Roman antiquity [Homer and Virgil], the Middle Ages [Dante], the modern period [Levi and the death camp], suggests a reassuring permanence and continuity." It provides "a lesson in dignity and survival, yet also a reminder that sheer physical survival is not enough— that what defines a human being is the need and ability to pursue higher aims."[13] However, one can be reassured by "permanence and continuity" in Auschwitz only by ignoring, as Brombert does, what precedes and follows "The Canto of Ulysses." In the previous chapter, called "The Chemical Examination," just when Levi thinks he has achieved a renewed status by being appointed to the chemical commando (a post that will restore some "permanence and continuity" to his life, as well as human dignity), the Kapo Alex, a green-triangle criminal inmate, wipes his grease-stained hand on Levi's shoulder, shattering the illusion that dignity is available to the Jewish prisoner in Auschwitz. In their earnest search for positive meaning in Levi's text, readers often tend to ignore the irony that undercuts his efforts to seize on an upbeat moment in his experience of the camp. Levi urges Philip Roth to grant him the right of inconsistency, and the literary device of irony that runs through his text like a persistent thread is its herald, especially in the "Canto of Ulysses."

Levi says that he finished "The Canto of Ulysses" in half an hour during a lunch break, and that it was the second chapter he wrote, following "The Last Ten Days." Robert Gordon speaks, accurately, I think, of the movement of Levi's mind in the text of *Survival in Auschwitz*, from "deposition as a witness to composition as a writer,"[14] though the need to get the Ulysses episode down on paper so early suggests that, despite his demurrals, the role of "composition as a writer" attracted Levi from the beginning. So powerful an impact did Dante have on his imagination that when he later came to write the second chapter, "On the Bottom," he was inspired to transform the poet's scenario into a death camp setting: "This is hell. Today, in our times, hell must be like this. A huge, empty room" (22). The point of the Canto of Ulysses is not to help us understand better Dante or Ulysses, or the importance of the *Inferno*, or even the value of art or poetry; the point of the Canto of Ulysses is to help us to understand better the nature of Auschwitz. To be "on the bottom" in the

Inferno (though Ulysses is near, not *at* the bottom) is to be punished for sin by divine will in a universe that also contains Purgatory and Paradise, a world where the reward of eternal bliss is assured for those who pursue knowledge and virtue within the limits of God's approval. To be "on the bottom" in Auschwitz, as Levi tells us very soon after his arrival, is as follows: "We are tired, standing on our feet, with a tap which drips while we cannot drink the water, and we wait for something which will certainly be terrible, and nothing happens and nothing continues to happen. What can one think about? One cannot think any more, it is like being already dead" (22). The lines remind us of the crucial role Levi reserves for *reader* memory in his narrative, since the mood of silence and nullity evoked here forms a stark contrast to the intense drama of Ulysses's story, and is not meant to be forgotten when we reach the later chapter. Indeed, a further link exists between the two, since in "On the Bottom," Levi introduces his first specific allusion to Dante, a brief citation from Canto 21: "No Sacred Face will help thee here! It's not / A Serchio bathing party" (29). In context, the lines are sarcastic with obscene implications, but Levi uses them for a different purpose. In Dante's hell, Virgil never tires of reminding his pupil that everything there happens according to God's will, a reassurance that helps him traverse the place, but Levi's citation from the *Inferno* here is a bleak reminder of the *absence* of the God in which he does not believe. In Auschwitz, there is no guide, no possibility of spiritual reprieve.

Dante's *Inferno* sheds its influence backward and forward in the text of *Survival in Auschwitz*, making the "Canto of Ulysses" not a special case but only an example of a theme that pervades the narrative. One of the earliest inmates introduced by Levi is named Null Achtzehn—018—the last three figures of the number engraved on his forearm, which translated into ordinary speech means "life is nothing," though one cannot expect all readers to realize that the numerical equivalent for the Hebrew word for "life" ("chai") is 18. Are we to believe that this is a coincidental fact and that the writer Levi did not know any of this? When we read Levi's description of Null Achtzehn, we have the odd feeling that the poet Dante has been imported to Auschwitz where he is describing one of the tormented souls in hell: "He has not even the rudimentary astuteness of a draught-horse, which stops pulling a little before it reaches exhaustion: he pulls or carries or pushes as long as his strength allows him, then he gives way at once, without a word of warning, without lifting his sad, opaque eyes from the ground" (43). We encounter the same strange sympathy that Dante evokes for certain punished sinners. But then Levi the writer displaces Dante the poet by adding a conscious literary allusion that one would never expect from the lips of someone in an oral testimony bearing witness to the fate of a fellow prisoner: "He made me think of the sledge-dogs in London's books, who slave until the last breath and die on the track" (43). Levi's theme is not the punishment of guilty sinners, but the reduction of innocent men to the condition of beasts, where human creatures struggle not for divine approval, but against a hostile or indifferent secular environment. Null Achtzehn, like Jack London's inhospitable arctic narratives, is a carefully chosen literary motif that resonates beyond its initial human reference.

The same must be said of Levi's use of the "Canto of Ulysses" from Dante's *Commedia*. Levi himself seemed ambivalent about the role of this chapter in his account of the death camp. In a section from "The Intellectual in Auschwitz" in *The Drowned and the Saved*, he insists that reciting the passage from Dante 40 years earlier "made it possible for me to reestablish a link with the past, saving it from oblivion and reinforcing my identity."[15] But by now, we should know that a contradictory rhythm governs Levi's text, alternating between glimmers of hope and moments of intense despair. Although Victor Brombert argues (and Levi's words just cited seem to confirm this) that "Levi the humanist found solace and salvation in Dante's poetry,"[16] to embrace this idea is to ignore Levi's own further words on the matter, which follow the lines just quoted: "[In Auschwitz] culture could be useful even in some marginal cases, and for brief periods; it could enhance an hour, establish a fleeting bond with a companion, keep the mind alive and healthy. It definitely was not useful in orienting oneself and understanding: on this score my experience as a foreigner is identical to that of the German [Austrian] Améry. [Levi must have in mind Améry's famous statement, *Es führte keine Brücke vom Tod in Venedig zum Tod in Auschwitz* (No bridge led from [Thomas Mann's novella] *Death in Venice* to death in Auschwitz.)] Reason, art, and poetry are no help in deciphering a place from which they are banned. In the daily life 'down there,' made up of boredom and interwoven with horror, it was salutary to forget them, just as it was salutary to forget home and family. By this I do not mean definitive oblivion, of which, for all that, no one is capable, but a relegation to that attic of memory where all the clutter of stuff that is no longer useful in everyday life is stored."[17]

Nevertheless, readers continue to celebrate the Canto of Ulysses as a spiritual summit, even as a redeeming factor in Levi's Auschwitz narrative. However, a careful examination of Canto 26 suggests that Levi may have had something else in mind, not a tribute to the enduring value of cultural memory or the art of poetry but an invitation to *differentiate*, to recognize how literature may invade and transform reality, in short, to acknowledge the distinction between literary vision and actual fact. Surely, Levi's own perception of this helps to explain his reluctance to consider himself a writer in his first work, but only one who bears witness.

The first thing the pilgrim Dante discerns as he enters the circle of false counselors where he encounters Ulysses is its fiery nature: its dominant image is flame, which encases the souls of those punished there. But Levi would have known that the prevailing image of Birkenau was also flame, belching forth from its chimneys the doom of its innocent victims, whose bodies were cremated there. Although Dante's hell is crowded with historical personalities, some of whom Dante knew, Levi chooses the story of a mythological figure to recapture its spirit for his companion Jean the Pikolo, overlooking the fact that Dante's Ulysses shares his forked flame with his fellow warrior Diomedes. And Virgil, not Dante, addresses the flames and asks to hear their tale, not inquiring about a heroic exploit or a courageous voyage, but specifically, "let one of you tell me where, lost, he went to die" (26, 83–84). But this is exactly the question that Levi must answer too, though there is nothing mythological (or indeed admirable) about the details of *his* journey. Indeed, the stories of Dante the pilgrim, of Ulysses, and of Primo Levi are saturated in the journey motif, and it is impossible to believe that the writer in Levi did not see or consciously make use of these connections.

Dante journeys from a "dark wood" with the aid of a protective guide down through the *Inferno* and up through *Purgatorio* to the shining bliss at the end of the *Paradiso*. Levi is transported from the bright, snow-capped mountains of northern Italy to the dismal Silesian plains of the Lager at Auschwitz, with no support and no prospect of escape. On his mini-journey from the soup kitchen to the work commando with Jean the Pikolo, he serves as a kind of cultural guide himself, but the meaning and effect of the lines he recaptures from the "Canto of Ulysses" remain in dispute. Ulysses, of course, is the archetypal sea voyager, especially in Homer, and by the time he became a "writer" in *La tregua* (*The Reawakening*), Levi offered no apologies for imitating his circuitous return to the place of his birth. However, because Dante did not know Homer's *Odyssey*, he invented an escapade commensurate with the sin of false counseling, though, as many critics point out, Dante seemed to have shared some sympathy for his Ulysses's bold heterodoxy. But it is impossible to overlook the fact that in Dante, Ulysses is steering his own fate and chooses to violate the spatial limitations of divine command, while Levi is deported against his will in a boxcar that, as Claude Lanzmann's film *Shoah* demonstrates, has become embedded in twentieth-century consciousness as a seminal image of fatal transportation. Given this obvious difference, could Levi really have wished us to see *parallels* between the two voyages? Finally, there is the story of the journey missed, barely implied, the evacuation of the camp, the death march that consumed the lives of Alberto and so many of his other fellow inmates, a journey through a hell that Dante could never have imagined.

Levi thus has two audiences for his citation of fragments from the "Canto of Ulysses"—Jean the Pikolo and ourselves. Jean is a naïve listener, thoroughly unfamiliar with Dante's text, and therefore possessing no context for what he is hearing. However, that is not true for Levi's readers, who are free to respond not only to what he includes, but also to what he leaves out, such as the passage when Virgil asks the sinner to tell him where he went to die. Indeed, Levi begins his recitation at exactly the next line: "'Then of that age-old fire the loftier horn/Began to mutter and move'" (112). Dante's readers, and many of Levi's, too, would know that Ulysses's sin is a grave one, being punished in one of the lowest reaches of the *Inferno*, the circle of the false counselors, whose principal transgression is manifested through speech—"'My little speech made everyone so keen,'"(114) Levi quotes from Dante—and Ulysses's talent for rhetorical persuasion enables him to convince his crew that his vision of the nature of reality constitutes a heroic challenge rather than a foolhardy adventure or a mortal sin. Had Levi already been familiar with *Moby-Dick* at this time, he would have had a perfect analogue in Melville's Captain Ahab, whose campaign and voyage of defiance still holds its romantic appeal. The last vestiges of skepticism about Levi's role as writer in this narrative should disappear as we realize how carefully he manipulates not only our response but also his own authorial voice, which completely abandons the tone of detached observer, swept up and carried away by what the imagination is capable of doing to ordinary experience. The "Canto of Ulysses" is a dramatic enactment of Levi's deepest fear in writing about Auschwitz: how literary strategies might threaten and tarnish one's credibility as a witness. The most memorable lines from Ulysses's "little speech," "'Think of your breed; for brutish ignorance / Your mettle was not made; you were made men, / To follow after knowledge and excellence,'"(113) sound like a clarion call of hope and encouragement to all the inmates of Auschwitz—but is it a summons to transfiguration, or a moment of temptation, similar to the one Ulysses issues to his companions? Our generation knows better than most how easy it is for victims of eloquence to lose their identity, to allow it to merge in a stronger will, and this is precisely what happens to Levi himself: "As if I also was hearing it for the first time: like the blast of a trumpet, like the voice of God. For the moment I forget who I am and where I am" (113). We are present at the birth—or the stillbirth—of an epiphany, but never granted the revelation, only teased by its possibility. The words "as pleased Another" that explain the shipwreck and drowning of Ulysses and his crew come as no surprise to Dante's readers who have been following Virgil's patient explanations of the moral and theological economy of the *Inferno*: they lie at the heart of the poem's Christian literary vision. But how are we to explain the consequent torrent of language that pours forth to Levi's silent auditor from a voice disarmed of rational control and sounding for all the world like the mystical summation of a soaring Mahler symphony: "I keep Pikolo back, it is vitally necessary and urgent that he listen, that he understand this 'as pleased Another' before it is too late . . . but still more something gigantic that I myself have only just seen, in a flash of intuition, perhaps the reason for our fate, for our being here today" (115). As I said, we are offered epiphany in the form of temptation, invited to succumb to the instinct for meaning that governs our response to the most inexplicable atrocities—and what is Jewish doom in Auschwitz if not that?—hoping to find in that "flash of intuition" an explanation for mass murder. But Levi the witness knows better: however praiseworthy Ulysses's quest for knowledge and excellence, one's aims in a German concentration camp are far more modest. Levi has already told us that the Lager is hunger: "We ourselves are hunger, living hunger" (74). Man in Auschwitz, Elie Wiesel later will write, is a starved stomach, confirming Levi's initial definition.

One reads with some amusement Ian Thomson's report of the response of Jean Samuel (the Pikolo of the episode) to the "Canto of Ulysses" that Levi sent him shortly after completing it. "Samuel," Thomson says, "was staggered that Dante had meant so much to Levi at Auschwitz; if anything the Frenchman had been faintly bemused at the time by Levi's attempt to interest him in a 600-year-old medieval poem that culminates in the mystical revelations of God in Paradise."[18] But Samuel could not have been expected to understand the writer at work, to have appreciated Levi's reasons for introducing his sudden paroxysm of enthusiasm for Dante's art with such ambivalent force: it at once celebrates the poet's literary achievement and warns against what Cynthia Ozick has called "the perils of the imagination,"[19] which Levi applies to writing about the Holocaust. The ever-present danger of such writing is to allow literary strategy to distort the historical truth of the event, to seduce us into believing that we can find, as Levi writes, "the reason for our fate. For our being here today." The Dante lesson finally dissipates as though it were a dream, because Levi realizes that the story of Ulysses is an intrusion on, rather than a mirror image of, his own catastrophe. Unlike Ulysses, he is in no way an agent of the disaster that engulfs him, and unlike Dante, he has no master narrative of salvation to console him.

In context, the Dante interval is immediately followed, as it must be, by the classic theme that pervades the camp experience: literal hunger, the desire for alimentary rather than artistic nourishment. The task for Levi and Pikolo in Auschwitz is not to study Dante but to fetch the soup: the language of the Lager reenters the narrative with "*Kraut und Rüben*," cabbage and turnips, a vocabulary that nurtures the stomach rather than the soul. Cultural memory may support abstract intellectual survival in

Auschwitz, but for the principal challenge of simply staying alive, *Kraut und Rüben* are far more vital. The "Canto of Ulysses" ends with a summation of the God-ordained climax to Ulysses's ill-fated voyage—"And over our heads the hollow seas closed up"—but neither art nor divinity intervenes to impose closure on Levi's unfinished journey in Auschwitz. Ulysses's sailing toward a world without people (*del mondo sanza gente*, 26, 117), toward a "*nova terra*" or "new land" (26, 137) is not an analogue to, but a distraction from, Levi's unwilled destination. Not even a Dante could have imagined its murderous agenda.

The next chapter instantly picks up the voyage motif, but it has shed all literary allusions, as the voice of the witness-bearer replaces the writer's vision, together with a distancing from Dante's poetic language: "Throughout the spring, convoys arrived from Hungary; one prisoner in two was Hungarian, and Hungarian had become the second language in the camp after Yiddish" (116). This explains why the last three foreign terms of the "Canto of Ulysses" chapter, *kápostza és répak*, are Hungarian for "cabbage and turnips." In other words, we are back in the world of mass murder, and Dante has been consigned to oblivion, a fading memory, an experiment that has done nothing to alter the fate of these doomed new arrivals, who within a few weeks will die by the hundreds of thousands, as pleased the Germans, not "Another." When Levi tells us that the news of the Allied landing in Normandy, of the Russian offensive, of the failed attempt on Hitler's life—which would bring us to the summer of 1944—"had given rise to waves of violent but ephemeral hope," surely he is also warning us not to make too much of our encounter with Dante's *Commedia*. Despite his optimistic temperament, Levi never allowed a false sense of promise to govern his talent for reclaiming the truth of his experience: "Day by day everyone felt his strength vanish, his desire to live melt away, his mind grow dim; and Normandy and Russia were so far away [Dante even further], and winter so near; hunger and desolation so concrete, and all the rest so unreal, that it did not seem possible that there could really exist any other world or time other than our world of mud and our sterile and stagnant time, whose end we were by now incapable of imagining" (116).

This brings us, finally, to the basic question Levi had to ask himself as he sat down to write *Survival in Auschwitz* shortly after his return home: What will my readers be capable of imagining, and how can I relate it to the reality that they already know? Dante may have asked himself the same question, but his genealogy of immorality in the *Inferno* furnished him with a pattern of sin and punishment unavailable to Levi. Indeed, when he began composing his own genealogy of morality in Auschwitz early in 1946, Levi had nothing but his own memory to rely on. The Nuremberg trials had scarcely begun, and the scope of the German atrocities was barely beginning to emerge. Almost everything Levi had to say would come as a shock to his Italian readers. There were few historical documents and no cultural framework called "the literature of the Holocaust." In the spring of 1946, while Levi was working on *Survival in Auschwitz*, a modest volume was published, in Polish, in Munich, Germany called "We Were in Auschwitz." It included the principal stories that were later part of Tadeusz Borowski's *This Way for the Gas, Ladies and Gentlemen*. Levi could not have known the work, but its three authors, all survivors, faced a dilemma similar to his, one lucidly expressed by the book's publisher, Anatole Girs, also a survivor: "Is this book necessary? I don't know. Whatever will be said about it, however, one thing is irrefutably clear: the art in it must be separated from the documentation."[20] Both Borowski and Levi recognized from the start the hybrid nature of Holocaust literature, in which the imagination would be forced to serve the facts, and not vice versa. Surely this helps to explain Levi's insistence throughout his life that the author of *Survival in Auschwitz* was not a writer.

For an audience that had never heard of Buna-Monowitz, to say nothing of Birkenau, who would have trouble comprehending selections, to say nothing of gas chambers and crematoria, who preferred, to use Nietzsche's image, "gazing haphazardly in the blue" to wandering in the gray fog of Auschwitz, Levi had to create a rhythm for easing the untutored imagination of his readers into such unappealing terrain. His narrative—and only a disciplined writer would be capable of this—pursues a principle of strategic orientation and disorientation, alternating moments of dignity with instants of shame, dread, and revulsion, giving his readers a chance to breathe normally in between their stifling gasps of horror. His portraits of individuals seem randomly interspersed throughout the text, but in fact they are distributed in such a way as to constantly shift the moral ground beneath us, duplicating for us his own question as a witness-writer of how to draw a genealogy of morality in such a place that would be faithful to its nature while also paying homage to our own need not to slide into a valley of despair. His "Canto of Ulysses" offers art as one refuge from the horror of Auschwitz; but the following chapter ends on a more durable high note, with the movement from literature back to life and a different kind of redemptive model, the "free" Italian laborer Lorenzo: "But Lorenzo was a man; his humanity was pure and uncontaminated, he was outside this world of negation. Thanks to Lorenzo, I managed not to forget that I myself was a man" (122).

Nevertheless, this very statement is followed by a chapter on the great selection of October 1944, in which Beppo the Greek is chosen by chance to die while Kuhn is spared and prays to God in gratitude, and the indifference of Kuhn to Beppo's fate, which outrages Levi, cancels much of the value of Lorenzo's loyalty to Primo. One finds oneself nostalgically drawn back to the moral stability of Dante's *Inferno*, where divine justice prevails, where one is consoled by the knowledge that virtue and faith can be rewarded. In Levi's camp milieu, however, Virgil's voice of reason is absent and, beyond Auschwitz, no Beatrice awaits the hopeful soul. Levi the writer finds himself obliged to discredit the world of his readers, where God chooses to punish the guilty, while Levi the witness is forced to recreate an alien locale where the Germans select the innocent to be murdered in gas chambers. It is an act, as he writes, that "nothing at all in the power of man can ever clean again" (130). This is about as definitive a statement as Levi will make concerning the impact of the death camp universe, what he will later call a "phase of anguish" that survival cannot assuage and the future will never erase from memory. Watching the hanging of a prisoner involved in an abortive rebellion in Birkenau confirms this image of the soiled self for Levi, who elaborates on what it means to be broken and conquered by such enforced witnessing, "even if we know how to adapt ourselves, even if we have finally learnt how to find our food and to resist the fatigue and cold, even if we return home" (150). To the very end, two voices struggled within the author of *Survival in Auschwitz*: the witness determined to get down the bare facts of what he and his companions had endured, and the writer consumed by a vision of the transformative power of the event: "We lay in a world of death and phantoms. The last trace of civilization had vanished around and inside us" (171). Generations of writers would embrace this legacy, tracing its implications in what we now call the literature of the Holocaust, but Levi's precise and modest language helped to lay its foundations, and for this, he deserves all the tribute he continues to receive.

Notes

1. Friedrich Nietzsche, *On the Genealogy of Morals*, trans. Walter Kaufmann and R. J. Hollingdale (New York: Vintage Books, 1989), 21. All passages quoted from Nietzsche can be found on this page in the *Genealogy*.
2. Primo Levi, *Survival in Auschwitz: The Nazi Assault on Humanity*, trans. Stuart Woolf (New York: Collier Books, 1993), 15. Subsequent page references to this edition will be included in the body of the text.
3. Marco Belpoliti and Robert Gordon, eds., *The Voice of Memory: Primo Levi—Interviews 1961–1987*, trans. Robert Gordon (New York: New Press, 2001), 250.
4. The original statement, "After Auschwitz, to write a poem is barbaric," was written in a 1949 essay entitled "Kulturkritik und Gesellschaft." It can be found in Adorno, *Gesammelte Schriften*, vol. 10, ed. Rolf Tiedemann (Frankfurt:

Suhrkamp, 1974), 30. In a 1962 radio broadcast, he modified this dictum as follows: "Through the aesthetic principle of stylization . . . an unimaginable fate still seems as if it has some meaning; it becomes transfigured, with something of the horror removed." For the full text, see "Engagement," in *Noten zur Literatur*, 2 (Frankfurt: Suhrkamp, 1965), 125–27.

5. Belpoliti and Gordon, *The Voice of Memory*, 224.
6. See Ian Thomson, *Primo Levi: A Life* (New York: Henry Holt, 2002), 208.
7. "A Conversation with Primo Levi," in Levi, *Survival in Auschwitz*, 179.
8. Ibid.
9. Ibid., 180.
10. Ibid., 181.
11. Ibid., 180–81.
12. Carole Angier, *The Double Bond: The Life of Primo Levi* (New York: Farrar, Straus, & Giroux, 2003), 330.
13. Victor Brombert, *In Praise of Anti-Heroes: Figures and Themes in Modern European Literature, 1830–1980* (Chicago: University of Chicago Press, 2001), 117.
14. Belpoliti and Gordon, *The Voice of Memory*, 11.
15. Primo Levi, *The Drowned and the Saved*, trans. Raymond Rosenthal (New York: Summit Books, 1988), 139.
16. Brombert, *In Praise of Anti-Heroes*, 122.
17. Levi, *The Drowned and the Saved*, 142.
18. Thomson, *Primo Levi*, 225.
19. Cynthia Ozick, "A Youthful Intoxication," *New York Times Book Review*, December 6, 2006, 35.
20. Tadeusz Borowski, Krystyn Olszewski, and Janusz Nel Siedlecki, *We Were in Auschwitz*, trans. Alicia Nitecki (New York: Welcome Rain, 2000), 1.

10

How It All Started

A Personal Reflection

Nicholas Patruno

Bryn Mawr College

To borrow Levi's own opening words in his Preface to *Se questo è un uomo* (*Survival in Auschwitz*), it was "per mia fortuna" that, in the fall of 1988, I received a phone call from Warren Slesinger, who at that time was acquisitions editor of the University of South Carolina Press. He was seeking the names of some recent prominent Italian writers whose works would be of interest to the American reading public. Besides Cesare Pavese and Alberto Moravia, he told me that, offhand, he could not recall the names of other modern Italian writers. The first two names that quickly came to mind to suggest to him were those of Italo Calvino and Primo Levi. His immediate response to the name of Primo Levi was "Why didn't I think of him?" And then came the surprise. What I thought was just a call of inquiry resulted in my being asked if I were interested in submitting a proposal for a book to add to the Press's series "Understanding Modern European and Latin American Literature," the companion to the "Understanding Contemporary American Literature" series.

Caught totally unprepared, I said I needed some time to consider it. Then, urged by a close friend and colleague, Rabbi Samuel Lachs, with whom I was already working on another translation project, I decided to submit a proposal, which was readily accepted. It was as the result of this "fortuna," therefore, that my book *Understanding Primo Levi* came out in 1995, the same year as Mirna Cicioni's excellent work, *Primo Levi, Bridges of Knowledge*, and five years after Risa Sodi's seminal book *A Dante of Our Time: Primo Levi and Auschwitz*.[1] It has been brought to my attention, though, that my work was the first book-length study of its kind (what I mean by this will be explained shortly) on Primo Levi to be published in English.

The guidelines I was given for writing the book were quite specific. It was to be a work that would serve as a guide "for undergraduate and graduate students and non-academic readers" and that would introduce them to the writer's life and writings and "explicate his most important works." Thus, the book was to be conceived as an introduction rather than "a comprehensive analysis" of Levi's works and it was meant to be used in conjunction with the reading of the works being treated, not "as a substitute for study of the original works."[2] Because my text was specifically directed at an American (or English) reading public, I focused on those writings of Levi's that had been translated into English, namely his major works, *Survival at Auschwitz, The Reawakening, The Periodic Table, The Monkey's Wrench, If Not Now, When?, The Drowned and the Saved,* and several of the short stories included in *Moments of Reprieve (Lilít e altri racconti), The Mirror Maker: Stories and Essays, Other People's Trades,* and *The Sixth Day and Other Stories.* In retrospect, I regret that I did not also include Levi's poetry, for it would have made for a more complete work and brought to light Levi's other side, the "unnatural" one, to use his own term, of his artistic persona.

In keeping with my responsibilities for the book, and, at the same time, to find out more about Primo Levi's private life, I was able to spend one month in Turin, in 1990, thanks to a grant I was awarded from Bryn Mawr College. There I met with some of Levi's acquaintances and friends, had an opportunity to speak by phone with his wife, and, at Einaudi publishers' headquarters, I was able to view, and permitted to photocopy, letters and documents of different sorts related to Levi's long and almost exclusive association with that publisher.

I cannot claim that any of these documents were of a crucially revealing nature, but that did not dampen the excitement I experienced when looking at some *prima facie* evidence. It was information not generally known (to me, at least, at that time) and interesting from the standpoint of assessing the extent of Levi's involvement in the production of his own works. Among those documents, I was excited to read Calvino's letter to Levi (signature erased, but sent from Paris) in which the former, as consultant to Einaudi, in commenting on *The Periodic Table,* writes, "Quanto ad Argon ho sempre le mie riserve sul fatto che sia in apertura" (regarding Argon, I still have my reservations about the fact that it is the opening chapter). But then he goes on to say, "se i capitoli seguono un ordinamento anche per peso atomico (con eccezioni, mi pare), non parlo più." (if the chapters follow an order also according to atomic weight [with exceptions, it seems to me], I won't say anything else.) This was one time, as we now know, when Levi, who had the highest regard for Calvino, held steadfast to his own judgment.

Of great interest was a letter that confirms Levi's involvement and concern with the accuracy of the translation of his works, a fact, parenthetically, clearly evidenced in the chapter "Lettere di tedeschi" (Letters from the Germans) in his *The Drowned and the Saved*, when he writes in reference to the German translation of *Survival in Auschwitz*. In that letter, Levi complains bitterly about the French translation of *Survival in Auschwitz*. Besides listing the several inaccuracies in the translation, which he attributes to the translator's "fretta" and "pigrizia" (haste and laziness), he adds a touch of sarcasm when, in commenting on the translator's omission of several of Dante's lines in the chapter "The Canto of Ulisse," he writes, "Troppa fatica . . . Il traduttore se la è cavata con il primo verso e con l'ultimo. Del resto, doveva avere con Dante un fatto personale" (Too much work . . . the translator got away with the first and last verses only. He must have had something against Dante).

I was also somewhat surprised by the degree of Levi's interest in how his writings were reviewed in other countries. In the case of *Survival in Auschwitz*, he translates portions of the reviews he deemed significant into Italian. For instance, from the *New York Herald Tribune*, dated December 28, 1959, Levi translates a section that states that no other writer's account of the concentration camp has the "stile ed efficacia" (style and incisiveness) of his book. From the *Rheinischer Merkur*, dated December 1, 1962, Levi translates the section that ends with "come possiamo vivere noi tedeschi, nel cui nome tutto questo è avvenuto?" (how can we Germans live, in whose name all this has taken place?).

From these documents, I also learned that of the 200,000 lire that Levi received as initial payment for the publication of *Survival in Auschwitz*, he agreed to accept the equivalent of 40,000 lire, and no more, in Einaudi stock. Moreover, on more than one occasion, Levi demonstrates his savvy in looking after his own financial interests by reminding the publisher of the correct amount he is due in royalties, and in making clear that the deadlines for these payments be respected.

These documents also reveal that Levi, who in one of his letters claims to be ignorant of the real function of a literary agent, was, at least for a time, a hands-on person when it came to negotiations for the publication of his works abroad. For instance, in connection with the negotiations between Levi and his American publisher, in discussing the possibilities for a fitting title for the American edition of his book *Lilít e altri racconti*, Arthur Samuelson of Summit Books, in a telex to Levi on July 23, 1985, writes, "Again I plead with you for 'Moments of Truce' as title. [. . .] Nothing works better because that is truly it [*sic*] title." In a telex dated July 29, 1985, Levi's gives a firm response to Samuelson: "As to title Einaudi and I insist avoid word *Truce*. Why not [use] one of the stories' titles, such as 'Il nostro sigillo' (Our Seal) or 'Stanco di finzioni' (Tired of Pretenses)?" In this case, as we know, the word "Truce" was replaced with "Reprieve." It would seem, though, that Levi was sensitive—and maybe for legitimate and possibly for copyright purposes—to having the same word appear in more than one of his book titles. The suggestion of a book title taken from one of the chapters contained therein might help explain the title *The Reawakening* for *La tregua*. As a marginal note in reference to this point, it is interesting that in the Italian version of the conversation between Levi and Philip Roth, Roth's objection to this title is omitted. And, as for the title *La tregua* itself, judging from the date (December 11, 1962) on a brief note accompanying a contract Einaudi sent to Levi, it would appear that the title being originally contemplated for that book was "Vento caldo" (Warm Wind). Still on the subject of titles, in another letter to Samuelson we learn that the original title that Levi had agreed to for the American edition of *La chiave a stella* was "The Riggers." We can only speculate as to why this title was not adopted.

At the offices of La Stampa of Turin, I met with Lorenzo Mondo, who provided me with an abundance of material that Levi published in that newspaper, now gathered, in book form, in *Terza pagina: Racconti e saggi di Primo Levi* (Torino: La Stampa, 1986).

In a conversation, Levi's wife, Lucia Morpurgo, confirmed to me (and perhaps she did so in order to gently cut short our chat because her mother-in-law needed her attention) that their son Renzo had been named after the Lorenzo about whom Levi writes in *Survival in Auschwitz* and in *Moments of Reprieve*.

In Turin, during my encounter with some of Levi's friends and colleagues, Renato Portesi, one of Levi's co-workers at the paint factory SIVA, showed me the daily logs Levi kept when he worked there. It was amazing to see the precision of these observations—handwritten and virtually totally free of erasures or revisions. Now that we know the importance that Levi placed in applying his experience as chemist to his own writings, we can better understand the clarity of his style. Portesi also shared with me an anecdote, reflective of Levi's moments of good humor and openness. According to Portesi, Levi welcomed the idea of showing what he was writing to his co-workers and receiving their comments. In *The Reawakening*, in the chapter "Vecchie strade" (Old Roads), Levi compares Cesare's action to that of an "eroe stendhaliano" (a Stendhalian hero). The comparison was not clear to Portesi and he asked Levi for an explanation. After giving it some thought, Levi admitted that he really did not know what he had meant, then adding "non sarei mica un millantatore?" (would this make me a braggart?).

My meetings with his friends Agnese Incisa and Giulio Bollati were of a more serious nature, for they discussed his recurring depression and how serious it had become just before his death.

The experience of Turin has served me well in providing an additional dimension, a kind of a more personal touch, to the course on Primo Levi I have been teaching, on alternate years, for over a decade, and offered more than once in the former University of Pennsylvania–Bryn Mawr Summer program in Florence. In fact, of my involvement with Primo Levi's works, most rewarding to me has been the influence I may have had in introducing the works of this extraordinary man to students, and the high enrolment that the course has enjoyed every time it has been offered (33 students in the semester of this writing) is suggestive of Levi's strong appeal to our young generation. In my case, this appeal has led me to offer another course, also well received, related to Levi, in our college seminar program for first-year students. With *The Periodic Table* as its centerpiece, this course focuses on the interaction, indispensable for Levi, between science and the humanities.

In addition to teaching, another reward resulting from my work on Primo Levi was my presence at the conference that gave rise to this volume of essays, and my participation in other fine symposia where, besides having had the pleasure and privilege of meeting colleagues, many of whom I also consider good friends, I have been given the opportunity of sharing my findings and at the same time of learning from and appreciating the contributions of others. I am sure we all agree that the circle of interest surrounding Levi and his writings, something that was already in clear evidence even before the publication of my book, has been widening steadily, and for good reasons. What Levi, the man and writer, offers continues to be a topic for discussion in various forums across different disciplines: literature, history, psychology, sociology, and science, just to mention some. Primo Levi has even turned up as a fictional character in other books. Here I am thinking of Thane Rosenbaum's *The Golems of Gotham*, a book I highly recommend, in which Levi is one of the golems loose in the streets of New York City.[3] As noted in other essays of this volume, Levi is the subject of films and of at least one play (Antony Sher, *Primo*). All this points to the fact that Levi, to borrow a word from the title of his most recent English publication, is indeed a "star," "tranquil" and still on the rise. Studies about him are plentiful and there are more to come. I, for one, am coediting a book of essays, *Approaches to Teaching the Writings of Primo Levi* for the MLA series "Approaches to Teaching World Literature," and I am grateful to several of my colleagues represented in this book (Millicent Marcus, Risa Sodi, Jonathan Druker, Lina Insana) for their invaluable contribution to the MLA project.

As one would expect, with all the new material that has come out on Primo Levi since 1995, my book may now be deemed somewhat out of date. It has been superseded by more thorough and perhaps more ambitious projects. This is how it should be. Now that he is universally recognized as one of the most eloquent voices on the Shoah, the attention on Levi seems to be turning more toward his creative genius, and deservedly so. One of the marks of a great author is when additional and meaningful nuances emerge with every reading of that writer's works. Levi certainly fits into this category with his inspiring words. Perhaps this is what may have led Al Filreis, professor of English at the University of Pennsylvania and director of that university's Center for Programs in Contemporary Writing, to state in an interview that appeared in the *Philadelphia Inquirer* on January 28, 2007 ("Influences: What Shapes the Minds that Make the News"), that Levi's *The Periodic Table* is the book that influenced him on the subject of how to live his own life and that he would recommend, had he "the power to order all of the Philadelphia region to read one book" (C 2).

I am gratified for whatever role I may have had in helping to make known Levi's importance and am grateful, at the same time, for whatever recognition I've received for my work—none, perhaps, more visible than my participation on NBC's "Today" show during the Turin Winter Olympics. For me, it was a metaphorical return to the city where it all started. It was another unexpected call, this time from one of the producers of NBC's daily coverage of the Olympics from Turin, who, in considering doing a piece on Primo Levi, wanted to know more about the man. The producer soon realized how important Levi was and asked if a local NBC-TV crew could come to Bryn Mawr to tape me for an interview and also take some shots of the class on Primo Levi that I was teaching. What had been a two-hour interview, with no prior preparation in terms of the questions being asked, when aired, was squeezed into footage lasting a minute or so.

In closing, I am grateful to have had the chance to reflect on the early years of Levi study in America. I do so in the spirit of an acknowledgement to all those who, with their contributions, are working to insure that Primo Levi will continue to receive the recognition he deserves.

Notes

1. Mirna Cicioni, *Primo Levi: Bridges of Knowledge* (Oxford: Berg Publishers, 1995), Risa Sodi, *A Dante of Our Time* (New York: Peter Lang, 1990).
2. Nicholas Patruno, *Understanding Primo Levi* (Columbia: University of South Carolina Press, 1995), ix.
3. Thane Rosenbaum, *The Golems of Gotham: A Novel* (New York: HarperCollins, 2002).

11

Levi's Western

"Professional Plot" and
History in *If Not Now, When?*

Mirna Cicioni

Independent Scholar

If Not Now, When?, published in 1982 and loosely based on historical facts, tells the story of a band of Eastern European Jewish partisans carrying out guerrilla activities against the German army between 1943 and 1945, in a westward progress from the forests of the Western Soviet Union to Milan, on their way to Palestine.[1] It is generally judged to be Levi's weakest work and it has not attracted significant critical attention, particularly in the English-speaking world. Its clear didactic aims are to show that some Jews, as Jews, did take up arms to fight the Germans, and to introduce the variety of Eastern European Jewish cultures to Levi's Italian readers.

These intentions have been judged too overt and too blatantly exposed in too many dialogues between the characters. In the United States, the novel was harshly dismissed by Fernanda Eberstadt as "a failure," where "men and women are wooden logs."[2] Qualified praise was given by Irving Howe ("less a depiction of events supposedly happening than [. . .] an exemplary fable, a story mediated through the desires of a writer") and Philip Roth ("the motive behind *If Not Now, When?* seems more narrowly tendentious [. . .] than the impulses that generate the autobiographical works").[3] Levi's English biographer, Ian Thomson, calls *If Not Now, When?* a "quixotic and ultimately ill-advised project" where "characters seem to exist for the sake of what they have to say."[4] In Italy, although the novel was a bestseller (four editions in the first two years) and won the prestigious Campiello and Viareggio literary prizes, and although it won enthusiastic praise from most early reviewers, a few critics pointed out that the characters were "without depth and without evolution" and that the novel as a whole was "almost a manifesto of socialist Zionism [. . .] [in which] the rhetorical and ideological component is too ponderous."[5]

Such reservations generally refer to some specific themes of the novel, in particular individual and collective Jewish identities or the representation of Eastern European *Yiddishkeit*. Without necessarily disagreeing with most of these evaluations, this chapter focuses on a different aspect of *If Not Now, When?* In an interview with his friend Roberto Vacca, Levi cheerfully admitted to another objective: "I wanted to write an adventure story, a Western" (Io volevo fare una storia di avventure, un western).[6] He expanded this notion in an interview with Stefano Jesurum: "I wanted an action novel, a Western full of passions, movement, travel, love affairs, conflicts" (Volevo un libro d'azione, un western pieno di passioni, spostamenti, viaggi, amori, conflitti).[7] The present discussion of *If Not Now, When?* starts from the assumption that by "Western," Levi meant Western *films* (which were extremely popular in Italy from the 1940s to the 1970s and therefore can be considered culturally assimilated texts). Irrespective of any authorial intention, *If Not Now, When?* can be read as a text that establishes, by means of thematic connections, an implicit dialogue with some self-questioning Western films of the 1960s. The novel also belongs to the category of twentieth-century historical fiction that has been variously called the antihistorical novel (romanzo antistorico), neohistorical novel (romanzo neostorico), or critical historical novel (romanzo storico critico) because it makes use of narrative strategies (such as the interplay of stereotypes and an explicit late twentieth-century perspective) to question "historical knowledge" as an absolute notion and to emphasize the partial and limited nature of historical representations.[8]

Although rigid definitions of genres have been problematized by postmodern critical theory, and although "the Western" is a very diverse genre, scholars tend to agree that Westerns are based on combinations of ideological tensions and contradictions arising from the notions of "violence" and "progress."[9] In specific narratives, these tensions take the form of oppositions and conflicts—between individual heroes and communities, between groups of people with different values and aims, or between the heroes' own past and present. These oppositions help the heroes define who and what they are, in an often difficult learning process, which is usually presented didactically in dialogues between the heroes or between heroes and enemies.[10]

Most comprehensive analyses of Westerns point out recurrent elements and patterns, and some argue that all Western narratives are variations on a limited number of basic plots.[11] One of these plots—a common one in the 1960s—is what Will Wright, in his influential (if now dated) structuralist study, *Six Guns and Society*, calls "the professional plot." In Wright's analysis, the heroes of the "professional plot" are a group of professional fighters who undertake to fight some strong villains; they defeat those villains and stay (or die) together.[12] Society is represented as weak and incapable of defending itself, and consequently the main emphasis is not on the relationship of the heroes to society and its values but on the relationships among the heroes.

Any attempt to read *If Not Now, When?* as a Western needs to establish an intertextual dialogue with "professional plot" films. This chapter concentrates on three classic American films released in the 1960s and very well known in Italy: *The Magnificent Seven* (1960), *The Professionals* (1966), and *The Wild Bunch* (1969). The plots are familiar and need only the briefest of summaries. In *The Magnificent Seven*, six hired guns and a young Mexican apprentice help a Mexican village fight off a group of bandits. At the end, four of the gunfighters are dead, two ride away, and the apprentice stays on in the village. *The Professionals* are four mercenaries hired for their fighting skills by a railroad owner who wants them to rescue his allegedly kidnapped wife. During the "rescue," they realize that she has in fact run away to join her lover, a guerrilla leader in the Mexican revolution. The mercenaries have a last-minute change of heart, defy their employer, and, forfeiting their reward, let his wife and her lover go back to Mexico and possibly follow them there. The members of *The Wild Bunch* are professional armed robbers with two opponents: a group of ineffectual bounty hunters on one side and an evil Mexican warlord on the other. The Bunch at first offers its services to the warlord, but when he captures and kills the youngest and most idealistic of them, the others take him and his men on, knowing that this is their last fight. Almost everyone perishes in a final apocalyptic shootout.[13]

Westerns, like all generic texts, usually rely on conventional characters, situations, and narrative structures in varying combinations.[14] In "professional plot" Westerns, the narrative tensions and oppositions are due to the different skills, ethnic identities, life histories, and personal conflicts that each member of the group brings to the job. In *The Magnificent Seven*, the seven gunfighters are variations on generic stock characters. Chris, the leader, is black-clad, laconic, and mysterious; Vin, his second-in-command, is easygoing and ironic as well as coolly competent; another gunfighter, half Irish and half Mexican, moves from one cultural identity to the other; another is silent and self-contained, and joins the fight to test himself; another hides his pathological fear of fighting; one is motivated by greed almost to the end of the narrative; and the Mexican apprentice is a young peon who hero-worships the hired guns and identifies with them until he is forced to acknowledge that there is little difference between gunfighters and marauding bandits. The four mercenaries in *The Professionals* represent more explicitly historical and political types. Rico, the leader, is an ex-military man and strategist; Bill is a dynamiter who fought beside Rico with Teddy Roosevelt's Rough Riders and then in Pancho Villa's revolution; Hans, a German rancher, loves horses and is horrified by violence; Jake, an African American, is a bounty hunter, a skilled tracker, and a dead shot with a bow and arrow. In *The Wild Bunch*, the Bunch consists of Pike, the quasi-military leader; Dutch, his loyal longtime companion; two amoral and callous brothers; an old man; and Angel, a young Mexican, the only man who is still relatively innocent.

In *If Not Now, When?*, the members of the Jewish band are not "professionals": each of them is a representative of a hitherto oppressed, powerless group and has made the specific choice to become involved in armed fighting for his or her own particular reasons. But, like the heroes of the three Westerns, they tend toward the stereotypical in that they are stock types both of various kinds of "partisan fighters" and of diverse cultural and ethnic identities. Five are ex-soldiers; one is a polyglot actor; one is a former ritual butcher who has transferred his skill in handling a knife to profane contexts; two have worked on farms; one—the leader—plays the fiddle. Nearly all are Russian; one is half Polish; three are survivors of destroyed *shtetlach*; one is a rabbi's widow; one is a Sephardic Jew; one is a socialist Zionist feminist; and one is the token non-Jew, whose function— not unlike the function of the Mexican apprentice vis-à-vis the rest of the *Magnificent Seven*—is to ask naïve questions, so that his comrades may enlighten him (and presumably Levi's Italian readers) about Jewish history and culture. The group finds itself in opposition not only to the soldiers of the Wehrmacht but also, at different times, to Russian partisans who do not accept Jews in their bands, Poles who mistrust Jews, Allied armies who attempt to neutralize and disarm the band, and finally, Western European Jews who do not share any of the band's culture and attitudes.

Another constant opposition is between who the band members are now and the memory of who and what they were before the war. The contrast between past and present identities is constructed as a source of learning and freedom—the freedom that comes from contradicting all the prevailing clichés of peaceful, defenseless Jewish victims: "children of merchants, tailors, rabbis, and cantors; they had armed themselves with weapons taken from the Germans, they had earned the right to wear those tattered uniforms [. . .]; in the *partisanka* adventure, different every day, in the frozen steppe, in snow and mud, they had found a new freedom, unknown to their fathers and grandfathers, a contact with friends and enemies, with nature and with action, which intoxicated them like the wine of Purim" (111).[15]

The notion of being the opposite of negative stereotypes is reiterated through a series of metaphors in a song that is sung and played by the leader, Gedaleh, and that had originally been written by a captured Jewish partisan a few minutes before he was executed:

Do you recognize us? We're the sheep of the ghetto,
Shorn for a thousand years, resigned to outrage.
We are the tailors, the scribes and the cantors,
Withered in the shadow of the Cross.
Now we have learned the paths of the forest,
We have learned to shoot, and we aim straight. (127)[16]

The song links the choice to fight to issues of dignity, identity, and ethics. An echo of its words underlies Gedaleh's explanation to a non-Jewish
Polish partisan: "We're fighting to save ourselves from the Germans, to get
revenge, to clear the way for ourselves, but most of all—and excuse the
solemn word—for dignity" (195; Combattiamo per salvarci dai tedeschi,
per vendicarci, per aprirci la strada; ma soprattutto, perdonami la parola
grossa, per dignità [422]). The theme of dignity echoes through Western
films, where it has central importance. In the individualistic Westerns of
the 1950s, the question for the loner hero was whether or not to fight; in
the "professional plots" of the 1960s, the question for the groups of fighters
becomes what they are fighting *for*.

In the didactic mode that prevails in this subgenre, the characters
repeatedly ask this question of themselves and of one another, and the
only answer they can come up with is the fact that the group has made a
commitment that must be honored to the end, even when the job appears
doomed to failure and defeat. "We took a contract," Chris says in *The Magnificent Seven* when Vin points out that the odds are against them. "It's not
the kind courts enforce," objects Vin. "That's just the kind you've got to
keep," Chris states quietly and forcefully. This ethical perspective takes on
a more overt political form in *The Professionals*, when the Mexican guerrilla leader—while exchanging gunfire with Bill, who had fought alongside
him in Pancho Villa's army—explains that violence needs to have meaning:
"We stay because we believe. We leave because we're disillusioned. We come
back because we're lost. We die because we're committed." The implication
is that, by contrast with the revolutionaries, the four mercenaries are alive
but are also disillusioned and lost. The theme underlying *The Wild Bunch* is
the fact that, until the very end, the actions of the Bunch are totally without
a purpose. "I need to make one good score and then back off," says Pike at
the beginning, after a carefully planned robbery has gone catastrophically
wrong. "Back off *to what*?" snaps Dutch. Pike's recurrent order "Let's go" is
consistently followed by the men, even though no one is sure where he is
going and why. They only find a meaning at the end, with their attempted
rescue of their captured comrade that means certain death for them all.
Pike's last "Let's go" is met with a grim "Why not?" before the men march
purposefully toward the final confrontation.

In *If Not Now, When?*, Gedaleh's certainties about what the band is fight-ing for is just one of the many discourses in a polyphonic text. In one of the first battles, the oldest man shouts an ironic challenge as the band faces overwhelming odds: "We're fighting for three lines in the history books" (66; Stiamo combattendo per tre righe nei libri di storia [282]). The irony of the understatement, "three lines," highlights one of the central aspects of Levi's writing: the passionate wish to contribute to preventing the erosion and loss of the Jewish past, and to ensure continuity by giving a voice to the people who are ignored by official records. Yet the statement is ambivalent: while overtly self-deprecating, it creates an implicit opposition between the dignity of the Jewish armed group and their erasure from the "big picture" of official history. Furthermore, the hope of a place—however small—in a future history provides little motivation to men and women who are all too aware that their past has been irrevocably destroyed and that their future is uncertain: "Their homes no longer existed: they had been swept away, burned by the war or by slaughter, bloodied by the squads of hunters of men; tomb houses, of which it was best not to think, houses of ashes. Why go on living, why fight? For what house, what country, what future?" (100).[17]

The text continually emphasizes the ambiguous position of the heroes, who have recently discovered determination and pride but who also see themselves as outsiders who do not belong anywhere: "Our homes don't exist any more, and neither do our families; and if we did go back, maybe nobody would want us, like when you take a wedge out of a log and the wood closes again" (165; le nostre case non ci sono più, e neanche le nostre famiglie; e se tornassimo, forse nessuno ci vorrebbe, come quando si toglie un cuneo da un ceppo, e poi il legno si richiude [390]). Uncertainty and lack of hope prevail in the musings of Mendel—the character through whose point of view the story is told, and the only character who evolves in the course of the narrative by acknowledging his own contradictions—as soon as he hears that the war is over: "He felt as if he had escaped a raging storm at sea, and had landed on a deserted and unknown land. Not ready, not prepared, empty [. . .] Our war, too, is over, the time of dying and killing is over, and yet I am not happy [. . .] Where is my house? It is in no place. [. . .] A man enters his house and hangs up his clothes and his memories; where do you hang your memories, Mendel, son of Nachman?" (213–14).[18]

Mendel's reflections are vaguely reminiscent of the somber way that Chris and Vin, in *The Magnificent Seven*, sum up their lives for the benefit of their apprentice: "After a while you can call bartenders and faro-dealers by their first name—maybe two hundred of 'em. Rented rooms you live in: five hundred. Meals you eat in hash houses: a thousand. Home: none. Wife: none. Kids: none. Prospects: zero. [. . .] Places you're tied down to: none. People with a hold on you: none. Men you step aside for: none."

A further intertextual reference to *The Magnificent Seven* in *If Not Now, When?* reinforces the theme of purposelessness and nonbelonging. After the Jewish partisan band has stopped for a few days in a Polish village and has helped the farmers with the harvest, the village mayor says, "I'm glad I met you. I'm glad you harvested for us. I'm glad I talked with you the way a man speaks with friends, but I'm also glad you're going away." In *The Magnificent Seven*, after the bandits have been defeated, the two surviving gunfighters take their leave from the wise old man of the Mexican village. "They [the farmers] wouldn't be sorry to have you stay," says the old man. "They won't be sorry to see us go, either," says Chris. "Yes. The fighting is over. [. . .] [The farmers] are like the land itself. [. . .] You are like the wind, blowing over the land and passing on" (Sono contento di avervi incontrato. Sono contento che voi abbiate mietuto per noi. Sono contento di aver parlato con voi come si parla con amici, ma sono anche contento che voi ve ne andiate).[19]

That the possibility of being part of a harmonious communal life is denied to professional groups foregrounds an inescapable contradiction. The core value of these groups is competence, doing the job right—what Levi often refers to as *l'amore per il lavoro ben fatto*, love for a job well done.[20] However, in action texts, "the job" involves killing. This is usually justified in terms of necessity and a lack of alternatives.[21] When action texts (such as *If Not Now, When?* and Westerns) are historical narratives set in the past, reflections about violence are an important element in the implied connection between the representations of the past and the political issues of the time when each text was produced. "Professional plot" Westerns belong to the 1960s and can easily be read as increasingly critical metaphors for US policies of intervention in Third World countries. Over the course of the flawlessly executed "rescue" of the runaway wife in *The Professionals*—a film made in 1966, when the Johnson administration was deploying increasing numbers of Marines in "search and destroy" missions in South Vietnam—the ethics of the job well done leads to the deaths of scores of innocent Mexicans, and the last-minute replacement of the ethics of competence with the ethics of solidarity is too abrupt to be totally convincing. *The Magnificent Seven* and *The Wild Bunch*—the former made in 1960, when the Kennedy administration was sending technical advisers to Vietnam and other Third World countries, and the latter made in 1969, at the height of the large-scale ground war in Vietnam—represent professional competence as something shared by heroes and villains alike, which makes any distinction between them blurred and problematic.[22]

In Levi's novel, doing the job right is central to survival and self-respect: "Mendel [. . .] admired the military preparation of the Gedalists. From what he had seen of their behavior so far, he would have expected them to be foolhardy, as they indeed were; but he hadn't foreseen the economy and the precision of their fire, and their correct technique with which they had stationed themselves. Tailors, scribes and cantors, their song said; but they had learned their new profession quickly and well" (131).[23]

At the same time—as Levi concludes in his last work, *The Drowned and the Saved*—"love for a job well done is a deeply ambiguous virtue" (98). Efficient killing in *If Not Now, When?* is presented as necessary, but always with a degree of ambivalence. When the young, non-Jewish Piotr asks Mendel how many Germans he has killed, Mendel explains his choices as inevitable retaliation: "In my village the Germans made the Jews dig a pit, then they lined them up along the edge, and they shot them all [. . .] And after that I think that killing is bad, but killing the Germans is something we can't avoid. [. . .] Because killing is the only language they understand, the only argument that convinces them. If I shoot at a German, he is forced to admit that I, a Jew, am worth more than he is: that's his logic, you understand, not mine" (78).[24]

However inevitable it may be, retaliatory violence inevitably soils and corrupts. When one of the band members, a young woman, is murdered in Germany immediately after the end of the war, her comrades avenge her by slaughtering a group of ten Germans. Mendel voices his doubts: "We did what they did: ten hostages for one German killed" (Abbiamo fatto come loro: dieci ostaggi per un tedesco ucciso). Gedaleh replies, "Maybe you're right, Mendel. But then how do you explain the fact that now I feel better?" (243; Forse hai ragione, Mendel. Ma allora, come si spiega che io adesso mi sento meglio?). And Mendel admits, "Yes, I feel better, too, but this doesn't prove anything" (Sì, anch'io mi sento meglio, ma questo non dimostra niente [473]).

The discourse on violence takes on additional significance in view of the fact that *If Not Now, When?* appeared in April 1982, two months before the Israeli invasion of Lebanon (with which Levi strongly disagreed, as evidenced in the open letter against the then-prime minister Begin, which he cosigned in mid June) and five months before the massacres in the refugee camps of Sabra and Shatila by Christian militias in Israeli-occupied West Beirut (which Levi strongly condemned in an interview in the left-of-center daily paper, *La Repubblica*). In the wake of these events, parallels were made by reviewers of all political persuasions between the armed Jews of the novel and the armed Israelis of Begin's army, usually with the conclusion that Levi's partisans "are unlike the self-assured Israelis, who have no doubts and no irony, and proudly emerge from the turrets of Begin's and Sharon's tanks" (non assomigliano agli israeliani sicuri di sé, senza dubbi, e senza ironia, che dominano dalle torrette dei carri armati di Begin e Sharon).[25]

Just as ambiguous and contradictory as the reflections on competence and violence is another aspect of action texts: the fact that discourses that

link self-respect to using weapons exclude all people who do not take part
in armed combat, such as women. In the three Western films examined
here, the only exception is the runaway wife in *The Professionals* (who is
Mexican and passionately explains her actions as a contribution to her
country's resistance to American power). In *If Not Now, When?*, the only
woman who speaks about dignity and commitment is the socialist Zionist
feminist Line, characterized as a very skilled fighter; at the same time, the
text constructs her as lacking compassion and tenderness, and not as "a
woman for a lifetime" (277; una donna per la vita [509]).[26] Mendel's prevailing point of view repeatedly presents women in terms of the support
and solace they can give men: "A woman is the best remedy for loneliness"
(203; una donna è il miglior rimedio contro la solitudine [430]).

Mendel's views of women represent one of several diverse prejudiced
opinions that are played off against one another in the novel without
any one discourse dominating; this produces ironic estrangement effects.
Oppositions between national stereotypes implicitly produce questions
about the nature of "historical knowledge." Readers who may laugh at the
superficial notions of Italy held by unsophisticated Eastern European Jews
("the land of the mild climate and notorious, open illegality; the affection-
ate mafioso land whose double reputation had reached even Norway and
the Ukraine and the sealed ghettoes of Eastern Europe" [252]) must then
reconsider the extent to which conceptualizations of Jews as "the tailors,
the scribes and the cantors / Withered in the shadow of the Cross" are also
misleading, in both Eastern and Western Europe.[27] Readers approaching
If Not Now, When? in and after 1982 may well be surprised by the band's
dream of Palestine, the destination of their journey, as a happy pastoral-
socialist utopia: "We don't want to become landowners: we want to make
fertile the sterile land of Palestine, plant orange trees and olive trees in the
desert and make it fruitful. [...] we want communities where you can work
during the day and, in the evening, play the violin; where there's no money,
but everyone does what work he can and is given what he needs" (195).[28]
This vision does not convince Mendel, who at the end of the journey is
still skeptical: "From the promised land he received no summons; perhaps
there, too, he would have to march and fight. Very well, it's my destiny, I
accept it, but it doesn't warm my heart" (252).[29]

The band's journey and the novel end in Italy, with the juxtaposition
of two transparent symbols: a baby (predictably, a boy) born to the two
most innocent members of the band, and a newspaper headline incomprehensible to the band members, which the authorial voice reveals to be a
report of the first atom bomb dropped on Hiroshima. The ambivalence of
the ending is primarily created by the obvious irony of the juxtaposition,
which challenges the notion of a war with one identifiable "good side" and

one identifiable enemy—what Levi in *The Drowned and the Saved* calls the "simple model" of history.[30] There is also, however, a total lack of reassuring certainties. By the final pages, readers are aware that, for most of the band, Palestine is a default solution: the members have gained independence and dignity but the future is uncertain for them and for the world. "Sarà guerra sempre," there will always be war, says the Polish partisan Edek, echoing Mordo Nahum in *The Truce*, "Guerra è sempre" (242), there is always war (52): there is little hope for change and renewal after the defeat of Germany. The only certainty for the band members is the loyalty and solidarity of their comrades: "Duty isn't a wealth. Neither is the future. They, yes. They are my riches; they remain to me. All of them: with their roughness and their faults, even those who have offended me, and those I have offended" (252).[31]

The endings of "professional plot" Westerns tend to be similarly tinged with pessimism: in all three films examined here, a group of villains was eliminated, but the system that produces the villains did not change. The oppressed Mexican people's chances for independence seem poor, while the professional fighters are left with, if anything, pride in their professionalism and the loyalty and solidarity of one or two friends. "We lost. We always lose," Chris in the *Magnificent Seven* says to Vin as they ride away from a village that no longer needs or wants them. Two former comrades of *The Wild Bunch* and the disenchanted mercenaries in *The Professionals* embrace the Mexican revolution as a default utopia because they have nowhere else to go, just as the survivors of the Jewish partisan band go to Palestine because antisemitism is still rife in Eastern Europe, Western Europe is too alien, and no other alternatives seem viable.

The dialogue between these texts produces a common view of history as consistently oppressive and uncertain, which encourages late twentieth-century viewers and readers—who have the benefit of hindsight—to make connections between past and present. The statement "We are fighting for three lines in the history books," so significant for the Jewish band, is remembered by Mendel when a Polish partisan says that he and his comrades are fighting because they want to demonstrate to the world, by dying if necessary, that they still exist (190). Readers in the 1980s would readily think of Polish Prime Minister Jaruzelski outlawing and attempting to silence the general union *Solidarnosc*. For Italian readers, the apparently self-deprecating understatement, "three lines," also establishes an implicit connection with the audience of "twenty-five readers" that the great nineteenth-century writer Alessandro Manzoni hypothesized for his historical novel, *I promessi sposi* (*The Betrothed*). *If Not Now, When?* establishes an intertextual dialogue with *The Betrothed* as well as with Westerns, because both novels question the grand narratives of official history and determinedly foreground the effects of political events on ordinary people (in Manzoni's ironic definition, "gente meccaniche e di piccol affare," or lowly, unimportant tradespeople).[32] For Manzoni, a Catholic convert, there is no chance of justice in human history. As he put it in his 1822 tragedy, *Adelchi*, the only possible choice for human beings is to oppress or to be oppressed—or, in other words, "all we can do / is wrong others, or be wronged" (non resta / che far torto o patirlo).[33] The only source of hope for Manzoni's characters is religious faith, and the question of why innocents are caused to suffer remains unanswered: the well-known conclusion of *The Betrothed* is that "when [troubles] come, either by our fault or by no fault of our own, faith in God makes them easier to bear and makes them useful for a better life" (quando [i guai] vengono, o per colpa o senza colpa, la fiducia in Dio li raddolcisce, e li rende utili per una vita migliore).[34] The question of why innocents suffer also remains unanswered in the humanist, nonreligious perspective of *If Not Now, When?*. Although there is evidence of human solidarity, a humanist outlook is repeatedly challenged by the persecution the characters suffered before they join the band and by the violence, prejudice, and hatred they experience during their journey.

"I am a naïve reader and I have written a book for naïve readers, an unsophisticated book" (Sono un lettore ingenuo e ho scritto un libro per lettori ingenui, un libro non sofisticato), Levi said in a 1982 interview with the Italian journalist Fiona Diwan.[35] Although it would be hard to disagree with Levi's self-deprecating assessment in view of the novel's ubiquitous didactic comments and the characters' lack of development, *If Not Now, When?* cannot be summarily dismissed as an unsophisticated work. The novel extends beyond the adventures of a specific group of people and challenges official history's criteria by representing history as a tangle of conflicting positions and ideologies rather than a linear grand narrative. Through its interplay of stock characters and cultural stereotypes, it shows the partial and "marked" nature of different perspectives on history. Above all, it encourages its readers to think in terms of historical ambiguity through its intertextual dialogue with the "professional plot" Westerns of 20 years earlier, which expressed political unease through heroes who were at the same time brave, quixotic, disenchanted with the ethics of professionalism, and disenchanted with their roles vis-à-vis their weaker neighbors.

Notes

1. All page references are to the Italian edition of *Se non ora, quando?* in volume 2 of Levi's *Opere*, ed. Marco Belpoliti (Turin: Einaudi, 1997) and to the English translation *If Not Now, When?*, trans. William Weaver (London: Abacus, 1987).

Many sincere thanks to Miriam Lang for her invaluable advice on the language, and occasionally the content, of this chapter. In 1980, Levi came across some notes on a story he had previously heard from his friend Emilio Vita-Finzi, who, in 1945, had worked in Milan for a welfare organization for Jewish refugees and camp survivors. Vita-Finzi had met and been impressed by a group of Russian Jews who had formed a partisan unit in the Soviet Union and had fought their way through Eastern Europe, stopping briefly in Italy on their way to Palestine. See Levi's afterword *to If Not Now, When?* (English: 511–13, Italian: 279–81).

2. Fernanda Eberstadt, "Reading Primo Levi," *Commentary* (October 1985): 47.
3. Irving Howe, "How To Write About the Holocaust," *New York Review of Books* March 28, 1985, 17; Philip Roth, "A Man Saved by His Skills" [1986], in *The Voice of Memory. Interviews 1961–87*, ed. Marco Belpoliti and Robert Gordon (Cambridge: Polity Press, 2001), 20.
4. Ian Thomson, *Primo Levi. A Life* (London: Hutchinson, 2002), 409, 419.
5. "Romano Luperini, "La lunga traversia non ha fine," review of *Se non ora, quando?*, *Gazzetta del Mezzogiorno* (May 27, 1982): 3. The 1982 Campiello prize was known as the Supercampiello, since the September 1982 award was the twentieth award. Alberto Cavaglion, "La scelta di Gedeone: appunti su Primo Levi e l'ebraismo," *Journal of the Institute of Romance Studies* 4 (1966): 194.
6. Roberto Vacca, "Un western dalla Russia a Milano," *Il Giorno*, May 18, 1982, 3, quoted in Gabriella Poli and Giorgio Calcagno, *Echi di una voce perduta: Incontri, interviste, e conversazioni con Primo Levi* (Milan: Mursia, 1992), 257. Romano Luperini, *La città* (Milano: Einaudi, 1999).
7. Stefano Jesurum, "Si è offuscata la luce della stella d'Israele," *Oggi*, July 14, 1982, 82. See also the interview with Philip Roth in Belpoliti and Gordon, *The Voice of Memory*, 20.
8. Vittorio Spinazzola, *Il romanzo antistorico* (Rome: Editori Riuniti, 1990); Margherita Ganeri, *Il romanzo storico in Italia: Il dibattito critico dalle origini al postmoderno* (Lecce: Piero Manni, 1999), 101–24; Cristina Della Coletta, *Plotting the Past: Metamorphoses of Historical Narrative in Modern Italian Fiction* (West Lafayette, IN: Purdue University Press, 1996), 15.
9. See Patrick McGee, *From Shane to Kill Bill: Rethinking the Western* (Oxford: Blackwell, 2007), xiv–xvii, and Lee Clark Mitchell, *Westerns: Making the Man in Fiction and Film* (Chicago: The University of Chicago Press, 1996), 3.
10. See André Glucksmann, "Le avventure della tragedia," trans. Gianni Volpi, in *Il Western: Fonti forme miti registi attori filmografia*, ed. Raymond Bellour (Milan: Feltrinelli, 1973).
11. See the essays collected in Bellour, *Il Western* (particularly the multi-authored "Miti," 137–239), and in Jim Kitses and Gregg Rickman, eds., *The Western Reader* (New York: Limelight, 1999), particularly "Authorship and Genre: Notes on the Western," by Jim Kitses (57–68) and "Pilgrims and the Promised Land: A Genealogy of the Western," by Doug Williams (93–114).
12. Adapted from Will Wright, *Six Guns and Society: A Structural Study of the Western* (Berkeley: University of California Press, 1975), 113.

13. For in-depth analyses of all three films, see Richard Slotkin, *Gunfighter Nation: The Myth of the Frontier in Twentieth-Century America* (New York: Atheneum, 1992), 474–86, 567–74, and 598–603, and McGee, *From* Shane *to* Kill Bill, 143–66. A useful analysis of *The Wild Bunch* is in Jim Kitses, *Horizons West*, 2nd ed. (London: BFI, 2004), 217–23.

14. See the multiauthored chapter "Miti" in Bellour, *Il Western*, and the chapter "A Man Is Being Beaten" in Mitchell, *Westerns*, 150–87.

15. "figli di mercanti, sarti, rabbini e cantori, si erano armati con le armi tolte ai tedeschi, si erano conquistati il diritto ad indossare quelle uniformi lacere [. . .]; nell'avventura ogni giorno diversa della *Partisanka*, nella steppa gelata, nella neve e nel fango avevano trovato una libertà nuova, sconosciuta ai loro padri e ai loro nonni, un contatto con uomini amici e nemici, con la natura e con l'azione, che li ubriacava come il vino di Purim." (Levi, *Se non ora, quando?*, in *Opere*, 2:331–32)

16. "Ci riconoscete? Siamo le pecore del ghetto, / Tosate per mille anni, rassegnate all'offesa. / Siamo i sarti, i copisti ed i cantori / Appassiti nell'ombra della Croce. / Ora abbiamo imparato i sentieri della foresta, / Abbiamo imparato a sparare, e colpiamo diritto" (Levi, *Se non ora, quando?*, in *Opere*, 2:348).

17. "Le loro case non c'erano più: erano state spazzate via, incendiate dalla guerra o dalla strage, insanguinate dalle squadre dei cacciatori d'uomini; case-tomba, a cui era meglio non pensare, case di cenere. Perché vivere ancora, perché combattere? Per quale casa, per quale patria, per quale avvenire?" (Levi, *Se non ora, quando?*, in *Opere*, 2:319).

18. "Si sentiva come sfuggito a un mare in tempesta, e approdato solo su una terra deserta e sconosciuta. Non pronto, non preparato, vuoto [. . .] Anche la nostra guerra è finita, è finito il tempo di morire e di uccidere, eppure io non sono contento [. . .] Dov'è la mia casa? è in nessun luogo. [. . .] Uno entra in una casa e appende gli abiti e i ricordi; dove appendi i tuoi ricordi, Mendel figlio di Nachman?" (Levi, *Se non ora, quando?*, in *Opere*, 2:440–41)

19. Levi, *Opere*, 2:391; English trans. by William Weaver, 166.

20. For a lucid discussion of Levi's ethics of work, see chapter 6, "Practice, or Trial and Error," in Robert Gordon, *Primo Levi's Ordinary Virtues: From Testimony to Ethics* (Oxford: Oxford University Press, 2001).

21. Jane Tompkins, *West of Everything: The Inner Life of Westerns* (Oxford: Oxford University Press, 1992) argues that Westerns "exist in order to provide a justification for violence" (227–28).

22. For a general reading of Westerns as historical-political metaphors and the problematic nature of professionalism, see Gianni Volpi's essay "L'ultima frontiera" in Bellour, *Il Western*, 92–134. For in-depth analyses of the echoes of American international politics in *The Magnificent Seven*, *The Professionals*, and *The Wild Bunch*, see Philip French, *Westerns: Aspects of a Movie Genre* (London: Secker and Warburg, 1973, especially chapter 1), Slotkin, *Gunfighter Nation* (especially 480–85, 570–74, and 600–602), and McGee, *From* Shane *to* Kill Bill (especially chapter 7).

23. "Mendel [...] ammirò la preparazione militare dei gedalisti. Da quanto aveva visto delle loro maniere fino a quel momento, si sarebbe aspettato che fossero spericolati, come infatti erano; ma non aveva previsto la precisione e l'economia del loro fuoco, e la tecnica corretta con cui si erano disposti. Sarti, copisti e cantori, diceva la loro canzone: ma avevano imparato presto e bene il loro nuovo mestiere" (Levi, *Se non ora, quando?*, in *Opere*, 2:352–53).

24. "Al mio paese i tedeschi hanno fatto scavare una fossa dagli ebrei, e poi li hanno messi in piedi sull'orlo, e li hanno fucilati tutti [...] E dopo di allora io penso che uccidere sia brutto, ma che di uccidere i tedeschi non ne possiamo fare a meno. [...] Perché uccidere è il solo linguaggio che capiscono, il solo ragionamento che li fa convinti. Se io sparo a un tedesco, lui è costretto ad ammettere che io ebreo valgo piú di lui: è la sua logica, capisci, non la mia" (Levi, *Se non ora, quando?*, in *Opere*, 2:295).

25. See Thomson, *Primo Levi*, 427–36, and Mirna Cicioni, *Primo Levi: Bridges of Knowledge* (Oxford: Berg, 1995), 127–30; Filippo Gentiloni, "Quando la stella di David era la bandiera dei perseguitati," *Il manifesto* (June 29, 1982): 6.

26. For a discussion of Line, see Enzo Neppi, "Sopravvivenza e vergogna in Primo Levi," in *Appartenenza e differenza: Ebrei d'Italia e letteratura*, ed. Juliette Hassine, Jacques Misan-Montefiore, and Sandra Debenedetti-Stow (Florence: La Giuntina, 1997), 123–24.

27. "Il paese del dolce clima e dell'illegalità notoria, aperta; il paese affettuoso-mafioso la cui fama bivalente era arrivata fino in Norvegia e in Ucraina e nei ghetti sigillati dell'Europa orientale" (Levi, *Se non ora, quando?*, in *Opere*, 2:482).

28. "Non desideriamo diventare proprietari: desideriamo rendere fertile la terra sterile della Palestina, piantare aranci e ulivi nel deserto e farlo fruttificare [...] vogliamo comunità in cui si possa faticare di giorno, e alla sera suonare il violino; in cui non ci sia denaro, ma ognuno lavori secondo le sue capacità e riceva secondo i suoi bisogni" (Levi, *Se non ora, quando?*, in *Opere*, 2:421–22).

29. "Dalla terra promessa non gli veniva alcun richiamo, forse anche laggiù avrebbe dovuto camminare e combattere. Bene, è il mio destino, lo accetto, ma non mi scalda il cuore" (Levi, *Se non ora, quando?*, in *Opere*, 2:482).

30. *The Drowned and the Saved*, in *Opere*, 2:1018 (23–24).

31. "Il dovere non è una ricchezza. neanche l'avvenire lo è; loro sí, di loro sono ricco, loro mi rimangono. Tutti: con le loro ruvidezze e difetti, anche quelli che mi hanno offeso, anche quelli che ho offeso io" (Levi, *Se non ora, quando?*, in *Opere*, 2:482).

32. Alessandro Manzoni, *I Promessi Sposi*, ed. Gilda Sbrilli (1841–1842; Florence: Bulgarini, 2000), 2.

33. Alessandro Manzoni, *Adelchi* (Milan: Garzanti, 2007), 354–55 (my translation).

34. Manzoni, *I Promessi Sposi*, 892 (my translation).

35. Fiona Diwan, "Sono un ebreo ma non sono mai stato sionista," *Corriere Medico* 3–4 (September 1982): 15.

12

Mind the Gap

Performance and Semiosis in Primo Levi

Ellen Nerenberg
Wesleyan University

I can say without fear of exaggeration or flattery that the television and especially the radio versions of my work have been of great importance to me, because they filled a void that I had never filled before, the space of live representation, of the theatre, that I have scarcely touched on, of cinema that I have never encountered. The experience of reaching an audience directly, not through the medium of the pages of a book, but through the eye and the ear, was extremely stimulating to me.

—Primo Levi, "The Little Theatre of Memory"

A lthough much has been said of Primo Levi's use of language, its epis-temological and ethical bases, and its negotiation of that which is unspeakable, his attempts at a performative mode have not enjoyed the same critical attention.[1] My chapter focuses on performance and its place in and its relation to Levi's work. The motif of performance in Levi's prose narrative has received some critical attention and the performances of Levi's works adapted for the stage have also enjoyed some critical consideration. Performances of Levi's work in other media, however, and especially for the radio, are as yet under-studied. In this chapter, I bring into proximity these varied types of live performance (as opposed to cinematic adaptation) to interrogate the shifts that these generic differences impose on linguistic codes and contexts. After investigating some key examples of theatrical performance in Levi's prose narrative, I focus principally on performances of his work that took place during his lifetime, and primarily on performances of *Se questo è un uomo* (*Survival at Auschwitz*).[2] I will have occasion, toward my conclusion, to briefly discuss Sir Antony Sher's 2004–2005 performances of his dramatic one-man show, *Primo*.

The gap I refer to in the title has several interrelated meanings that are geographical, historical, and linguistic in nature. Chief among these is the potential opening, or aporia, between the two constitutive parts of the linguistic sign, the signifier (a word in either graphic or acoustical context) and the signified (the concept or the meaning the signifier indicates). Levi believed mightily in clear language, especially for a topic like the representation of the Lager. In his 1976 essay "Dello scrivere oscuro" (On Obscure Writing), Levi observes that "He who does not know how to communicate, or communicates badly, in a code that belongs only to him or a few others, is unhappy, and spreads unhappiness around him. If he communicates badly deliberately, he is *wicked*, or at least a discourteous person, because he imposes labor, anguish, or boredom on his readers."[3] Levi found clarity essential, but also asserted the imperative for accuracy in the portrayal of Nazi violence, as his 1977 excoriation of Liliana Cavani's film *Il portiere di notte* (*The Night Porter*) of three years earlier illustrates.[4]

Performances in and of Levi's works, I argue, illuminate this drive for clarity.[5] At the same time, performance by its very nature defies attempts to control signification, for the proliferation of semiotic signs found in performance exceeds such control. As a semiotician of the theater, Tadeusz Kowzan has observed, "Everything is sign in theatrical presentation . . . [The] spectacle uses the word as well as non-linguistic systems of signification."[6] Study of performance in and of Levi's writing reveals the tension inherent in the adaptation of prose to a performative medium. However, and perhaps more valuably, study of a fuller spectrum of live performance in and of Levi allows us to evaluate Levi's changing relationship to linguistic signification of the Holocaust over time.

The performances of Levi's work during his lifetime derive principally, but not exclusively, from his testimonial, *Survival in Auschwitz*, and may be considered in the context of the author's own re-elaboration of that text over time.[7] Levi's participation in the adaptation of this material differed markedly from, for example, the performances of his texts not treating the Camp, a point I return to shortly. Levi's control over artistic decisions about the adaptation of his works may obviate concerns like those voiced by Bryan Cheyette in a recent essay concerning the various "appropriations" of Levi as "text and totem" of the Holocaust.[8] Levi's enthusiasm about the potential of performance and participation in adaptations of his work notwithstanding, examination of the performances produced during his life reveal a need for control over meaning and meaning-making (signification *tout court*). This is demonstrated by Levi's hesitation at releasing the linguistic sign from its "home" in prose, where meaning may arguably be more easily anchored and therefore greater control over it maintained, into the less predictable arena of performance.

Scholarship on Levi's work has fruitfully addressed some aspects of the issue of performance and translation between generic forms.[9] Recent biographies of Levi chart the chronology of the works, their performances, and Levi's location in time and space vis-à-vis those performances.[10] In her excellent study, theater anthropologist Helga Finter focuses exclusively on the Turin production of *Se questo è un uomo*, placing it in the context not of other works within Levi's oeuvre, as I do, but of other European dramatic representations of the Shoah.[11] As Finter fits Levi into an extra-Italian context, Paolo Puppa's examination of Levi's "hidden theater" situates his work within the history and development of Italian theater. Lina Insana, on the other hand, details shifts between adaptations of Levi's texts, with special focus on post-1987 productions, specifically on Sir Antony Sher's 2004–2005 performances of his dramatic monologue *Primo*, Davide Ferrario and Marco Belpoliti's 2007 film *La strada di Levi* (Primo Levi's Journey), and Belpoliti's chronicle of the making of that film, *La prova*, published the same year. My focus on the semiotic potential of Levi's work as illustrated by the examples of performance found in his prose, how this potential is tapped at various points in his career as a writer, and what this reveals about Levi's understanding of representation of the Shoah fits between and adjacent to the research that has preceded it.

Levi's performed works travel a route that outlines another gap, in addition to the linguistic one, between signified and signifier described earlier. The path of performance moves between media (stage, radio, television) as well as between companies and theaters that are privately owned and operated and those that are publicly funded. Concerning their Italian reception, the itinerary of performance brings Levi's works increasingly toward a center. For example, the starting point of performance—on Canadian Public Radio—is radically marginal, geographically speaking, to both Levi as well as to Italian society. The subsequent move to RAI Radio, however, marks reentry into Italy of Levi's performed work and reveals a willingness to commit state funding (albeit regionally disbursed) to Levi's testimony of the Holocaust. Finally, yet another gap emerges between Levi, sober scientist and survivor, and Levi the writer. Although Levi appears not to have observed great distinctions between the varied media, as noted earlier, it is useful to remember the differing conditions of access for the radio and the theater, and what Peppino Ortoleva has described as the "geography" of the media in this period.[12]

Like the radio broadcasts, stage performances of Levi's work move to increasingly centralized locales after their beginnings on the margins. The first staged performances of Levi's works took place, quite literally, underground. In 1966, the Teatro delle Dieci, a privately funded avant-garde theater company, presented three of Levi's science fiction stories at the Ridotto del Romano (the basement of the Romano cinema). Later the same year, performances of *Se questo è un uomo* were presented by Turin's Teatro Stabile (hereafter TST), the city's municipally funded theater company, at the venerable Teatro Carignano. We might also see this relocation to a more geographically central, municipally ordained location as an act corresponding to the ways in which European and specifically Italian society in this period opened to receive testimony of the Shoah, as Fabio Girelli-Carasi and Millicent Marcus have detailed.[13] Yet if this is the case, and Levi's testimony was at last making its way to a more central and consequently visible location, it was not without obstacles. As Levi biographer Ian Thomson details, even cataclysmic events of such magnitude as the November 1966 engorgement of the Arno River and the flooding of Florence that followed played a role, requiring the relocation of the premier of *Se questo è un uomo* from Florence to Levi's own Turin.[14] Not to belabor the point, but it almost seems as though a *force majeure* was required to bring Levi's Holocaust show home from its scheduled opening out of town.

Performance in Levi's Prose

Levi's prose narrative teems with semiotic markers rooted in performance. As Puppa remarks, like Dickens and Henry James, Levi's "true theater is not to be found in [his] plays."[15] In fact, use of performativity as a device spans the oeuvre, reaching from the chapter of *Survival in Auschwitz*, titled "L'ultimo" (The Last One) to, as Giuseppe Mazzotta suggests in a forthcoming essay, *The Drowned and the Saved*. The 1947 edition of *Survival in Auschwitz* concludes with "The Last One" and offers a very different textual conclusion from that of the 1958 edition.[16]

"The Last One" begins with commentary on Primo and Alberto's developing commercial acumen (their "organization" of the menashka, a sort of bucket, and the brooms) and ends with the public hanging—the thirteenth Levi had witnessed—of "Der Letzte," an inmate suspected of involvement in the Birkenau explosions of October 1944. The camp guards make a spectacle of the hanging, complete with a band that plays music at the beginning and end of the show, an announcement over the loudspeaker of the act about to take the stage, an audience of the forcibly convened detainees, and Der Letzte, the main attraction, who appears "nel fascio di luce del faro" (in the beam of the spot light).

The trajectory of the chapter, first Levi's commerce and then Der Letzte's hanging, is significant. Part of the shame that rises in him at the display of Der Letzte's courage attaches to Levi's acknowledgment of the distance between his actions and those of the man about to hang. "Vergogna," shame, is the word upon which the chapter—and the 1947 volume—close. Levi writes that the detainees watched while "at the foot of the gallows, the SS watch us pass with indifferent eyes: their work is finished, and well finished. The Russians can come now: they will only find us, the slaves, the worn-out, worthy of the unarmed death which awaits us."[17] Unlike the salvific "The Story of Ten Days," the chapter Levi added to the end of the 1958 edition, "The Last One" charts the annihilation of the noble and is the note upon which the first edition of *Survival in Auschwitz* ends. Der Letzte's cry from the gallows—"Kamaraden, ich bin der Letzte! (Comrades, I am the last one!)—dramatizes Levi's belief that those who survive are the most unfit, the weakest, those who had succumbed to the anti-logic of the dehumanizing process of the Camps.

Michel Foucault notes in *Discipline and Punish* that the disappearance of the spectacle of public execution resulted in the internalization of disciplining norms. Apparatus like Bentham's panopticon, developed in the last decade of the eighteenth century, help in the successful disciplining of delinquency that the State, influenced by Enlightenment ideals of justice and punishment, set to remove from public view. As the site for the inversion of Enlightenment philosophical ideals, Auschwitz resurrected public execution for its heuristic value, informing Levi's construction of the camps as "the world turned upside down." This inversion and the demonstrated futility of Enlightenment ideals is perhaps most clearly articulated in the chapter from *The Drowned and the Saved* titled "An Intellectual in Auschwitz" (Un intellettuale a Auschwitz), in which Levi demonstrates the uselessness of philosophy and literature in the Lager, and on which Mazzotta meditates in his aforementioned essay.

Many of the most salient passages exemplifying Levi's use of theatricality in prose are found in *The Reawakening*, the companion text to *Survival in Auschwitz* that Levi published in 1963, as Puppa and others have detailed. Performance lies at the very heart of this picaresque memoir and sheds light on the renascence of the refugees. This may provide a rationale for bestowing the title "The Reawakening" for the US market. Examples from *The Reawakening* indicate the salutary intrusion of the theatrical in the lives of the refugees. As Levi writes in the chapter "Victory Day," "uscimmo dal teatro leggermente intronati, ma *quasi commossi*" (we left the theater dazed and *almost moved;* emphasis added). A reawakening different from the horrible "Wstàwach," the Polish command that marks the text's beginning and conclusion, is possible and theatrical display is its vehicle. Performance is so crucial to the very structure of *The Reawakening* that the news the former prisoners may return home emerges from the navel of the performance of "Il naufragio degli abulici" (The Shipwreck of the Spirit-less).[18] Moreover, the publication date of 1963 stands out within the history of Levi's re-elaboration of his Holocaust experience, corresponding to an important period in the European reception of the Holocaust, as Robert Gordon points out in his essay in this collection. Levi had, in fact, already tasted the possibilities of performance in the RAI radio broadcast of the dramatic reading of "La bella addormentata nel frigo" (Sleeping Beauty in the Fridge) in 1961. Finally, 1963 is also the year in which George Whalley began his adaptation of *Survival in Auschwitz* for the Canadian Broadcast-ing Company, whose early 1964 broadcast I return to at a later point.

Puppa charts the manifestations of "hidden theater" throughout Levi's oeuvre, resonating across time of composition and generic considerations. However, as a way into an examination of Levi's system of spectacular and performative signs, I wish to meditate on "The Juggler" (Il giocaliere), a short story from *Moments of Reprieve* (Lilít e altri racconti), that has not received critical attention for its unveiling of the sort of semiosis that I have been describing. In this story, written between 1975 and 1981, the year the collection was published, Levi uses performance to distinguish between communications of all types: spoken, written, gestural, and performative.

Eddy the Juggler is a "green triangle," which, according to the Auschwitz sign system, signifies a "common thief," someone of the ranks of Befauer, who are, Levi tells us in that memorably calm and measured tone, "genta-glia," or scum. Eddy, whose name, Levi allows, was "probably for the stage," possessed "uncommon qualities" and he gives us the following description:

> Dazzlingly handsome, he was blond, of medium height, but slim, strong and very agile. He had aristocratic features and skin so light it looked translu-cent. He could not have been more than twenty-three, and he didn't give a damn about anything or anyone: the SS, work, or us. He had a serene and self-absorbed look that set him apart. The very day of his arrival he became famous. In the washroom, completely naked, after washing himself carefully with a piece of scented soap, he set it on the top of his head, which was shaved like ours, bent forward and, with imperceptible practiced and precise undulations of his back, made the luxurious piece of soap slide little by little from head to neck, then down, along the entire spinal column all the way to his coccyx, at which point he made it fall into his hand. Two or three of us applauded but he showed no sign of noticing and went off to dress, slowly and abstractedly.[19]

Eddy's considerable agility and the contortions he carefully executes transform the shower (surely not the Lager's most felicitous space and even less so for the newly arrived) into a kind of theater, complete with a performance (Eddy's undulations), a performer (Eddy himself), spectators (fellow inmates), and even applause. Without uttering a word in this story devoid of any dialogue, Eddy's body speaks a language of its own, with each articulation of the spine an enunciated syllable. In the place where spoken language is largely unintelligible (even to someone like Eddy, who speaks the Camp's hegemonic tongue), his articulating spine announces a sovereignty of the body that his fellow prisoners can only faintly remember.

The sight of Eddy's mastery of his body and the memory it evokes transfixes the onlookers, Levi among them. Indeed, the scene from Sher's 2004–2005 performances of *Primo*, famously reprised for posters advertising the New York run of the show, display the actor with one hand over his heart (or breast), the other over his genitals, recalling the affront, even outrage, of the stripping bare of the detainee's body upon arrival at Auschwitz. Sher intones, paraphrasing directly from *Survival in Auschwitz*, "already my body is not my own." If the outrage of transit, in all its "excremental horror," as Levi calls it in *The Drowned and the Saved*, were not enough, then entry into the Camp systematically stripped the body of protection and identity. We might ask whether this sign system of the body, more expressive than the spoken language surrounding him, functions for Levi as a homologue to the Italian language that, as Sander Gilman has remarked, reminds him of his former and "intact self."[20]

In "The Juggler," Levi privileges the gesture and its performance over speech, and scrutinizes Eddy's every movement. At work, he unpredictably breaks into a jig, throws a somersault, rolls a hoop, juggles, and all with the same distracted air. When Eddy, who is vice-Kapò of the squad, discovers Levi writing a letter—hazardous Lager activity, it goes without saying—he slaps him and thus gives Levi occasion to tell us about yet another dialect of Lagerspeak. He writes that "Punches and slaps passed among us as a daily language and we soon learned to distinguish meaningful blows from the others inflicted out of savagery. [. . .] A slap like Eddy's was akin to the friendly slap you give a dog" (*Moments of Reprieve*, 13).[21]

Eddy does not, as Levi fears, denounce him to the Political Section. Although Eddy communicates verbally to him, Levi, significantly, does not reproduce this oral communication in the story and writes that Eddy "mi tenne un discorso difficile da riportare" (*Lilìt*,17). [He made a speech to me that I find difficult to repeat] (*Moments of Reprieve*, 14). This story about nonverbal communication ends with a performance of another kind, a sort of *tableau vivant* or pantomime, where the sign system of the Reich and that of performance collide. Levi last sees Eddy who

> Stava in piedi nel corridoio fra il filo spinato ed il reticolato elettrico e portava appeso al collo in cartello con uno scritto "Urning," e cioè pederasta,

ma non sembrava nè afflitto nè preoccupato. Assisteva al rientro della nostra schiera con aria svagata, insolente, e indolente, come se nulla di quanto che avveniva intorno a lui lo riguardasse. (*Lilít*,17)

[(was) standing in the passage between the barbed wire and the electrified fence, and around his neck hung a sign on which was written *Urning* (pederast), but he appeared neither upset nor anxious. He watched the reentry of our work-group with a distracted, insolent, and lazy look, as though nothing that was happening around him concerned him in the slightest.] (*Moments of Reprieve*, 15)

Levi fashions a system in "The Juggler" that explicitly substitutes spoken language with the nonverbal sign of the gesture. It is no accident that Eddy is an entertainer, one trained in the re-presentation, through performance, of signs. What is Eddy "il giocaliere" juggling? Through performance, the sign customarily widens and a gap emerges between its two component parts, the signifier and the signified and they are, as it were, the balls Eddy (and Levi) keep in the air. This gap resonates within Levi's oeuvre: between signified and signifier, between spectator and spectacle, between the emitter of the sign (variously, the playwright, the actor) and its destination (the perceiving audience). This is the gap between intention and interpretation, between meaning and accountability, a gap that emerges at the heart of the discourse concerning the ethics of representing the Shoah.[22]

As the temporal gap widens between the Shoah and the present, the question of how events will be portrayed (from which perspective, using which documents, in which genre, etc.) becomes increasingly complicated. Cinematic representation seems particularly to pressure this point, perhaps because of the way cinema reifies the image on celluloid. The pliant nature of theatrical representation (an ever-changing live performance for an ever-changing and ever-evolving audience), as Levi himself noted, makes the ethical considerations of cinematic representation all the more pointed and makes the theater a rich source for a way to sublate often unproductive tensions.[23]

Eddy the Juggler indicates the potential gap in the sign of performance most effectively. His body epitomizes the kinesthetic sign of the actor's body in performance, whose significance continually shifts in meaning with regard to its position vis-à-vis the audience.[24] Caught in a very hostile gap indeed, between the barbed wire and the electric fence, Eddy shows how the signifier strays from that which it seeks to express. Even if the Camp meant to discipline him publicly for pederasty, Eddy's performance, here conveyed through the infinite indifference of his facial expression, belies the accusation and, importantly, the apparatus of power that lies behind it.

The performance of the non-linguistic sign in "The Juggler" subverts the regulation of expression and interpretation that Levi appears to exact in the essay "Dello scrivere oscuro," to which I referred previously and that was written more or less within the same time frame as the stories in *Moments of Reprieve*.[25] I am not suggesting that in this essay Levi does not understand what Sausurre would describe as the arbitrariness of the bond between the signifier and the signified, for "The Juggler" shows that a sign can plainly point in one direction and end up by going in another, a desirably ironic and often deployed writerly device. Rather, just as the problematic Lina Insana has outlined, the trouble is the nature of the sign as it travels (or "adapts" or "translates") from one genre to another—from the nonfiction essay in *Other People's Trades*, to the fictionalized story set in Auschwitz ("The Juggler" and the other stories of *Moments of Reprieve*), and beyond.[26] Compounded by the conditions of performance, the arbitrariness of the linguistic sign sets up a difficult task for Levi to negotiate, especially insofar as the representation of Auschwitz is concerned.

Performance of Levi's Works

Survival in Auschwitz: From Page to Stage

As illustrated by the quotation at the start of this chapter, taken from the interview he gave in 1982, Levi found the immediacy of performance stimulating. The appeal of live performance does not vary for Levi according to media, and he makes no distinction between the differing conditions of theatrical performance and broadcast, which are in fact considerable. The review that follows of the performances of Levi's work separates performances of *Survival in Auschwitz* from those of texts that do not treat the Holocaust, and follows the chronology of presentation or broadcast.

Unlike the dynamic established by the writer-reader relation, broadcast and especially live performances afforded Levi immediate access to the addressee, the recipient of the linguistic utterance, whether oral or scripted, that was "unmediated by the page," as noted in the quotation with which this chapter begins. Proximity to the reader was not singular; rather, the experience was one of the shared spaces of performance. "Of all the 'arts,'" performance studies scholar Samuel Weber writes, "theater most directly resembles politics insofar as traditionally it has been understood to involve the assemblage of people in a shared space."[27] The space of performance has the potential to make reception of Levi's work less of an atomized experience than in its reading. The same shared experience was available to the author. Remarking on the happiness he felt in collaboration, Levi writes that "the hours and days spent here, working in a team, were among the happiest of my postwar career, of my career as a writer—and that was new for me too, working as a team, with others, not the lone writer at his desk."[28]

The gaps I have already mentioned are joined by another that an account of the performance of Levi's works helps particularly to illuminate: the gap that emerged between the survivor chemist, the sober author of a Holocaust testimonial that was growing in import, and the writer. These two entities seem particularly prominent between 1963 and 1966, as Levi shifts between recognition of his Holocaust testimonial and its re-presentation in varied modes and authorship of his science fiction.

Survival on the Radio: Canadian Broadcast Corporation and RAI Radio (1964–1965)

Survival in Auschwitz was first readied for performance on the Canadian radio network. Levi appreciated this radio play that aired January 24, 1965, written by George Whalley, performed by Douglas Rain, and produced by John Reeves, taking note of how the medium of radio underscored the importance of oral communication and aural comprehension.[29] Whalley's script elucidated the confusion of languages that so colored Levi's experience of the Lager, as Thomson and Lepschy and Lepschy also observe.[30] Concerning the script for the CBC, Levi wrote in the program notes for the 1966 TST performances that, "[t]he enterprise, its result, and the medium of the radio, which was new to me, all filled me with enthusiasm, and a few months later I offered RAI an Italian adaptation."[31] Levi's adaptation of Whalley's adaptation complicates notions of the "appropriation" of the author that I referred to previously and invites us to probe more deeply into this episode.

John Reeves' program notes for the week's CBC broadcasts describe the technical considerations in detail. Remarkable in Reeves' notes is the reappearance of the gap I have been describing, both in terms of the script for the audio play as well as its editing for final broadcast. The radio script, which took folio or book format, laid out directions latent in Levi's text on the left page and dialogue and other sound effects on the right. Reeves noted that, "Nearly every action has a reference to it in the commentary, and these references were made to coincide."[32] The script thus sought to maintain the unity of the story in prose but parse it for performance, drawing into proximity these two genres rather than reinforcing a gap between them.

The recording process sought a similar unity. Although the performance was broadcast in mono, the CBC production was recorded in stereo, dedicating one channel to the "left" side of the script, that is, Levi's narrative, and the other to the script's right-hand page, that is, dialogue and sound. Reeves perceived two advantages to this production technique. First, "we were able to pre-record the commentary by itself, and thus free the actor who played Levi (Rain) to take part in the action, too."[33] This allowed Rain to be audible simultaneously as retrospective narrator and actor in the present. Reeves believed that this technique contributed to the "authority of his comments, since it becomes movingly clear that he is speaking out of direct personal experience."[34] Finally, Reeves observed that this technique also made "time disappear, as though the years between the events and the commentary had shrunk to nothing. And the events were an ever-present reality in the mind."[35]

The second advantage of using stereo to record the production was, as Reeves points out, purely technical. Shifting between the two stereo channels made it possible to "precisely [...] shade with meaning one line or one phrase or even a single word."[36] Reeves adds that although it made editing the recording more complicated—a process that took over one hundred hours—he believed that it ensured greater clarity of meaning. One could also say that the stereo recording technically ensured the presence of Levi's intention in ways that otherwise could have been diminished. Reeves concludes his program note by observing that decorum urged him to dwell on the formal and technical aspects of the recording. As if drawing from the sort of decorum Levi himself puts into practices in the chapter "The Journey" in *Survival in Auschwitz*, where he does not reproduce the conversation between him and his female traveling companion in transit from Fossoli to Auschwitz, Reeves says that his focus in the notes is on technical aspects because "Of our feelings on the subject, I don't think it is proper to speak." He concludes by noting that "all of us, cast, adaptor, production staff, knew that we were in the presence of a great and noble response to a terrible evil and that these things speak for themselves."[37]

The dramatic reading of *Se questo è un uomo*, broadcast for the first time on RAI in April 1964, is approximately 63 minutes long and maintains both the structure of the prose text as well as, to a certain extent, the presence of Levi as a narrator. The troupe of radio actors, still intact as of 1966, performed, with Nanni Bertorelli in the role of Levi, as well as actors of other nationalities, an aspect that will be taken up in the various staged versions of the drama. Levi had heard Bertorelli in a dramatic reading of *Se questo è un uomo* staged by the Teatro delle Dieci and had proposed him as the lead when the RAI found other, better-known actors to be less available.[38]

In order to abridge the prose text so that it would conform to general parameters of other dramatic presentations (in play and other formats) broadcast by the RAI, the first chapter—until Levi's arrival in Auschwitz—is narrated by Bertorelli with very few dramatizations of the text. This has the effect of establishing and preserving the primacy of the observing voice, making it recognizable in the "confusion of tongues" that follows. After arrival in the camp, Levi is successfully folded into the mix of voices, helping sculpt the "everyman" that becomes even more evident in the 1966 staged version.

The alternating focus on Levi's observations and his fellow detainees' dramatizations of specific points in the text is balanced and efficient. This balance shifts subtly to Levi when the radio play reaches "The Story of Ten Days" and moves toward its conclusion. The prose text signals a reentry into time and history with the definitive dates attached to each day. The radio drama underscores this reentry by an echo effect hallowing each proclaimed date. Although dramatic dialogue continues as a feature of this last section of the play, the Levi character, though anonymous, reemerges as a single observing and documenting individual at the end of the radio drama with the declamation of the Shemà. Nearing the end of the poem, the echo effect is engaged again, producing several results. First, the ring and raised volume solemnizes the already somber poem. Second, for anyone familiar with the Shemà (or shema, the call to daily prayer for Jews that stands as epigram to the prose text of Survival in Auschwitz) and its prosody, the cadence invokes a more liturgical tone to mark the conclusion of the work than does "The Story of Ten Days." Third, as noted, is the return to the individual voice of the documenting narration after its blend with the others of the camp. The allegorical journey begins and ends with an individual who has, along the way, joined in the collective human suffering.

Sound plays an important role elsewhere in the radio drama. As Thomson has noted in his biography of Levi, sounds were gathered in the hillsides of Turin in a way that one could call neorealist in use, given the audible mono-recording that is folded into the studio mix.[39] It is interesting that the realistic touch this adds should accompany the part of the broadcast that marks the merging of the Levi character with his fellow inmates and establishes a parallel correspondence of content and craft, or audio technique.

The medium of the radio, in which sound is of signal importance, is particularly remarkable in the episodes "The Canto of Ulysses" and "Selection." In the first, Levi's voice is more amplified, while Pikolo's fades in and out, which highlights both the dialogic form (and therefore the presence of another) and the act of retrieving Dante from oblivion. Such alternation allows the two consciousnesses to be present concurrently in a way the prose text cannot: the text defers the union of Pikolo and Levi, but the radio is able to synthesize so that when we arrive at the moment when Levi perceives having reached Pikolo by way of Dante, the consciousness of Pikolo, always present by way of his remote voice asking questions, comes again to the fore. The superimposition of the voices is valuable and imitates live conversation, even a didactic one like that of "The Canto of Ulysses." This has the effect of making Pikolo more present than he might otherwise be. He seems like an appendage in the text, but the radio play does not make him secondary.

"Selection" also profitably uses sound to center and direct the inter-pretation. The diegetic sound is not surprising: the babble of the voices in the background, the steps of the inmates running and jumping during the moment of selection. The addition of the extradiegetic echo, mentioned previously and that returns in "The Story of Ten Days," produces the effect of acoustically isolating Levi in his disdain for Kuhn. Levi clearly and starkly pronounces sentence on Kuhn and his repugnant prayer. Kuhn's singsong Hebrew prayer of thanks following the selection of October is gibberish, made unintelligible by both the reduced amplification of that actor's voice and the increased amplification of Bertorelli's. After "Selection," as Kuhn thanks God he has not been chosen yet to die, Levi's voice emerges singly. The absence of diegetic sound marks the first difference. Like the CBC's stereo recording, Levi's voice is isolated from the Buna-Monowitz "Babel" and, consequently, imbued with a greater clarity that is also literal. More-over, the addition of the echo effect further distinguishes this section. The effect is sure: Levi does indeed judge Kuhn and his blasphemy.

Levi's judgment of, and rage about, the crime of the Nazi deportation, detention, and murder of European Jews has often been portrayed as man-ifest *interlinea*, between the lines. The radio broadcast of *Se questo è un uomo* makes this rage and judgment patent from, as it were, the start of the memory of the offense. That is, it is not deferred to another genre (poetry, short story) or another time (decades after the first drafting of *Se questo è un uomo*). On the contrary, it is portrayed as concurrent with the drafting.

Natural Histories (*Storie naturali*; Turin: Ridotto del Romano, February 1966)

The debut of any stagings of Levi's texts was an honor reserved for the Teatro delle Dieci, directed by Massimo Scaglione since its founding in 1958. Although my focus in these pages is principally on the history of *Sur-vival in Auschwitz*, performances of Levi's work in this period pivot between his Holocaust testimonial and his science fiction, as yet pseudonymously authored by "Damiano Malabaila." As artistic director, Scaglione had asked Levi repeatedly for a script that the Teatro delle Dieci could put into production. Since *Natural Histories* was due out imminently, Levi suggested it as a text for the company, and Scaglione then chose three stories to present: "Il sesto giorno" (The Sixth Day), already in play form in the original; "La bella addormentata nel frigo" (Sleeping Beauty in the Fridge), which had already served as the basis of a dramatic reading for RAI radio five years earlier; and "Il versificatore" (The Versifier).

Moving from the Teatro delle Dieci at the Ridotto del Romano to Turin's Teatro Stabile (TST) and performances at the refurbished Teatro Carignano constituted more than a change of address, as observed earlier. The aims of the Teatro delle Dieci as a theatrical company, as well as the material conditions of production, differed from those of the TST, where many of the Teatro delle Dieci troupe had trained.[40] The choice of texts for performance reveals a company's mission. Almost immediately after its founding, the theater began performing works of contemporary European avant-garde playwrights, including Ionesco, Beckett, Adamov, Tardieu, and Cocteau, among others, and, among Italians, works by Flaiano and Pavese. Scaglione and the Teatro delle Dieci went on to perform works by Breton and Tzara, in addition to those of Sciascia, Behan, and Genet. Concerning the adaptation for the stage of prose works, subsequent to its collaboration with Levi the company staged performances based on works by Gina Lagorio and Giovanni Arpino.

In February 1966, the Teatro delle Dieci presented the one-act plays. The conditions for collaboration, which Levi later remembered fondly, were as felicitous as the reception of the play. Levi found the theatre beguiling, Scaglione recalled, saying that, "Primo was like a child with new toys."[41] Given the interest in tracing Levi's control over the representation of his Holocaust testimonial, the curious disavowal that occurred at the end of the science fiction one-acts is significant. Levi the author had not yet disclaimed these texts by publishing them pseudonymously as Damiano Malabaila, so that the Teatro delle Dieci performances antedated publication of *Natural Histories* and, consequently, Levi was the publicly acknowledged author of the texts that Scaglione adapted. As a twist, however, at the close of *The Versifier*, the poetaster-robot of the title squeaks out that it, the Versifier, not Levi (and certainly not Malabaila), had authored the evening's presentations.

Se questo è un uomo (Turin: Teatro Carignano, November 1966)

Levi's re-adaptation of *Survival in Auschwitz* for RAI Radio in April 1964 prepared the way for the notion of a *riduzione*, or an adaptation of the testimonial for the stage. The dramatic version of *Survival in Auschwitz*, coauthored by Primo Levi and his actor-friend, Pieralberto Marché, premiered at Turin's Teatro Carignano on November 18, 1966.[42]

I observed earlier that transfer to the TST and the Teatro Carignano constituted moving to a more central location, but this center was not simply geographical. The TST was founded in 1955 and charged with the resuscitation of the city's theatrical activity, once thriving, but which had suffered under Fascist suppression. The City of Turin committed an annual subvention of 20 million lire to underwrite its activity and donated the venerable (if outmoded) space of the Teatro Gobetti.[43] The actor Nico Pepe, known for his performances of Goldoni, served as the company's first director and lasted two seasons. Pepe was followed by Gianfranco De Bosio and it was under his artistic direction that the company successfully staged productions of Ruzante.[44] But if, over time and with the passing of artistic directors, the TST demonstrated a commitment to the classical theater of Goldoni, Chekhov, Pirandello, and Shakespeare (with Vittorio Gassman's acclaimed 1968 performance of *Richard III* in a Luca Ronconi production), it was not to the exclusion of more contemporary or even avant-garde drama, as illustrated, for example, by the production of Brecht's *The Resistible Rise of Arturo Ui* that inaugurated the 1955–1956 season. Concerning the dramatization of works by contemporary writers, the TST also adapted works by Natalia Ginzburg and Alberto Moravia, in addition to Levi.

Marché and Levi's 1966 script for *Se questo è un uomo* departs from the prose text in several ways. The play consists of two acts, which roughly correspond to a balanced division of the 17 chapters in the 1958 text. Unlike its predecessor in prose—which interrupts the story by way of chapter breaks and further frames and interrupts the story with chapter titles—the lighting design proposed by the dramatic text calls for an uninterrupted flow of action between scenes. Whereas the prose text offers a protagonist-narrator through its use of first-person narration, Primo is not only not the protagonist of the play; he is not a character in the play, contrasting sharply with Sher's *Primo*, as I observe shortly. Levi's dramatization calls for two different characters, The Author, who addresses the audience at the beginning of the play (something that significantly parallels the Author's Preface in the 1958 expanded edition) and another character named Aldo.

The dramatic text for *Se questo è un uomo* aims at a similar diminution of the protagonist by calling for a chorus and by dividing between its members (which vary in number throughout the play) what the prose text puts forward as the protagonist-narrator's meditations. Levi and Marché seemed fixed on multiplying the number of voices that tell this story and De Bosio appeared intent on widening that scope even further by casting 53 actors to play the parts. The drive toward an ever-increasing plurality of voices marks the end of the play, which, unlike the prose text, finishes with a refrain from the *Shemà*. Literalizing Levi's poem, which asks us to "Consider if this is a man [. . .] if this is a woman," the script calls for a chorus of six men and six women to read the poem at the opening. As the lights fade at the end of the Act II, as many as 24 actors share the stage and the declamation of the poem, which is recited not in unison but in succession, meaningfully accumulating the voices.

Levi's first adaptation of *Se questo è un uomo* for the radio exploited that medium's potential for capturing the horror of Camp cacophony. The sound design for the TST production, however, did not include extradiegetic music. As Thomson reminds us, the avant-garde composer Luigi Nono eventually withdrew his commitment to the production, contributing to the production's state of "shambles" before its relocation to Turin from Florence.[45] The exclusion of a corporeal German presence onstage identifies an important aspect of the use of sound for the TST production. The script cordons off from the space of performance any bodily intrusion identified as German: no onstage presence of a German character is called for and Germans and the German language are made present only through sound. This clearly recalls the conditions of radio, where voices and sound are invisible but nonetheless tangibly present. In the TST production, German becomes the disembodied sound of power that decides the fate of the actor-prisoner during the moment of selection.

The decision to rid the stage of the corporeal presence of Germans is a matter of some ethical moment. Although De Bosio could have double cast some of the roles, he chose instead to hire a complete cast of 53; as a consequence, each character was portrayed uniquely. The absence of German embodiment stands against such individuation of the detainees. To be sure, the prisoners are dominated by German force, but the space of the stage is nevertheless quarantined from the taint of the kinesthetic sign of Germans.

The critical reception of the 1966 production was respectful but mixed, or, as Puppa asserts, "tepid."[46] Writing in *Vie nuove* on December 1, theater critic Ettore Capriolo offers a divided opinion about both the script and the performance. Capriolo finds that Levi and Marché have not learned to "rethink the book's episodes in terms appropriate to the language of the stage," and found the performance an impoverished recapitulation of a rich and moving prose text. Nonetheless, Capriolo finishes his review with a pious flourish, invoking the "alto impegno civile," or the "high civic engagement" that the performance affords the spectator, and seems, on these grounds, to encourage readers to attend.[47] Despite its civic import, the production closed early and became a subject of a contractual dispute in the period that followed.[48]

The elements that critics singled out for praise derived not from Levi's choices but, rather, from Marché's artistic decisions. Indeed, in an unpublished article that Finter initially brought to light, we learn that "the main ideas for stage adaptation—the absence of the SS from the stage, the new conception of the 'Levi' character and the choral structure"—were all the contributions of Marché.[49] This does not mean that all blame for the infelicitous aspects of the production can be laid at Levi's doorstep, but it does help distinguish the collaborators' contributions.

The script illustrates the desire to determine the meaning and intention of the performance. This is evident in the stage directions, which are as copious as they are impossible to disregard. While the stereo recording of George Whalley's script for the CBC had found a felicitous solution, the introduction of the kinesthetic sign of the actors (their embodied presence on stage) complicated the 1966 stage production. The extensive stage directions in *Se questo è un uomo* eclipse dialogue. This does not bode well for a script in general, nor did it serve the script for the TST performances. Roman Ingarden divided the dramatic text for purposes of study into the *Haupttext* (chiefly dialogue) and the *Nebentext* (everything else). The *Nebentext* breaks down further into intradialogic and extradialogic stage direction.[50] This means that stage directions either come couched within dialogue (e.g., one character says to another, "Here, let me open the door for you") or they are offered in an external form, typically didascalics, or stage directions. Capriolo and the eminent dramaturge Guido Davico Bonino point out the success of those scenes in which dialogue, the *Haupttext*, has some function. For example, in the scenes with Roberto, Lorenzo's proxy, and the Canto of Ulysses that Davico Bonino found particularly affecting, the *Nebentext* does not insist on any particular form of semiosis; rather, the dialogue allows for a different semiotic process to take place.[51]

On balance, the dramatic text for *Se questo è un uomo* labors hard to take control of semiotic signification. Judging from this text, Levi believes that not only do parameters of interpretation exist, but he also proves that, at least at this juncture in his career and at this point in his rewriting of the Lager experience, he wants to have a hand in establishing them. The extensive and meticulous extradialogic stage directions oppose Marché's impulse to distribute the narrator's reflections among multiple characters. On one hand, such distribution seems to suggest that the story is not just Levi's, it is Every Survivor's. On the other, Levi will not relinquish authorship and the itemized stage directions reveal a need to assert authority in a different form. If the 1966 script signals Levi's attempts to control signification, it contrasts with the disavowal of authorship performed by the science fiction one-acts at Teatro delle Dieci. This "underground" material lacks the gravitas of *Se questo è un uomo*. The greater critical success of the Teatro delle Dieci performances may be attributed to the greater freedom of interpretation consonant with the company's avant-garde practice, or it may be the result of the author's greater willingness to "disappear" behind (or into) the Versifier or, eventually, his alter ego, Malabaila.

Primo, Sir Antony Sher (London and New York, 2004–2005)

My examination of semiosis in and of Levi's work has focused principally on performances in varied media of *Survival at Auschwitz* that took place during his lifetime in an attempt to illuminate the issue of control over the production of meaning. Clearly, all such control is lost upon the author's death. A full review of the adaptation of Levi's work in the post-1987 period is outside the scope of this chapter; nevertheless, it is interesting to note the similar struggles over signification that take place in Sir Antony Sher's adaptation, *Primo*. I will work toward my conclusion by pointing out some of the contrasts between Sher's choices and those Levi made in the 1966 dramatization.[52] No performance of Levi's work should be slavishly bound to precedent and, it is clear that Sher did not intend to recreate the TST production, the critical reception for which had, after all, been lukewarm. However, for purposes of illustrating the problems that Sher's production both creates and faces, some comparison to the 1966 dramatization is useful.

Sher's adaptation offers a retrospective and synthetic vision of Levi's life and thoughts and was performed in the most canonical and most commercially ordained of venues: in London, at the National Theater of Great Britain, and in New York, at The Music Box Theater on West Forty-Fifth Street, operated by the powerful theater conglomerate, the Shubert Organization. With the New York run, the itinerary of performed Levi came full circle, returning to North America. To judge from the performance venues, Levi in (or as) performance has "arrived." But what brand of Levi is re-presented?

Although 95 percent of the text of the performance derives from *Survival in Auschwitz*, Sher's interpretation of Levi is filtered through *The Drowned and the Saved*, which Levi began to write 35 years after liberation. This is a dangerous collapse of a historical and temporal gap that requires greater mindfulness. The decision to recreate a Levi circa 1986 is understandable from several points of view. The South African actor and playwright is himself middle-aged, and not, as Robert Brustein observed, a starveling twenty-something chemist.[53]

The staging of Sher's monologue shares some technical characteristics with the 1966 dramatization, specifically lighting design and, to a certain extent, sound (designed by Rich Walsh). Hildegard Bechtler's set was minimalistic, with David Howe's lighting design creating discrete areas meant to represent varied locales within the Camp (the rail yard, the showers, etc.). Unlike the 1966 production, which saw Luigi Nono's nonparticipation, music figures prominently in the sound design, with Jonathan Goldstein's elegiac score assisting in movement and flow between scenes.

It is in the area of sound that other, more striking differences between the productions occur, revealing a slippage in accuracy that affects signification. The crucial difference between the 1966 dramatization and Sher's production lies in the shift from a cast of 53 to a cast of one. Gone is the accumulation of voices and multiplication of experience, the element of sound that had initially, by his own account, drawn Levi to a dramatization of *Survival in Auschwitz* in the first place. In its stead is a definitively identified individual, the Primo of the title. One cannot fail to see the parallel between this Primo and another so audaciously named in Carole Angier's incendiary 2002 biography.[54] Individualizing Levi's story in this way disallows the "uomo" of *Se questo è un uomo*, a mere carrier of carbon molecules like so many others on the planet. Sher's rich and fulsome voice is the only one the audience hears. Absent the choral, Everyman aspect, one senses Sher's wish to assign something like an existential loneliness in Levi near the end of his life. It is ironic—perhaps even tragically so—that performance, which Levi appreciated for the way it beckoned him from isolation, as noted earlier, should simply reinforce that isolation. This, however, is the infelicitous consequence.[55]

Sher's Levi is a singular spokesperson with an obvious burden, the Levi who will commit suicide several months later. This teleological reading collapses the gap created by history that I mentioned earlier. In *Primo*, Sher projects the 1986 Levi back onto his 1946 incarnation and flags there the trailhead of the path that ineluctably leads to suicide. In brief, Sher has stripped Levi's *Se questo è un uomo* project in each of its incarnations of the work's "chiunquismo," its "Everyman" aim. Perhaps the personalizing drive and winnowing down of Sher's *Primo* brings it into proximity with Daniel Mendelsohn's *The Lost: A Search for Six of Six Million*, published the following year. Mendelsohn's brave 2006 study, however, documented the hunt for six relatives lost in the Holocaust and did not aim, it should be noted, to create a leading role for one of the most acclaimed actors of English-language theater.

Primo Levi's history of and with performances of his works during his lifetime illustrates how the status of language evolves during his career as a writer. The 1966 script of *Se questo è un uomo* hesitates between releasing the semiotic sign into the space of the theater where the spectator might interpret it more freely, and reining it in, controlling it, its presentation, and its subsequent interpretation. However, as Levi retreats from testimony, he appears to overcome the need to assert his control over the performative sign, whether on stage or in his prose. Levi's use of performance and the performance of his works illustrates how, by allowing the textual linguistic sign to cede to the performative gesture, Levi permits the theater to produce, as Susan Melrose observes, "A body of chaos of a short-lived kind. Something painful in its pleasing."[56]

Notes

1. For Levi's language, see Marco Belpoliti and Robert S. C. Gordon, "Primo Levi's Holocaust Vocabularies," in *The Cambridge Companion to Primo Levi*, ed. Robert S. C. Gordon (Cambridge: Cambridge University Press, 2007), 51–65; Cesare Cases, "L'ordine delle cose e l'ordine delle parole," in *Primo Levi: Un'antologia della critica* (Turin: Einaudi, 1997), 5–33; Sander Gilman, "The Special Language of the Camps and After," in *Reason and Light*, ed. Susan Tarrow (Cornell: Cornell University Press, 1990), 59–81; Fabio Girelli-Carasi, "The Anti-Linguistic Nature of the Lager in the Language of Primo Levi's *Se questo è un uomo*," in *Reason and Light*, 40–59; Anna Laura Lepschy and Giulio Lepschy, "Primo Levi's Languages," in *The Cambridge Companion to Primo Levi*, 121–36; Pier Vincenzo Mengaldo,"Lingua e scrittura in Levi," in *Primo Levi: Un'antologia della critica,* 169–242; Lawrence Schehr, "Primo Levi's Strenuous Clarity," *Italica* 66, no. 4 (Winter 1989): 429–43; Cesare Segre, "Lettura di *Se questo è un uomo*," in *Primo Levi: Un'antologia della critica*, 91–116.
2. I account for a greater range of texts adapted for performance in my forthcoming *Primo Levi on the Air*, which explores broadcast (radio and television) performances and staged versions of Primo Levi's works in the 1961 to 1980 period.
3. Primo Levi, *Other's People's Trades*, trans. Raymond Rosenthal (London: Michael Joseph, 1989), 174 (emphasis added).
4. See Primo Levi's, *The Black Hole of Auschwitz*, ed. Marco Belpoliti and trans. Sharon Wood (Malden, MA: Polity Press, 2005), 37–38.
5. For a consonant reading of the role of "Dello scrivere oscuro" and Levi's linguistic aims, see Lepschy and Lepschy, "Primo Levi's Languages," 134.
6. Tadeusz Kowzan, "The Sign in the Theater: An Introduction to the Semiology of the Art of the Spectacle," trans. Simon Pleasance, *Diogène* 61 (1968): 57.
7. All titles of Levi's texts are given in English, followed by Italian, save the theatrical performances of the Holocaust testimonial, which is given as *Se questo è*

un uomo. It is generally accepted that Levi elaborated on the initial 1947 text in the following ways: the addition of his Author's Preface and an additional, last chapter, "The Story of Ten Days" (La storia di dieci giorni) to the 1958 edition; the 1966 script for the stage, coauthored with Pieralberto Marché; and the Appendix added to editions published after 1976. See Judith Woolf's "From *If This is a Man* to *The Drowned and the Saved*," in *The Cambridge Companion to Primo Levi*, 35–49 for an appraisal of the author's trajectory, and the bibliography in *The Cambridge Companion to Primo Levi*, 189.

8. See Bryan Cheyette, "Appropriating Primo Levi," in *The Cambridge Companion to Primo Levi*, 67–85.

9. See Lina Insana's *Arduous Tasks: Primo Levi, Translation, and the Transmission of Holocaust Testimony* (Toronto: University of Toronto Press, 2009).

10. See Carole Angier, *The Double Bond: Primo Levi, a Biography* (London: Viking, 2002), 558–64, and Ian Thomson, *Primo Levi: A Life* (London: Hutchinson, 2002), 315–19.

11. Levi's own thoughts about the production are found in "Note to the Theater Version of *If This is a Man*," in Levi's *The Black Hole of Auschwitz*, 23–27. On Holocaust drama in general, see Claude Schumacher, ed., *Staging the Holocaust: The Shoah in Drama and Performance* (Cambridge: Cambridge University Press, 1998) and Christian Rogowski, "Teaching the Drama of the Holocaust," in *Teaching the Representation of the Holocaust*, ed. Marianne Hirsch and Irene Kacandes (New York: MLA Press, 2004). The term "hidden theater" is Paolo Puppa's. See his "Primo Levi's Hidden Theater," in *Primo Levi. The Austere Humanist*, ed. Joseph Farrell (Oxford: Peter Lang, 2004), 183–201. See also Helga Finter, "Primo Levi's Stage Version of *Se questo è un uomo*," in *Staging the Holocaust*, 229–53. See also Lina Insana, "In Levi's Wake: Adaptation, Simulacrum, Postmemory," *Italica* 86, no. 2 (2009): 212–38.

12. Peppino Ortoleva, "A Geography of the Media Since 1945," in *Italian Cultural Studies*, ed. David Forgacs and Robert Lumley (Oxford: Oxford University Press, 1996), 185–98, and E. Menduini, *La radio nell'era della televisione* (Bologna: Il Mulino, 1994).

13. See Millicent Marcus, *Italian Film in the Shadow of Auschwitz* (Toronto: University of Toronto Press, 2007). esp. 13–20, and Fabio Girelli-Carasi, "Italian-Jewish Memoirs and the Discourse of Identity," in *The Most Ancient of Minorities*, ed. Stanislao Pugliese (Westport, CT: Greenwood Press, 2002), 191–99.

14. Thomson, *Primo Levi*, 315.

15. Puppa, "Primo Levi's Hidden Theater," 199.

16. Levi's materials in the Einaudi archives include a typescript of *Il sesto giorno* [The Sixth Day], the creation story in play form, published in 1966. The manuscript is dated 1957 but is believed to have been written a decade earlier, making dramatic dialogue part of Levi's earliest genres. For a complete assessment of the variants and editions of *Se questo è un uomo*, see Giovanni Tesio, "Su alcune giunte e varianti di *Se questo è un uomo*," in *Studi piemontesi* 6 (1977): 270–78.

17. This passage comes from the British translation of *Se questo è un* uomo: Primo Levi, *If this is a Man*, trans. Stuart Woolf (London: Orion, 1960) 150.
18. In addition to Puppa, see also Robert Gordon, *Primo Levi's Ordinary Virtues. From Testimony to Ethics* (Oxford: Oxford University Press, 2001), 284, for a consonant reading of the importance of these moments in *The Reawakening*.
19. "Era di una bellezza smagliante: biondo, di media statura ma snello, robusto ed agilissimo, aveva tratti nobili ed una pelle così chiara da apparire traslucida; non doveva avere più di 23 anni. Si infischiava di tutto e di tutti, delle SS, del lavoro, di noi; aveva un'aria insieme serena e assorta che lo distingueva. Divenne celebre il giorno stesso del suo arrivo: nel lavatoio, tutto nudo, dopo essersi lavato accuratamente con una saponetta profumata, se l'appoggiò sul vertice del cranio, che aveva rasato come tutti noi; poi si curvò in avanti, e con ondulazioni impercettibili del dorso, sapienti e precise, fece scivolare la sontuosa saponetta piano piano, dal capo al collo, poi giù giù lungo tutto il filo della schiena, fino a coccige, dove la fece cadere in una mano. Due o tre fra noi applaudirono, ma lui non mostrò di accorgersene e se ne andò a rivestirsi, lento e distratto." Primo Levi, *Lilít e altri racconti* (Turin: Einaudi, 1981), 12–13. Further references to *Lilít* will be from this edition, and page numbers will be included in the body of the text. Primo Levi, *Moments of Reprieve*, trans. Ruth Feldman (New York: Penguin, 1995), 10. Further English translations of passages from *Lilít e altri racconti* come from this Feldman edition, and page numbers will be included in the text.
20. See Gilman, "The Special Language of the Camps and After," 61–62. For some brief thoughts on the relation between the "semiotics" of corporeal language and performative gesture and Levi's essay "Dello scrivere oscuro," see Lepschy and Lepschy, "Primo Levi's Languages," 135.
21. "[p]ugni e schiaffi correvano fra noi come linguaggio quotidiano; ed avevamo imparato presto a distinguere le percosse "espressive" da quelle altre, che venivano inflitte per ferocia [. . .] Uno schiaffo come quello di Eddy era affine alla pacca si dà al cane" (*Lilít*,15).
22. Cf. Amy Hungerford, "Teaching Fiction, Teaching the Holocaust," in *Teaching the Representation of the Holocaust*, eds. Marianne Hirsch and Irene Kacandes (New York: MLA, 2004), 182.
23. Much of the tension concerning cinematic representation of the Holocaust has centered on Roberto Benigni's 1997 *La vita è bella* [Life is Beautiful], which closely adheres to a sense of theatrical decorum handed down since the Renaissance: gross atrocities are not witnessed by the audience but, rather, are declaimed and described by the actors: they are *oscena*, ob-scena meaning destined for representation off-stage. See also Millicent Marcus, *Italian Film in the Shadow of Auschwitz*, esp. 77–78; Sander Gilman, "Is Life Beautiful? Can the Shoah Be Funny? Some Thoughts on Recent and Older Films," *Critical Inquiry* 26 (Winter 2000): esp. 291–93; and Maurizio Viano, "*Life is Beautiful*: Reception, Allegory, and Holocaust Laughter," *Annali d'Italianistica* 17 (1999): 155–72. See also Levi's thoughts on the mini-series Holocaust in *The Black Hole of Auschwitz*, 59–66.

24. For the kinesthetic sign as illustrated by the actor's body see, among others, Jean Alter, *A Sociosemiotic Theory of Theater* (Philadelphia: University of Pennsylvania Press, 1991); Elaine Aston and George Savona, *Theater as a Sign System: A Semiotics of Text and Performance* (London: Routledge, 1991); and Erika Fischer-Lichte, *The Semiotics of Theater*, trans. Jeremy Gaines and Doris Jones (Bloomington: Indiana University Press, 1992).

25. See Primo Levi, *Opere*, ed. Marco Belpoliti, intro. by Daniele Del Giudice (Turin: Einaudi, 1997), 2:1531–32.

26. Insana, *Arduous Tasks*, esp. 4–11.

27. Samuel Weber, *Theatricality as Medium* (New York: Fordham University Press, 2004), 31.

28. Levi, "The Little Theatre of Memory," 55.

29. The genesis of the idea for performance on the radio is generally attributed to the impression Levi drew from the CBC recording. Thomson writes (*Primo Levi*, 310) that "in early 1964 a tape reached [Levi] of the Canadian Broadcast Corporation's radio version of *If This is a Man*. It was a revelation." The CBC archives, however, show the date of first transmission as Sunday, January 24, 1965. Levi's notes for the theatrical performances in Turin confirm this chronology, but there exists some archival equivocation as to the date of the CBC's first actual broadcast. I am thankful to Keith Hart of the CBC Radio archives for his assistance on this matter.

30. Thomson, *Primo Levi*, 310; Lepschy and Lepschy, "Primo Levi's Languages" 132.

31. See Levi, *The Black Hole of Auschwitz*, 26.

32. John Reeves, "If This is a Man," *CBC Times*, January 23–29, 1965.

33. Ibid.

34. Ibid.

35. Ibid.

36. Ibid.

37. It is worth noting that a largely similar cast and crew reassembled to produce an approximately 90-minute radio performance of *The Truce* for the CBC, broadcast for the first time on March 12, 1968 (Accession number 940703-15 [43], Canadian Broadcast Corporation archives). It is perhaps only coincidental that another recording of Levi's work encouraged innovative recording techniques: *The Truce* was the first radio drama to be recorded on four-track tape by the CBC.

38. Per my own 2008 interview with Massimo Scaglione, December 6, 2008. See also Scaglione's note "L'altra metà del 'centauro' Primo Levi: Intervista a Massimo Scaglione," *Sistemateatrotorino* April–May 2007, n.p.

39. Thomson, *Primo Levi: A Life*, 310–11.

40. These included Franco Alpestre, Wilma D'Eusebio, Bob Marchese, Piera Cravignani, Giovanni Moretti, Annamaria Mion, Luciano Donalisio, Carla Torrero, and Adolfo Fenoglio. See http://www.teatrodelledieci.it/storia.htm, accessed March 24, 2011.

41. Thomson, *Primo Levi: A Life*, 315.

42. See Guido Davico Bonino, "Primo Levi, come per caso, a teatro," in *Primo Levi: Il presente del passato*, ed. Alberto Cavaglion (Milan: Franco Angeli, 1991), 141–46.

43. For a history of the general setting of Turin and Levi's work situated within the city, see David Ward, "Primo Levi's Turin," in *The Cambridge Companion to Primo Levi*, 3–16. For the TST, see also http://www.teatrostabiletorino.it, accessed November 24, 2009. See also Nico Orengo, *Chi è di scena!* (Turin: Einaudi, 2006).

44. El Ruzante was the nickname for Angelo Beolco, a sixteenth-century playwright who composed rustic comedies in the Paduan dialect.

45. Thomson, *Primo Levi: A Life*, 318.

46. Puppa, "Primo Levi's Hidden Theater," 199.

47. Bonino, "Primo Levi," 141–46. The original reads, "La riduzione di Levi e Marché seguendo abbastanza da vicino gli episodi rievocati nel libro (molti ne elimina e pochissimi ne aggiunge(non ha saputo ripensarli in termini propri al linguaggio del palcoscenico." And "Resta ovviamente una serata di alto impegno civico."

48. See Puppa, "Primo Levi's Hidden Theater," 199.

49. Finter, "Primo Levi's Stage Version," 236–37n23.

50. See Aston and Savona, "The Sign in the Theater," in *Theater as a Sign System*.

51. See Bonino, "Primo Levi per caso," 144–45. See also Finter, "Primo Levi's Stage Version," 252.

52. For a compelling and fully detailed reading of the Sher production, see Insana, "In Levi's Wake," who also details Sher's *Primo Time*, a made-for-television film.

53. Robert Brustein, "Primo Levi: The Staged and the Damned," in *Millennial Stages. Essays and Reviews 2001–2005* (New Haven: Yale University Press, 2006), 245–49.

54. See also Millicent Marcus, "Primo Levi: The Biographer's Challenge and the Reader's Double Bind," *Italica*, 80, no. 1 (2003): 67–72.

55. See Primo Levi, "The Little Theatre of Memory," 55.

56. Susan Melrose, "Theater and Language," in *A Semiotics of the Dramatic Text* (New York: St. Martin's, 1994), 51.

Bibliography

"About the Righteous: Statistics (Righteous Among the Nations—per Country & Ethnic Origin January 1, 2010)." http://www1.yadvashem.org/yv/en/righteous/statistics.asp#detailed.

Adorno, Theodor W. "Cultural Criticism and Society." In *Prisms*, translated by Samuel and Shierry Weber, 17–34. Cambridge, MA: MIT Press, 1981.

———. *Negative Dialectics*. Translated by E. B. Ashton. New York: Seabury Press, 1973.

Agamben, Giorgio. *Homo Sacer: Sovereign Power and Bare Life*. Translated by Daniel Heller-Roazen. Stanford, CA: Meridian: Crossing Aesthetics, 1998.

———. *Remnants of Auschwitz*. Translated by Daniel Heller-Roazen. New York: Zone Books, 2002.

———. *State of Exception*. Translated by Kevin Attell. Chicago, IL: University of Chicago Press, 2005.

Alter, Jean. *A Sociosemiotic Theory of Theater*. Philadelphia: University of Pennsylvania Press, 1991.

Angier, Carole. *The Double Bond: Primo Levi, a Biography*. London: Viking, 2002.

Anissimov, Myriam. *Primo Levi: The Tragedy of an Optimist*. Translated by Steve Cox. London: Aurum Press, 1996.

Anonymous. "Pantera nera." *L'espresso*, April 16, 1960, 21–23.

Anonymous. *L'espresso*, April 30, 1961, 7.

Antelme, Robert. *La specie umana*. Turin: Einaudi, 1954; 1st ed., *L'Espèce umaine*, 1947.

Antonicelli, Franco, ed. *Trent'anni di storia italiana: 1915–1945: Dall'antifascismo alla Resistenza*. Turin: Einaudi, 1961.

Aston, Elaine, and George Savona. *Theater as a Sign System: A Semiotics of Text and Performance*. London: Routledge, 1991.

Barenghi, Mario. *Italo Calvino: Le linee e i margini*. Bologna: Il Mulino, 2007.

Bassani, Giorgio. *Cinque storie ferraresi*. Turin: Einaudi, 1956.

———. *Il giardino dei Finzi-Contini*. Turin: Einaudi, 1962.

———. *Gli occhiali d'oro*. Turin: Einaudi, 1958.

Battini, Michele. *The Missing Italian Nuremberg: Cultural Amnesia and Postwar Politics*. New York: Palgrave Macmillan, 2007.

Beer, Marina. "Memoria, cronaca e storia: Forme della memoria e della testimonianza." In *Il Novecento: Le forme del realismo*, vol. 11 of *Storia della letteratura italiana*, edited by Nino Borsellino and Walter Pedullà, 595–691. Milan: Federico Motta Editore, 2001.

Bellour, Raymond, ed. *Il Western: Fonti forme miti registi attori filmografia*. Translated and edited by Gianni Volpi. Milan: Feltrinelli, 1973.

Belpoliti, Marco, and Robert S. C. Gordon. "Primo Levi's Holocaust Vocabularies." In *The Cambridge Companion to Primo Levi*, edited by Robert S. C. Gordon, 51–65. Cambridge: Cambridge University Press, 2007.

———, eds. *The Voice of Memory: Interviews 1961–1987*. Translated by Robert S. C. Gordon. New York: New Press, 2001.

Benjamin, Walter. "The Task of the Translator." In *Illuminations: Essays and Reflections*, edited by Hannah Arendt, translated by Harry Zohn, 69–82. New York: Schocken, 1969.

Berlin, Isaiah. "Notes on Prejudice." *New York Review of Books*, October 18, 2001, 12.

Bernadini, Paolo. "The Jews in Nineteenth-Century Italy: Towards a Reappraisal." *Journal of Modern Italian Studies* 1, no. 2 (1996): 292–310.

Bertoletti, Isabella. "Primo Levi's Odyssey: The Drowned and the Saved." In *The Legacy of Primo Levi*, edited by Stanislao Pugliese, 105–18. New York: Palgrave Macmillan, 2005.

Bettelheim, Bruno. *The Informed Heart*. 2nd ed. London: Paladin, 1970.

Biasin, Gian-Paolo. "The Haunted Journey of Primo Levi." In *Memory and Mastery: Primo Levi as Writer and Witness*, edited by Roberta S. Kremer, 3–19. Albany: State University of New York Press, 2001.

Bonfantini, Mario. *Un salto nel buio*. Milan: Feltrinelli, 1959.

Bonino, Guido Davico. "Primo Levi, come per caso, a teatro." In *The Cambridge Companion to Primo Levi*, edited by Robert S. C. Gordon, 141–46. Cambridge: Cambridge University Press, 2007.

Bravo, Anna, and Daniele Jalla, eds. *Una misura onesta*. Milan: Franco Angeli, 1993.

Brombert, Victor. *In Praise of Anti-Heroes: Figures and Themes in Modern European Literature, 1830–1980*. Chicago, IL: University of Chicago Press, 2001.

Brooks, Richard, director. *The Professionals*. Columbia, 1966. Film.

Bruck, Edith. *Andremo in città*. Milan: Lerici, 1962.

———. *Chi ti ama così*. Milan: Lerici, 1959.

Brustein, Robert. "Primo Levi: The Staged and the Damned." In *Millennial Stages: Essays and Reviews 2001–2005*, 245–49. New Haven, CT: Yale University Press, 2006.

Caleffi, Piero, and Albe Steiner. *Pensaci, uomo!* Turin: Einaudi, 1960.

———. *Si fa presto a dire fame*. Milan: Edizioni Avanti!, 1958.

Calvino, Italo. *Le cosmicomiche*. Turin: Einaudi, 1965.

———. *La giornata di uno scrutatore*. Turin: Einaudi, 1963.

———. *Lettere*. 2 vols. Milan: Mondadori, 2000.

———. *Romanzi e racconti*. 2 vols. Milan: Mondadori, 1994.

———. *Saggi*. 2 vols. Edited by Mario Barenghi. Milan: Mondadori, 1995.

Camon, Ferdinando. *Conversazione con Primo Levi*. Milano: Garzanti, 1991.

———. *Conversations with Primo Levi*. Translated by John Shepley. Marlboro, VT: Marlboro Press, 1989.

Cannon, JoAnn. "Storytelling and the Picaresque in Levi's *La tregua.*" *Modern Language Studies* 31, no. 2 (2001): 1–10.

Caruth, Cathy. "Trauma and Experience: Introduction." In *Trauma: Explorations in Memory,* edited by Cathy Caruth, 3–12. Baltimore, MD: Johns Hopkins University Press, 1995.

———. *Unclaimed Experience: Trauma, Narrative, and History.* Baltimore, MD: Johns Hopkins University Press, 1996.

Cases, Cesare. "L'ordine delle cose e l'ordine delle parole." In *Primo Levi: Un'antologia della critica,* edited by Ernesto Ferrero, 5–33. Turin: Einaudi, 1997.

Cavaglion, Alberto. *Notizie su Argon: Gli antenati di Primo Levi da Francesco Petrarca a Cesare Lombroso.* Turin: Instar Libri, 2006.

———. *Primo Levi: Il presente del passato.* Milan: Franco Angeli, 1991.

———. "La scelta di Gedeone: Appunti su Primo Levi e l'ebraismo." *Journal of the Institute of Romance Studies* 4 (1996): 187–98.

Celli, Carlo. *Gillo Pontecorvo.* Lanham, MD: Scarecrow, 2005.

Cheyette, Bryan. "Appropriating Primo Levi." In *The Cambridge Companion to Primo Levi,* edited by Robert S. C. Gordon, 67–85. Cambridge: Cambridge University Press, 2007.

Chiodi, Piero. *Banditi.* Turin: Einaudi, 1961; 1st ed. 1946.

Cicioni, Mirna. *Primo Levi: Bridges of Knowledge.* Oxford: Berg, 1995.

Consonni, Manuela. "The Impact of the 'Eichmann Event' in Italy, 1961." *Journal of Israeli History* 23, no. 1 (2004): 91–99.

Coslovich, Marco. *Giovanni Palatucci: Una giusta memoria.* Atripalda: Mephite, 2008.

Costa, Fabrizio, director. *Senza confine.* Sacha Film, 2001. Film.

Crowther, Bosley. "War Panorama: 'Italiani Brava Gente Bows at 2 Theaters.'" *New York Times,* February 4, 1966. http://movies.nytimes.com/movie/review?res =9E01E1DC1338E637A25757C0A9649C946791D6CF.

Dawidowicz, Lucy S. *The War against the Jews, 1933–1945.* New York: Bantam Books, 1976.

De Felice, Renzo. *Rosso e nero.* Milan: Baldini e Castoldi, 1995.

———. *Storia degli ebrei italiani sotto il fascismo.* Turin: Einaudi, 1961.

———. "L'ultima maschera." *Rassegna Mensile di Israel* 1 (1963): 63–68.

Deaglio, Enrico. *La banalità del bene.* Milan: Feltrinelli, 1991.

———. *The Banality of Goodness: The Story of Giorgio Perlasca.* Translated by Gregory Conti. Notre Dame, IN: University of Notre Dame Press, 1998.

Debenedetti, Giacomo. *16 ottobre 43.* Milan: Il Saggiatore, 1959; 1st ed. 1944.

Della Coletta, Cristina. *Plotting the Past: Metamorphoses of Historical Narrative in Modern Italian Fiction.* West Lafayette, IN: Purdue University Press, 1996.

Derrida, Jacques. "Des Tours de Babel." In *Difference in Translation,* edited and translated by Joseph Graham, 209–48. Ithaca, NY: Cornell University Press, 1985.

Des Pres, Terence. *The Survivor: An Anatomy of Life in the Death Camps.* New York: Oxford University Press, 1976.

Diwan, Fiona. "Sono un ebreo ma non sono mai stato sionista." *Corriere Medico* (September 3–4, 1982): 15.

Druker, Jonathan. *Primo Levi and the Fate of Humanism after Auschwitz*. New York: Palgrave, 2009.

Dundovich, Elena. "Khrushchev: Contemporary Perspectives in the Western Press." In *Europe, Cold War, and Coexistence, 1953–1965*, edited by Wilfried Loth, 190–200. New York: Frank Cass, 2004.

Eco, Umberto. "Ur-Fascism." *New York Review of Books*, June 22, 1995, 12–15.

Eberstadt, Fernanda. "Reading Primo Levi." *Commentary*, October 1985: 41–47.

Fabre, Giorgio. *Il contratto: Mussolini editore di Hitler*. Bari: Dedalo, 2004.

———. *Mussolini razzista: Dal socialismo al fascismo: La formazione di un antisemita*. Milan: Garzanti, 2005.

Fackenheim, Emil L. *To Mend the World: Foundations of Post-Holocaust Jewish Thought*. Bloomington, IN: Indiana University Press, 1994.

Farrell, Joseph, ed. *Primo Levi: The Austere Humanist*. Oxford: Peter Lang, 2004.

Ferrario, Davide, director and adaptor. *La strada di Levi* [Primo Levi's Journey]. Screenplay by Marco Belpoliti, Primo Levi, and Davide Ferrario. Rossofuoco Productions, 2006. Film.

Ferrero, Ernesto, ed. *Primo Levi: Un'antologia della critica*. Turin: Einaudi, 1997.

Fini, Marco, ed. *1945–1975: Fascismo, antifascismo, Resistenza, rinnovamento*. Milan: Feltrinelli, 1962.

Finter, Helga. "Primo Levi's Stage Version of *Se questo è un uomo*." In *Staging the Holocaust: The Shoah in Drama and Performance*, edited by Claude Schumacher, 229–53. Cambridge: Cambridge University Press, 1998.

Fischer-Lichte, Erika. *The Semiotics of Theater*. Translated by Jeremy Gaines and Doris Jones. Bloomington: Indiana University Press, 1992.

Forgacs, David. "Building the Body of a Nation: Lombroso's *L'antisemitismo* and Fin-de-Siècle Italy." *Jewish Culture and History* 6 (2003): 96–110.

Forgacs, David, and Robert Lumley, eds. *Italian Cultural Studies*. Oxford: Oxford University Press, 1996.

Frank, Anne. *Diario*. Turin: Einaudi, 1954; 1st ed., *Het Achterhuis*, 1947.

French, Philip. *Westerns: Aspects of a Movie Genre*. London: Secker and Warburg, 1973.

Freud, Sigmund. "Beyond the Pleasure Principle" (excerpt). In *The Freud Reader*, edited by Peter Gay, 594–625. New York: W. W. Norton, 1989.

———. *Moses and Monotheism*. Translated by Katherine Jones. New York: Vintage Books, 1967.

Frigessi, Delia. *Cesare Lombroso*. Milano: Einaudi, 2003.

Ganeri, Margherita. *Il romanzo storico in Italia: Il dibattito critico dalle origini al postmoderno*. Lecce: Piero Manni, 1999.

Gentiloni, Filippo. "Quando la stella di David era la bandiera dei perseguitati," *Il manifesto*, June 29, 1982, 6.

Gibson, Mary. *Born to Crime: Cesare Lombroso and the Origins of Biological Criminality*. Westport, CT.: Praeger, 2002.

Gilman, Sander. "Is Life Beautiful? Can the Shoah Be Funny? Some Thoughts on Recent and Older Films." *Critical Inquiry* 26 (Winter 2000): 279–308.

———. *The Jew's Body.* New York: Routledge, 1991.

———. "The Special Language of the Camps and After." In *Reason and Light*, edited by Susan Tarrow, 59–81. Ithaca, NY: Cornell University Press, 1990.

Ginzburg, Natalia. *Lessico famigliare.* Turin: Einaudi, 1963.

Girelli-Carasi, Fabio. "The Anti-Linguistic Nature of the Lager in the Language of Primo Levi's *Se questo è un uomo.*" In *Reason and Light*, edited by Susan Tarrow, 40–59. Ithaca, NY: Cornell University Press, 1990.

———. "Italian-Jewish Memoirs and the Discourse of Identity." In *The Most Ancient of Minorities*, edited by Stanislao Pugliese, 191–99. Westport, CT: Greenwood Press, 2002.

Glucksmann, André. "Le avventure della tragedia," translated by Gianni Volpi, 75–91. In *Il Western: Fonti forme miti registi attori filmografia*, edited by Raymond Bellour. Milan: Feltrinelli, 1973.

Gordon, Robert S. C. *Primo Levi's Ordinary Virtues: From Testimony to Ethics.* Oxford: Oxford University Press, 2001.

———. "Which Holocaust? Primo Levi and the Field of Holocaust Memory in Post-War Italy." *Italian Studies* 61, no. 1 (Spring 2006): 85–113.

———, ed. *The Cambridge Companion to Primo Levi.* Cambridge: Cambridge University Press, 2007.

Gramsci, Antonio. *Further Selections from the Prison Notebooks.* Edited and translated by Derek Boothman. Minneapolis: University of Minnesota Press, 1995.

Israel Gutman, ed., *I giusti d'Italia: I non ebrei che salvarono gli ebrei, 1943–1945.* Milan: Mondadori, 2004, 193–194

Harrowitz, Nancy. *Anti-Semitism, Misogyny, and the Logic of Cultural Difference: Cesare Lombroso and Matilde Serao.* Lincoln: University of Nebraska Press, 1994.

Hausner, Gideon. *Sei milioni di accusatori.* Turin: Einaudi, 1961.

Hirsch, Marianne, and Irene Kacandes, eds. *Teaching the Representation of the Holocaust.* New York: MLA Press, 2004.

Hochhuth, Rolf. *Der Stellvetreter.* Hamburg: Reinbek, 1963.

———. *Il vicario.* Milan: Feltrinelli, 1964.

Hoffman, Eva. *After Such Knowledge: Memory, History, and the Legacy of the Holocaust.* New York: Public Affairs, 2004.

Horkheimer, Max, and Theodor W. Adorno. *Dialectic of Enlightenment: Philosophical Fragments.* Edited by Gunzelin Schmid Noerr. Translated by Edmund Jephcott. Stanford, CA: Stanford University Press, 2002.

Höss, Rudolf. *Comandante ad Auschwitz.* Turin: Einaudi, 1960; 1st German ed. 1958.

Howe, Irving. "How To Write About the Holocaust." *New York Review of Books*, March 28, 1985, 14–17.

———. "Introduction." In Primo Levi, *If Not Now, When?*, translated by William Weaver, 3–16. New York: Summit Books, 1985.

Hungerford, Amy. "Teaching Fiction, Teaching the Holocaust." In *Teaching the Representation of the Holocaust*, edited by Marianne Hirsch and Irene Kacandes, 180–90. New York: MLA, 2004.

Insana, Lina N. *Arduous Tasks: Primo Levi, Translation, and the Transmission of Holocaust Testimony*. Toronto: University of Toronto Press, 2009.

———. "In Levi's Wake: Adaptation, Simulacrum, Postmemory." *Italica* 86, no. 2 (2009): 212–38.

Jani, Emilio. *Mi ha salvato la voce*. Milan: Ceschina, 1960.

Jesurum, Stefano. "Si è offuscata la luce della stella d'Israele," *Oggi*, July 14, 1982, 82–84.

Ka-Tzetnik 135633. *La casa delle bambole*. Milan: Mondadori, 1959; 1st ed. 1953.

Kaplan, Harold. *Conscience & Memory: Meditation in a Museum of the Holocaust*. Chicago, IL: University of Chicago Press, 1994.

Kertész, Imre. *Fateless*. Translated by Tim Wilkinson. London: Vintage Books, 2006.

———. *Fatelessness*. Translated by Tim Wilkinson. London: Harvill, 2005.

Kidd, Dustin. "The Aesthetics of Truth, The Athletics of Time: George Steiner and the Retreat from the Word." Unpublished student essay, December 7, 1998. http://xroads.virginia.edu/~ma99/kidd/resume/steiner.html.

Kitses, Jim. "Authorship and Genre: Notes on the Western." In *The Western Reader*, edited by Jim Kitses and Gregg Rickman, 57–68. New York: Limelight, 1999.

———. *Horizons West: Directing the Western from John Ford to Clint Eastwood*. 2nd ed. London: BFI, 2004.

Kitses, Jim, and Gregg Rickman, eds. *The Western Reader*. New York: Limelight, 1999.

Kowzan, Tadeusz. "The Sign in the Theater: An Introduction to the Semiology of the Art of the Spectacle," translated by Simon Pleasance. *Diogène* 61 (1968): 52–80.

Lattes, Dante. "Tu quoque Quasimodo?" *Rassegna Mensile di Israel* 1 (1961): 3–5.

Lepschy, Anna, and Giulio Lepschy. "Primo Levi's Languages." In *The Cambridge Companion to Primo Levi*, edited by Robert S. C. Gordon, 121–36. Cambridge: Cambridge University Press, 2007.

Levi, Carlo. *Christ Stopped at Eboli*. Translated by Frances Frenaye, with a new introduction by Mark Rotella. New York: Fararr, Straus, & Giroux, 2006.

———. *Fear of Freedom*. Translated by Adophe Gourevitch. Edited by Stanislao G. Pugliese. New York: Columbia University Press, 2008.

———. *Paura della libertà* (Turin: Einaudi, 1946); reprinted in *Scritti politici*, edited by David Bidussa, 132–204. Turin: Einaudi, 2001.

Levi, Primo. *The Black Hole of Auschwitz*. Edited by Marco Belpoliti. Translated by Sharon Wood. Malden, MA: Polity Press, 2005.

———. *Collected Poems*. Translated by Ruth Feldman and Brian Swann. London: Faber and Faber, 1988.

———. "A Conversation with Primo Levi." In *Survival in Auschwitz: The Nazi Assault on Humanity*, translated by Stuart Woolf, 175–87. New York: Touchstone Books, 1986.

———. "'Deportazione e sterminio di ebrei,' with a note by Alberto Cavaglion." *Lo straniero* 11, no. 85 (July 2007), 5–12.

———. *The Drowned and the Saved.* Translated by Raymond Rosenthal. London: Abacus, 1988.

———. *The Drowned and the Saved.* Translated by Raymond Rosenthal. London: Michael Joseph, 1988.

———. *The Drowned and the Saved.* Translated by Raymond Rosenthal. New York: Summit Books, 1988.

———. *The Drowned and the Saved.* Translated by Raymond Rosenthal. New York: Random House, 1989.

———. *If Not Now, When?* Translated by William Weaver. London: Abacus, 1987.

———. *If This Is a Man* and *The Truce.* Translated by Stuart Woolf. London: Penguin Books, 1979.

———. "Itinerary of a Jewish Writer." In Primo Levi, *The Black Hole of Auschwitz*, 155–69. Malden, MA: Polity Press, 2006.

———. "Lasciapassare per Babele," *La Stampa*, November 5, 1980.

———. *Lilít e altri racconti.* Turin: Einaudi, 1981.

———. "The Little Theatre of Memory." In *The Voice of Memory: Interviews 1961– 1987*, edited by Marco Belpoliti and Robert Gordon and translated by Robert Gordon, 47–56. New York: New Press, 2001.

———. *The Mirror Maker: Stories and Essays.* Translated by Raymond Rosenthal. New York: Schocken Books, 1989.

———. *Moments of Reprieve: A Memoir of Auschwitz.* Translated by Ruth Feldman. New York: Penguin, 1995.

———. "Note to the Theater Version of *If This is a Man*." In *The Black Hole of Auschwitz*, edited by Marco Belpoliti and translated by Sharon Wood, 23–27. Malden, MA: Polity Press, 2005, 23–27.

———. *Opere.* 3 vols. Turin: Einaudi "Biblioteca dell'Orsa," 1987–1990.

———. *Opere.* Edited by Marco Belpoliti with an introduction by Daniele del Giudice. Torino: Einaudi, 1997.

———. *Other People's Trades.* Translated by Raymond Rosenthal. London: Michael Joseph, 1989.

———. "The Past We Thought Would Never Return." In *The Black Hole of Auschwitz*, translated by Sharon Wood, 31–34. New York: Polity Press, 2005.

———. *The Periodic Table.* Translated by Raymond Rosenthal. New York: Schocken Books, 1984.

———. *I racconti: Storie naturali, Vizio di forma, Lilít.* Turin: Einaudi, 1996.

———. *The Reawakening.* Translated by Stuart Woolf with an afterword, "The Author's Answers to His Readers' Questions," translated by Ruth Feldman. New York: Macmillan, 1987.

———. *La ricerca delle radici.* Torino: Einaudi, 1981.

———. *The Search for Roots.* Translated with an introduction by Peter Forbes. Lanham, MD: Ivan R. Dee, 2003.

———. *Il sistema periodico.* Torino: Einaudi, 1975.

———. *I sommersi e i salvati.* Torino: Einaudi, 1986.

————. *Storie naturali*. Torino: Einaudi, 1966.

————. *Survival in Auschwitz*. Translated by Stuart Woolf. New York: Collier, 1961.

————. *Survival in Auschwitz*. Translated by Stuart Woolf. New York: Touchstone, 1996.

————. *Survival in Auschwitz: The Nazi Assault on Humanity*. Translated by Stuart Woolf. New York: Collier Books, 1993.

————. "Tradurre ed essere tradotti." In Primo Levi, *L'altrui mestiere*, 109–14. Torino: Einaudi, 1985.

————. *A Tranquil Star*. Translated by Ann Goldstein and Alessandra Bastagli. New York: W. W. Norton, 2007.

————. *La tregua*. Turin: Einaudi, 1963.

————. "Un passato che credevamo non dovesse tornare più." In *L'assimetria e la vita*, edited by Marco Belpoliti, 47–50. Turin: Einaudi, 2002.

————. "Vanadium." In Primo Levi, *The Periodic Table*, translated by Raymond Rosenthal, 211–23. New York: Schocken Books, 1984.

————. "Why Auschwitz?" (Afterword). In *Shema: Collected Poems of Primo Levi*, translated by Ruth Feldman and Brian Swann. London: Menard Press, 1976.

Lewinska, Pelagia. *Twenty Months at Auschwitz*. New York: Lyle Stuart, 1989.

Lizzani, Carlo, director. *L'oro di Roma*. Ager Cinematografica, 1961. Film.

Lombroso, Cesare. *L'antisemitismo e le scienze moderne*. Torino: Roux, 1894.

Luperini, Romano. *La città*. Turin: Einaudi, 1999.

————. "La lunga traversia non ha fine." Review of *Se non ora, quando?*, *Gazzetta del Mezzogiorno*, May 27, 1982, 3.

Luppi, Marzia, and Elisabetta Ruffini, eds. *Immagini dal silenzio: La prima mostra nazionale dei Lager nazisti attraverso l'Italia 1955–1960*. Modena: Nuovagrafica, 2005.

Luzzatto, G. L. "Il giardino dei Finzi-Contini." *Rassegna Mensile di Israel* 5 (1962): 239–40.

Manzoni, Alessandro. *Adelchi*. Milan: Garzanti, 2007.

————. *I Promessi Sposi*. Edited by Gilda Sbrilli. Florence: Bulgarini, 2000.

Marcus, Millicent. *Italian Film in the Shadow of Auschwitz*. Toronto: University of Toronto Press, 2007.

————. "Primo Levi: The Biographer's Challenge and the Reader's Double Bind." *Italica* 80, no.1 (2003): 67–72.

McGee, Patrick. *From Shane to Kill Bill: Rethinking the Western*. Oxford: Blackwell, 2007.

Melrose, Susan. "Theater and Language." In *A Semiotics of the Dramatic Text*, 36–64. New York: St. Martin's, 1994.

Menduini, E. *La radio nell'era della televisione*. Bologna: Il Mulino, 1994.

Mengaldo, Pier Vincenzo. "Lingua e scrittura in Levi." In *Primo Levi: Un'antologia della critica*, edited by Ernesto Ferrero, 169–242. Turin: Einaudi, 1997.

Michaelis, Meir. *Mussolini and the Jews: German-Italian Relations and the Jewish Question in Italy, 1922–1945*. Oxford: Oxford University Press, 1978.

Minerbi, Sergio. *La belva in gabbia: Eichmann*. Milan: Longanesi, 1962.

Mitchell, Lee Clark. *Westerns: Making the Man in Fiction and Film*. Chicago, IL: University of Chicago Press, 1996.

Momigliano, Arnaldo. *Essays on Ancient and Modern Judaism*. Edited by Silvia Berti. Translated by Maura Masella-Gayley. Chicago, IL: University of Chicago Press, 1994.

———. "The Jews of Italy." In *Essays on Ancient and Modern Judaism*, edited by Silvia Berti, translated by Maura Masella-Gayley, 121–34. Chicago, IL: University of Chicago Press, 1994.

———. *Pagine ebraiche*. Edited by Silvia Berti. Turin: Einaudi, 1987.

Moyn, Samuel. *A Holocaust Controversy: The Treblinka Affair in Postwar France*. Waltham, MA: Brandeis University Press, 2005.

Negrin, Alberto, director. *Perlasca: Un eroe italiano*. RAI Fiction, 2002. Film.

Nel Siedlecki 6643, Janusz, 75817 Krystyn Olszewski, and 119198 Tadeusz Borowski. *We Were in Auschwitz*. Translated by Alicia Nitecki. New York: Welcome Rain, 2000.

Neppi, Enzo. "Sopravvivenza e vergogna in Primo Levi." In *Appartenenza e differenza: Ebrei d'Italia e letteratura*, edited by Juliette Hassine, Jacques Misan-Montefiore, and Sandra Debenedetti-Stow, 111–33. Florence: La Giuntina, 1997.

Neumann, Iver B. *Russia and the Idea of Europe: A Study in Identity and International Relations*. London: Routledge, 1996.

———. "Russia as Europe's Other." *Journal of Contemporary European Studies* 6, no. 12 (Spring 1998): 26–73.

Nietzsche, Friedrich. *On the Genealogy of Morals*. Translated by Walter Kaufmann and R. J. Hollingdale. New York: Vintage Books, 1989.

Nirenstajn, Alberto. *Ricorda che ti ha fatto Amalek*. Turin: Einaudi, 1958.

Nyiszli, Miklós. *Auschwitz: A Doctor's Eyewitness Account*. New York: Arcade, 1993.

Orengo, Nico. *Chi è di scena!* Turin: Einaudi, 2006.

Ortoleva, Peppino. "A Geography of the Media Since 1945." In *Italian Cultural Studies*, edited by David Forgacs and Robert Lumley, 185–98. Oxford: Oxford University Press, 1996.

Ozick, Cynthia. "A Youthful Intoxication." *New York Times Book Review*, December 6, 2006.

Pasolini, Pier Paolo. *Opere*. 10 vols. Edited by Walter Siti. Milan: Mondadori, 1998–2003.

Patruno, Nicholas. *Understanding Primo Levi*. Columbia: University of South Carolina Press, 1995.

Peckinpah, Sam, director. *The Wild Bunch*. Warner Bros., 1969. Film.

Permoli, Piergiovanni, ed. *Lezioni sull'antifascismo*. Rome: Laterza, 1960.

Piazza, Bruno. *Perché gli altri dimenticano*. Milan: Feltrinelli, 1956.

Picciotto Fargion, Liliana. *Il libro della memoria: Gli ebrei deportati dall'Italia (1943–1945)*, 2nd ed. Milan: Mursia, 1992.

Pinay, Maurice. *Complotto contro la chiesa*. Rome, 1962.

Poli, Gabriella, and Giorgio Calcagno. *Echi di una voce perduta: Incontri, interviste e conversazioni con Primo Levi*. Milan: Mursia, 1992.

Poliakov, Léon. *La Bréviaire de la haine*. Paris: Calmann-Lévy, 1951.

————. *Il nazismo e lo sterminio degli ebrei*. Turin: Einaudi, 1955.

Pontecorvo, Gillo, director. *Kapò*. Cineriz, 1961. Film.

Porto, Bruno Di. "Il problema ebraico in Nello Rosselli." In *Giustizia e Libertà nella lotta antifascista*, edited by Carlo Francovich, 491–99. Florence: La Nuova Italia, 1978.

Pugliese, Stanislao G. "The Antidote to Fascism." In *My Version of the Facts*, by Carla Pekelis, vii–xii. Evanston, IL: Marlboro Press/Northwestern, 2004.

————. *Carlo Rosselli: Socialist Heretic and Antifascist Exile*. Cambridge, MA: Harvard University Press, 1999.

————, ed. *The Most Ancient of Minorities: The Jews of Italy*. Westport, CT: Greenwood Press, 2002.

————. "Trauma/Transgression/Testimony." In *The Legacy of Primo Levi*, edited by Stanislao G. Pugliese, 3–14. New York: Palgrave, 2005.

Puppa, Paolo. "Primo Levi's Hidden Theater." In *Primo Levi: The Austere Humanist*, edited by Joseph Farrell, 183–201. Oxford: Peter Lang, 2004.

Quasimodo, Salvatore. *Il falso e vero verde* (Milan: Mondadori, 1956).

————. *Tutte le poesie*. Milan: Mondadori, 1984.

Reeves, John. "If This is a Man." *CBC Times*. January 23–29, 1965.

Reitlinger, Gerald. *The Final Solution*. New York: Beechhurst Press, 1953.

————. *La soluzione finale*. Milan: Il Saggiatore, 1962.

Ringelblum, Emmanuel. *Sepolti a Varsavia*. Milan: Mondadori, 1962.

Rogowski, Christian. "Teaching the Drama of the Holocaust." In *Teaching the Representation of the Holocaust*, edited by Marianne Hirsch and Irene Kacandes. New York: MLA Press, 2004.

Romano, Giorgio. "Rassegna delle riviste" [on Giacomo Debenedetti in *Rinascita*]. *Rassegna Mensile di Israel* 5 (1960), 228.

Rondini, Andrea. "La scrittura e la sfida: Una lettura di '*Lilìt*' di Primo Levi." *Studi novecenteschi* 59 (2002): 239–76.

Rosenbaum, Thane. *The Golems of Gotham: A Novel*. New York: HarperCollins, 2002.

Rosenfeld, Alvin H. *A Double Dying: Reflections on Holocaust Literature*. Bloomington: Indiana University Press, 1988.

Rosi, Francesco, director. *La Tregua* ["The Reawakening"]. Miramax Films, 1997. Film.

Rossellini, Roberto, director. *Generale della Rovere*. Zebra Film, 1959. Film.

Roth, Philip. "A Man Saved by His Skills." In *The Voice of Memory. Interviews 1961–87*, edited by Marco Belpoliti and Robert Gordon, 13–22. Cambridge: Polity Press, 2001.

Rubinowicz, David. *Il diario*. Turin: Einaudi, 1960.

Russell of Liverpool, Edward. *Il flagello della svastica*. Milan: Feltrinelli, 1955.

————. *The Scourge of the Swastika*. New York: Philosophical Library, 1954.

Scaglione, Massimo. "L'altra metà del 'centauro' Primo Levi: Intervista a Massimo Scaglione." *Sistemateatrotorino*, April–May, 2007, n.p.

Schehr, Laurence. "Primo Levi's Strenuous Clarity." *Italica* 66, no. 4 (Winter 1989): 429–43.

Schleiermacher, Friedrich. "On the different methods of translating." In *Western Translation Theory from Herodotus to Nietzsche*, edited and translated by Douglas Robinson, 225–38. Manchester: St. Jerome, 2002.

Schumacher, Claude, ed. *Staging the Holocaust: The Shoah in Drama and Performance*. Cambridge: Cambridge University Press, 1998.

Schwarz-Bart, André. *Le Dernier des Justes*. Paris: Seuil, 1959 (*L'ultimo dei giusti*. Milan: Feltrinelli, 1960).

Segre, Cesare. "Lettura di *Se questo è un uomo*." In *Primo Levi: Un'antologia della critica*, edited by Ernesto Ferrero, 55–75. Turin: Einaudi, 1997, 91–116.

Sereny, Gitta. *Into that Darkness: An Examination of Conscience*. New York: Random House, 1983.

Shirer, William L. *The Rise and Fall of the Third Reich*. New York: Simon and Schuster, 1960.

———. *Storia del Terzo Reich*. Turin: Einaudi, 1962.

Slotkin, Richard. *Gunfighter Nation: The Myth of the Frontier in Twentieth-Century America*. New York: Atheneum, 1992.

Sodi, Risa. *A Dante of Our Time*. New York: Peter Lang, 1990.

Spinazzola, Vittorio. *Il romanzo antistorico*. Rome: Editori Riuniti, 1990.

Stille, Alexander. "The Biographical Fallacy." In *The Legacy of Primo Levi*, edited by Stanislao Pugliese, 209–20. New York: Palgrave Macmillan, 2005.

———. "The Double Bind of Italian Jews: Acceptance and Assimilation." In *Jews in Italy under Fascist and Nazi Rule: 1922–1945*, edited by Joshua Zimmerman, 19–34. Cambridge: Cambridge University Press, 2005.

Stone, Marla. "Primo Levi, Roberto Benigni, and the Politics of Holocaust Representation." In *The Legacy of Primo Levi*, edited by Stanislao Pugliese, 135–46. New York: Palgrave Macmillan, 2005.

Sturges, John, director. *The Magnificent Seven*. Mirisch Corporation, 1960. Film.

Tarrow, Susan, ed. *Reason and Light*. Ithaca, NY: Cornell University Press, 1990.

Tarzizzo, Domenico, ed. *Ideologia della morte: Storia e documenti dei campi di sterminio*. Milan: Il Saggiatore, 1962.

Tesio, Giovanni. "Su alcune giunte e varianti di *Se questo è un uomo*." In *Studi Piemontesi* 6 (1977): 270–78

Thomson, Ian. *Primo Levi: A Life*. London: Hutchinson, 2002.

———. *Primo Levi*. London: Random House, 2002.

Tompkins, Jane. *West of Everything: The Inner Life of Westerns*. Oxford: Oxford University Press, 1992.

Todorov, Tzvetan. *Imperfect Garden: The Legacy of Humanism*. Princeton, NJ: Princeton University Press, 2002.

Toscano, Mario. *Ebraismo e antisemitismo in Italia: Dal 1848 alla guerra dei sei giorni*. Milano: Franco Angeli, 2003.

———. "Italian Jewish Identity." In *Jews in Italy under Fascist and Nazi Rule: 1922–1945*, edited by Joshua Zimmerman, 35–54. Cambridge: Cambridge University Press, 2005.

Vacca, Roberto. "Un western dalla Russia a Milano," *Il giorno*, May, 1982, 3.

Valabrega, Guido, ed. *Gli ebrei in italia durante il fascismo*. Milan: CDEC, 1961–63.

van Alphen, Ernst. "Second-Generation Testimony, Transmission of Trauma, and Postmemory." *Poetics Today* 27, no. 2 (2006): 473–88.

Varnai, Ugo (pseud. of Luigi Meneghello). "Lo sterminio degli ebrei d'Europa, I-III." In *Comunità*, 22 (December 1953), 16–23; 23 (February 1954), 10–15; 24 (April 1954), 36–39.

Viano, Maurizio. "*Life is Beautiful*: Reception, Allegory, and Holocaust Laughter." *Annali d'Italianistica* 17 (1999): 155–72.

Vivanti, Corrado, ed. *Gli ebrei in Italia, vol. 11 of Storia d'Italia.* Turin: Einaudi, 1996.

Volpi, Gianni. "L'ultima frontiera." In *Il Western: Fonti forme miti registi attori filmografia*, edited by Raymond Bellour, 92–134. Milan: Feltrinelli, 1973.

Ward, David. "Primo Levi's Turin." In *The Cambridge Companion to Primo Levi*, edited by Robert S. C. Gordon, 3–16. Cambridge: Cambridge University Press, 2007, 5–33.

Weber, Samuel. *Theatricality as Medium.* New York: Fordham University Press, 2004.

Weiner, Rebecca. "The Virtual Jewish History Tour: France." http://www.jewishvirtuallibrary.org/jsource/vjw/France.html#Holocaust

Wiesel, Elie. *Legends of Our Time.* Translated by Stephen Donadio. New York: Avon, 1970.

Williams, Doug. "Pilgrims and the Promised Land: A Genealogy of the Western." In *The Western Reader*, edited by Jim Kitses and Gregg Rickman, 93–114. New York: Limelight, 1999.

Woolf, Judith. "From *If This is a Man* to *The Drowned and the Saved*." In *The Cambridge Companion to Primo Levi*, edited by Robert S. C. Gordon, 35–49. Cambridge: Cambridge University Press, 2007.

Wright, Will. *Six Guns and Society: A Structural Study of the Western.* Berkeley: University of California Press, 1975.

Zuccotti, Susan. *The Italians and the Holocaust.* New York: Basic Books, 1987.

Index